"Mateo, oh, Mateo!" She arched. She clutched at him. She throbbed.

In answer, he softly cupped her breast, then let the flat of his palm smooth down over her rib cage to her belly. When his hand slipped farther down, stroking the silkiness between her thighs, Charlotte all but stopped breathing. She writhed against his palm.

Suddenly Mateo, holding Charlotte firmly in his arms, rolled onto his back.

"Do with me as you will, my little love," he whispered.

Barbara Critiques said of Becky Lee Weyrich's SUMMER LIGHTNING: "SUMMER LIGHTNING is as refreshing as a spring rain. Ms. Weyrich rivals the best comedian as she creates two intelligent characters that are human enough to laugh at themselves as well as seeing the situations for what they really are.... This is one that you'll not only keep, you'll probably not loan out for fear it won't get returned! Savor and enjoy!"

GYPSY MOON

Becky Lee Weyrich

FAWCETT GOLD MEDAL • NEW YORK

*To the memory of
Ruth Tucker Herbert,
my wonderful teacher and very,
very, very, very, very
good friend*

Prologue

A Gypsy Camp Somewhere in the Balkans—1797

The ghosts of a thousand Gypsy dancers whirled in the green-black arms of their evergreen lovers, growing tall upon the hills surrounding and sheltering the Romany camp. A full moon lit this ethereal *czardas* of love.

Wisps of fragrant wood smoke spiraled upward into the darkness from the dying embers of the campfire. Violins lay quiet next to beribboned tambourines. Midnight and sleep cloaked the Gypsy caravans.

Inside her tent, Valencia tossed restlessly on her bed of wolf skins. The day had been long and hot, the night and the dancing charged with a certain unsettling tension. Her dreams warned of mysterious evil and coming catastrophe. She clutched an ivory-and-gold icon of the good saint, Sara-la-Kali, to her bosom, hoping to ward off the black spirits of night.

*   *   *

Thinking Valencia fast asleep, her husband, Xendar, rose from their pallet and slipped silently out into the night. With the stealth of a hunting beast, he made his way to the tent of his wife's sister, Kavà. He had watched the girl grow from a pretty nymph into a beautiful pagan, ripe for love.

Earlier in the day, he had chanced upon her bathing naked in the stream. That sight fired his blood and chased all caution from his mind. She had spied him watching but made no move to cover herself. She wanted him, too. He was sure of it. No longer could he deny the smoldering Gypsy fires that threatened his sanity while searing his loins with desire.

Without a sound, Xendar maneuvered his large frame through the unlaced flap of Kavà's tent. He crouched low, letting his Romany-black eyes adjust to the darkness. Before him lay the object of his lust—as wantonly lovely in sleep as she had been whirling in the orange glow of the campfire a short time before.

But now her clinging peasant blouse was gone and the rise and fall of her bare breasts made him long to taste the ripe, forbidden fruits. Her shapely legs, which had flashed tantalizingly from beneath swirling skirts as she danced, rested in magnificent nudity, pale against the bear rug, causing a painful hunger in his body. Xendar, involuntarily, gave a low groaning sound deep in his throat.

Kavà's eyes flickered open. She saw a dark shape looming over her and tried to scream. But the man fell on her, devouring the sound of her terror and turning it with ravenous lips into a whimper of desire.

She relaxed, yielded. She knew this man. She ached for him. How often she had dreamed of the time when he would seek her out and give her the love only their eyes had dared speak of in the past.

"Xendar," she moaned between kisses. "Xendar, I am yours. Take me!"

Sensing her husband's absence, Valencia touched the empty spot next to her and found the coarse animal hair still warm from his body. Where did he go these nights when he left her? What did he do? In a part of her heart that she kept guardedly locked, Valencia held the answers to these questions. But she dared not turn the key and confront the truth.

The whispers of Xendar's transgressions were never spoken to Valencia's face. But a Gypsy woman hears all . . . knows all. Had it not been for her insatiable passion for the man, she would have cast him from her tent long ago. But the few times she had tried to accuse him, the stroke of his wondrous hands, the touch of his lips to her breast, and all was lost. She craved him the way a drunkard craves his wine. Still, tonight something was different. She had sensed it for hours.

She rose from her bed, still holding Saint Sara to her breast, and peered out. The wind was on the rise, sending strange, silver-edged clouds scudding across the wizened face of the moon. On nights like this, her body ached for the nearness of Xendar, for the strength of his arms about her and the reassurance of his heart beating its fierceness next to her own. Suddenly, the blood pounded in her ears like waves of the great sea battering the sands. She felt her need rising with the nerve-shattering force of an erupting volcano.

It was then that Valencia heard his urgent whispers: "Yes, my wild one. Bite me! Scratch me like a cat in heat! Move with me. . . . Ride with me. Feel my fire enter your flesh!"

The words and a woman's accompaniment of sighs seemed to come from everywhere and nowhere. Valencia's dark eyes surveyed the calm scene—fancifully carved and painted *vardos* drawn up around the camp; a circle of tents like her own around the fire; horses standing at rest after their long day's haul into the mountains; stiff-haired, yellow mongrels drowsing in the shifting moon shadows. But no sign of Xendar.

The sighs grew louder, more urgent. Valencia knew the woman was nearing that magic moment when the world exploded, leaving only blinding bits of stardust in its wake and a feeling beyond the words to describe it.

Gathering her whispering skirts about her, Valencia crept toward the sounds. She stopped suddenly, feeling something like death clutching at her heart.

"No, Xendar!" she breathed.

Valencia recognized the ecstatic cry that rent the silence of the night. Her bare feet hardly touched the ground as she flew toward Kavà's tent. She threw back the flap and stood frozen in sick horror and disbelief. The sacred icon dropped from her hand, shattering into two jagged pieces at her feet.

Her husband lay atop her sister, sending the last seeds of his passion flooding through her.

Now it was Valencia's scream that filled the night. "*Marimé!* Unclean! *Marimé!*"

Instantly, Xendar rolled away from Kavà, covering his face with his crossed arms at the sound of his wife's accusing words.

"No, Valencia!" His voice quivered with terror. "Please, no!"

Kavà, her delicate golden body naked and shivering, lay where Xendar had left her. Valencia noted the smear of blood on her thighs, proclaiming the death of her virginity.

"He *raped* you!" Valencia whispered, horror seeping through her like the venom of a poisonous snake. "My own husband!"

4

Valencia stared from one to the other. Kavà made no move to defend her lover. Her plum-colored lips parted, but no sound came from them. She lay rigid while Xendar cringed away, his taut muscles glistening still with the sweat of his lust. Surely, Valencia thought, her sister's glazed eyes reflected her terror of the man.

Aroused by the wronged woman's screams, the others in the camp gathered at the tent. They waited silently to hear Valencia's pronouncement—the women with a feeling of the rightness of it in their hearts, the men shrinking back in dread at the thought of the certain curse to come.

The wind hushed and Valencia's voice echoed in the stillness: "I pronounce Rom Xendar *marimé*—unclean! For breaking his marriage vows and tainting the virgin body of my own sister, he will be cast out. No more one of the *Rom*—not of our race—and without *familia*, he shall roam the woods alone forevermore. And should fruit come of this forbidden union, it will carry the curse of the father from generation to generation. In the name of Sara-la-Kali, Sara the Black, handmaiden to the sisters of the Virgin Mary and patron saint of all Gypsies, I call down this curse upon the one whom I have called husband!"

A tortured sound escaped Xendar's lips. The fire hissed and flames leaped upward as Valencia whirled from her pleading husband to point a golden-ringed finger at the moon, which was now as naked as Xendar himself.

Her words came out in a mournful chant. "At the time of the full moon, your suffering shall be great, even as mine is this night. You will feel the shame my sister has felt. You will quake and cry for mercy as your mind and heart relive this unspeakable deed. A thousand demons shall possess your soul."

With Valencia, the rest of the Gypsies picked up the chant: "Xendar is *marimé, marimé, marimé!* Xendar is unclean, unclean, unclean! Xendar is cast out, cast out, cast out!''

They drew his blood, throwing rocks and sticks at the "rapist," chasing him out of the camp. As he stood alone at the edge of the deep woods, Xendar turned a final, pleading gaze upon his wife. At his look, Valencia's heart twisted with pain, then softened as she recalled their exquisite nights of love.

Raising her arms for silence, Valencia gave Xendar a parting gift—a hope, faint as it was, for the future.

"This curse which I lay upon the head of Xendar will be lifted from him and those who issue from the strength of his passions only through the love—true and faithful—of a golden Gypsy. He may search the earth for such Gypsy fire as it will take to cleanse him, and may Sara-la-Kali aid him in his quest."

Out of the night, a lone raven with wings as black as Valencia's hair swooped down, screaming, his grating cry punctuating the curse. The Gypsies covered their heads to protect themselves from the diving fiend— perhaps the spirit of Sara the Black herself, called up by Valencia's angry words.

Valencia, ignoring the fear of the others, turned her back on her husband, never to see him again, but to be reminded of him for the rest of her life.

For out of Xendar's unholy union with Kavà came a son, Croate. And Croate fathered Lassim, and the son of Lassim was named Strombol. When Strombol married Zolande, queen of the Gypsies, their child—dark and beautiful—was called Mateo.

Mateo inherited Valencia's curse . . . and learned to fear the full moon.

Chapter 1

The same fiery Gypsy moon that had cast its spell over Xendar, Kavà, and Valencia, enflaming their passions almost a century before, now shone down with a gentler light on the bluegrass fields of Fairview Plantation in the heart of Kentucky's horse country.

The moonlight softened the scene—glossing over the fences that needed mending and the peeling paint of the once proud white-columned mansion standing on the hill. The fortunes of the Buckland clan of Fairview had shifted with the tides of the Civil War, which had taken its master and consumed its riches. But on such a soft summer night, one could still imagine Fairview's former glory—the elegant balls, the festive horse shows, the golden-haired daughter breaking hearts with a sigh and a smile.

A stray moonbeam laced its way through the curtains at a second-story window to weave a pattern of silver and shadow over Charlotte Buckland's face and gleam in the silky hair fanned out over her pillow. The light caught one of the tears on her cheek and turned it for an instant into a tiny diamond.

Charlotte wasn't sleeping. How could she sleep? Jemima Buckland's announcement at dinner had shaken her too dreadfully. She was still struggling to comprehend her mother's news.

Yes, she loved Fairview, and yes, she would do *anything* to save her family home from the auction block. Those were the impassioned words she had spoken to her mother not a week before. And she had meant what she'd said. But never—not in her wildest nightmares—had Charlotte imagined that her mother would take the word "anything" so literally and use it against her in such a way.

Now she was trapped . . . imprisoned . . . held powerless in the brutal arms of fate!

Charlotte's storm of protest at her mother's pronouncement had gotten her nowhere. Jemima Buckland, her determination not shaken in the least by her daughter's outcry, had calmly responded, "You may leave the table now, Charlotte, and go to your room. And while you are up there. you might consider the fact that your choice of husbands has been limited, to say the very least, since the war. As for finding a man for you with enough money to save Fairview, I had given up all hope of that until now. Winston Krantz is the answer to my prayers."

Charlotte had not been surprised by this last statement. Jemima Buckland had been encouraging Major Krantz's attentions since he first arrived in the area, seeking out Fairview and its owner because of the horse farm's reputation for fine thoroughbreds. Charlotte had sensed all along that her mother had secret plans for the U.S. Cavalry officer. But she had assumed that Jemima wanted the man for herself. At something over thirty,

Major Krantz was, after all, much closer to Jemima's matronly age than Charlotte's tender nineteen years. He was attractive enough, for an older man, and what he lacked in wit, charm, and hair he made up for with his eagerness to please. It hardly seemed strange to Charlotte that her mother had determinedly flirted with him, encouraging the major to woo her.

Winston Krantz had lost his wife to scarlet fever the same year that Jemima was widowed when Federal bullets cut down Albert Buckland on the bloody field of Shiloh. They seemed a perfect match. It would be a comfortable and companionable second marriage for them both, Charlotte had reasoned maturely. She had even allowed herself to grow accustomed to the idea of the major as her mother's husband, even if she couldn't visualize him as a replacement for her beloved father. But to think of marrying him herself . . . Why, she couldn't begin to imagine such a thing!

A breeze ruffled the lace curtain, drawing Charlotte's attention to the bright Kentucky moon peeking in her window. When she was no more than three, her father had taught her to wish on the moon. He'd always tell her, with a broad grin and a flash of his almost black eyes, "Most people say to wish on a star. But we Bucklands are a bold clan, with big dreams. We make big, bold wishes. To get what we want, it takes a wish on the full moon."

Charlotte felt a new lump in her throat at the thought of her father. She missed him desperately, especially at times like these when she needed his help. He would never have forced her to marry without love. Albert Buckland had been a sentimental romantic who believed that the world turned for love alone. And Charlotte was, indeed, her father's daughter in this above all else.

Tying the curtains back so that her words would have clear passage to the moon, Charlotte leaned her elbows on the sill and stared up, her hands folded as if in prayer. "Now, listen to me, moon," she began, feeling only slightly foolish. "I'm in *big* trouble, and my daddy promised you'd help. You've got to get me out of this. I will not marry Major Winston Krantz! I don't care if—"

A quiet knock at the bedroom door cut off Charlotte's plea in midsentence.

"Who's there?" She bristled, sure that her mother had come up to reinforce her earlier command. But she relaxed, sighing with relief, when her grandmother answered, "Open up, child. It's Granny Fate."

Fatima Lee Buckland, her father's mother, had disappointed Charlotte by uttering no word of protest after Jemima had announced her startling news at dinner. Granny Fate, like her son, had always taken Charlotte's side in the frequent disagreements between mother and daughter. However, Charlotte had supposed, because of her silence earlier tonight, that Granny Fate had known of the marriage plans in advance and approved.

But perhaps the moon wasn't Charlotte's only ally in this matter after all. She scrambled out of bed to open the door for her grandmother.

Fatima Buckland swept into the dark room like a miniature whirlwind—silk skirts snapping and gold bracelets jangling while her heavy gardenia perfume swam in the air.

Without a word, she lit the bedside lamp and turned to her granddaughter. "There! That's better. I like to look into those Buckland-brown eyes when I'm talking to you."

Charlotte didn't want Granny Fate to see that she'd been crying. She cast her gaze down, whispering, "Mama always says I should have been born with blue eyes like hers . . . that brown eyes don't become a blonde."

"There's nothing wrong with brown eyes!" Fatima snapped, defending her own as well as Charlotte's. "A man can stare deep and long into dark eyes and never see the bottom of the secret pool where a woman keeps her heart hid. But you look into blue eyes and everything's just laying right there on the surface for the taking. I was gazing into your mama's blue eyes all evening, and I didn't care a bit for what I saw there.''

"I won't marry him, Granny Fate." Charlotte's statement was a faint whisper in the quiet room, but for all her lack of force her point was clear.

"Jemima says he's rich."

Charlotte couldn't tell from her grandmother's statement whose side the fiery old woman was on. She looked carefully into Fatima Buckland's lined face but could read nothing there.

"If she wants his money, why doesn't *she* marry him?" Charlotte's voice was a near wail now.

"Don't think she wouldn't—in a minute—if he asked. That was 'Mima's plan in the beginning. But it turned on her. She still thinks of you as a child, and she hadn't considered that her beau might be more taken with a younger, sprightlier filly than a saddle mare that's long since been broke and rode.''

"But if Mother loves Major Krantz, how could she bear to let me marry him, much less force me into it?''

"Love's got nothing to do with this, child. It's a simple matter of economics to 'Mima now. Your mother's a hard woman. She needs the tax money for Fairview, and she's willing to put her own daughter on the block to get what she wants. It's just like in the old days of the slave market. The bed wench brings the highest price, and the older and more foolish the buyer, the more he's willing to pay.''

Charlotte felt her cheeks burning at her grandmother's frank comparison. And besides being embarrassed, she felt confused. She hardly knew her own mind, or so it seemed at the moment. She could see her mother's point. Fairview *must* be saved! She couldn't agree more with that. But at the same time, the idea of marrying a man she knew she could never love, for financial security alone, filled her with a kind of sick rage. This was *her* life! And she was a human being—not horseflesh to be bartered and bid over.

"I won't marry him," she repeated. Her hands clenched into fists as she said the words, as if she were holding tight to her freedom, her very life.

A slow smile started deep in Fatima Lee Buckland's eyes and soon lit her whole face. Gold rings glittered in the lamplight as the old woman reached out and stroked her granddaughter's cheek with long, slender fingers. Her voice held a warm, quiet force. "No Buckland woman in history has ever been sold into marriage against her will. And I certainly will not allow my own granddaughter to be the first!"

"Oh, Granny!" Charlotte cried. She rushed into her grandmother's open arms, her whole body suddenly feeling weightless with relief.

"Hush now! No more tears. That time is past."

"I'm sorry," Charlotte said. "It's just that I'm so relieved. I thought you agreed with Mother. That the two of you were going to force me. . . ."

"*Agree with 'Mima? Me?* Lord, honey, if that woman said the night was black, I'd swear it was white just to get her goat! I haven't agreed with your mama since the day she wormed her way into the Buckland family."

"Granny Fate!" Charlotte stood away, shocked by her grandmother's vehemence and her choice of words. She'd always known that there was no love lost between the two women, but since that often worked to her advantage, she had never questioned the cause of their antipathy.

"I'm sorry, child. I shouldn't have let that slip." Fatima Buckland studied her granddaughter's face for several moments, as if trying to decide whether or not to go on. Finally she said, "Charlotte, you're a grown woman now, and I'm *not* sorry I said that! It's time you realized that the world isn't made up of fairy tales and sugar plums. I think your daddy'd want you to know how things were so you won't feel any guilt about going against your mama on this marriage." She paused and nodded agreement with herself before continuing. "An eye for an eye and a bride for a bride, that's what it comes down to."

"Granny, I don't understand."

"You're fixing to, honey." Fatima Buckland grasped Charlotte's hand and led her to the bed, where they both sat down. Granny Fate took a pillow in her hands and toyed with the tattered lace on its edge, not meeting her granddaughter's gaze as she went on. "My Albert missed his chance at love. Your mama trapped him into marrying her, honey!"

Charlotte gasped but said nothing.

"Jemima Lewis came out here from Maryland to visit some cousins and find a husband. She was a pretty-enough thing and bright, too. But seems there'd been some scandal about her back home, we found out later, and she wasn't considered proper marriage material where she came from. So 'Mima came here on her matrimonial mission. The Bucklands being the wealthiest landowners in these parts, she zeroed right in on my boy. Albert had his heart set on another, a sweet, dark-haired girl named Valinda. But that didn't faze Miss Jemima Lewis. She flashed those big blue eyes and flirted with Albert till the whole county was talking about it."

Granny Fate paused, shook her head, and took a deep breath, as if she were about to plunge into deep water.

" 'Mima'd been here near to the end of her stay—a *long hot* summer. I was getting ready to breathe a sigh of relief at seeing the last of her, too, I can tell you.

13

Then just the day before she was to go, up she flounced to the front door of Fairview, that aunt and uncle of hers escorting her, real formal-like. I felt a storm brewing before the full blow struck. Sure enough, it came! Announced to me, she did, in the presence of her aunt, with those big blue eyes of hers shining bright, that my Albert'd got her with child.''

Charlotte couldn't contain her shock, but Granny Fate's full attention was on her tale.

"I figured it was an out-and-out lie, but when I confronted Albert, he admitted that there was a chance her story might be true. Poor boy! My heart went out to him. He said that at a barbecue early in the summer he'd got liquored up pretty good with some of the other boys and couldn't remember anything about that night except that he'd spent a good deal of it with 'Mima Lewis and she'd been mighty flirtatious and tempting. He knew his duty, even though it pained his heart to do it. He went straight off over to Bluefield to tell Valinda their engagement was off. He knew the only honorable course was to marry 'Mima. He did, but he was a sad-eyed groom, if I ever saw one.''

"Oh, Granny!" Charlotte was near tears again at the thought of her chance conception causing her father such pain. "I wish I'd never been born!"

The old woman hugged her tight and shushed her. "Wasn't your fault, honey. You didn't come along for four long years. No, sir! As I suspected from the first, 'Mima's story was pure fiction. Those kinfolks of hers must have been laughing through their teeth at the wedding. Imagine, marrying off used goods to the only son of the wealthiest family in these parts! She was no more carrying Albert's child than I'm carrying a striped mule right this minute! She even admitted to Albert, first time they had a fight, that he'd never touched her that night.''

Charlotte sat silent, feeling numb, when her grandmother finished.

Suddenly, Fatima Lee Buckland bolted up from the bed and whirled about the room in an unexpected show of pleasure and excitement. Falling to her knees before Charlotte with her skirts flared in a bright circle on the floor, she clasped her granddaughter's hands and smiled up at her.

"Don't you see, honey? All that's in the past. So many years I've been holding all this bottled up inside me, just bursting to let out all the hurt and disappointment to make room for hope. Now's our chance—yours and mine! My Albert loved you better than life itself. He must have curled up in his grave tonight to hear what 'Mima was planning for his daughter. He wouldn't have allowed it, and neither will I! You're going to know the love your daddy missed when he had to give up his Valinda."

Charlotte laughed with glee at her grandmother's slightly malevolent enthusiasm. Then her mirth faded as she remembered that Fairview was at stake as much as her own future.

"But Granny Fate, Mama says we'll lose Fairview if I don't marry Major Krantz. She said you'd be out in the cold and we'd all be begging for bread to keep from starving."

Fatima Buckland's laughter echoed about the room like fairies dancing. Her dark eyes glittered mischievously. "It wouldn't be the first time I've begged! Do you think we were always rich, girl? Your grandpa and me didn't have a penny when we got off the boat in this country. But Slome was a good horse trader, and I have many talents. We built this place, so it's my say what happens to it."

Her voice trailed off as her mind traveled some distant

path through the past. "Yes, it's only just. A bride for a bride!"

When Granny Fate rose, Charlotte noticed that she looked far younger than the ancient soul she had seemed only moments before. Her grandmother's long, bejeweled fingers snapped at the air and her laughter rippled through the silence. She whirled once and then again, sending her gay skirts flaring. Her feet were bare and tanned by the sun. She danced a few steps, then said, "Come child. I have a secret to impart!"

Charlotte followed her to a far corner of the room, where a doll's crib sat on a braided rug. She watched Granny Fate pull the floor covering aside and press one end of a wide floorboard. A trap door popped open.

"I never knew that was there," Charlotte said.

"Neither did your mama. That's why the contents are still safe. If she'd sell you to that Yankee to get the tax money, she surely wouldn't blink an eye at selling off the few remaining family heirlooms."

Granny Fate removed a small gold key from a ribbon around her neck. Carefully, she fit it into the lock of the small leather-bound and brass-studded trunk she had taken from hiding. She turned the key with a sort of religious reverence. The lid came open easily, releasing the tinkling notes of a music box. Inside, Charlotte saw the glitter of gold and ivory. Antique jewelry gleamed among folds of old lace. Granny Fate held up the fragile fabric for Charlotte to see.

"This was handmade in Spain nearly a hundred years ago. In the old country they call it a *mantilla*. It's your wedding veil, child. I wore it when I married your grandpa, God rest his soul."

"It's lovely, Granny."

"Always remember your heritage, child. Remember that the Buckland family goes back more generations than you could count. As a Buckland, you hold yourself proud."

"I will. I promise," Charlotte replied.

Granny Fate filled a pouch with gold coins and placed a golden serpent bracelet with ruby eyes about Charlotte's arm.

"Take the trunk. It contains your past and your future, child."

She embraced her granddaughter briefly, and Charlotte knew by the trembling of her body that the old woman was weeping.

"Follow your heart and your fancy, Charlotte. Ride the wind, the way we did in the old days. I've saddled your horse. He's waiting behind the barn. It's not a long ride to the crossroads. You can flag down the train and get on board. But you must go quickly!"

Everything was happening so fast, Charlotte couldn't think straight. "Go where, Granny Fate?"

"Go west, Charlotte! Seek out your fortune . . . and your love!"

After one final embrace, Granny Fate disappeared through the door as quickly as she had come. Charlotte, her heart pounding with excitement and a certain amount of dread, dressed in a traveling suit and packed a few things in the trunk. She stood for a moment in the tiny bedroom that had been her nursery as a child. Would she ever see this room again? Tears sprang to her eyes at the thought. But the mournful whistle of a train far off in the distance forced her mind back from the past to the present. As for the future, she hardly dared ponder its uncertainties.

In moments, she had slipped out of the house by the back way and was racing for the big white barn. She could hear Caesar's impatient snort as she neared.

"Easy, boy," she whispered. "It's only me. We're

going for a little midnight ride." Quickly she strapped the little trunk behind the saddle.

The moon was low, but Charlotte slipped up into the sidesaddle with the expertise of one born to ride. She would have preferred riding bareback, but her skirts hindered her. She gave Caesar his head, urging him to speed. The surefooted stallion raced away into the night, with Charlotte Buckland like a female centaur on his back.

The damp night wind kissed her cheeks and her hair blew free, as untamed as her spirits and her heart. Gone was the depression, the feeling of being trapped and tricked by fate. Ahead, somewhere along those shining tracks, lay her future. She would rush to meet it and embrace it joyfully . . . lovingly.

Chapter 2

Charlotte felt numb all over. The steady clickity-clack of the iron monster's rotating feet and its deep rumbling, which muffled all other sounds, seemed a part of her after many days' travel. Other passengers boarded and detrained. But still she sat as the minutes ticked by with the rhythm of the wheels.

At first she'd felt nervous and strangely out of place on the westward-bound train. Before the war, she wouldn't have dreamed of traveling without a chaperone— not even for a short distance, let alone across the entire country. But this was 1870—the dawn of a new era. Never again would she fall back on her Southern-belle ways. This new land was tough. Charlotte Buckland would be just as tough. She saw herself as one of a new breed—a refugee of the ravaged South, hungry for adventure, longing to leave the torment of the war years behind and experience the exotic wonders of the golden West. If she found love along the way, that would be all right, too.

But gazing out of the dust-and-cinder-frosted windows of the Kansas & Pacific Railroad coach, the diminutive beauty with hair the color of the last two gold coins left in her purse didn't feel quite as brave as she pretended. For the first time in her life, she was completely alone. And the brown plains and wide rivers outside were alien to her after a lifetime spent in the Bluegrass State.

Still, she had made her choice. Now she would live with it. Better to be alone in a strange land, she thought, than married to Major Winston Krantz. And what a narrow escape she'd had from becoming the bride of that U.S. Cavalry officer! One more day and . . .

"Leavenworth! Next stop!" the leathery old conductor called out tonelessly.

"How long, please?" Charlotte asked.

He looked her up and down with rheumy eyes before he replied, " 'Bout a half hour, miss. But you ain't gettin' off there, are you? Thought you were going on down the line a piece."

Charlotte felt a pink tinge stain her cheeks. Never would she get over her embarrassment at having to admit her straitened circumstances. But she lifted her head to a proud tilt, offered the man a radiant smile, and answered, "I'm afraid my dreams stretch farther than my purse strings. But I'll find work. I'll get where I'm going. Don't you worry."

"You mean you're all on your own . . . no family or friends hereabouts?"

"I make friends easily." She gave the conductor such a confident look that he couldn't doubt her.

"Well, you just watch yourself, miss. Leavenworth's a rough place. A circus town, you know."

"Circus town?" Charlotte's curiosity was piqued.

"And worse! Seems like the whole world's moving west and Leavenworth's the jumping-off spot. This town gets every kind. Even them wild Romany folk that come over from Europe right after the war.''

Charlotte frowned slightly, not understanding.

The conductor looked this way and that, as if to make sure none of the other passengers could hear, before he leaned toward her and whispered, ''You know—Gypsies! A bad lot. I'd hate to see my daughter stopping over in Leavenworth all by herself.''

Charlotte was fascinated. ''What are Gypsies doing way out here?''

''They're carney types. Great horse people, you know. And out of that comes their traveling shows—circuses. C. W. Parker Company of Leavenworth caters to their kind, mending tents and selling all manner of stuff you can't get nowhere else.'' He straightened up and made a clucking sound of disapproval with his tongue. ''Draws a bad crowd. You be mighty careful, miss. I hear tell they ain't above stealing an occasional pretty girl, 'specially one that's got hair like a summer noontime.''

''I will,'' she promised, controlling a wayward laugh at the old man's outrageous fears.

He moved on down the aisle, secure in the thought that his warning was well placed.

Charlotte leaned back with a sigh and watched the Missouri River slide past outside. Her mind left Leavenworth and the Gypsies and returned to Fairview Plantation, to her mother and grandmother. Would she ever see them again? Of course she would! She had to believe that. Nothing in life meant anything without family and roots. And Charlotte Buckland's roots grew deep in the fertile soil of Kentucky. Yes, she would return—someday —once she'd proven herself.

But now that all ties with home and family had been broken—now that she had literally and figuratively stamped her foot and stormed out—Fairview seemed a lifetime away, more fantasy than reality. The only tangible things in her life this minute were the wide stretches of country outside and the rumble of the train. She wondered what awaited her in Leavenworth, Kansas. Had Granny Fate done right to help her run out on her old life?

Charlotte shook her head as if to clear it of all doubts. Her neat curls bounced beneath the faded green velvet bonnet perched upon them. She looked down at the small trunk at her feet, which contained, as Granny Fate had told her, "your past and your future."

What had Fatima Lee Buckland meant? Charlotte still didn't understand. Maybe she never would. Her grandmother had a way of talking in riddles.

"Leavenworth . . . coming up!" wailed the conductor.

Charlotte reached down and touched the trunk. Everything she owned in the world was safely locked inside. Granny Fate had given her something of home and family so that Charlotte wouldn't feel lonely once she was far away.

Sudden excitement gripped Charlotte. All sad thoughts vanished, leaving a kind of childlike wonder in their wake. She leaned forward in her seat, anxious to see this new place. As the train puffed into the station, she knew by a sign on the corner that she would be stepping out on Olive Street. She hurried to get her things together.

When the fatherly old conductor offered a hand to help her down, she thanked him and smiled brightly.

"You mind yourself now, young lady," he admonished.

"Oh, I will. You don't have to worry about me."

Leavenworth came as a surprise to Charlotte. She had imagined a sleepy, rough little crossroads, where men sat in the shade playing checkers and mongrel dogs lazed in the sun. But the town bustled with activity. Steamboats lined the wharf near the tracks. Teams of oxen lumbered to and from the station, and wagons of every size and description waited to load or unload.

People hurried in all directions, busy at every conceivable task.

Once she got over her amazement and caught her breath, finding a hotel was her first order of business. She looked about for someone to ask, but everyone was in such a hurry. Three rough-looking men on the platform were passing a bottle around and eyeing her. She thought of the conductor's warning and started to move away.

"Hey, pretty lady!" One of the dirty loiterers, his breath stale with rotgut whiskey, reached out and grabbed her arm. "If you're sellin', me and my buddies are sure in the market for whatever you got to offer."

Charlotte's heart seemed to shrink inside her breast. She pulled away from the man, but he moved in to block her way. She was about to scream for help when a stranger pushed through the crowd and shoved the masher away.

In a voice exotically accented, the tall stranger ordered, "On your way, mister. I would not want to have to hurt you."

What the man's quiet tone failed to convey, the crack of his bullwhip added with authority. The drunken trail hand stumbled away without an argument.

Charlotte turned toward the man with the whip to thank him, but her breath caught in her throat, choking her words. The stranger who had rescued her was out of another time and place. He towered over her, gazing down, his sun-bronzed face unsmiling. She thought with an odd sadness that had he not been so ruggedly built and hardened by the elements, he might have been called beautiful, though never to his face. A riptide of black curls swirled about his collar, bringing out the mysterious darkness of his eyes. He wore golden earrings and a heavy chain, hand-wrought, about his neck. The jewelry was no more in keeping with his rough workman's britches, shirt, and knee-high boots than was the vivid scarlet silk kerchief wound about his neck.

She realized suddenly that he was examining her with a curiosity equal in intensity to her own. She felt as if his jet eyes were piercing her very soul. Unsettled by his scrutiny, she looked away.

"You are unharmed?" His voice was as mellow and rich as aged Kentucky bourbon.

"Yes . . . thank you . . . sir," she stammered.

"It is not wise for a woman to be alone in this part of town. If you do not live far, I will see you safely home."

Without waiting for Charlotte to give her consent, he hoisted her trunk to his broad shoulder, grasped her arm, and hauled her along with him toward the main part of town.

"Wait a minute! Where are you taking me?" she asked, annoyed by his brusqueness. "I don't have a place to stay yet. I just got off the train."

"Then I will see to your lodgings myself." He never slowed his pace, hurrying her along the bustling thoroughfare.

Charlotte Buckland could do nothing. The man seemed set on his mission. She wasn't sure whether to be grateful or terrified. Hadn't she heard tales of girls traveling alone who were kidnapped, forced into brothels, and never heard from again? She might have handled the drunken man earlier, but she was powerless against her present captor.

"Please!" she cried, pulling back to slow his progress. "You must tell me where you're taking me."

"Please indeed!" he replied, moving on, hauling her with him along the wooden sidewalk. "I do not have time to answer questions. I will see to it that you are taken care of."

Suddenly, a woman's scream from across the street

distracted Charlotte's attention. "Mateo!" the woman yelled. "Mateo, answer me!"

"A thousand devils!" Charlotte's dark stranger muttered angrily, but he neither turned nor responded to the summons.

"Come back here, you!" the woman demanded angrily.

"When I finish my business, Phaedra," he called back. But he still refused even to glance in her direction.

Charlotte did manage a glimpse of her and gasped at what she saw. The exotic beauty stood on the far curb, holding her skirts up to keep them out of the dust. And *such* skirts! Charlotte had never seen anything like this person's costume. She wore a tight-fitting bodice of silver, her full breasts straining at the fabric and threatening to spill out over the top when she leaned forward to shout again. From the tight waist, layer upon layer of heliotrope-and-emerald gauze flared about her. Charlotte recognized the unmistakable outline of shapely bare limbs through the gossamer skirts.

But amazingly enough, Charlotte seemed to be the only person in town who even gave the woman named Phaedra a second look. And obviously this man—what had Phaedra called him . . . *Mateo?*—was trying to avoid her.

"Aren't you going to answer?" Charlotte said.

"Pay her no mind," Mateo ordered. "If luck is with us, she will go away."

"But she sounds desperate. Shouldn't you find out what she wants?"

A laugh rumbled from his full lips. "Phaedra is always desperate and she always wants the same thing—to start trouble. Believe me, it is of no importance."

As Mateo hurried Charlotte down Delaware Street, she happened to glimpse a "Help Wanted" sign in the window of C. Clark's china and glassware shop. She decided to return later and inquire about the position.

Beyond the buildings on the far side of the street, she saw a collection of brightly painted wagons and tents set up at the edge of town. She was reminded of the horse fairs back home.

Suddenly, everything became very clear to Charlotte Buckland. The tents and wagons, the woman called Phaedra in her outlandish garb, and Mateo with his golden earrings and fancy whip.

"Why, you're with the circus, aren't you?"

"Some call it that."

"You're one of the Gypsies!" The thought both thrilled and frightened her.

He stopped and turned Charlotte, none too gently, to face him before he answered, "I am Rom Mateo, son of Queen Zolande. I work with horses, so I am known by the title *Graiengeri*. It is an old and honorable profession among my people."

Charlotte could tell by his tone that she had offended him in some way. "I'm sorry, Rom Mateo. I didn't mean any insult."

He let go of her arm and looked directly into her brown eyes for a moment—long enough to make something inside her warm under his gaze.

"I, too, am sorry. You did not speak the name Gypsy in the ugly manner of most *gajos*. I was too quick to defend what needed no defense. But my people—my *familia*—are dear to me. I will allow no slur on the Gypsy name."

Charlotte felt somewhat embarrassed by the passion of his words. She cast about for another subject and said, "My father was a horse breeder and trainer, and his father before him. We have a farm in Kentucky."

He nodded gravely. "It is a good life with the horses. But your father is gone now?"

"In the war," she answered quietly, her eyes downcast.

"Do not be sad. He left a daughter to be proud of,"

Mateo declared, pressing Charlotte's hand with his for the briefest moment.

"Thank you, Mateo."

"Ma-te-o!" Phaedra was at it again. *"Dinilo!"*

Mateo threw back his head and laughed, then shook his fist in Phaedra's direction. Charlotte looked at him quizzically.

"She called me 'stupid one,' " he said. "I will get her for that!"

"Is she your sister, Mateo?" Charlotte was frowning, puzzling over the connection between this wild Gypsy pair.

Mateo shook his head until his dark curls tossed in the breeze. He laughed. "God forbid we should be from the same womb! She is only my cousin." Then the humor in his voice vanished. "But we will be closer than that soon. Now I will take you into the hotel. Phaedra, for once, is correct. It is time I was about my business."

Mateo ushered Charlotte into the cool, spacious lobby of the Planters Hotel. The clerk, looking very staid and officious in his celluloid collar and spectacles, presided over the wide mahogany desk. The place seemed entirely respectable; her worry had been wasted.

"This is quite nice, Mateo. I'm sure I'll be comfortable here. Thank you so much for helping me."

When Mateo didn't reply, Charlotte turned to find him leaving.

"Wait!" she cried. "Will I see you again?"

He turned slowly toward her and seemed to be looking her through and through, memorizing her face and form. His eyes, heavy-lidded, measured her inch for inch, until Charlotte felt herself quivering inside her worn velvet traveling suit. It was almost as if his gaze had the power to touch her physically and in the most intimate places.

"You don't want to see me again, *sunaki bal*—golden-

27

haired one." The sound of his coiled whip slapping the top of his boot was the only noise in the quiet lobby. "I can bring nothing but trouble to you."

Before Charlotte could say another word, Mateo was gone.

"They're odd ones, them Gypsies," the desk clerk remarked, shoving the ledger toward Charlotte.

She was quick to come to Mateo's defense. "They are a proud people. That one in particular is a fine man."

"Know him right well, do you, *Miss* Buckland?" the clerk asked, after a quick glance at the register to get her name and marital status. He peered at her over his wire-rimmed spectacles with accusing eyes. "This here's a high-class hotel, miss. The best one north of St. Louis. We got a reputation to uphold. Don't cotton to no hanky-panky, if you get my drift."

The man was being absolutely insulting. No one spoke to Charlotte Buckland in such a manner and got away with it. She gave him a level gaze in return and snapped, "I'm quite afraid I do! You can rest assured that as soon as I find a decent boardinghouse, I'll be leaving your high-class hotel!"

Struggling with her trunk, Charlotte started from the lobby to find her room without assistance. The desk clerk got in the parting shot: "That's up to you, Miss Buckland. But until you're out of here, that Gypsy boyfriend of yours is to stay clear! We don't allow his kind on the premises!"

Too angry to reply, Charlotte swept down the hallway in seething silence, wondering at the same time why she had been so quick to defend a man she hardly knew and would probably never see again.

Chapter 3

The Planters Hotel offered a very real luxury after days of travel on the sooty train—a porcelain bathtub. Charlotte shed her grimy clothes and climbed in for a good scrub and soak. Slowly, her travel-weary body revived. By the time she emerged from the water, her whole outlook had changed for the better—all gloom washed away with the grime of her trip.

What could be so terrible? Here she was in an exciting new place that absolutely vibrated with life. She had a comfortable room and enough money left to buy herself the best steak in town at Delmonico's. On her way to supper, she would stop on Delaware Street and speak to Mr. C. Clark about that position. How could he turn down a freshly scrubbed, rosewater-scented woman with a polished eastern accent? She was accustomed to drinking from Waterford and eating off Sevres before the war. She was a natural for the glass and china trade, Charlotte assured herself.

She hand-pressed the wrinkles out of her best dress—a spring-green afternoon gown of crisp lawn. It was a few years out of style and rather tight, since her figure was more mature now at nineteen than when Granny Fate had made the dress. Still, the color looked good on her, contrasting nicely with her shining hair and bringing out the flecks of gold dust in her brown eyes. And the fullness of her breasts was quite becoming, she decided, rather than shocking like Phaedra's.

That thought focused her mind on the Gypsies once more. From her window Charlotte could see the red-and-blue tents, their bright flags fluttering in the afternoon breeze. The crowds gathering in the area must mean a matinee was about to begin.

She looked in the mirror over the washstand and smoothed back her curls, pinning each side in place with a pair of ivory combs. As she watched her reflection, she saw a mischievous smile playing about her lips. She tried frowning it away, but the devilish grin refused to be banished.

"Dare I?" she asked of her bemused mirror image. It replied with an immediate, affirmative nod.

What harm could there be in attending a matinee? There were dozens—possibly hundreds—of people down there buying tickets. Men, women, even children. It would be perfectly respectable, she decided, not without a slight shudder at the delicious impropriety of it all. Why, she might even see Mateo again!

She paused before opening the door. What had he meant when he'd told her she didn't want to see him again—that he could only bring her trouble? Then she shrugged all doubts away and hurried down the hallway.

"Mateo talks in riddles just like Granny Fate."

In spite of her determination to find a job and her pressing need for money, Charlotte wasn't disappointed in the least when she found the china shop closed for the rest of the afternoon. She promised herself faithfully that her first stop the next morning would be to inquire about the position, then she hurried toward the tents in the distance, fairly bursting with excitement.

She felt the same elation now that she had experienced as a child back in Kentucky when her father had taken her to the horse fairs. Was there really any difference, after all?

As she neared the grounds, a swarm of dark, tousle-haired children surrounded her. They were a ragtag lot of barefoot cherubs, all pleading eyes, clutching hands, and wide, white smiles. They engulfed her like a shifting rainbow in their bright, outlandish costumes.

The tiniest girl, no more than four, gripped Charlotte's fingers and begged, "Please, *gajo* lady, a penny is all we ask. Our papa will beat us if we do not bring home something."

The little beggar's eyes, wide and shimmering with tears, struck at Charlotte's heart for a moment. Then she spied the twitch of a grin just below the surface of that pitifully angelic face. She recognized some of the same mischief in the child's expression that she had seen in her own face such a short time before. But Charlotte decided to play along with the moppets. She feigned a horrified look.

"*Beat you?* You poor little child! What's your name?"

"You guessed my name," the girl said, nodding vigorously. "I am Pesha, but they all call me *Poor Little Pesha*. Even my papa, who beats me—*regularly!*"

"Well, *Poor Little Pesha,*" Charlotte said in a mock stern voice, "I want to know your father's name, too. I'd like to have a word with him about these beatings."

Pesha squinted at her through beautiful, dewy tears and drew herself up with pride. "My papa is the great Prince Mateo!"

Charlotte was taken aback. *Mateo?* She hadn't guessed that he might be married and a father. But why not? He was certainly a handsome, virile man. Women must have thrown themselves at him all his life.

"Prince Mateo, he is my papa, too!" volunteered a lad of about ten.

"And mine!"

"Mine, too!"

"Yes, all our papas!" they chorused.

"And he beats us every one!" Poor Little Pesha added in a voice loud enough to silence the others, who were usurping her center-stage position.

Charlotte felt numb—not because she believed for a moment that Mateo beat his children, but at the alarming thought that he *had* them. And so many! Were Gypsies allowed more than one wife? She didn't know. But surely, if Mateo had fathered such a brood, he had shared the magnificent effort with a number of women.

"Only a penny," Pesha persisted. "Please, pretty *gajo!*"

Anxious to put an end to the scene, Charlotte fished out a copper coin and pressed it into the girl's tiny palm. The giggling, jostling band of urchins immediately scurried away like tiny fish in a school.

Charlotte refused to let this incident mar her afternoon. She simply wouldn't think about Mateo . . . or his numerous offspring. She hurried to join the crowd, still pondering the man's prolificacy, in spite of herself.

The ticket line was long and stretched across a patch of dusty, sunlit ground. Charlotte hesitated, not wanting to wilt her dress. Glancing about, she spotted a smaller tent, off by itself. A hand-lettered sign out front read "Your Future Told By TAMARA."

"A fortune-teller!" Charlotte cried, then glanced about self-consciously to make sure no one had heard.

Without giving her more sensible side a chance to

block the exciting impulse, Charlotte hurried into the tent. When she entered the cramped quarters, her eyes met those of a darkly beautiful woman about her own age.

Tamara nodded without smiling. "You will take the chair."

Quickly Charlotte sat down across a small table from the Gypsy woman. She squirmed uncomfortably for several moments as Tamara eyed her up and down. Unable to meet the dark eyes examining her, Charlotte focused her gaze on the table, where Tamara's ringed fingers gently caressed the white cloth. Soon the clamor of the crowd outside seemed to fade. Only the silence that stretched between the two women and the whisper of flesh against fabric held sway inside the tent.

"You wish to know your future." Tamara's sudden rich voice uttered it as a statement rather than a question.

"Yes, please."

"You have come a very long way to find your fortune, miss."

Once more Tamara stated facts rather than asking questions. But how could she know? Charlotte wondered. She studied the woman—her bold features, the golden rings and necklaces, and the bright scarf tied about her ebony hair.

"Well, lady?"

Charlotte looked up. "What?"

"Gold! If I am to tell your fortune, my mind must be helped by your gold . . . freely offered. I take not. I only give. Such is the way of the Gypsy fortune-teller. But your gift will help my powers to help you."

Hesitantly Charlotte dropped her last gold coin into Tamara's open palm. The woman studied it intently, then bit it to make sure it was real. When she looked up into Charlotte's face, there was a strange, faraway quality to her expression.

"You have just ended a journey which you think has taken you away from danger and unhappiness."

A bit disappointed that the last of her gold had bought her only information that she already knew, Charlotte asked, "Is that all?"

Taking a small crystal ball out of the ample pocket of the apron covering her flowered skirt, Tamara gazed into it with her night-colored eyes almost closed.

Her voice took on a trancelike tone. "I see a ring blazing about you, but many other things—a screaming raven, a wild stallion, and a brilliant sunburst. Two people. Two hearts breaking. Love and hate shall mingle and mate. Beware the night! The night of the full moon!" Suddenly Tamara cried out a strangled sob and collapsed to the table. "That is all," she whispered. "Go! Leave this place before it is too late. There is great danger for you here!"

Unnerved by the words of the Gypsy fortune-teller, Charlotte hurried from the tent. She almost turned away, back toward the hotel. The few coppers she had left would buy her supper. She had heard entirely too much about danger for one day. Her excited anticipation of seeing the circus acts had fled with the Gypsy's warnings.

Then, just as she turned to head back toward the main part of town, she spied Mateo. Gone were his workingman's clothes. The tall *Rom* now wore a costume of scarlet and gold—his tights form-fitting, his chest bare beneath a flowing cape of matching colors that bedazzled her eyes in the afternoon sun.

She caught only a brief, glittering glimpse of him as he led his six black horses into the tent. But it was enough. She could not deny her curiosity about him or her desire to see him perform. There was no longer any doubt in Charlotte's mind as to how she would spend her remaining coins.

"One, please," she said to the copper-skinned girl in the ticket box.

She hurried inside and found a seat on a wooden bench in time to hear the ringmaster cry out, "And now from the capitals of the Continent, where he has appeared before the crowned heads of Europe, it is with great pleasure I present to you Prince Mateo and his performing *grai*."

Mateo, who had stood like a statue at the far entrance, a curtain of devil-black stallions forming the perfect backdrop for his glittering costume of scarlet and gold, now whirled his cape away. The whip, which Charlotte had seen him use earlier, whistled over his head before slicing the dusty air with a sharp report. The horses reared over him, poised in midair for one magnificent, terrifying instant. Then, with a precise command in his native tongue, Mateo set the stallions circling around the ring until their galloping pace created a black blur before Charlotte's eyes.

She applauded loudly, in a most unladylike fashion, as Mateo leaped onto the back of one of the moving horses and balanced there, his arms spread wide, displaying the strong contours of his bare chest. The hard muscles in his thighs strained at the fabric of his tights as he fought for and gained control of his own body and that of the high-strung animal beneath him.

Charlotte held her breath. How could he possibly maintain his stance? The horses seemed to be flying. If he fell, he would be crushed beneath their savage hooves.

With all the grace and beauty of a ballet dancer, Mateo maneuvered to the horse's hind quarters, poised there for a moment to make sure of his balance, then did a breathtaking flip, high into the air. Charlotte gasped, feeling for a moment as if her heart had stopped altogether.

A thunder of applause followed the daring stunt. She sat back, breathing deeply, weak with relief. There followed a series of exquisitely executed dismounts and remounts, flips, and hurtles through the dust-choked air. Charlotte thought she could take little more as she watched him mount the great black in the lead for a final somersaulting round of the horses' backs. But he never missed a step or lost his balance for a moment. It was as if Mateo had invisible wings.

As a final stunt, he stood upright once more on the back of his lead horse and whistled a command. A second stallion of equal, magnificent proportions moved in alongside until the two horses' flanks were amost touching. Eight hooves beat with a perfectly matched, galloping rhythm, echoing the thunder of Charlotte's heart. With flawless timing and daredevil bravado, Mateo placed one foot on the back of the second animal. Around and around they dashed, with their master balanced between the two, a wide and triumphant smile on his face as he waved his arms above his head, acknowledging the audience's appreciative cheers.

At last he back-flipped off the pair, giving another shrill whistle as he landed on his feet directly before Charlotte. At his signal, all six horses stopped, posed with one foreleg raised, then bowed their graceful necks to the audience.

Mateo, his sweating chest heaving, stood so close to Charlotte that had she dared reach out to touch him, as she longed to, her trembling fingers might easily have brushed away the droplets of perspiration from the damp curls about his face. His arousing scent of heated horse-flesh and leather seemed to envelop her. Their eyes met for one galvanic moment, seeming to bond their souls. To Charlotte it was like a physical jolt.

Then the instant passed. Mateo's lips curved upward at the corners in a kind of wild, heathen joy. It was as if no one else in the world existed in his eyes. She felt his gaze—a tangible force pressing against her heart and awakening unexplained longings deep within her. No man had ever looked at her this way . . . or made her feel this way.

"You were wonderful, Mateo," she whispered, barely conscious that she had spoken the words aloud.

"For you alone, my *sunaki bal*," he answered, clasping her hand and bringing it to his lips.

The cheering throng within the tent seemed to be in another dimension, with Charlotte and Mateo suspended somewhere in between physical planes. This space they occupied offered tingling thrills and rarefied air. Best of all, it was exclusively theirs.

Charlotte couldn't force her gaze away. She caressed him visually, from the tensing of his muscled thighs to the wild disarray of his gleaming hair. And as she devoured his form with her eyes, he made love to her with his. She felt weak, confused, out of her element, but very much a part of his, as he touched his fingers to his lips and blew her a parting kiss.

Suddenly, the crowd around her made itself known to Charlotte. They hadn't missed Mateo's special attention to her. Their applause and lewd jeers were now meant for her. She looked up and saw that even Poor Little Pesha and one of her Gypsy brothers had noticed Mateo's special favors to her. The two children stood nearby, miming the scene they had witnessed. Pesha's large eyes gave her an all-knowing look.

In utter shame, Charlotte rose to flee from the tent, but at the exit a strong hand caught her arm.

"No, golden one! You will not leave yet. You have cheered my cousin Mateo. You will show Petronovich the same courtesy. Please to stay and observe my performance. I promise to show you my most extravagant gratitude."

Charlotte stared, unable to move, as this equally dark and handsome man brought her fingers to his lips, imitating Mateo's gesture. Still holding her hand, but now in a less than gentle grip, he looked into her eyes with a fierceness that sent chills through her. Trying to pull away, she cast about frantically in search of Mateo. But he and his horses were gone from the tent.

"No, please!" she begged. "I must go!"

"No! You must stay!"

This man was so much like Mateo, yet so different. His Gypsy eyes held a threat not to be taken lightly. Mateo's voice was deep and musical, while that of this stranger held menace in its depths. Charlotte struggled against him, but his grip proved as powerful as his gaze.

"Let me go!" she demanded. He would not.

Almost dragging her now, he placed her firmly back in her front-row seat and ordered, "You will stay right here!"

Petronovich moved away from her, and Charlotte rose to leave. But he had anticipated this and made a slight motion toward the tent flap. At his signal, two burly men took up posts in front of Charlotte's only escape route. She saw the Gypsy's smile of victory as she took her seat once more.

Leaping into the ring, the menacing stranger postured before his audience as the ringmaster announced, "We have now for you the masterful, the magnificent, the marvelous Rom Petronovich and his trained bruin, Boski, aided most deliciously by the ravishing Princess Phaedra."

The men in the crowd stomped, cheered, and whistled at Phaedra's name. A moment later, Charlotte watched the tall beauty lead a great black bear into the center of the tent, tugging him along by a chain attached to a large ring through his nose.

Petronovich and Phaedra bowed to each other, their Romany-black eyes flashing sensually in defiant lust. The moment became so naked in its passion that Charlotte looked away. She couldn't explain why this pair gave her such a fearful feeling, but there was no denying her discomfort.

When Petronovich shouted an order and the bear gave a loud growl, Charlotte looked up again. The exotic Phaedra, dressed in a flowing costume of purple, green, and silver that matched her partner's tights, whirled about the ring in a pagan dance, pulling the ungainly bear along behind her. He ambled on his hind legs, front paws flailing the air in an effort to keep his balance. When he faltered from time to time, Phaedra jerked the chain cruelly.

Suddenly Petronovich grasped Phaedra about her slender waist and raised her high in the air above his head. The bear stumbled about, making pitiful noises, trying to rescue his mistress.

Petronovich taunted the frantic animal, saying, "You want her, eh, Boski? You want your lovely Phaedra? Ah, but don't be so anxious, my furry friend. You say you will die without her?" Petronovich flashed a meaningful look at the audience and said, "Many men have said the same, among them the great *graiengeri*, Rom Mateo! So, if she can have such a prince of Romany, why should she desire you? Eh, Boski?"

When he spoke Mateo's name, Petronovich shifted his gaze to Charlotte Buckland. Again she would have fled, but a quick glance at the exit told her the guards were still on duty.

"Boski, my Boski, come save me!" Phaedra cried in a teasing voice, sending the poor bear into paroxysms.

Suddenly Petronovich whirled Phaedra around, then placed her on his discarded cape in the center of the ring. The bear master stepped back, allowing the frantic Boski to run to his mistress, Phaedra stretched out her shapely white arms to the creature, who proceeded to lick her all over with his long purple tongue. The woman moved her body as if she were in a lover's embrace. She sighed and moaned her feigned pleasure.

The men in the crowd went wild, stamping and shouting as they watched the clumsy bear tease Phaedra's tempting flesh.

Charlotte turned her head away. She couldn't stand to watch. The exchange between two men sitting behind her proved even more embarrassing.

"You reckon she really gets her kicks from havin' that varmint slobberin' all over her, Gus?"

"Couldn't say," Gus answered. "But I'll fill that there bear's skin any-damn-time them Gypsies want to give me the job. I guaran-damn-tee you I'd do it for free! That there Princess Phaedra's some piece of female!"

A wild yell from Petronovich silenced the audience and brought Charlotte's attention back to the ring.

"Enough, Boski! Away from her! She is mine!"

A mock battle ensued between man and beast. They wrestled about the ring, vying for the attentions of the still reclining Phaedra, who shouted encouragement to each in turn.

With a sudden roar of rage—mock or real, Charlotte couldn't decide which—Petronovich shoved the bear away from him and grabbed his whip. He lashed Boski brutally until the creature roared out in pain. The crowd cheered and yelled their approval.

Charlotte's stomach turned. She had to get out of the tent—away from this vicious man, whose maniacal black eyes were now on her once more. She jumped up from her seat and dashed not for the guarded exit but directly across the ring—past bear and performers—and hurried through the far tent flap, used only by the members of the troupe.

She thought she heard Mateo call after her, but she dared not stop, for fear Petronovich might be in pursuit. She never slowed her pace but ran all the way back to the Planters Hotel. What had begun as an exciting after-noon had ended in humiliating disaster.

The sun was sinking low by the time Charlotte reached her room and locked herself in. She had no money left to buy supper. It didn't matter—she couldn't have eaten anyway. Her nerves were ragged, her emotions in a turmoil.

Tomorrow, she decided, when she had calmed herself enough to think, she would set her new life in order—find a job and a homey rooming house. She would stay away from the Gypsies. *All of them!* Mateo had been right: they could only bring trouble!

Having a bed to sleep in for the first time in many nights, Charlotte wasted little time thinking of Fairview, her grueling trip west, or her empty stomach. Neither did she dwell on Mateo's mysterious attraction, nor Petronovich's cruelty. As soon as her head touched the pillow, she fell into a deep sleep.

Hours later, the full moon crept through her window, silvering her face. But she didn't feel its touch. Neither did she hear the rattling of the window opening, nor the soft thud of boots approaching her bed. Not until she felt searching hands upon her body did she try to scream.

But unknown lips, pressed tightly to her own, refused to allow any sound of protest. Only then did she come fully out of her dreams to awake in a nightmare.

Chapter 4

Charlotte Buckland fought like a tigress, trying to escape. But strong arms held her fast. The prolonged and demanding kiss smothered her cries. Never before had any man touched her this way. Now, in one terrifying moment, a stranger was about to possess her totally.

Grasping both her wrists in one hand while still clinging to her lips with his own, the man tore open her linen nightgown. Charlotte experienced a moment of shock when cool air found her exposed breasts. Then a hand was there, teasing, taunting her nipples to erection. She strained away, trying to bury herself in the mattress, but there was no escaping him. His hard bare chest pressed down on her, taking her breath away.

He broke off the kiss at last, but the hand that had tortured her breasts quickly covered her mouth.

"Not to struggle, my beauty. I wish you no harm. I have come to love you." His voice was a husky growl against her ear.

The heavy accent brought instant recognition. *Mateo!* But no. He would never force a woman. He would never have to! Then her mind grasped her attacker's true identity. Her defiler was Petronovich, the cruel bear master!

Shock and terror possessed her, robbing her of survival instincts for a moment. She stopped fighting him and lay still, staring up at the rugged profile and the mass of black hair tumbling over his forehead.

"Ah, is better now." He crooned the words suggestively, tracing the contour of one cheek with his fingertip. "You remember Petronovich. You want me . . . no?"

Believing that Charlotte understood and accepted what he meant to do, Petronovich relaxed his guard, releasing his hand from her mouth to find her lips with his again. But in that split second before he leaned down to kiss her, Charlotte filled the room with her screams. She fought like a wild thing, scratching his face and neck, sinking her teeth into his arm. Petronovich let fly a stream of *Romani* curses, adding to the fracas. Immediately the sound reached them of doors opening and feet running in the hallway.

Mindless of the pain he was causing her, Petronovich grabbed Charlotte roughly in his arms and pressed her face into his hard chest. Though she continued to scream for help, her voice was muffled. Her struggles proved useless.

"Now you have done it!" her abductor snarled through clenched teeth. "Big trouble for both of us! But I will have you—one way or another!"

The next moment, Charlotte felt herself falling through the air, still in Petronovich's arms. He landed on his feet on the ground below, jolting her to the very core, then took off running. Her whole body ached from his rough treatment. Her mind fought to deny this terrible reality.

Surely, someone would stop this madman and rescue her!

But when she recognized the voice of the surly desk clerk coming from her open window, her heart sank.

"Well, I could have told you this would happen," she heard him say. "She come sashayin' in here this afternoon with one of them Gypsy fellers! And that's the same one making off with her now. She'll be in his wolf skins in no time!"

Another voice argued, "But Jess, the girl's screamin' her head off. Shouldn't we do something?"

"Hell, no, Chester! It's all part of the ceremony."

The sounds from the hotel faded. A moment later, Petronovich hoisted Charlotte up over the high wheel of his painted caravan and shoved her through the door behind the porchlike front of the wagon.

"You let me out of here!" she screamed, pounding with all her might on the locked door.

"All in good time, my fiery beauty!"

She sank down in one corner, too furious to continue her hopeless battle. The darkness was oppressive inside the wagon. As her eyes adjusted to it she suddenly realized that she was not alone. A huge shape blocked the moonlight that tried to filter in through the thick curtain over one window.

Already the wagon was rumbling through the night. She could hear Petronovich's whip cracking and his growling voice encouraging the horses to more speed. Where was he taking her? She dared not think about it.

The one thing that she had to concentrate on was escape. She forced her mind into a calm mode while never taking her eyes off the dark shape a few feet away from her. She had to be rational if she hoped to save herself from this mad Gypsy. She noticed a slight movement from her fellow passenger. Was it a man sleeping there? No, it was too huge. What, then?

With her sudden realization, Charlotte's breath froze in her chest. She should have guessed from the smell— the gamy, earthy odor that permeated the wagon's interior. But it couldn't be! Not even Petronovich would do such a thing!

She shrank back in the corner. Perhaps if she stayed perfectly still and didn't make a sound . . .

But Charlotte couldn't help herself. When the thing moved and coarse fur brushed against her bare legs, she screamed as she never had before. Boski, as terrified as Charlotte herself, moved away from her. From the far side of the wagon, she could hear the bear sniffing the air, trying to identify her scent.

Oh, God! she thought. Why didn't I stay in Kentucky?

Just then, the caravan lurched to a jolting halt. Charlotte was thrown across the floor, landing in a heap against Boski's heavy haunch. The bear put a paw across her, caressing and licking her gently as if she were his Phaedra. Charlotte held her breath, not daring to move a muscle.

Mateo lay in his tent, alternately burning with an inexplicable fever and shivering with chills. His body ached as if it were possessed by devils, their pitchforks stabbing him from inside. He tossed on his pallet, thrashing his arms, biting hard on a piece of twisted rawhide to keep from screaming in his agony. His eyes refused to focus, but it didn't matter. He had secured the tent flap against the painful glow of the full moon. If one single ray fell upon him, he would be lost to the madness completely.

For a moment he lay quiet, breathing deeply, trying to clear his fogged senses. Why was he cursed? How could he spend the rest of his life this way? He was a strong man . . . a man of reason. But neither his strength nor his reasonable mind could win out over this hideous, nameless foe that attacked his body and soul with each full moon.

"An ancient curse," his mother, Zolande, had explained gently when he was still a small boy. "In time, you may find a way to banish it. But for now there is only endurance. I am sorry, my son."

Mateo remembered that he had seen silver tears in his mother's eyes as she'd spoken to him. It was the only time in his life that he had ever seen the noble queen of the Gypsies cry.

The full moon hushed the camp. Every man, woman, and child knew of Mateo's struggle with the spirits. They crept into their tents early, hiding their heads beneath the covers, praying for dawn and an end to their prince's suffering.

So the woman's screams rending the still night came as a shock. Mateo, eased somewhat by the waning of the moon, sat up and listened. Had he imagined the sounds? No! They came again—louder and more frantic.

Struggling to his feet, Mateo threw back the flap and looked out. On the far side of the camp, he saw Petronovich's caravan pulled up outside of the circle. His cousin, cursing loudly, was struggling with a woman.

Suddenly she spied him and cried out, "Mateo, help me!"

He knew that voice. It was the golden-haired *gajo* woman he had taken to the hotel—the same fair-haired beauty who had watched his act and praised him.

He summoned all his strength and made a rush for Petronovich, tackling him about the knees. More startled than hurt, Petronovich let go of Charlotte Buckland. She staggered backward, falling to the ground beside the wagon. The two men wrestled in the tall grass near where she lay. Finally, Mateo got the better of his cousin.

He sat astride the downed Petronovich, daring him to make another move.

"This is none of your affair, Mateo," Petronovich snarled. "She is mine! I took her!"

"*Took* her?" Mateo repeated, glancing quickly toward the sobbing girl.

What he saw made him want to take her in his arms and soothe away her tears and her grief. Her shining hair, loosened from its pins, tumbled in wild abandon about her face. Her great eyes, the color of aged brandy, stared up at him, pleading for his protection. She wore only a thin nightgown, torn open at the neck. Her heavy breathing caused her breasts to rise and fall, offering a glimpse of pale rosettes from time to time.

God help me, Mateo thought, she arouses far more than my sympathy!

But no! She was not one of his kind. He shouldn't be thinking such thoughts about her. She would have to be returned to her own people. Then he looked down at Petronovich and saw the malicious smile twisting his cousin's lips. Perhaps it was already too late to take her back.

"What is this?" demanded a low, female voice.

Charlotte looked up at the old woman. Her face was brown and lined, but aristocratic. Though she wore nightclothes, huge hoops of gold dangled from her ears, and her neck and arms were elaborately adorned. Obviously she was a leader of the clan. She ignored Charlotte for the moment and glared down at her son and nephew.

"Does the *phuri dai*, the ruler of you and all your kin, not deserve some explanation? Mateo? Petronovich?"

"I am sorry, Mother, that we disturbed you." Mateo stood up, allowing his cousin to rise, also. "It seems the moon madness did double duty tonight. Petronovich left camp and stole a woman—a *gajo*."

The old queen's gnarled hands flew to her lips. "In

the holy name of Sara-la-Kali!" she swore. "I should have known it would come to this someday. How many times in your youth, Petronovich, did I have to cross some farmer's palm with gold after you stole his chicken? But a woman! How do I repay that debt?"

Queen Zolande stood directly in front of Petronovich, her glittering black eyes seeming to pierce him through. Her voice quivered with rage.

"It may be worse than you know, Mother," Mateo said quietly. "Look at her."

Zolande swung around. Her lips drew back in a tight line as she took in Charlotte's disheveled appearance and torn gown.

Feeling self-conscious under the woman's blazing stare, Charlotte tried to smooth the wild tangle of her hair from her face.

"So, it was not enough to steal her; you have used her as well?" the queen said to Petronovich while still gazing at his victim.

When Petronovich made no answer, Zolande demanded of Charlotte, "Well, has he bedded you?"

Still stunned and not fully understanding what the woman meant, but wanting her attacker punished, Charlotte cried, "Yes! He sneaked in through my window while I slept and climbed right into my bed! When I tried to fight him off, he tore my gown. My arms and mouth are all bruised, he held me so tight and used me so savagely!"

"She lies!" Petronovich snarled. "That may have been my plan, but I haven't touched her. Mateo saw to that!"

"You did!" Charlotte yelled at Petronovich. "You forced me to . . ."

Zolande watched dispassionately as Charlotte lapsed into angry tears.

"So, we see as well as hear what you have done to this woman, Petronovich. I now have choices to consider. I could return her to the town and have you jailed."

"Please, no!" Petronovich cried. "You know that I would die in jail as quickly as any other Gypsy. I must have my freedom, Queen Zolande!"

"Allow me to finish," she said, a cold edge to her voice. "I cannot have you jailed, for fear it would bring trouble to all of us. As I have heard the *gajos* say, 'One rotten apple spoils the barrel.' I am afraid they believe that, and you may be the rottenest fruit to taint our family tree since Xendar the Accursed." She glanced at Charlotte and added in a low tone, as if speaking to herself, "And, too, she may be with child even now."

Petronovich had lost his cool, superior air. "No, Queen Zolande! I did not lie with her! I swear it on my own mother's grave!"

The *phuri dai*'s bejeweled hand lashed out like lightning to slap Petronovich's mouth.

"How dare you speak in desecration of sacred ground? Do not whine to me about your punishment. The least you can do is act the man!"

"Mother," Mateo broke in, "she needs warmth and rest. She's shivering. Can't we continue this later?"

"Here, Mateo," a soft voice answered. "Put this blanket around her." It was the fortune-teller, Tamara.

Mateo took the blanket and went to Charlotte. Gently, he wrapped her in its warmth, then took her cold hands between his. His touch was reassuring. She knew he'd never let them harm her.

"*Phuri, dai*, I know this woman," Tamara said in her quiet voice. "I read her fortune only yesterday."

Queen Zolande's features softened when she looked at Tamara. The girl was like a timid bird, she mused. Strong enough to see and tell the sadness in the futures of others, but not willful enough to hold her own man. If only Mateo could have been cast with Tamara, how different their lives would be. But Fate would have her way, Zolande thought with a shrug.

"Did you see Petronovich, your own betrothed, in this woman's stars, Tamara?" asked Zolande. "Were you warned that he might do such a shameful thing, my dear?"

Tamara looked down, wanting to avoid Petronovich's defiant eyes. "I saw one of the *Rom*, Queen Zolande. I felt ill winds. I warned her to leave this place before it was too late."

Queen Zolande clutched her shawl about her as if she felt a sudden chill. "Then it is so! We cannot turn her away. She must stay with us until we know for certain if she carries Romany seed. And *you*!" She whirled about, pointing an accusing finger at Petronovich. "You will remain in camp at all times unless we are performing. Am I understood?"

Petronovich only nodded, but his eyes flashed dark anger. Why should they believe the *gajo* woman instead of him? Couldn't they see she was out to make trouble? Very well! he thought. They had accused him of the crime. He would see that it was committed!

Charlotte had all but forgotten the others. Mateo's handsome face looking down into hers was all that mattered. Why not stay with the Gypsies, if they would have her? That way she could get to know Mateo—understand the troubled look in his wonderful eyes. Those very eyes now hypnotized her, making her forget that Mateo might not have room in his life or his heart for her.

"Mateo, will you keep me with you? Protect me?" she begged.

He shook his head. "I cannot. I am sorry, but the queen would forbid it."

"But you must!" she insisted.

"Shhh! don't upset yourself, little one. You won't be

badly treated. And Petronovich will not be allowed near you . . . not until . . .''

Charlotte stared at him. "Until *what*? I don't want Petronovich near me ever again!"

He gave her a strange half smile. "How like a Gypsy woman you are, to protest so. He will be forced to stay away from you until he earns your brideprice and can marry you."

"*Marry me?* You're crazy! You're all crazy! I'm not going to marry him. I'd sooner marry his trained bear!" Charlotte's voice broke suddenly and she clutched at Mateo as if for protection.

Something deep inside him seemed to tear loose from its moorings. His heart thudded loudly, pulsing against Charlotte's soft, warm breasts. He slipped one arm around her waist and smoothed her hair. He could feel little gasps of breath on his neck, like the softest of kisses. She was weeping.

"Hush now," he urged. "The others will hear you. Gypsy women don't cry."

"But I'm not a Gypsy. And I'll cry if I feel like it!"

"You are strong for one who looks so frail and vulnerable. I saw that in you right away." His lips brushed her hair and she could feel his words whispered against her forehead. His breath was like a hot brand.

Charlotte clung to him, feeling some of her panic subside. If only he would marry her! The thought shocked and thrilled her at the same time. What had come over her? She had traveled hundreds of miles to escape a forced marriage planned by her own mother. Now these strangers seemed to take it for granted that she would marry the crazy man who had kidnapped her. And she was no better than they were—wishing she could marry Mateo, a wild Gypsy horse trainer she knew nothing about, except that he might have fathered a sizable army of dark-eyed children already. Still, it felt too wonderful to be in his arms and feel his heart beating against her own to worry about that right now.

Suddenly she was wrenched out of Mateo's embrace. Sharp nails flew at her face and neck, scratching painfully. A scream that could have come from a wild animal filled the dawn. Charlotte looked up into Phaedra's hateful black eyes.

"So, you pale-haired witch, you are not satisfied with taking little Tamara's man! You want my Mateo, too! Well, you will not have him! He is mine—*all mine*!"

Charlotte cringed away from the spitting, clawing woman. Had Mateo not grasped Phaedra's arms, she might have ripped Charlotte's throat out with her long nails.

A bitter smile curved Mateo's lips. Still holding tight to Phaedra, he said in a loveless tone, "Why, my dearest, how you surprise me! I thought your eyes and body were for Petronovich alone. But here you are acting and sounding like a jealous lover. How sweet!"

Phaedra's eyes narrowed. Her head swayed on her graceful neck as if she meant to strike like a snake. She turned to look at Mateo and hissed, "My body is my own. What I do with it is only my concern. But you belong to me. It was written at my birth. I do not share my possessions!"

Mateo released her abruptly. Phaedra turned for a moment to glare at Charlotte. Then, throwing her arms around Mateo's neck, she sought his lips in a deep, lingering kiss. Charlotte wanted to turn away, but fascination won out over propriety. She stared fixedly as Phaedra's long-nailed fingers dug into the flesh of Mateo's bare back.

Mateo's arms remained stiffly at his sides, his fists clenched. He refused to respond, even when Phaedra pressed her breasts tightly to his chest and rotated her hips against him suggestively. Charlotte felt her pulse pounding and blood rushing up to color her cheeks. At the same time, unfamiliar stirrings warmed her deepest parts.

As suddenly as Phaedra had captured her prey, she released him. Mateo's eyes blazed his anger. The Gypsy woman laughed and turned to Charlotte.

"There, my fine *gajo* lady! Now you know what a real *Rom* expects of his woman. Of course, no one would expect it of you. Poor, pale little creature!" She turned back to Mateo, taunting, "Why, darling, this one would faint dead away at the mere thought of such passion! But then perhaps you aren't up to it either, my wretched, moon-mad dear!"

Charlotte Buckland had inherited a hot temper. Her mother swore it came from her father's side of the family. She worked hard at controlling it and tried to remain ladylike at all times. But Phaedra had pushed her past her limits. Something—no *everything*—about Phaedra boiled her blood.

Without even thinking about what she was going to do, Charlotte threw off the blanket covering her torn gown. She walked past Phaedra to where Mateo waited, sensing her intention. When they were facing each other, Charlotte looked up into Mateo's warm eyes. For several seconds, their gazes locked.

"What is it, golden-haired one?" he questioned. He lifted his fingers to her face, brushing a damp strand of hair from her lips.

In answer, Charlotte let her hands touch his waist tentatively. As if the test had proven safe, her fingers moved up to his bare chest, stopping for a moment to entwine themselves through the black hair that glinted golden red in the dawn. Slowly, inch by inch, her hands crept up until her fingers laced behind his neck. Then, with only slight pressure, she drew his mouth down on hers.

His lips were soft, full, and enveloped hers with a caressing tenderness. She felt his tongue testing, teasing, until she responded, parting a way for his intimate exploration. Her head felt light. Warmth from their mingled lips suffused her body. She could feel her own heart pounding in her breast like some Gypsy rhapsody.

Still their bodies had not met, though they stood so close that Charlotte could feel a delicious heat radiating from Mateo's nearness. Then, as the kiss possessed them both, she felt his strong hands grasp her hips, pulling her to him. It seemed to Charlotte that their very souls touched and clung to each other at that moment. Their hearts throbbed together to a frantic Gypsy rhythm. She became aware of another throb against her thigh—pulsing heat that made her ache for something she didn't understand.

Mateo drew away slowly. They stood staring at each other. Charlotte thought she would always remember that moment—the rising sun, a halo behind his raven mane, tingeing it with Gypsy gold. The misty light obscured his face—all except those wonderful eyes. She could see her own reflection in those deep black pools, as if he had locked her within himself and sealed her enchanted prison forever with his kiss.

"Bravo! Bravo!" Phaedra cried. "The little *gajo* did not swoon!" Then her voice dropped to a low, suggestive whisper as she spoke directly to Charlotte. "You may kiss him here to taunt me, but I dare you to go to Mateo's bed! What would you do—all pale and tender— when he crushed those pristine breasts against his hard chest, making them throb and ache? Would you cry out when he stroked your quivering thighs with his powerful *graiengeri*'s hands, forcing from you the same obedience he demands of his horses? And what if you did have the courage to open your delicate petals to the great Rom Mateo? Would he ride you gently or with wild abandon as he gallops his stallions in the ring?"

Seeing Charlotte start to pale, Mateo warned, "Enough, Phaedra!"

"Enough? For your little white Anglo, perhaps, Mateo, but not enough for Princess Phaedra! I am all woman. And I demand *all* from my man!"

As the Gypsy woman flipped her bright skirts and stalked away, Charlotte stood trembling at the pictures Phaedra had evoked in her mind.

What had she done? What must Mateo think of her now? And what would he expect from her next? Was she no better than Phaedra—throwing herself at him? She could feel his gaze still on her, but she dared not look at him.

"What is your true name, *sunaki bal?*" he asked gently.

She swallowed hard, trying to find her voice. "Charlotte Buckland," she answered in a whisper.

"Very well, Charlotte. I will see you to the brides' tent now. You will remain there for the time being."

She turned to him, suddenly overwhelmed with joy. This must be the way Gypsy men asked women to become their wives. She hadn't displeased him after all. He wanted her for his own! She was more than willing. She had heard of love at first sight, but never had she believed it could happen to her. Now she knew it was possible. Anything was possible as long as she had Mateo!

Throwing her arms around his neck, she kissed him again, deeply. But this time his lips were motionless upon her own. She stepped away and looked at him, bewildered. She couldn't read his closed expression. His eyes seemed clouded by a mysterious veil.

As if the second kiss had never interrupted what he had been saying, Mateo continued, "You will live in the brides' tent and Tamara will see to your needs until Petronovich is able to raise the brideprice and claim you for his wife.''

His words came like a physical blow. Charlotte could only stare at him in stunned silence.

Chapter 5

Staggered by Mateo's pronouncement, Charlotte meekly allowed herself to be led toward the bright blue brides' tent. She felt numb and strange, as if her spirit were disconnected from her body and she were viewing the whole scene from the top branches of one of the tall cottonwoods that grew along the stream near camp.

She was keenly aware of the sound of the breeze stirring the trees, of the aroma of wood smoke and rabbit stew cooking, of the feel of rough buffalo grass stabbing her bare feet. But Mateo, although his guiding hand rested on the small of her back, seemed only an indistinct shape, hazy and undefined in her mind's eye. Her whole existence had taken on a dreamlike quality in the past hours—tipping back and forth from fantasy to nightmare at a moment's notice.

What quirk of fate had put her on a collision course with these Gypsies? Had this queer turn in her life been written in the stars since the beginning of time? Or had the whole direction of her future detoured the instant she'd stepped down from the train in Leavenworth, Kansas? Just thinking of so many unanswerable questions made her head ache.

"Wait here, please," Mateo said, snapping Charlotte out of her trancelike state.

She watched him walk ahead several paces. To her eyes, Mateo resembled some pagan woods god with his broad shoulders gleaming rich bronze in the early-morning light and his hair like a dark crown forged in Hades but brushed with the pure gold of Heaven. His buckskin britches fit like a second skin over narrow hips and well-developed thigh muscles before disappearing into soft leather boots.

The sheer animal power of his physique sent a tremor through Charlotte. She tried to look away, to deny her own thoughts and desires. But try as she might to put Phaedra's words from her mind, the suggested vision of her own naked flesh, pale beneath the Gypsy-copper of Mateo's strong, demanding body, persisted.

He turned suddenly, as if sensing the drift of her thoughts. In that instant, their gazes met and held. Although Mateo's face was unlined, Charlotte could see the troubled frown deep in his black eyes, like storm clouds on the far horizon. Then the expression changed, growing softer, almost pleading with her to understand.

But how could she understand a man whose eyes held love while his lips refused to speak the words? What kind of man would turn the woman he desired over to await the coming of her marriage to another?

"Mateo," Charlotte whispered. She moved toward him, one hand outstretched in supplication.

He looked away, breaking the fragile spell between them, and turned to the fancifully painted wooden door set into the side of the brides' tent. Reaching for the string of small, hammered-silver bells that hung there, he gave them a vicious jerk. Even while the merry chimes echoed through the early-morning stillness, Tamara opened the door and motioned for Charlotte to enter.

A brief, uncertain moment passed as Charlotte reached the entrance and Mateo. His fingers brushed her hand with a feather-light touch as if his impulse were to grab hold and keep her with him. Surrounded by a misty haze of morning sunshine, they stood staring at each other with an intimate intensity that shut out the rest of the world.

Charlotte's very soul ached when Mateo offered her a melancholy smile. Slowly he bent toward her, his lips parted, beckoning hers. She closed her eyes and her whole body tensed, awaiting the sweet pressure, longing for the taste and feel of him once more.

But only his breath teased her waiting lips as he said, "Good-bye, Charlotte. I must leave you now."

Unbidden tears sprang to her eyes. She felt as if he were casting her into the yawning black depths of a whirlpool instead of showing her to a comfortable place to rest.

"You will be safe here, little one, until the time comes for—"

Charlotte drew herself up with all the dignity she could muster and cut off the words she didn't want to hear.

"I won't marry him, Mateo!"

"As Fate wills," he answered softly.

She watched as he turned and strode away, her heart feeling unaccountably empty.

"Mateo is right, you know," Tamara said, ushering Charlotte into her new quarters.

"Right about what?" Charlotte lashed out. "If you mean marrying Petronovich, you're as dead wrong as he is!"

The shy Gypsy girl busied herself with the teapot and didn't meet Charlotte's fiery gaze. "No. I meant that Mateo is right about Fate. Our lives and fortunes are all dictated by what was written ages ago. We cannot change it. There is no reason to try."

"That doesn't make any sense, Tamara. Think about it. I heard what Queen Zolande said about you and Petronovich. You were destined to be his bride. If that's so, I have no place with him. And I certainly have no desire to be his wife!"

Tamara's gentle sable eyes grew moist. She smiled at Charlotte and shook her head. "Fate can be fickle, my friend. At my birth, it was written that I should be Mateo's bride. But I was a sickly child, and certain signs forecast my early doom. Since Mateo will be king someday, it would not be right for his queen to have clouds in her future. Therefore, I was given to Petronovich. But the very fact that my fate was altered that way may mean that nothing will ever be certain in my life. It is of no consequence." She shrugged eloquently. "Petronovich is in no hurry to marry me. He earned my brideprice once, but gambled it away. Perhaps he did so on purpose because he doesn't want me. Perhaps I was never meant to wed anyone."

"And you accept all this without question?" The very thought made Charlotte furious.

"It is not for me to accept or reject. We exist in the eternal now, living each day as it comes—without expectations, without regrets. I am simply thankful to see the sun rise again each morning. You will learn our ways and be happy, too, eventually."

"Never!"

Seeing that Charlotte Buckland was not a willing student of her fatalistic tutoring, Tamara changed the subject. "Come sit down and have some tea. You've had an exhausting night. We will break our fast, then you must sleep."

Delicious aromas from the cooking fires drifted into the tent, making Charlotte's stomach rumble insistently. She remembered suddenly that she hadn't eaten since arriving in Leavenworth the day before. She sat down at the small table in the center of the tent and accepted the red-and-gold china cup that Tamara offered. Unlike the dark Bohea tea her mother brewed back home, this was topaz in color and spiced with wild herbs and mint. It went down smoothly, leaving Charlotte with a warm, drowsy feeling.

"Another cup?" Tamara offered.

"Please. It's delicious."

Tamara smiled her appreciation of the compliment. "I make it myself from herbs and grasses I pick and dry. I'll show them to you when you've rested enough to go out for a walk in the *vesh*. Now I'll go bring our food."

"Wait, Tamara!" Charlotte put a restraining hand on the girl's arm. "Stay and talk to me for a bit."

The lovely Gypsy woman nodded and took her seat again.

"Tell me about the Gypsies—where you came from, how you got here."

Tamara's beautiful face took on a wistful, faraway look. "To tell you of Gypsies is to talk to you of the wind, for so we come and move on unknown and unknowing. Some say we suffer this fate because we are descended from Cain—that we wander the earth ever trying to escape the guilt of his mortal sin. Perhaps this is so, or perhaps since we have been mistrusted and sent away so often, we have adopted the nomadic life out of self-defense, moving on before others cast us out. Whatever the reason, we flow like the water and move like the trembling branches of a tree in a storm.

"Those of us in this camp are of the Lowara tribe—the

horse traders—and the *kumpania* of Valencia. Once our people roamed the Transylvania plains at the foot of the Carpathian Mountains. We know Russia, the Balkans, the Sacro Monte caves of Spain. Most recently we came from Wales. Only one year have we been in America." Tamara's face clouded suddenly and she shook her head. "I do not wish to speak of the sea voyage. Gypsies are not good sailors, I'm afraid. But we traveled from Liverpool to the great city of New York, then on to meet the other circus people in Philadelphia before heading for this wild country."

"All of you came together, Tamara?"

She nodded. "Thirty-six of us, counting little Svetslav, who was born on the boat. A few others joined us from a circus troupe in Philadelphia."

"But Mateo has been with you all along?"

Tamara smiled. "Ah, so now we get to your real interest, Charlotte Buckland! Yes, Mateo came from Wales, where he bred and trained horses for the racecourses of England."

"He's a fine man," Charlotte said, hoping to prod Tamara into further discussion of Mateo.

"As well he should be! The only son of the queen has grave responsibilities to the *familia*."

The family, Charlotte thought. Always the family! She felt a sudden overwhelming resentment at being an outsider—a *gajo*.

"Do Mateo's responsibilities to the *familia* extend to populating the entire western territory with hordes of little Gypsies?" Even to her own ears, the question sounded harsher than she had intended.

Tamara stared at her, perplexed. "I'm sorry. I don't understand."

Charlotte got up and paced for a moment, embarrassed at having to discuss the subject with such an innocent. "I met a mob of children at the circus—at least a dozen. They all claimed their father was Mateo. They said he would beat them if I didn't give them money."

To Charlotte's total consternation, Tamara laughed out loud.

"I didn't think it was funny, Tamara! How many children does Mateo have? How many wives? Or is the son of the queen free to take his pleasure wherever he finds it?"

Tamara caught Charlotte's hand and coaxed her back into her chair before she said, "I'm sorry, my friend. I shouldn't have laughed. I can see that the experience upset you terribly. You met many children, you say. Poor Little Pesha?"

Charlotte nodded.

"That child! At times I think she should be beaten! But of course, we don't believe in such cruel punishment, not even for naughty little liars."

"Then you mean Pesha isn't Mateo's daughter?"

"Certainly not! Nor are any of her accomplices who besieged you. They are a crafty pack of high-spirited con artists. They know that Mateo is the star of the circus. So they call him their father, thinking that the *gajo* customers will give them more, out of respect for his high position and great talent in the ring. Mateo has never married, although he is well past the age when most of the *Rom* take brides. He must marry soon. He is a child of Queen Zolande's autumn years. She is very old and infirm. The *familia* cannot be left without a leader, and Mateo is the chosen one."

"He'll marry Phaedra?"

Tamara shrugged. "As Fate wills. She is his, if he wants her. But there are unusual factors to be considered in Mateo's choice of a bride, for she will also be queen. I think he has delayed his final decision, hoping against hope that some ancient prophecy will be fulfilled."

Charlotte slumped back in her chair, weak with relief, and smiled. "Thank you, Tamara. I was so worried about those children, even though I only half believed what they said." She didn't mention that most of her relief came from knowing that Mateo had not yet chosen the woman with whom he wished to share his life.

"A word of caution, my friend. Only half believe *anything* that a Gypsy tells you. We have kept ourselves safe from the world by never letting the *gajos* know the full truth on any subject."

Charlotte eyed the other woman speculatively. If this was so, how much of Tamara's story could she believe? And how could she live in an atmosphere of falsehood and fairy tales?

Once again, Tamara seemed to be reading Charlotte's thoughts. Quietly she said, "One thing I will tell you about Mateo which you can believe, totally. Always his people will come first—before personal desires, ambitions . . . even before love."

Charlotte felt a blush stain her cheeks. Was this a warning from the perceptive Gypsy fortune-teller?

"How can love even be considered in a family that still *arranges* marriages?" Charlotte answered, an edge of bitterness in her voice.

Tamara patted her hand in understanding. "Our ways are our own. The very fact that you question them shows that you could never give your heart to Mateo without reservations, Charlotte. Besides, he is different from the others—" Tamara quickly cut off her words as if she'd said more than she should have to an outsider.

"Different? How? I don't understand, Tamara."

"I'm sorry, my friend. It is for Mateo himself to explain, if he should choose to. Now I'll go for our food."

Left alone, Charlotte had time to examine her surroundings while she mulled over Tamara's words. The tent was partitioned by colorful curtains into several small rooms. The earthen floor was hard-packed and covered by lush Brussels carpets. The table and four chairs were beautifully carved, with touches of gilt on the trim. An oil lamp with rose-tinted glass and heavy, leaded-crystal prisms hung from the ridgepole. A glassed-in china cupboard held the dishes, and two other chests, painted blue, completed the furnishings in the main room.

Charlotte pulled aside the deep-amethyst–colored curtain. There on the floor, like a cozy nest, lay a pallet of soft rabbit skins. A heavy robe of black fur served as blanket and counterpane. Charlotte couldn't resist the urge to lie down for just a moment. In spite of her gnawing hunger pangs, weariness took priority. Within seconds after she'd settled herself in the warm, caressing pelts, she was asleep.

Charlotte awoke disoriented. The room was dark and close with the dry heat of autumn. Music drifted to her from somewhere beyond the walls. She listened, trying to place the unfamiliar sounds. She could make out the sad sighs of a violin, accompanied by the low throb of a drum and the trills of a flute. From time to time, she heard wild yelps interspersed through the song.

Indians! she thought, clutching the pelts beneath her. But the feel of the fur in her fingers soon brought her back to reality. Not Indians, but *Gypsies*! Could one be less of a threat to her than the other? A kind of hopelessness settled over her, but she forced herself to shake it off. There must be a way out of this. She would bide her time and pick the moment for her escape.

"Oh, you have awakened at last," Tamara said, peering in around the edge of the curtain.

"At last? How long have I slept?"

"Through a day, a night, and a second day. I was

worried, but Mateo said I should leave you to your rest. He said your journey was long and your strength dissipated by the manner in which you came to us.''

Charlotte laughed out loud at the delicate phrasing Tamara used to refer to her kidnapping by Petronovich. The girl misunderstood her reaction.

"Ah, good! You're feeling better. Mateo will be so pleased."

Charlotte walked into the lighted room, taking stock of her ruined nightgown and wondering what she would do for clothes, since everything she owned was still at the Planters Hotel in Leavenworth.

"Why should Mateo care? He's washed his hands of me."

Tamara frowned at her guest. "I do not understand about this washing of Mateo's hands you speak of."

"It's an American saying. What I mean is that I didn't think Mateo cared in the least about what happened to me from now on."

"Oh, you are wrong! He cares a great deal. He has such plans for you!" Tamara's pretty eyes sparkled like bright bits of glass and she smiled mysteriously.

"Plans? What plans?"

"It is a secret . . . for Mateo alone to tell you. Hurry now. Eat the stew I've brought. Then you must bathe and dress and join the others around the campfire. Hear? They are already playing and singing. Mateo has planned a *patshiva*—a celebration to honor you as our special guest."

"I have no clothes, Tamara," Charlotte said between bites of delicious stew spiced with wild garlic and onion. But the other woman was busy pouring steaming water from a copper pail into a basin.

"From now on, you will bathe in the stream as the rest of us do. But for tonight, I thought you would like to refresh yourself indoors with hot water."

"Thank you!" Charlotte had never spoken the words with more sincerity.

The warm water and scented soap renewed her spirit and refreshed her body. When she finished and had wrapped herself in a blanket, Tamara appeared from behind one of the curtains, carrying a beautiful costume.

"This is for you."

Charlotte could only stare in awe. The full-sleeved peasant blouse was as white as snow and embroidered with golden threads. Two tiny bells dangled from the drawstring at the wide neck. The skirt gleamed the colors of the rainbow—from golden yellow to fiery crimson to deep violet. Yards and yards of the luxurious material were gathered at the tiny waistband, and the lacy, scarlet petticoats Tamara provided would flounce the skirt beautifully.

"Tamara," Charlotte said, fingering the soft cotton blouse, "this is too kind of you . . . to let me wear your best clothes. Really, I couldn't."

Tamara giggled. "These are not *my* clothes. Mateo had them made for you specially."

"Mateo? I don't understand."

"Get dressed. All will be explained soon enough," Tamara assured her.

Not until Charlotte slipped the blouse over her head did it dawn on her that some articles of clothing were missing. Without a corset or even a thin camisole, her dark nipples made pronounced shadows through the light cotton. Tamara, noting her frown, adjusted the neckline, pulling the blouse off her shoulders and tying the drawstring securely. Then she gathered the fullness in front for modesty's sake.

"Lovely!" Tamara sighed, standing back to gaze at her handiwork.

Charlotte wasn't so sure, but there was nothing she

could do about it. At least she would have the darkness outside to give her some measure of cover.

As a final touch, when Charlotte was dressed, Tamara placed golden hoops in her ears and draped several finely crafted chains about her neck.

"One more thing is needed," said the fortune-teller after closely examining the effect of Charlotte's costume.

She brought out a chain from which several small coins dangled. Carefully she pinned it in place so that the circles of gold lay evenly across Charlotte's forehead.

"There!" she said with satisfaction. "Mateo will be pleased."

All this talk of Mateo, when Petronovich's name had yet to be mentioned, gave Charlotte fresh hope. Maybe things had changed while she'd slept. Perhaps even now she was on her way to wed Mateo before his approving *familia*. A strange but not unwelcome thrill fluttered her heart. Would she be with Mateo—as his wife—this very night?

The blue-black sky was moonless, but stars twinkled above like silver sequins sewn on velvet. The whole scene seemed a vision of enchantment as Charlotte and Tamara left the brides' tent. A huge bonfire glowed fiery orange in the very center of the camp, and colorfully dressed Gypsies whirled and leaped about its perimeter to the pulse of the bizarre Romany music.

Charlotte immediately spotted Mateo and Petronovich in a clear space near the fire. The two seemed locked in a duel to the death. But they used no weapons. Sweat glistened on their determined faces as they stamped the packed earth with dancing feet. Their bodies moved in undulating rhythms while they clapped their hands over their heads and whirled in dizzying circles.

She watched, transfixed by the power and sensual

beauty of Mateo's body. His bare chest, etched with dark hair, glistened, bronzed by the firelight, while his thigh muscles rippled with each move. She noted shyly the obvious bulge in his tight buckskins that displayed his aroused manhood, proclaiming him a true and powerful *Rom*. He moved through the dance with all the power and elegance of one of his own horses. She felt faint just watching him and thought how he and Petronovich resembled two stallions vying for a choice mare.

The music built to a frenzy and the pair of dancers whirled and stamped with ever more zeal. Charlotte could see the strain of exertion etched in Petronovich's face, but Mateo's expression was still nonchalant, though his dark eyes radiated a certain mocking irony. At last, Petronovich spun away and stumbled out of the circle, leaving Mateo to finish his exhibition alone. The cheers and applause grew louder. On and on he danced, until the earth seemed to tremble with each stamp of his boots. Then, suddenly, the music crashed into silence. Mateo gave a wild yelp and leaped high in the air. Total quiet gave way to pandemonium as wave after wave of cheers rose and everyone rushed to congratulate the victor.

"He will be coming for you now," Tamara whispered.

The lovely Gypsy spoke the truth on this occasion. As soon as he could extricate himself from the mob, Mateo strode directly toward Charlotte. With his face gleaming in the firelight and the bulge in his trousers making it obvious that he was still aroused, Charlotte had a moment's inclination to flee. But his eyes held her riveted to the spot. Whatever he was about to offer, she would have to accept. Before she could move or even force her mind to think any organized thoughts, he was there, reaching out a hand to caress her cheek. She closed her eyes a moment, luxuriating in his touch.

"You were well worth waiting for, *sunaki bal*," Mateo said. "Thank you, Tamara. You have done a magnificent job."

With only a smile and a nod, Tamara slipped away, leaving Mateo and Charlotte alone together. She stood before him, aware that his eyes were examining every article of her clothing and jewelry. He nodded his approval almost imperceptibly.

"Yes, it is as I imagined," he said. "You will be the most exotically beautiful woman in our *kumpania*, Charlotte Buckland. A queen in your own right."

His final statement made her breath catch and her heart pound so that the concealing gathers at the front of her blouse actually fluttered over her taut nipples. "A queen," he had said. How else could she became a queen? She would have to marry a king!

He cupped her face in his warm palms and smiled down into her eyes, caressing her with his gaze until she thought her heart would burst from wanting his kiss. She closed her eyes. Unconsciously, her lips parted and her chin tilted upward, ready for his sweet assault. But instead of kissing her, Mateo let his hands slide down to rest on her bare shoulders. The touch of his fingers felt hot to her flesh. She trembled deliciously and made no protest or attempt at false modesty when his gaze shifted downward to scorch her thinly clad breasts. She felt her nipples ache as they strained at the fabric.

"Beautiful!" he breathed. "Beyond words!"

"Mateo," she began, not knowing what she would say.

He gave her no opportunity to get beyond his name. His beautiful dark face came down over hers, blocking out the light of the campfire. As its warmth faded from her flesh, another kind of heat took its place. Charlotte felt Mateo's lips capture hers and send flames of desire raging through her. He was ever so gentle, but the sensations aroused by his kiss sent her reeling, plummeting through a soft, black void where only stardust lit the path back to reality.

Never had she felt such wonder and enchantment. His full lips moved over hers as if he were an explorer, staking his claim on previously undiscovered ground. He ventured cautiously at first, touching lightly, testing her reaction. But when she responded eagerly to the delicious taste of him, he grew bolder, tempting her lips to part for him while his arms stole about her to cradle her close to his hard chest.

Charlotte felt as if some magical door to worlds unknown had just swung open for her. Being in Mateo's arms, savoring his ardent kiss, seemed so right, so good. She never wanted the moment to end. She wanted to taste the heady wine of his breath and inhale his woodsy essence forevermore, while his strong arms held her close, pulsing new, exciting life through her whole body, making it ache with the sweetest of needs.

When Mateo finally broke the embrace, they stood for a long moment staring at each other. Their eyes spoke eloquently of the wonders of love.

"Ah, victory is sweet," he whispered. Then, taking her hand in his and smoothing her satiny skin with sensitive, knowing fingers, he ordered, "Follow me!"

For a moment, she realized she had no voice. Her senses seemed to have taken flight, like some night bird rejoicing in the splendor of the free-blowing winds. When she could find words, they came from deep within her soul—a soul filled with love and longing.

"Always, Mateo," she breathed. "I'll always follow you."

Chapter 6

The moment Charlotte and Mateo entered the circle of firelight, a multitude of Romany-dark eyes focused on them. The musicians, just as curious as the others, let their song trail off into silence. Charlotte hung back, hiding in Mateo's shadow, uncomfortable with the heat of so many gazes upon her. What, she wondered, did they imagine her to be? Some golden-haired freak for their sideshow or, perhaps, a sorceress from some misty land beyond their far-reaching pale? Nervously, she slowed her step, but Mateo urged her on.

"Come along, Charlotte. The hour grows late. We must speak with the *phuri dai*."

"Your mother?" Charlotte asked, puzzled. Probably, she reasoned, it was a formality for visitors to pay their respects to the formidable old lady.

"Not only my mother, but my queen as well. She must give final approval to any decisions made within the *familia*." Mateo paused for a moment and gave

Charlotte a grave look. "I would never dream of speaking my mind to you without her permission."

Charlotte forgot all about the staring Gypsy eyes and the rest of the world. Mateo's expression remained a mystery to her, but his words seemed to indicate that he had made an important decision while she'd slept, unknowing. Her heartbeat accelerated, but cautiously, as if it were afraid to let her believe what she hoped to be true. Like a sleepwalker in a happy dream, she followed Mateo, still clutching his hand.

Then she was standing directly before Queen Zolande. The old matriarch sat on a thronelike chair, a bear robe draped over her lap, although the night air was warm. A scarlet cape hugged her thin shoulders, and gold chains, hoops, and coins festooned about her person glinted their ancient mysteries in the firelight. Her face was placid except for her eyes—tiny, piercing bits of black glass like miniature crystal balls, seeing past, present, and future all in the same unblinking instant. Her gaze darted quickly over her tall son but soon locked on Charlotte.

Mateo leaned forward and kissed his mother on one cheek and then the other. She acknowledged his filial homage by clasping his hand with long fingers that seemed covered with brittle, blue-lined parchment. She spoke softly to him in the *Romani* dialect. Although Charlotte couldn't understand the words, she recognized the deep love in the queen's tone.

"I would speak to you, Queen Zolande," Mateo said formally.

The woman's expression changed, the light of mother-love curtained by the sterner countenance of the *phuri dai.*

"I will hear you, Prince Mateo," she answered, sitting up with more authority and nodding slightly.

"It has to do with the *gajo* woman."

Once more Queen Zolande pierced Charlotte with an intense, dark look. She did not smile. Charlotte felt her discomfort growing. Why didn't Mateo just get on with it?

"Petronovich's woman?" she said, narrowing her eyes as if to take better measure of the girl standing before her.

Charlotte's head jerked up and her level gaze jousted with the queen's piercing stare. "No!" she cried impulsively. "I am *not* Petronovich's woman!"

Mateo turned a warning frown on her and whispered, "You will remain silent!"

Fury boiled up inside Charlotte's breast. How could he speak to her that way? Surely Mateo no longer thought of her as "Petronovich's woman"! She was her own woman! But Mateo's warning look stopped her tongue. He offered her a reassuring smile, and she felt a sudden softening inside. She returned his fond look, thinking that she would never be angered by anyone calling her "Mateo's woman."

"I am in need of her, Queen Zolande," Mateo continued.

Charlotte winced at his choice of words. An odd way, she thought, to express love and a desire to marry.

The queen's eyebrows arched and her lips pursed in disapproval. "You will have Phaedra soon enough."

"Phaedra has chosen to be with Petronovich. Besides, she doesn't like my horses. They terrify her. But Charlotte Buckland comes from a line of horse breeders and trainers. She and I will be a perfect team."

Charlotte was confused. She realized that ancient cultures that still arranged marriages and haggled over brideprice were totally foreign to her, but what did her relationship with Mateo's horses have to do with whether or not the queen would give her permission for them to marry? Charlotte shrugged off her misgivings. She loved horses! She loved Mateo, too. If her expertise as an equestrienne enhanced her chances of becoming Mateo's bride, then she loved him all the more for being wise enough to use this argument with Queen Zolande.

"And what if she is too delicate?"

Mateo turned his eyes on Charlotte as if measuring her physical capabilities, then looked back to his mother. "I will be most careful with her. She will not be hurt; that I promise you."

Charlotte felt herself blushing all over. How *could* they discuss such a matter—the very difficulties of a virgin bride on her wedding night—and right in front of her? Still, Mateo seemed to know exactly how to handle the old queen. Zolande was almost smiling now. Yes, she even gave a slight nod of approval.

"We will see how it works out, Mateo. You understand, though, that there is still Petronovich to be considered. He brought her here; he is responsible for her. But I will speak to him."

Mateo bowed his head, acknowledging the *phuri dai*'s words. "I understand."

"Then let it be," she said. Turning back to Charlotte, the queen commanded, "I will abide no more trouble from your presence in this camp. If you are to become as one of us, you will follow our ways. You will obey Mateo at all times!"

Charlotte, who had experienced a growing joy as the talk progressed and imagined herself about to become Mateo's bride, suddenly felt fury flood her being. Obey indeed! Words she knew she shouldn't say were trembling on her lips, ready to burst out before the old queen, when Mateo took her by the arm and led her quickly away.

In an instant, the peculiar form of the marriage request was forgotten. She was aware only of the man next to her, his strong arm about her waist, guiding her away from the others.

"So, it is done, my *sunaki bal*!" he said with obvious satisfaction in his voice. "Now we need time to be alone . . . to talk . . . to learn of each other."

"Yes, Mateo," she answered meekly—not because Queen Zolande had ordered her to obey this man but because he spoke to her needs as well as his own.

He led her away from the campfire and the curious onlookers. They walked the woodland path for a long time in silence. Charlotte was too transported by her feelings, her longing for Mateo, to speak. And he seemed happy simply to have her beside him, all to himself. They owned these silent woods, the gentle breeze whispering its night song, and every one of the millions of stars overhead. They were in love. And that love made them wealthy beyond belief.

Charlotte had never realized she possessed such depths of emotion. Her mind and heart sang with joy, relief, excitement, and a slight quickening fear at the thought of becoming this Gypsy's bride. Would he be gentle with her as he had promised the queen? Or would the deep passions she sensed smoldering within him surface to claim her with ruthless abandon once they were alone and away from the others? The thought sent a shiver through her.

But as they strode on through the forest, side by side and hand in hand, her fears fled and her whole body responded to Mateo's warmth. She quivered in anticipation of what she guessed was about to happen.

Had she been home in Kentucky, safely shielded by old standards and archaic values, she would never have allowed herself to be put in this position. She could never have walked out into the night with any man. Certainly she would not be thinking the thoughts that now mesmerized her. She would have demanded that they wait until *after* their wedding.

But this was not Kentucky, and the old values meant nothing. And this was not just any man. This was Mateo—*her* Mateo!

Behind them, Charlotte could hear the bittersweet sound of a Gypsy love song. Though she couldn't understand the words, the weeping strains of the music relayed a universal theme. The violin told of sweethearts loving, parting, sobbing out their longing for each other.

How happy it made her to know that she and Mateo were about to be joined! She squeezed his hand and felt the pressure returned. He, too, was aware of the mournful lovers' song.

"Beautiful, is it not?" he said in a hushed voice. "Beautiful, but so very, very sad."

"What do the words mean, Mateo?"

He paused on the trail and took both her hands in his. "She is young and very lovely and innocent. She is also very poor—daughter of a *rashai,* a parson. Her lover is older, but not so old, and his family is not so poor as hers. They say he must marry a *rawnie,* a great lady, who will bring much *sunaki,* Gypsy gold, to their *familia.* But the young man and his lover refuse to listen. They sing to each other that they will live on golden honey instead of *sunaki* and be rich with the silver of the moon and stars. As they flee, a *Romani chiriklo,* the Gypsy bird of happiness, flies over their heads, singing out his blessing."

"The flute—I hear it," Charlotte said.

"We call that instrument a *chavora,* but, yes, you are right. That is the little bird singing."

"Then why does the song sound so sad, Mateo?"

"Gypsy love songs are always sad. I haven't finished the story, little one. His parents have engaged the *ababina,* the village sorceress, to put a spell over him so that he will leave his lover and return to them. While the runaway couple is making love one night beside the *dariav,* the great sea, the evil spell comes over him. He thrusts the girl away and calls her *'fuli tschai,'* 'bad girl.' She weeps and pleads. Hear even now the sighing of the violin? But her young man can only hear what the *ababina* allows.'' He paused and gave a heavy sigh.

''What happens next, Mateo?''

Shaking his head, he answered, ''It is a very sad tale, as I said. The beautiful girl drinks *drab*—poison. Only as she is breathing her last does her lover come out of the spell. It is too late. He sobs and wails, tears his clothes, yanks out his hair. Then, while embracing her cold body, he takes his *churi* and stabs himself in the heart, dying upon her still breast.''

''And that's the end?'' Charlotte asked with tears brimming in her eyes.

When the first tear escaped to trickle down her cheek, Mateo caught it with his finger and smiled at her. ''It is only the end for those who do not believe as we Gypsies do. We know what comes next. And believe it or not, this is one of our happier songs.''

''I don't believe it!'' Charlotte answered. ''There's nothing happy about it!''

''Ah, wait, little dove. Hear me out! *Develesa,* the one you call God, is too kind-hearted to have mere mortals treat each other so badly without His intervention. True, the boy and the girl are dead, but better off for it. Alive, they would not have been allowed together, but in death they share the same tomb. And as the priest pronounces, *'Talgin al-mayit,'* instructing them how to answer the angels of the grave, they are transported to *ravnos,* Gypsy heaven, to live happily together forevermore among the stars.''

Charlotte was silent after he finished. Her hands felt cold, even with Mateo holding them. She wasn't sure

she would ever understand his Gypsy logic—or lack of
it. She didn't want to have to die to be happy. Living
was what happiness was all about to her—living with
and for Mateo.

"It's only a song, a very ancient one, Charlotte. Don't
take it so seriously."

"I can't help it," she answered. "It is serious to you.
You believe it, don't you, Mateo?"

"Believe a fable? No. Not completely."

"But you believe it enough to think that happiness on
earth is unimportant as long as you can count on it
beyond the grave."

"I don't understand what you're trying to say."

"I'm saying what I believe. The queen mentioned that
Petronovich would have to be consulted about us. What
if he objects? I think that you would give me to another
man for the sake of fate, destiny, whatever name you
wish to call it, rather than upsetting the grand scheme of
things by admitting that you love me and want me for
yourself!"

Charlotte was trembling by the time she finished her
impassioned speech. Never before had she spoken with
such fiery conviction. But she was fighting for her future—
indeed, for her very life.

Mateo closed his arms around her in a crushing embrace as if she might flee into the night if he didn't hold
her. For several long, flaming moments they stood there—
Charlotte trembling in his arms, feeling heat rise from
his body to warm her own. She couldn't move, couldn't
speak. She could only cling to him, breathing in his
wonderful woodsy musk, not wanting to believe that he
could ever let her go.

Mateo felt her trembling, her heart quivering against
his chest. He felt wounded, angry, torn. What did she
expect of him? He was not a man made of stone with ice
water in his veins. Since their first meeting, Charlotte

Buckland had tortured him with her beauty and her need to be loved. Did she think she was the only one with needs? He was not a weak man, but she had tested his strength to its limits. If he had his way, he would take her this minute! Damn Fate and Gypsy traditions!

Yes, he thought, smiling grimly, he would mount her as his great stallions did their mares—without guilt or worry over the consequences. His big hand sought her breast and it quivered in his palm. A tremendous ache shot through him and he pressed his body close to her willing warmth. She was ready for him, he could tell. Ah, how he wanted her!

When Mateo broke the extended silence, his words and their fierce tone jarred Charlotte to the core. "Don't ever accuse me of fearing to speak my love for you! You force me now with your challenge to say words better off unspoken. I felt this time would come, and I have dreaded it for your sake."

He paused and Charlotte held her breath, fearing the denial his words seemed to imply. He caught her chin in his less-than-tender grasp and forced her to look into his eyes. His savage expression terrified her. He devoured her with his gaze before he spoke again.

"I do love you, Charlotte Buckland! God help us both, I do! As a man should only love one woman in his life. But . . ."

"But what, Mateo?" The words were not loud enough even to be called a whisper. Charlotte was numb from his unexpected declaration, from longing, and from a kind of heart-fluttering fear.

Instead of answering her, he pressed her face between his palms until she cried out in pain. His wild expression became at once terrifying and exciting. She had no idea what to expect from him next.

"You are an *ababina*, a sorceress, little one. All cream and honey covering deep-burning fires. If you knew how much I want you at this very moment, you would flee for your life!" A low growl rumbled in his throat. "No! I do not wish to wait for death to know happiness. But were that the only way . . ." He paused in midsentence and jerked a silver stiletto from his scarlet waist sash, letting the pointed tip press his throat dangerously. "I would die by my own hand this moment."

Charlotte's eyes widened as she watched a single drop of blood trickle down from below his neck scarf, staining his bronze skin. "Mateo, don't!" she cried, struggling to wrest the knife from his hand. The point caught in her blouse, ripping a long slash, but she continued to fight him until the thin dagger fell to the ground between them. Then she collapsed, sobbing, against Mateo's chest, her mind spinning wildly. Had he really meant to kill himself? Or had he meant to kill her? Maybe she was supposed to be some heathen Gypsy sacrifice—an offering to *Fate*.

"Forgive me, darling," he whispered against her hair. "I was only trying to make a point." He held her at arm's length so that he could look into her face and reassure her. "Tongue of a jackal! I've hurt you!" he cried, staring at the blood staining the jagged rip in her blouse.

Before Charlotte could tell him that it was nothing, Mateo swooped her into his arms and headed for the nearby stream. She relaxed against him. The night had been so emotionally charged that she truly felt she might faint.

When they reached the stream, Mateo laid her gently on the bank. Tearing off the *diklo* from around his neck, he dipped the silken scarf into the water. Suddenly Charlotte realized his intent.

She clutched her torn blouse and said, "Mateo, I'm all right, really. It's only a scratch."

Gently but insistently, he removed her hands from the neck of her blouse and pressed them down to her lap.

"Only a scratch can become a nasty infection out here in the wilds. It must be cleansed immediately. Relax now. I won't hurt you. I promise to be gentle."

Relax? Charlotte thought. How could she relax? Already she could feel the heat from his hands radiating to her breasts as he worked carefully to untie the drawstring holding her blouse. She sat rigid, her eyes averted from his face, and felt a blush tinge her cheeks.

Slowly, Mateo eased the blouse down over her left shoulder. The slight pressure of his fingertips sent a shiver through her.

"Easy now." He gentled her as he would an injured mare.

"Mateo, really, it's nothing," Charlotte protested.

"Good, my little dove. Then it will not take me long to tend it."

She breathed deeply, steeling herself for the delicious ordeal. Mateo would see soon that the wound was just above the nipple of her left breast. She tensed when his hands touched the area but relaxed with the soothing feeling of the cool, damp silk pressed to her flesh. She closed her eyes and let Mateo tend her, achingly aware of the liquid fire spreading through her body with each stroke of his ministering fingers.

Mateo, for all his cool detachment, could not deny that the soft pale mound laid bare before his eyes aroused him deeply. When the heel of his hand brushed Charlotte's nipple and it stiffened against his palm, he jerked his hand away as if he had touched fire. Fire was, indeed, what he was dealing with here. The fire of passion fanned by soul-deep love—a love made more painfully exquisite by the inevitable fact that it would be denied him.

He wanted her . . . oh, yes! He, too, remembered

Phaedra's graphic words and wondered what it would be like to possess this lovely, golden woman. If he dared, he might find out this very night. By the change in her breathing, he could tell that she was not unaffected by the intimacy of his hands upon her. Even in the dim starlight, he could see that her eyes were closed, her full lips pouted as if anticipating his kiss. It would be so simple to disarm her with his own lips while he filled his hungry hands with her tender breasts—stroking, kneading, taunting their velvety nipples to quivering surrender before his mouth possessed them. And then . . .

No! he thought. I must not allow myself to think such things!

"Have you finished with me, Mateo?" came her soft, innocent voice.

He looked at her through eyes glazed with desire. She sat there, one breast still partially exposed—still tempting him with its ripeness. How could he let such a moment pass? He must fight these lustful demons to the limits of his endurance.

"No, not yet," he replied. "Proper herbs pressed to the wound will draw out the pain."

"But there's no pain, Mateo."

Liar! she thought to herself. You've never known such pain in your life! Pain of heart, soul, and body. Only Mateo can ease it, and it will take more from him than his special herbs!

Charlotte leaned on her elbows and let her head fall back, inhaling deeply, trying to slow the rapid rate of her heart. Her breasts strained forward, rising and falling dramatically with each breath. When Mateo returned with his poultice of sweet grasses for her wound, the sight of her stopped him in his tracks. Never had he seen such languid, sensual beauty—her pale gold hair cascading over her bare shoulders, eyes closed and face upturned as if star-bathing, her breasts at a proud jut with their crested peaks straining against the confines of her thin bodice.

Mateo moved quickly, his feet, even in their heavy boots, as silent as if they were bare. Standing over her, he gazed down, keenly aware of the desire throbbing through his body—a desire that refused to be banished in spite of all his efforts to control himself.

He dropped to his knees beside her and eased the blouse down to free her breasts, his fingers trembling against her bare flesh. She opened her eyes but made no protest.

Charlotte could feel his gaze fondling her. The sensation centered in her breasts but massed and intensified in a lower region until her thighs quivered and her legs felt weak. When he leaned over her to press the cool, moist grasses on her wound, she could feel his breath, warm against her skin. She sighed his name.

"Charlotte, my darling," he whispered. "You are too beautiful! No man should be denied. . . ." There was a long pause; then, in a husky whisper, he said, "I want to touch you."

She watched his hand in tingling fascination as it hovered, fingers splayed, above her naked breast. She nodded silently, looking now into his wonderfully solemn face.

A long silence ensued. Charlotte closed her eyes and lay very still, hardly daring to breathe. His touch was feather-light. She barely felt it at first. But soon she realized with a burning certainty that his fingertips were cautiously exploring the very tips of her nipples. They stood erect for him, begging for more demanding caresses. Slowly, his fondling intensified. He stroked her boldly, masterfully, and white-hot fire raged through her. He squeezed, and the torment was exquisite. Charlotte was hard-pressed to lie still and complacent. When he cupped both breasts in his hands, circling their crowns with his thumbs, her hips, as if with a will of their own, thrust forward toward him and she moaned.

"Charlotte, oh, my sweet Charlotte," he crooned, lowering his head to let his lips scorch a trail down the steamy valley from her throat.

The next moment explosions of delicious sensation erupted through her. His hard, pointed tongue stabbed the tender tip of her breast, then flailed wildly, battering her aching nipple into a supple mound of surrender. He left off his attack at that moment, permitting his victim to relax her defenses. But when she allowed a satisfied sigh to escape her lips, her loving tormentor struck once more, sucking the tender nipple into the hot, moist darkness of his mouth. He licked, he probed, he suckled until she thought he would draw the very soul out of her body.

Charlotte cried aloud with the magnificent feeling, throwing herself on his tender mercy. But her pleading only encouraged Mateo's tongue to bolder insinuations. Carefully, he imprisoned the throbbing nipple between his teeth, breathing in and out deeply so that the sensations of cool and warm, moist and dry, titillated her with each breath he took. She writhed and thrashed beneath him until he released his hold. Capturing her lips, he quieted her with his eager mouth and the hard, throbbing pressure of his body.

One of Mateo's strong arms encircled her waist and he pillowed her head against his shoulder. Charlotte felt his other hand touch her bare back. It began its tantalizing progress downward. Gooseflesh covered her as his fingers slithered along her backbone. At the band of her skirt, his hand stopped, resting for a moment. Then his widespread palm cupped her buttocks, bringing her firmly against his thighs. Charlotte stiffened, feeling the throb of his desire even through her skirts. But she forced all reserve from her mind. This was not Kentucky! Her

Mateo—her husband-to-be—wanted her as much as she wanted him. Why should she force him to wait? Already their souls were married by their love for each other.

His lips moved from hers and rasped, "Fate be damned! I want you now, Charlotte Buckland! Nothing else matters anymore. Not the *familia,* not even knowing you belong to Petronovich!"

His words slashed her with deadly aim and inflicted far more pain than his dagger. The sudden shock shattered her mesmerized state. She pushed him away, pounding at his chest when he tried to hold her.

"Charlotte, what's wrong?" he begged.

"Everything, Mateo," she answered as she stood up on shaky legs and adjusted her blouse. "Everything in the world! What do you mean, I *belong* to Petronovich?"

He looked angry and confounded. "It is our custom. The wife belongs to the husband. He pays the brideprice and she is his property from then on. It has always been so!"

Charlotte stared at him, unbelieving. Hadn't she heard Mateo ask Queen Zolande for permission to marry her only an hour ago? True, it had been a strange conversation between them and Mateo had yet to ask her to be his wife, but still . . .

She wanted to scream and tear her clothes as the Gypsy in the song had done. Mateo stood so tall and handsome before her, with the stream forming a silver ribbon backdrop. She could still taste his mouth on hers . . . still feel the tingle where his gentle hands had caressed her flesh so lovingly. But now he was beyond her reach.

Was he so different from other men that she had mistaken his words of love? Had his actions been spurred by lust alone? Her mind whirled. Suddenly, all she could think of was escape. She spun away from him.

"Where are you going?" Mateo called.

"I'm leaving!"

"Wait!" He ran after her, catching up in a few long strides. He grasped her arms and pulled her to him, not roughly, but with a certain undeniably masculine command.

His lips captured hers once more, and their breath mingled, weakening Charlotte's resolve. Holding her close with one arm, he sought her breast with his free hand, stroking new sparks to flame.

"You forced me to admit my love tonight. I would not have spoken so openly to you and put this burden upon us both. But now it is done. We owe something of ourselves to each other. Can you say you don't love me, Charlotte?" he whispered.

She tossed her head defiantly, determined to say the words. "I don't . . ." she began, but the rest trailed off into nothingness as scalding tears brimmed in her eyes. "No, I can't, Mateo."

"Then it is as I thought. But we will press each other no more on that subject. Now I want you to listen to me, Charlotte." His hand was still fondling her, draining the defiance from her soul. "I have wronged you tonight. I want you, yes. But I should never have tried to take advantage of the situation."

"Take advantage? But I thought . . ." She couldn't finish. How could she tell him that she believed he had brought her to the woods to make love to her . . . that she wanted him to?

"Sometimes I go a little crazy. The others call it moon madness. Perhaps we can blame my behavior on that. At any rate, I promise you it will not happen again. I have no right. I had a special reason for wanting to see you alone tonight."

Charlotte's hopes caught flame once more. Of course! she thought. Gypsy men lived by high standards. That was why Queen Zolande was so angry with Petronovich for kidnapping her. Now Mateo was furious with himself for trying to seduce her before they were married. Her obstinate mind refused to acknowledge that Mateo still referred to her as "Petronovich's woman." She didn't choose to remember that undesirable detail.

"As I told the *phuri dai,* I want you, Charlotte."

She clung to him, weak with relief and happiness.

"I want you to be my partner."

She stared up at him, not comprehending. "Of course we'll be partners, Mateo. In everything!"

"The horses . . ."

"Yes, the horses! I'll feed them, groom them for you, exercise them, whatever you ask me to do."

"Oh, little one," he said, laughing, "you are not to be a water boy, a groom! I'd never expect such menial tasks of you. You'll have a much more exalted position. Since Phaedra joined Petronovich's act some weeks ago, I have been working alone. But I need a woman."

Charlotte stared up at Mateo. He was serious! Everything that had happened now became clear as crystal to her. Tamara had said Mateo had big plans for her. He had asked the old queen for her approval of something that was important to the *familia*. He had called her "Petronovich's woman," even after admitting his own love for her. But he had brought her into the woods not to make love to her but to ask her to be a part of his act!

"You need a partner to work in the ring with you, Mateo?"

"Not just any partner—*you*!"

Her whole body was shaking uncontrollably. She had run the gamut of emotions since arriving in this place. And tonight had left her exhausted. She took a long time answering, thinking her situation through, coolly, logically. If she left the Gypsy camp, where would she go? Certainly not back to the Planters Hotel. She had no money, no friends or family. She was totally alone and destitute.

"Well, *sunaki bal*? I would want to begin rehearsing tomorrow."

"Why not?" she replied, throwing up her hands in resignation.

Mateo caught her in his arms again and hugged her. "Then we are a team!"

Charlotte shook her head, thinking to herself, We certainly are!

But the very thought left a bitter taste in her mouth. Never before had she loved a man. And tonight she might willingly have given her all to Mateo. Yet what good did it do for him to say he loved her if he still considered her the property of another?

Yes, she loved Mateo. Yes, she wanted Mateo. And because of that love she had almost made a terrible mistake just now. She had led with her heart instead of using her head. But as Mateo had said, it would never happen again. Charlotte Buckland would make sure of that!

"What time and where tomorrow, Mateo?" she asked with cool reserve.

"At first light. Tamara will show you the place." He was staring at her with an odd expression on his face. "Is something wrong, my *sunaki bal*?"

She winced; although she loved to hear him call her by the pet name he favored, right now it hurt terribly.

"Please don't call me that anymore, Mateo. My name is Charlotte."

"As you wish, Charlotte." He reached for her hand to lead her back through the woods, but she drew away.

"No." Only a slight tremor in her voice betrayed her. He couldn't see the tears in her eyes through the darkness. "I know the way back, Mateo."

For a long time, he stood like a statue before her. She couldn't see his face and had no idea what he meant to do. When he spoke at last, his voice sounded strangely sad.

"Does anyone know the way back from where you and I have been tonight, Charlotte? I doubt it!"

She doubted it, too.

Chapter 7

Leavenworth was sleeping by the time Mateo spurred his horse into town later that night. The plank sidewalks, which usually resounded with many hurried, tramping feet, were silent, empty. The shops looked like staring ghost houses, their windows, blank and silvery black, reflecting only a muted image of horse and rider passing in the night.

He tugged the reins gently to the right, turning his horse into Shawnee Street. The wide, dusty thoroughfare, which bustled in daylight hours with ox and wagon trains headed farther west, lay broad and still. Only the jail, the two hotels, and the Star of the West saloon offered light and life at this hour. As if the horse could sense his rider's needs, the great black stallion headed straight for the saloon.

Seldom, if ever, did Mateo frequent *gajo* watering holes alone. He preferred the company of his fellow *Rom*, be it in an English pub, in a cow town pleasure palace, or beside a roaring campfire. But tonight he felt the need of solitude and a drink—stronger stuff than the brown beer or wine he drank with his friends. It would take the sting of the white man's whiskey to quench the fire in his gut and the pain in his heart put there by Charlotte Buckland.

He wanted her, by Develesa, *how he wanted her*! Never had any other woman cast such a spell over him. But so many things stood between them. He had obligations to so many—his mother, Phaedra, even to Petronovich. Queen Zolande would have the final say in whom he married, and the bride of the future king must be of Gypsy blood, with the same fires that drove him burning brightly in her soul.

As for Phaedra, their birth contract could be broken at his discretion. They were not right for each other; Mateo knew that. But still, she had waited a long time for him. She might not love him, but she coveted the title and the power his wife would possess.

Then there was Petronovich. In spite of the evil manner in which he had abducted Charlotte Buckland, the very act gave him priority when it came to who would have her. If indeed she was carrying his child, there would be no question as to her fate. She would be required to wed Petronovich on a properly moonlit night before the assembled *familia*.

And if that happens, he thought, I will lose my place among my people. Mateo knew he would have to leave. He could never bear the pain of seeing her night and day as another man's wife.

But even if all other obstacles could be overcome, there was still his recurring madness. How could he subject the woman he loved to those ugly nights when the full moon cast its spell?

Yes indeed! He needed a drink!

He dismounted slowly and tied his horse to the hitching rail in front of the Star of the West. Instinctively, he glanced up the street and down, ever wary of being out of his element in the *gajo* world. Here, he was not the great Romany prince, but a foreigner, most often the object of scorn and ridicule. He never looked for trouble, but he never ran away from it, either. Still, it was the middle ground he trod most often, avoiding unpleasant confrontations whenever he could.

He'd been in the West long enough to recognize the signs to look and listen for. He would turn back toward camp at the sounds of angry voices or gunshots coming from the saloon. He knew to stay away when he saw many hard-ridden horses outside, a sure indication that trail hands would be two deep at the bar with money in their pockets and an itch that could only be scratched by liquor, women, and a good dirty fight.

But the saloon seemed quiet tonight. Only faint laughter and the tinny notes of a nickelodeon drifted out the open door to mar the silence of Shawnee Street. By the bright gaslights inside, he could see several of the barroom girls in their colorful dresses and the blue uniforms of a number of cavalrymen from Fort Leavenworth. Most of them, he knew, would be officers, men with no interest in brawling. He would have his drink, he decided.

Everyone looked, but no one spoke when he entered. The men immediately went back to their drinks and their poker games. The girls offered him shy, flirtatious smiles but drew away to let him pass. They knew who he was. And although they might like to get better acquainted with just another handsome drifter, most *gajo* women looked on Gypsies with the same fear and doubt they harbored toward Indians.

Mateo took a seat at the very end of the bar. The saloon keeper, Solange, approached him. She was a dusky beauty who, rumor had it, had once been a slave on a cane plantation in Louisiana until her master had taken her from the fields to warm his bed.

"Your pleasure, *monsieur*?"

Her soft, Creole-accented French reminded Mateo of long-ago days when he was innocent of the pain women could cause and much happier for it.

"Whiskey, *s'il vous plaît*, Mademoiselle Solange."

"Ah, you speak French, *mon ami*!" she said, placing a brown bottle and a heavy shot glass on the counter.

Mateo poured a shot and tossed it off before he answered. "I speak the language of the person I wish to hear me. French, Spanish, Russian, Italian." He paused and downed another drink, sighed as it seared his throat, and raised his empty glass to her. "Too bad, eh, that I've never mastered the language of love?"

Her smile was enchanting—full, bright red lips that puckered, trembled slightly, then stretched to frame perfect white teeth. "But Prince Mateo, I have always heard that yours *is* the language of love!"

He gave an approving, hearty laugh and flashed a sardonic smile at Solange. "If only that were true! We have a saying in *Romani*: *'Si khohaimo may patshivalo sar o tshatshimo.'* It translates loosely to 'There are lies more believable than the truth.' "

"Meaning you believed your own myth and it has let you down?"

"*Exactement, mademoiselle*! The lady, I am quite sure, will never look on me with love in her eyes again. And why should she? I acted the fool with her!"

"And so now you have come to Solange to confess all and drown your sorrows." She clucked her tongue disapprovingly and threw up her hands in an impatient gesture. "You men! You are all alike! Here you sit, pouring out your heart to me, when you should be pleading with the lady in question for her forgiveness."

He stared hard at Solange. She was very beautiful,

with skin even more dark and coppery than a Gypsy's, flashing brown eyes, and a magnificent figure. For a moment he let his gaze caress the mounds of velvety flesh straining to be free of the ruby satin of her low-cut bodice. He was reminded for an agonizing instant that Charlotte's breasts felt more like cool silk than velvet to his touch, and that they tasted of honey and warm clover.

He was still mulling over Solange's words and thinking of Charlotte Buckland when a heavyset soldier took the seat next to his and demanded, "What does a thirsty man have to do to get a drink in this place?"

"Forgive me, Major," Solange said in a subservient tone, which Mateo realized was heavily laced with sarcasm. "You will want whiskey, of course. The cavalry drinks nothing else."

"Your best Kentucky bourbon, madam!" he bellowed. "I am—as you people so quaintly put it out here in the West—saddle-sore, dog-tired, and bone-dry. I just rode into Leavenworth, and I can tell you, I've had one helluva trip! Plain whiskey won't do it for me—not in the shape I'm in."

Mateo gave the officer a sidelong glance. He was a burly man, bulging at the seams of his dust-caked blue uniform. His hair, rusty blond in color, was thinning on top and cropped short and stiff at the sides, reminding Mateo of the unkempt coats of the mongrel dogs in camp. The soldier's fair complexion, companion to his fiery hair, was sunburned to a raw, painful pink, and his nose was peeling like old plaster. The man smelled of horseflesh and long days on the trail without a bath. Still, he didn't appear to be a troublesome sort. Mateo kept his seat and his own counsel.

After some searching beneath the counter, Solange produced a bottle, the label proudly proclaiming it "Kentucky's Finest." "Will this do, Major?"

He whisked the bottle from her, unstoppered it, and drank, not waiting for a glass. Solange and Mateo exchanged bemused smiles.

"Ahh!" sighed the major. "That's good stuff! Smooth as a baby's bottom! Just like back in Kentucky."

"You are from Kentucky, then, Major?"

The officer grinned, looking almost boyish for all his thirty-or-more years. "Boston, actually, but I'm an adopted son of the Bluegrass State and proud of it, ma'am!"

His face disappeared behind the upturned bottle once more. Solange and Mateo glanced at each other. He knew what she was thinking. If the major kept drinking at this rate—probably with little more than a bit of beef jerky in his stomach—she might have a mean drunk to deal with in short order. Or, if he passed out, she would have a nonpaying customer in one of the bedrooms upstairs for the night. Mateo nodded slightly, agreeing to help Solange.

"Welcome to Leavenworth, Major," Mateo said in a big, friendly voice he reserved for unsuspecting *gajos*. "Allow me to introduce myself. Mateo Porado, at your service."

Even while the major shook Mateo's offered hand, Solange found herself fighting to stifle a laugh. She had no idea what the Gypsy prince's surname really was, but she'd learned enough *Romani* from her golden-earringed customers to know that "Porado" was not a name at all. This was a ribald joke the *Rom* often played on naive strangers. Porado was one of the Gypsies' words for "erection."

"Glad to meet you, Señor Porado. You're Mexican, eh? Indian scout out at the post?"

Mateo's quick anger showed only in his dark eyes and completely escaped the major's notice.

The officer continued jovially, "Winston Krantz here;

major, United States Army, about to report for duty with George Armstrong Custer's Seventh Cavalry—the finest damn troop in the service. I expect you and I'll be putting in some time together, tracking down those filthy, murdering redskins.''

Mateo let Major Krantz think what he would. Instead of correcting the man's mistaken impression, he said, ''Will you be riding out to Fort Leavenworth tonight, Major, or staying in town?''

''Damned if I'd thought about it one way or the other. My mind's been focused on finding a bottle for the past ten hours. How far is it out to the post?''

''About three miles,'' Mateo answered.

Major Krantz took another long pull on the bottle of bourbon while he considered. At last he groaned, then said, ''Hell, I don't think I could sit that horse for another yard, much less three miles. Is there a hotel in this burg?''

''The Planters Hotel is not far and is very comfortable, Major,'' Solange offered.

The liquor was already making his pale blue eyes watery. His speech was beginning to slur. And the major was obviously a man who turned amorous from spirits. He reached across the bar and caught Solange's hand in his, squeezing it with drunken affection. ''You can call me Winnie, little lady. All my friends do.''

Neither Solange nor Mateo missed the fact that he had not accorded the same privilege to the ''Mexican Indian scout.'' It made little difference to Mateo. Under no circumstances could he imagine himself becoming friendly with this *gajo* officer or any other who was out to ''track down those filthy, murdering redskins,'' as the major had so bluntly put it.

Mateo knew little of the cause of difficulties between the U.S. Army and the Indians. It was none of his business, after all, and Gypsies never meddled in the affairs of others. But it seemed to him that this was a one-sided fight. What he had gleaned of the ugly situation came from talk at the forts, where he went to sell horses to the cavalry. Most of the officers he had come in contact with were much like Major Krantz—cocky, pompous, and out for Indian blood. On the other hand, the Indians he had met were noble men—a proud, ancient people, not unlike the Gypsies.

Lately, he had heard disturbing talk at the post about this Lieutenant Colonel Custer. It was rumored that the yellow-haired officer soon planned to break the treaty signed with the Sioux in 1867, in order to seize sacred burial grounds in the Black Hills and mine the area for gold. And this Major Krantz would be helping to decimate the Indians in order to desecrate their land.

"I suppose the Planters Hotel will be adequate for one night," said Winston Krantz. "How do I find it?"

"I'll take you," Mateo answered. "I was going there anyway tonight on some business."

Major Krantz had finished almost the entire bottle of "Kentucky's Finest." When he stepped down from the bar, his knees buckled. Mateo caught him before he fell.

Krantz bellowed a drunken laugh. "Riding that blasted horse has got me bow-legged."

"Don't worry, Major. The hotel is not far. We'll walk."

Throwing his arm about Mateo's broad shoulders for support, Krantz yelled, "Charge!" The other officers in the room looked up but only laughed at their besotted comrade.

Outside the bar, the night air had turned cool with a hint of autumn in its bite. But instead of having a sobering effect on the major, it seemed to intensify his intoxication. He was silent for a time, then Mateo heard him sniff loudly, as if the man were fighting back tears. The idea made Mateo uncomfortable. The *Rom* only wept on special occasions—funerals, weddings, the birth of a first son.

"We are almost there," he said, trying to head off the major's emotional outburst.

"Did I ever tell you I was supposed to be married?" Major Krantz managed to say.

"You have told me nothing. It is a man's right to keep his privacy with strangers." Mateo did not want to hear the major's sad tales. He had problems enough of his own.

"She was so beautiful—long yellow hair and warm brown eyes. And her skin was clear and pale."

Mateo's mind reverted to Charlotte Buckland. The major could have been describing her. But no! Yellow was no fit description of her hair. It was golden—like a field of ripe wheat in the sun. And *brown eyes*? No! She might think her eyes were simply brown, but to him they reflected nature's perfect spectrum—the green of new leaves, the gold of the sun, the blue of the skies.

"I have a picture of her here somewhere," the major persisted, fumbling through his pockets. "I'll show you sometime. I thought she loved me. But she ran off— right before our wedding day." A sob choked his words.

"It is best not to dwell on the past, but look to the future," Mateo said rather harshly. The major was beginning to get heavy, and he was becoming boring. One or the other Mateo could stand, but not both at the same time.

Just ahead, the lights of the Planters Hotel shone brightly. Mateo paused and allowed the major to adjust his uniform and his emotions before they entered the lobby. Then he waited and let Major Krantz go in alone. He had no desire to be associated with this *gajo*. He followed a moment later, seemingly having arrived by himself.

Mateo's errand might have seemed foolish to most at

this hour of the night. And maybe it was. But at the time he had decided to fetch her trunk from the hotel, a hard ride alone through the darkness had seemed the only way to exorcise Charlotte Buckland from his senses. Sleep would have been hard put to find him, much less soothe him with pleasant dreams. And it seemed only right that her property be returned to her.

Mateo stood back, waiting for the night clerk to take care of Major Krantz before he approached the desk to state his business. To his chagrin, he saw it was the same clerk who had been there the day he'd brought Charlotte. And this one had a reputation for hating Gypsies. Mateo knew he would have to act mild and meek and watch his temper.

Major Krantz was soon checked in. He headed for his room without so much as a backward glance at Mateo, much less a thank-you. But Mateo didn't expect any thanks. So it went with the *gajos*.

When Mateo stepped forward, the clerk said with a leering grin, "Well, by damn, if it ain't the bridegroom! What you doin' in town? Sniffing around for a new piece already, are you? I figured you'd have that fiery little filly saddle broke and be ridin' the wolf skin range by now."

Mateo stared at the man uncomprehendingly.

"Did she keep up that hollering all night, like she was doin' when you hauled her off from here?"

Charlotte! He was talking about Charlotte and Petronovich. Mateo bristled. The desk clerk must have seen his cousin taking her away and done nothing to stop the kidnapping.

"I've come for her trunk," Mateo said, his voice deadly calm.

The clerk leaned his bald head to one side and gave Mateo a hard look through his thick glasses. "Well now! I don't know as I can be handing over the little lady's property to just anybody. Might be it's valuable. And how'm I to know if you mean to return it to her? Hell! I know you thieving Gypsies and how you operate! You probably mean to take her things over to the saloon and trade 'em for whiskey. Nope! Can't do it! Now get on outta here!"

Mateo stood where he was. Only the narrowing of his eyes and the warning twitch of a muscle in his neck betrayed his mounting rage.

"The lady's trunk . . . *now!*" He spoke the words with such calm control that the underlying threat was barely discernible.

"See here!" said the clerk, backing away from Mateo, who was now leaning over the counter. "You nor none of your kind can come in here making demands! I said you ain't gettin' that trunk, and *you ain't!*"

Mateo's big hands shot out with lightning speed to grasp the clerk's frayed lapels. He drew the man up and off the floor until he was half sprawled on the counter and they were eye to eye.

"I am a patient man . . . a man of peace. But you test my control! My patience will extend for exactly two more minutes. By that time you will either bring the trunk or find yourself with your rather large nose—which I find offensive in itself—flattened, and your body broken in a number of places. I will also see to it that our queen places a curse on you which will haunt you even after your wretched body mends."

The clerk's pockmarked face had gone deathly white. He feared physical pain, but more than that he was terrified at Mateo's mention of a curse. Everyone had heard the tale of old Jake Kincaid, the prospector who had knocked up a Gypsy gal. Poor old Jake had sworn he never knew she was one of them, and besides, he'd been blind drunk when he'd jumped her. Didn't matter! He'd never tossed another skirt to the day he died! They'd put a curse on him that purely shriveled him up to nothing. Jake'd sworn he had trouble finding it when he needed to piss!

The clerk nodded his head vigorously, too frightened to find his voice. Mateo released him and stood back, waiting patiently, as if nothing untoward had happened. The man, shaking badly, turned for the office door to retrieve Charlotte Buckland's belongings. As soon as his back was to Mateo, he grabbed his crotch to make sure everything was still intact.

Charlotte awoke the next morning not to wild Gypsy music but to the familiar tinkling strains of a music box. She thought she must be dreaming. She knew that tune, but she had never heard it anywhere except when she opened the lid of the antique trunk Granny Fate had given her. She opened her eyes.

There it was. And kneeling beside it was Mateo, his dark hair tousled, his face unsmiling, but so handsome it made her want to reach out and draw his lips to hers. But no! She would not think such thoughts. Not ever again!

"Good morning," he said, his tone husky, caressing.

Charlotte didn't trust her voice. She merely nodded and clutched the fur blanket to her bare breasts.

"I have brought your things from the hotel."

"Thank you, Mateo," she managed at last.

She watched one sun-browned hand reach out toward her, as if he meant to touch her cheek. "Charlotte . . ." he began.

Suddenly, all her resolve from the night before vanished. Yes, she wanted him! No, it didn't matter why he came to her or under what circumstances! She possessed little apart from her self-respect, but she would sacrifice even that to have Mateo.

She reached out to him, eagerly, longing to be taken into his strong, demanding arms. She was ready to finish with love what had last night been preempted by anger. How could she have been so foolish?

But Mateo ignored her gesture. He rose to his feet, towering over her, looking completely unattainable.

"I am going to exercise the stallions now so they will be ready when you arrive to begin your training. Please hurry. It is quite late. You've overslept."

He turned on his heel and strode out of the brides' tent, slapping the soft leather of his boot top impatiently with his whip. Charlotte felt that she would prefer lashes from that whip to Mateo's indifference. Tears welled up in her eyes.

For comfort, she turned to familiar things. Slowly, she removed the clothes from her trunk, sorting and refolding them. At last she reached the bottom. There was the ruby-eyed snake bracelet and the delicate *mantilla*—her wedding veil. Would she ever get to wear it?

"Mateo!" Charlotte sighed wistfully. She could visualize him standing tall and handsome beside her and the bridal veil covering her happy tears.

But no! She would never be his bride, only his partner in the ring. The thought filled her with blind fury.

What kind of man was he to steal her heart even as he refused to accept her love? Like none she had ever known before—or was likely to meet again.

Very well, she decided. She would join his act, perform for his adoring fans. But in the end, she would demand far more from him than he had stolen from her!

Chapter 8

The hot morning sun beat down on Mateo's bare shoulders, deepening his dark gold skin to bronze. But he hardly felt the heat, even though sweat ran in rivulets down his chest, soaking the tight waistband of his buckskin britches. He stood in the center of the clearing where he exercised his horses, a lead rope in his right hand, guiding one of his great stallions through its paces.

The intelligent animal knew that Mateo's mind was not on his work this morning. The usual smooth, even rhythm of the master's body was ever-so-slightly off. He held the rein in too tight a grip. And today his eyes were not those of the eagle.

Try as Mateo might, he could not force his thoughts from the night before, from Charlotte. Where had he gone wrong? It was all the same, in the ring with his horses or in love with a woman—one missed step and all was lost. Now here he was, waiting for her, about to introduce her to a dangerous business, and his mind was so steeped in desire and frustration that even his best horse was snorting in reproof at his inept handling. It wouldn't do. He must get his mind on his *grai* so as not to endanger the woman he loved.

He unhooked the lead rein and slapped the big black fondly on the rump. "Go, you Black Devil! Find a pretty mare in the meadow and make her happy."

The beautiful animal reared and pawed the air as if thanking Mateo before the sleek muscles bunched in his haunches and he streaked off to freedom. Mateo stared after him, wishing love could be so simple and straightforward an act between a man and a woman.

"Is that what you think makes a woman happy?" Charlotte's quiet voice behind him made Mateo whirl around.

His eyes narrowed. He wasn't used to people eavesdropping when he talked to his horses. Theirs was a sacred bond, he felt, not to be intruded upon by outsiders. But Charlotte Buckland was about to become a part of this closed society. He had no cause to be angry with her.

"Well, do you, Mateo?" she persisted.

His face was solemn as he answered her. "Yes, I believe it can make a woman very happy . . . with the right lover."

Tension stretched between them like the tightrope far up in the circus tent. Charlotte was so tempted to ask him who he thought was the right lover for her—himself or Petronovich? The question trembled just behind her lips, begging to be asked. But she had sworn to hold her tongue on such matters. It would not do to begin their partnership in the ring with such a query.

"You look fit this morning." Mateo walked around her, sizing her up with appreciative eyes as if she were a mare he was considering for purchase.

Charlotte stood very still, allowing his inspection, although he was embarrassing her terribly. She felt almost naked in the outfit he had provided as her practice costume. The flesh-colored doeskin britches fit every curve and contour of her legs, thighs, and buttocks. The second piece of the suit, a sleeveless jerkin, molded itself to her breasts, which strained at the low-cut neckline. Never before had she worn such a revealing costume. When she rode back in Kentucky, she was always dressed appropriately in a long riding skirt with a shot-weighted hemline, so that even her ankles were modestly hidden. Now, it seemed, Mateo wasn't satisfied with making her wear such an outrageous outfit; he must also make her uncomfortable by his scrutiny.

"Are you ready to begin?" she snapped, whirling to face him.

A slow, almost mocking smile curved his full lips. "I've already begun, little one."

For some reason she couldn't figure out, his words embarrassed her further. Perhaps it was his sultry tone of voice or the way his bare chest heaved and the dark curls there glinted in the sun.

Away in the distance, she heard the amorous snorts of the great black horse and the nervous whinny of his mare. She glanced toward the meadow, and Mateo's eyes followed hers. The Black Devil, as Mateo called his favorite, was mounting the smaller black mare. Although Charlotte had witnessed the coupling of horses all her life, the fact that Mateo was so close and watching with her made her cheeks flame and caused an uneasy heat to rise in her body.

"When her time comes, the foal is yours, Charlotte. It is only just, since you and I shared this mating."

"Thank you, Mateo." Her answer was simple, although her thoughts and emotions were not. Mateo's generous offer pricked her conscience. He seemed to be pointing out the obvious, unspoken fact—that this mating was the *only* one they had shared or ever would.

"Now! Shall we begin, Charlotte?"

She nodded. She was more than ready! Anything to get her mind on something other than—than what she had been thinking about.

Mateo gave a sharp whistle, and all his stallions—except for the Black Devil, still busy in the meadow—came galloping out of the woods. They clustered around their master like children greeting a much-loved grown-up.

He laughed and patted necks, muzzles, and flanks as the stallions closed in on him. "You won't get a thing that way," he told them. "Back off. Give me room. You are worse than Poor Little Pesha . . . always mongering for handouts."

The horses, seeming to understand his every word, backed away and allowed Mateo to retrieve his jacket from a nearby limb. Charlotte watched him, smiling, as he held the coat high above his head, taunting the eager horses.

"Ah, you want sweets, eh? Well, come, then. One at a time. Here." He reached into a pocket, bringing out several hard lumps of sugar. "Here it is for you, my beauties."

Charlotte watched in amazement as Mateo's well-trained horses lined up, each awaiting its turn to take a treat from his palm.

"That's marvelous, Mateo. They listen to every word you say. I've been around horses all my life, but I've never seen anything like this. What's your secret?"

"There is no secret. These animals love me and I return that affection, openly and honestly. I treat them with the respect I desire from them, and they respond. They must come to love you, too, Charlotte, if we are to work together." He looked at her suddenly with a solemn expression. "There must be a great deal of understanding and love among all of us."

Oh, Mateo, there is! Charlotte thought. But she said nothing, only nodded.

Charlotte spent the next hour getting to know Mateo's horses and letting them get used to her. She rode each one, bareback, around the clearing several times. Even the Black Devil came in from the meadow, but Mateo warned Charlotte never to try to ride him. By the time she'd been around and around the ring until her head was spinning, Mateo was grinning broadly.

"Yes, you will do, Charlotte Buckland! My *grai* know a horse person. There is no fooling them. Phaedra tried to win them over, but she could never conquer her fear. They sensed that and rejected her for it. But you are quite a different matter."

Charlotte experienced the same delight she had always known when her father praised her. "Thank you, Mateo. I'll try very hard. I want to be the best!" Suddenly she felt almost shy with him.

He walked over and patted the horse she was on, then gave it a lump of sugar. And just as casually, he reached up and patted Charlotte's thigh, letting his big hand rest there. It seemed the most natural gesture in the world, but it sent a charge through her whole body. How could she ever hope to succeed in the ring if she couldn't learn to control her emotions? Somehow she had to force herself to keep cool, calm, and in control. Yes, Mateo was the most desirable man she had ever met. She admitted that without the slightest hesitation. But *he* and *she* were not meant to be *they*! The sooner she reconciled herself to that, the better off she would be.

Mateo removed his hand as casually as he had placed it there and said, "Now that they know you, shall we try one thing more today before we let them rest? I think that will be all, then. I don't want them to get overheated."

Charlotte wiped the perspiration from her face with the back of her hand. She wondered if Mateo had given the slightest thought to how tired and hot *she* was.

"What next?" she asked. "I'm in your hands."

He gave a great laugh. "How true, little dove!"

The next moment he leaped onto the back of Velacore, the horse she was sitting on, and positioned himself behind her. He placed both hands on her waist and pulled her so close that his chest molded itself to her back and his thighs clamped themselves to hers. The two of them became one with each other and the horse. Again Charlotte grew conscious of intense heat, but this time it wasn't coming from the sun.

Mateo gave a signal and the horse began a gentle canter around the ring. Charlotte was acutely aware of Mateo's body. He urged Velacore to more speed, and the friction between them increased. They were flying now, the trees at the edge of the clearing no more than a gold-and-green blur.

"You're all right?" Mateo said close to Charlotte's ear.

"Fine."

"Very well, then. Velacore will continue at this pace until I signal otherwise. I will dismount and remount while you remain in place and guide him around the track. Keep an even hold on the reins. Are you ready to try it?"

Charlotte's heart was thundering. She could do as Mateo instructed, but she feared for his safety. The horse was moving so fast. He might dismount without injury, but how would he ever be able to get back on?

"Charlotte? Are you ready?"

She pushed the fears from her mind; Mateo knew what he was doing. "Yes!" she shouted into the wind.

A moment later, she felt his weight shift against her. Now his hands were on her shoulders. He rose to a crouch on the back of the prancing horse. Then he was standing. As they neared a pile of straw beside the track, Mateo launched himself off the horse with the same ecstatic cry she had heard from him at the circus. She wanted to look to see if he'd landed safely, but she dared not turn her attention from horse and track.

"You are doing fine!" she heard him shout. "Steady on the reins now. I will be remounting from a second horse. Don't be distracted when we move in beside you."

Charlotte didn't answer; she merely hung on, her heart pounding, her legs aching from gripping her mount. Around and around the track—sun blazing, dust flying, muscles straining—horse and rider flew. She had ridden all her life, but never like this. Never before had she felt one with a horse, known its effort and total coordination with its rider. The feeling was more than physical; it was deeply emotional as well.

She heard a second set of hooves pounding like a twin heartbeat. Again she dared not look. Closer and closer it came. The earth seemed to be shaking beneath her. She felt the heat of the horse's breath on her leg. Then the great head came into view at the corner of her vision. Mateo made his transfer from one horse to the other with such perfection of timing that there was not one false step. He slid on behind her and gave another of his war whoops.

"We did it!" he cried, hugging the breath out of her.

Suddenly Charlotte found herself laughing and crying at the same time. "Yes! We did it!" She leaned back, luxuriating in Mateo's embrace.

Before either of them realized what was happening, Mateo had turned Charlotte in his arms until his lips found hers. The unexpected joining came as naturally and spontaneously as their joy and excitement at success.

At first, Mateo's kiss was nothing more than the congratulatory buss one friend bestows upon another. But the shock of flesh finding willing flesh soon flamed into a deep, sweet prelude to love.

Charlotte's hands crept up Mateo's bare back. Her breathing changed from deep drafts to shallow bursts as his strong fingers twined through her hair, gently forcing her head back, holding her in a grip that forbade her to turn away. So lovingly imprisoned, there was little else for her to do but respond, parting her lips for his intimate possession.

The noon sun burned down on them. The horse continued its slow rounds of the practice ring. And Charlotte Buckland, clasped tightly in the embrace she had sworn to deny, surrendered to Mateo's forceful lips, his knowing hands, and her own desperate desires.

After the strenuous night she had spent in her lover's arms, Phaedra slept until noon. Now, seated before the polished brass plate she used for a mirror, she prepared herself carefully for a special mission.

She would speak with Queen Zolande.

Carefully, Phaedra scrubbed the paint from her face. She brushed out her long, night-colored hair and parted it in the middle—a style she abhorred. But she knew that twin braids were favored by young girls and stately matrons. The queen must see her as pure and worthy—untainted by the slightest hint of passion.

"The queen . . ." Phaedra murmured to her own image. A smile parted her full lips and one eyebrow arched thoughtfully. She wasn't thinking of old Zolande, however; she was visualizing a younger, stronger, more beautiful woman—and she was dreaming of the power of the Gypsy throne.

Phaedra had known of Mateo's new partnership only an instant after the *phuri dai* had given her nod of approval. The news had traveled like wildfire through the Gypsy camp. Phaedra had chafed at the imagined rejection from the moment she'd heard. Granted, the decision to leave Mateo's act had been hers and hers alone. But the idea that she was about to be replaced—and by the *gajo* woman, of all people—set her temper raging.

She couldn't possibly have slept last night; she'd been far too upset. So the purple veil had seemed the logical solution. Only with Petronovich could she spend her angry passions. But this time even Petronovich's willing lust had failed to dispel her fury. Mateo's affront still rankled.

Angrily she tossed the braids over her shoulders. Why should she care? She had detested working with the horses—the heat, the dust, the constant practice for hours on end with Mateo always driving, issuing orders, and pointing out her slightest fault. She could never please him. Working with Petronovich's Boski was so much more enjoyable. The crowds loved her. She was the star of the act. And she could manipulate the dumb, adoring beast as easily as she did its master.

Phaedra smiled wickedly, remembering her lover's eagerness to please her all through the night. He had stroked and fondled, kissed and caressed, begging her to find her pleasure so that he could take his. She gave a low laugh, thinking back over those dark hours of ecstasy. If only Petronovich knew how his touch made her breasts tingle and her thighs ache until the final rush of fulfillment engulfed her. How pleased with himself he would be! But no. Never! She would keep him at bay . . . keep him in need. Only when the sun was peeking into the tent to gild their damp, naked bodies, only when the camp was beginning to stir, had she allowed him to take her and spend his own passions. And although she had reached the heights time after time, she'd never let Petronovich know that he had satisfied her needs. This control she had taught herself proved most useful. When Petronovich had left her, he had been smarting with guilt, thinking that she still lay aching for him. He would return whenever she beckoned to right this wrong.

In more ways than this, her relationship with Petronovich was of her own design. He came to her when and if she called. Otherwise, he was forbidden access to her tent. And on the nights when she left her purple veil before her tent flap as a signal to him, he always gave; she only took. So would it be with Mateo! she vowed.

Phaedra rose slowly, composing her features as she did so. Queen Zolande would not be allowed to see beyond the humble, maidenly façade. Phaedra's plea would be heard, considered, and granted. There was little else the queen could do. And by the next full moon, when Mateo succumbed to the madness, a new queen would take the throne and be hailed as the *phuri dai*.

Queen Zolande was still puzzling over Phaedra's request for an audience when her dead sister's daughter entered the tent. Inside herself the *phuri dai* smiled, but her face remained as passive and expressionless as if it were carved in stone. What was Phaedra up to with her calculated girlish appearance? Zolande had no idea, but she could not betray her curiosity.

"Come, Princess Phaedra. Stand before me and I will hear you," she commanded.

Only Phaedra's walk as she approached the queen betrayed the sensual woman beneath the innocent disguise. Seeing her arrogant stride and the seductive sway of her hips, it would have been clear to a perfect fool what kind of person Phaedra was—and Queen Zolande was no fool. The braids, the shining face, were only lamb's fleece hiding the she-wolf.

"My queen," Phaedra said in a respectful whisper as she bowed before Zolande. "I beg you not to close your mind or your heart to the words I am about to say, even if my plea should sound impertinent."

Zolande nodded. "Speak, girl, and we shall see."

"I find myself in a difficult position—pledged to Mateo, but with no word from his lips to tell me when my destiny from birth will be fulfilled. Or even if it will ever be. I have seen all my sisters wed. I am an aunt many times over. Yet still I am without husband, without child." Phaedra paused and forced a look of sorrow to her face. "I am no longer a young girl, my queen. My childbearing years are at their zenith now, but soon they will pass. What will happen to me if I am forced to grow old all alone—with no husband to protect me and no sons to care for me in my declining years?"

Once more Queen Zolande was forced to hide a smile. At eighteen, Phaedra was hardly declining! Still, the girl had a point. Most Gypsy women were married by thirteen, some at a much earlier age.

"So what have you in mind, Princess Phaedra?"

"Please, Queen Zolande. If you could speak to Mateo on my behalf . . . I would have him in an instant. I love him." Now it was Phaedra's turn to bite her lip to keep it from curving upward. Her ability as an actress, developed for the circus ring, was being tested to the limit. She cast down her gaze in an attitude of humility. Her voice lowered to the barest whisper. "If, by some chance, Mateo finds me unworthy, then let him break our contract and free me to wed another."

"And is there another you favor over my son, Phaedra?" The queen narrowed her eyes and leaned forward as if she had the power to see into the other woman's heart. "Petronovich, perhaps?"

"Oh, no!" Phaedra gasped. "There is no other, my queen. My heart and soul are Mateo's, but for his asking."

Queen Zolande's black eyes glittered knowingly. The fact that Phaedra made no mention of her body's owner did not escape the old woman.

"What of my son's madness?" she demanded.

Phaedra shrugged in the time-honored fatalistic manner of the Gypsies and turned her palms to heaven. "Can any man be perfect? I have seen Mateo's suffering. I will do what must be done to ease his pain when the full moon afflicts him. Beyond that, what can anyone do?"

The queen felt a sharp stab in her heart. What indeed? She had been so sure that Mateo would find his golden Gypsy and end the curse forever. But her own time was growing short. Mateo must wed—and soon.

As if Phaedra could read the old queen's thoughts, she said, "We have all wished for the coming of this golden Gypsy, but how can we imagine that Mateo will be the one to find her when almost a century has passed without relief from the curse? I have waited this long to approach you on the subject of my marriage, praying every night that this special Gypsy woman would present herself to become my own beloved's bride. I would gladly sacrifice my happiness to see Mateo free of the curse. But it has not happened. And now, my queen, I feel my turn has come. Please, will you help me?"

Queen Zolande squirmed slightly in her discomfort. She would as soon see her son remain forever without a wife than force him to marry Phaedra. But a contract was a contract. She had reinforced the betrothal as her poor sister lay dying. With her final breath, Phaedra's mother had asked for Zolande's promise to see their son and daughter made man and wife. And soon, the old queen knew from the shortness of her breath and the fire in her chest, she would be joining her sister in *ravnos*. How could she face that dear woman on the other side if she had failed to keep her vow?

"You may go now, Phaedra," Zolande said suddenly, sternly.

"But—" Phaedra's placid façade slipped when she was dismissed so abruptly. She had humbled herself before this senile old woman, but she would not be refused. Her black eyes flashed angrily, and the full line of her lips tightened.

"You have spoken your plea," interrupted the queen. "Now I must consider and, if I decide to, speak with my son on this matter. Go!"

Phaedra relaxed. She bowed and backed slowly away from the *phuri dai*. So it was done! Queen Zolande might detest the very thought of it, but she had no choice other than to order Mateo to marry. And Phaedra, of course, would be his bride . . . *his queen*.

"May your days be long and free of care," Phaedra said in *Romani*, and then she left the tent.

"What can I say to you to make things right?" Mateo was still holding Charlotte, although now they lay beneath a cottonwood tree at the edge of the clearing. She leaned against his shoulder. While one arm supported her, with his other hand Mateo stroked the rise of softness at the opening of her doeskin jerkin. His dark eyes smoldered as he caressed her. "A very wise woman last night told me that if I loved you, I had better tell you and set things straight between us. So I'm telling you now, *sunaki bal*. I love you!"

Charlotte was having trouble thinking clearly. Granted, she was an innocent, untouched by any man when she left Kentucky. She had no way to compare Mateo's kisses or the way his hands felt on her flesh. But even little girls have imaginings. And Charlotte had long since left behind playtime musings for the more erotic fantasies of a mature young woman. However, even those wild flights of fancy paled before the real emotions and sensations Mateo stirred within her.

"I thought we agreed last night that we wouldn't speak of love again," she said.

Mateo's hand crept up her throat, making her tremble. Lifting her chin, he turned her face toward his. There was no denying the love she saw in those coal-black eyes, and she knew that her own mirrored his.

"Charlotte, my love, it is easy enough to speak lies to oneself and to others under cover of darkness. The real test comes beneath the burning eye of the sun. Believe my words now. They are true . . . the only real truth."

Charlotte's heart quickened for a moment. Then Tamara's soft voice came to mind, telling her that no Gypsy will ever speak the full truth to a *gajo*.

"And what are you feeling?" asked Mateo.

Charlotte tried to turn her eyes away so he couldn't read her thoughts. How could she tell him? Would he believe her if she said she loved him more than life itself? Would he be shocked if she told him that every inch of her ached to have him hold her and kiss her and touch her? Would it matter to him that marriage *didn't* matter to her?

"Mateo," she began, her voice trembling. "You know my feelings. You've known that I love you since the first moment we met. You looked into my soul and helped yourself to all my secrets. I could see it in your eyes that day. What more can I say to you?"

Suddenly Charlotte felt tears welling up in her eyes. She felt defenseless, naked, talking to him this way.

What did he want of her? Hadn't she offered everything she had to give?

"No, my darling," he whispered, wiping away her tears. "This is not a time for weeping. Our hearts are in tune; our destinies are entwined. Fate has meant this to be."

His words shocked her. She pulled away, staring. Was he mocking her? What had happened to all the obstacles of a few hours ago . . . Petronovich, Phaedra, his own Gypsy heritage?

As so often happened, Mateo seemed to be reading her mind. "Phaedra will be no problem. To marry her or not to marry her is my decision alone. I choose not to. As for Petronovich and his claim on you, I don't believe he has one. He told me that he did not . . . accomplish what he set out to do. There will be no child."

Charlotte gasped. "Of course not!"

He smiled at her shock and kissed her gently. "So there is nothing for us to worry about, little dove. We love each other. We will be together."

For a moment, Charlotte was confused by the odd way he put it. Why didn't he say they would be married? Then the final, greatest obstacle came back to her. *Mateo must marry a Gypsy.* Again tears stung her eyes, but she blinked them back. Did a few words spoken over them matter so much? No! The most important thing was being with the man she loved.

Mateo bent down and kissed her temple, then whispered, "There are some things more important than my place in the *familia.* We will go away together. We will have all our years to love each other . . . as man and wife."

"Oh, Mateo!" Charlotte cried. She flung her arms around his neck, sobbing with joy.

He crushed her to his chest and sought her lips for a

deep, soul-filling kiss. Charlotte felt as if she were floating somewhere among the thin wisps of clouds high
above them. Never, not in her most exotic fantasies,
had she dreamed that she could love or want or need
any man this much. But now here he was—holding her,
kissing her, promising her a shining future. She pressed
close to him, never wanting the wonder to end.

"Mateo!" It was Tamara, calling to him from just
beyond the clearing.

Charlotte wrenched herself free, her cheeks burning
with embarrassment that the shy girl who had once been
chosen as Mateo's bride should find them locked in such
an embrace, with Mateo's hand inside the jerkin pressing her breast and his mouth consuming hers.

"At last I've found you," Tamara said, her own discomfort evident in her tone. "Queen Zolande wishes to
speak with you immediately, Mateo."

"My mother wants me? Now?"

Charlotte didn't like the look of the tight lines around
Tamara's mouth as she answered, "No, Mateo. *The
queen* wants you."

"But she never holds audiences this time of day,
Tamara. What's going on?"

Tamara shook her head. "I cannot say, Mateo. But
her summons was urgent."

Mateo sprang to his feet, anxiety plain in his face.
"She isn't ill?"

"She didn't appear so. But would she tell us, if she
were?"

Mateo clasped Charlotte's hand for a moment. "I
shouldn't be long, darling. You go with Tamara for now.
I'll come to the brides' tent when I finish so we can
make our plans."

Charlotte nodded and rose. She stood silently beside
Tamara and watched as Mateo hurried toward the camp

with long strides. The happiness she had felt only moments before vanished. Something was wrong. She knew it.

"What's happened, Tamara?" she asked, fearing the answer.

"What Fate has willed." Tamara slipped her arm about Charlotte's waist and gave her a compassionate squeeze. "I'm sorry, my friend."

Charlotte turned toward the young fortune-teller and saw tears in her eyes. In that instant she knew, though she refused to accept the truth.

Chapter 9

Mateo pulled on his shirt and jacket as he strode toward his mother's tent. Every step felt leaden. Although he had no inkling as to the nature of the queen's summons, he knew trouble awaited him. The hair rose on the back of his neck like the hackles on a Gypsy mongrel when a *gajo* draws too near. His heart thudded in his chest. And the deep, hollow ache inside him that always presaged disaster painfully returned.

Mateo glanced about the camp. Everything looked normal enough. The women sat hunched over the fire, preparing buffalo stew. Most of the men lazed about, smoking their pipes and exchanging gossip. A few naked or near-naked children were chasing a dog and squealing in their excitement. The scene gave no hint of trouble.

Mateo entered the large tent without asking permission, forgetting even the amenities in his haste. Inside, no lamps were lit. It took his eyes a moment to adjust to the dim interior after the bright sun outside. While he was still squinting and trying to see, his mother's voice greeted him.

"It is well that you have come so quickly, Prince Mateo. This matter can wait no longer."

He bowed before her, then kissed her on each cheek. She was not smiling. Neither was he.

"You're not ill, Mother?"

"No. Only sick at heart, my son."

The old queen sat on her thronelike chair, enveloped in her scarlet cape. She looked frail and even more ancient than her years, Mateo noted. She sat motionless, her usually animated hands still and quiet in her lap. Her head sagged at a dejected angle and her eyes looked red and tired.

"Have I done something to cause you pain?"

One thin hand stretched toward him. "Never, my son. No, never. But I am afraid that what I am about to say will bring you great suffering, if not now, later. If I had any other path, believe me, I would take it. But my heart is slowing its beat with every shift of the sands in the hourglass. I may live to see the first snow, but I will not smell the flowers of another spring."

Mateo grasped her hand and kissed it. "Mother, please . . . don't . . ."

A faint smile hovered about her mouth. "Don't what, my son? Die, or talk about it? I must do both. I have lived a long, happy life, and you have been my shining light since the day I gave birth to you. Fate has been kind to me. And now the time is growing short before I will once more join the rest of our family—my own love, Strombol, your sisters, and even my own dear sister . . . Phaedra's mother."

There was a catch in Zolande's voice as she mentioned Phaedra. She looked at Mateo with pleading eyes, hoping that he would understand.

"Are you asking me to prepare myself, Mother? I

don't think I can. I know that for each of us the time comes. But to think of life without you . . ."

"Is to think of your own life as king," she finished for him.

He knelt before her, letting his head rest on her lap. She stroked his thick hair, the way she had when he was a small boy. They were so much alike, this pair—strong, just, passionate in love or hate.

"Hear me now, Mateo," the queen said softly. "It seems that I am to be denied the one thing in life that would have brought me the greatest joy. All these years I have prayed for the golden Gypsy to take your curse away. Still, she has not come. We can wait no longer, my son. I'm sorry."

Mateo's head jerked up and he stared into his mother's face. For the second time in his life he saw tears on her cheeks.

"What are you saying, Mother?"

"You must be wed, Mateo."

Suddenly his mind returned to the sight of Charlotte Buckland riding his great black horse, her shining hair streaming in the wind. He could still taste her honeyed kisses and feel the warm silk of her breasts against his palms. A hot rush of blood pulsed through him. Yes, he must be wed, and he planned to.

"Mateo, you aren't listening to me," the queen said, breaking into his thoughts.

"I'm sorry, Mother. But your words set me thinking. It seems that as always our minds are traveling the same paths. I decided only this morning that it is time I was married. I've already asked her, in fact, and she has accepted my proposal."

Queen Zolande frowned. This was not possible. Phaedra had left her only moments before she'd summoned Mateo. Or had Phaedra taken the matter into her own manipulating hands, as she so often did—not waiting even for the queen to have her say?

"Perhaps it is just as well," Zolande said as much to herself as to Mateo. "If you have spoken to her already, then you must be reconciled to this match."

"Reconciled?" Mateo jumped to his feet and gave a great laugh. "My dear mother, I am ecstatic! Grown men aren't supposed to feel this way. Why, I'm like a boy again! Every minute will drag by until she's my wife." He quieted and said, "I love her more than I can tell you, Mother."

Queen Zolande only shook her head. How could any man love a woman like Phaedra? But then love was often blind, or so she'd heard.

"Well, Mateo, I must say I'm relieved." She stood and embraced him. "Every mother wants happiness for her son. But I never dreamed that you cared so much for Phaedra."

Mateo pulled away from his mother's arms and stared at her, his face clouding suddenly. *"Phaedra?* No! It's Charlotte Buckland I plan to marry."

The old queen's heart sank at his words. She knew it had been too easy.

"No, Prince Mateo," she said firmly, "you will *not* marry a *gajo!*"

For several moments, as Queen Zolande's words hung in the still air, a clash of wills took place. In silence, two pairs of glittering black eyes locked in challenge. The old ways battled the new.

Mateo broke the silence. "Then I will not marry at all!" His words, though spoken quietly, transmitted a harsh finality.

Queen Zolande took a deep breath that hurt her weak chest. She drew herself up, ready to use her last ounce of strength and authority to defend her much loved son from his own foolishness.

"You are not just another *Rom*. You will be king, Mateo! You must marry, but you may not marry out of the *familia*. There has never been any question of this, nor will there ever be. As you bear Valencia's curse, so must you bear this honor and this obligation. And even if all that were not so, Petronovich has first claim on the *gajo* woman."

"He does not! I have questioned him closely on what happened that night. He did set out intent upon having her. But she fought him off quite effectively. I believe him when he says he did not lie with her."

"Then you are a *fool*, Mateo!"

The words stung. Never had his mother spoken to him so sharply. He could see the pain in her eyes even as she accused him. His feelings and his voice softened.

"Mother, Charlotte herself told me that it was all a terrible mistake—that he didn't take her. Perhaps Petronovich would lie to me, but not the woman I love."

Queen Zolande held one hand pressed to her heart. The pain was bad now. Her words came out breathlessly. "Think about it, Mateo. If she truly loves you, would she hurt you by telling you this particular truth? What man wants to know that the woman he loves has been with another? She would lie to spare you the pain of knowing. No! We can believe neither of them. Only the next man to take her to his bed will ever know for sure."

"Then I will—"

"*You will not!*" The queen's voice rose to a dangerous pitch. "Mateo, the moon is not full now, but you are acting out of madness all the same. So you test this woman and find her a virgin still, what then? Would you leave her soiled and at the mercy of some future lover when he finds he is not the first? You cannot marry her! She is not a Gypsy! You *will* marry Princess

Phaedra!'' Zolande slumped to her throne chair. "That is my final word. Go now. Leave me to rest."

Mateo stumbled from the tent, his mind in an angry blaze. This couldn't be happening! Phaedra as his wife? He couldn't begin to imagine it. He'd known all his life of the birth contract. But contracts, he also knew, could be broken. Phaedra cared nothing for him or for anyone other than herself. And the thought that his mother was questioning Charlotte Buckland's virginity while proposing he marry Phaedra was laughable. Phaedra dropped to the wolf skins as often as leaves fell from the trees.

Granted, it was not unthinkable for a Gypsy woman to lie with more than one man, even if she was married, but *only for money*, never for pleasure. Women served the *familia* in any way they could. When bad times came, the married ones would go to the towns and seek out strangers. But only for needed gold! No respectable Gypsy would ever give her body to appease her own carnal appetites as Phaedra did.

"No! On the holy breast of Sara-la-Kali I will not marry her!"

Mateo stormed back into the queen's tent. Again he was like a blind man, but he could see that his mother no longer sat in her chair. A faint rasping filled the tent, drawing his attention.

"Mother!" He hurried to where she lay sprawled on her bed of skins, struggling for breath.

"Mateo," she gasped, "go for Tamara. She will help me."

All the words he had meant to say dissolved, leaving only a bitter taste in his mouth and a deep ache in his heart. He could not go against his mother now. It would kill her as surely as if he were to plunge his dagger into her heart. He bent and kissed her fevered brow, then went to find Tamara.

*   *   *

The bells on the door of the brides' tent tinkled gaily. Charlotte, bathed and dressed in a bright yellow skirt and white drawstring blouse, hurried to answer, sure that Mateo had come for her. She still felt as if she were floating about on some gilt-lined cloud. She had ached to confide her secret to Tamara, but the girl's somber demeanor had warned her away. It was better this way, after all. If the others found out, they might try to dissuade Mateo from marrying her.

She'd refused to let the nagging worry she'd felt when Mateo was called to the queen's tent stay with her. There should be no happier time in a woman's life than the day she decides to marry. And Charlotte Buckland was bound and determined to enjoy the full measure of that happiness.

She hurried toward the door, but Tamara intercepted her.

"I will answer it, Charlotte."

"But I know it's Mateo."

"That may be, but how do you know his business is with you?"

Tamara's usually sweet voice sounded strange, almost harsh, to Charlotte's ears. She hung back, allowing the Gypsy girl to answer the call of the bells. It was Mateo, but he never mentioned Charlotte's name or even glanced inside to see if she was there. Her heart ached as Tamara hurried back in to fetch the dried herbs she needed to tend the queen.

"Tamara, doesn't Mateo want to see me?"

The fortune-teller, her face solemn, swept past Charlotte. "There's no time. The queen is ill. Mateo and I must go to her."

"But when will you be back?"

"I have no idea. Please, I can't answer questions now."

Then they were gone, leaving Charlotte alone, her lovely plans for an afternoon with her future husband crushed. Still, she took heart. She knew how it was between mothers and sons. Hadn't Granny Fate doted on Charlotte's own father, her only son? It was the same with Mateo and Queen Zolande. Even after they were married, Charlotte promised herself, she would never try to come between him and the queen. And she certainly had no right to now. She would wait for Mateo, until he had cared for his mother.

Charlotte sat alone in the tent, watching the afternoon shadows lengthen as they inched across the carpets. Soon the golden sunshine was tinged with the orange and lavender of sunset and still Mateo had not returned. She was restless, bored, and feeling somewhat sorry for herself.

"This won't do!" Resolutely, Charlotte grabbed a basket and headed for the door. She would go to the forest—the *vesh,* as Tamara called it—and pick wildflowers for Queen Zolande. There was little else she could do. But flowers always made a sick person feel better, she reasoned. Besides, Mateo would appreciate her thoughtful gesture.

Glancing toward the center of the camp as she came out, she saw that a large group was gathered outside Queen Zolande's tent. They talked in hushed voices, milling slowly about. Mateo and Tamara were not among those holding the vigil. As much as she wanted to go to the others and ask about Mateo's mother, she couldn't. She was still "the *gajo* woman," still the outsider. And although the Gypsies never treated her unkindly, they made it clear that she did not belong among them. They looked through her when she passed, as if she were as invisible as the wind. No, they would not welcome her intrusion now. She hurried away.

Twilight was already creeping into the woods when she arrived at the stream. Birds sang far up in the trees in hushed, sleepy tones. The day's heat had been preserved in the earth and warmed her bare feet, but the breeze felt chilly about her shoulders. Evening was slipping its cool, blue velvet mantle over the forest.

Searching the banks for flowers, Charlotte followed an animal path beside the stream. She found a few buttercups and a patch of Queen Anne's lace. Farther ahead, she saw the bright scarlet of a bed of wild poppies. She would have a lovely, colorful bouquet for Mateo's mother. She dropped to her knees, spreading her skirt to catch the poppies as she picked them. Suddenly, something drew her attention—some faint sound.

Charlotte stopped her gathering and listened. The sound was water splashing just up ahead. She strained her eyes but could see nothing for the trees and the encroaching gloom. Rising, she started toward the sounds. By the time she saw who it was, it was too late to retreat. Phaedra, her naked body gleaming wet, sat on the bank, her face upturned to one last beam of sunlight. Her eyes were closed and she seemed lost in some pleasant world all her own.

Although she wanted to turn and flee, Charlotte found herself rooted to the spot. Like one of these weeds I've picked for the queen, she thought dismally. She was dreadfully embarrassed to have come upon the other woman at such a private moment. But the sight of Phaedra's voluptuous body—her large-nippled breasts, rounded thighs, and tiny waist—was both entrancing and intimidating. Charlotte couldn't help but compare Phaedra's beauty to her own. She thought again of the things Phaedra had said about making love. Surely this woman was right: Mateo must find Charlotte's charm a pale imitation next to Phaedra's Gypsy sensuality.

Just as Charlotte started to turn, Phaedra spotted her and said, "Well, if it isn't the little *gajo* spying on me! Aren't you afraid to be out this late in the woods all alone? For all you know, some lust-crazed *Rom* could be lurking behind any tree, just waiting to jump out and rape you!"

Charlotte felt utterly flustered. "I'm sorry. I—I didn't mean to disturb you," she stammered.

Phaedra drew one long leg up, rested her chin on it in a decidedly wanton pose, and laughed. "You've never disturbed me! And I doubt you ever will. You won't be here that much longer."

Charlotte brightened. "Oh, then Mateo told you?"

"Told me what?" Phaedra sat up and stretched, thrusting her full breasts forward. She yawned to indicate that she found both the blonde *gajo* and her conversation boring.

"Mateo has asked me to marry him." Charlotte hadn't meant to say it, but her old rebellious nature surfaced to force the secret out.

Phaedra was on her feet in an instant, bored no longer. "He *what*?"

"He says we'll go away together . . . just the two of us, as man and wife."

In spite of the pleasure she had taken in telling Phaedra her news, Charlotte was instantly sorry. The woman's eyes narrowed to slits, her long-nailed fingers drew back into talons, and her breasts heaved with rage. The fact that she was naked—and obviously unashamed to be— further added to the bestial quality of her anger. For some time, she stood before Charlotte, seemingly unable to find her voice over the deep growl in her throat. She looked like a dangerous, wild creature with her wet hair tossed about her bare shoulders and her lips curled in a threatening sneer.

Charlotte was frightened. She wanted to turn and run, but she refused to give ground to this woman. Then suddenly Phaedra began to laugh. The unpleasant sound echoed through the quiet forest, startling the birds into silence, unnerving Charlotte further.

"*My* Mateo, marry *you*?" Phaedra choked out through her laughter. Then her ugly mirth vanished. "You're as mad as he is! No, you're not mad. You're just stupid! I told you what Mateo wants from his woman. I can see you now, all pale and cringing, begging him to be gentle on your wedding night."

"I really don't see that my wedding night is any of your concern!" Charlotte snapped.

"No, I doubt that it will be, since my Mateo will certainly not be a part of it! You see, he's going to marry *me*!"

Charlotte couldn't believe her ears, but she wasn't about to let her would-be rival have the last word. "Mateo does not love you!"

Phaedra offered Charlotte a bemused smirk. "I never said he loved me, only that he will marry me."

"Of all the . . ." Charlotte was too outraged to go on. She whirled away, wanting to break into a run but forcing herself to act with a certain amount of decorum.

"I suppose you imagine that he loves *you*?" Phaedra called after her.

"*He does!*"

Phaedra laughed again. "Poor little *gajo*!" she crooned. "Mateo is a man who takes what he wants. If he loved you, if he even desired you, he would have ordered you to his bed already. Has he?"

"No! Of course not!"

"Then he doesn't love you," Phaedra said with finality.

Charlotte was so angry now that she couldn't even

think of a reply. She turned and started to run back to the village.

"Hey, you!" Phaedra called. "Where do you think you're going? I'm not finished with you yet!" She caught up with Charlotte and, taking her by the arm, whirled her around. "No one turns her back on Princess Phaedra. Especially not now that I am about to become the queen. Do you hear?"

"Take your hands off me!" Charlotte yelled, struggling against the other woman.

"First, you promise me that you will go away."

"I will not! I'll stay here as long as Mateo wants me!"

"He does *not* want you! You are no Gypsy! What would he do with you? Settle down and live in a white man's house? Ha! You are crazy if you think my Mateo could live that way. He must be free like the wind."

Charlotte was battling now to retain her reason and her trust in Mateo. She pushed Phaedra away from her and quickly grabbed up her basket of flowers.

"I refuse to stand here and argue with a . . . with a *naked woman*!"

Charlotte didn't hear what Phaedra shouted after her. Her heart was pounding with her feet. She had to be away from that woman. She had to find Mateo. Surely he would reassure her of his love. He wouldn't lie to her. And he wouldn't marry Phaedra. He detested her.

Still, the other woman's words echoed in her mind: "*You are no Gypsy!*"

There was a change in the camp when Charlotte returned. The cluster of people had left the front of Queen Zolande's tent. The women were at their fires, the men at their pipes and mugs. Nicolai, the blind guitarist, strolled among them, strumming his wires softly. His tune, though typically Gypsy-sad, was not a song of mourning, Charlotte knew. She walked to the queen's tent to leave her basket of flowers. Perhaps, if she was quick about it, no one would notice her.

But just as she stooped down to deposit her bouquet, the tent flap flew open. Startled, she looked up into the dark contours of Mateo's troubled face.

"The queen wishes to speak with you." His statement came in the cold, stern form of a command.

"Mateo?" Charlotte said, but he was gone.

She stood there uncertainly. Should she call through the flap for permission to enter or just go in unannounced? Did Mateo mean that the queen wanted to see her this very minute or at some time in the future? Tamara solved her dilemma.

"Please come in now, Charlotte. Queen Zolande is feeling much better, but she swears she won't rest until she's spoken to you."

"About what, Tamara?"

The Gypsy girl shook her head. "That is for her to say and you alone to hear, my friend."

When Charlotte entered, both Tamara and Mateo left. It wounded her deeply that Mateo didn't speak to her and even seemed to be avoiding her. She needed reassurance now more than ever before. And she would have it. But first she must face the queen.

"Come closer, Charlotte Buckland," rasped the ailing woman. "These old eyes are not as keen as they once were. Turn up the wick in the lamp. I want to see the beauty of this face which my son holds so dear."

At that moment, Charlotte had the sudden urge to hug the frail old lady, who lay on her bed of skins looking as fragile as a china doll. So Mateo had spoken to his mother. This explained everything—even Mateo's coolness toward her just now. He wanted his mother's approval, and Zolande had probably not yet given him a hint as to what her answer would be. Charlotte turned up the lamp as ordered and went to stand near the queen.

"I promise to make your son happy," Charlotte said hesitantly. "I love Mateo very much, Queen Zolande."

Mateo's mother waved a thin hand in the air, dismissing Charlotte's words.

"Who taught you manners, girl? Don't you know not to speak until spoken to in the presence of the queen?"

"I'm sorry," she whispered, blushing from head to toe.

"As for this great and powerful love you profess for my son, what does one of your youth know of real love, child?" She raised her hand once more to show this was a rhetorical question. "Your world is so different from ours. The people are different; the rules are different. You will love a dozen times before you marry. But for a Gypsy love comes only once. And without the honor and respect of his fellow *Roms,* a man can know no love worth having. Love and marriage are for the benefit of the *familia*—first, last, and always."

The queen stopped for breath and Charlotte seized the opportunity to speak. She knew where Mateo's mother was headed. She did not want to hear it.

"Don't you think I know something of respect and family honor? I'm not some heathen out to ensnare your son. Please, I want only to make him happy, to love him, to bear his sons."

"Ah, there! That is just my point. Would you have the great Prince Mateo sire sons with pale hair and skin, sons with the thin blood of the *gajo*? It cannot be! He is prince of his people. If you wish to marry into our clan, I will see that Petronovich—"

"No! Never! I don't love Petronovich. I am Mateo's woman!" Charlotte cringed at her own words. Only a short time ago, she had sworn that she belonged to no one. Already, through her love of a Gypsy, she had fallen into their way of thinking and speaking.

"*Phaedra* is Mateo's woman."

The queen's voice was quiet, but her words hit Charlotte with the force of the bullets that had felled her father on the field of battle. She felt pain twist through her heart.

She tried not to remember how lovely Phaedra was. The Gypsy woman's curvaceous bronze body, Charlotte was sure, was what men's dreams were made of. Mateo might never love Phaedra, but if forced to marry her, he would take great pleasure in bedding her. The thought was almost too much for Charlotte to bear. She would fight for him!

"Mateo told me we would go away. He knew that our marriage would never be accepted."

"Poor child," the queen said, sighing. "My son is a man in years, but a boy in his heart. He knew that was not possible. He should never have made such wild promises. His life is here. His destiny is to be king of the Gypsies. There is no place for you in his life or his destiny. I am truly sorry, Charlotte Buckland."

Queen Zolande's eyes closed, signaling that the interview was at an end. But the matter was far from settled for the lovely, golden-haired woman who stood beside the bed watching the old queen's breathing grow even in sleep.

Tears gathered in Charlotte's dark eyes, but she refused to let them flow. She had fought to be free of one marriage. She would fight all the harder to have this one. No Queen Zolande, no Princess Phaedra, no moon madness or Gypsy curse would take Mateo from her.

"Life is life," she had heard the Gypsies say time and again. "Sing, dance! Who knows what will happen tomorrow?"

"Who knows, indeed?" Charlotte whispered, and a smile curved her lips.

Chapter 10

A strange pall hung over the Gypsy camp in the coming weeks. Queen Zolande lay abed in her tent, struggling against the Dark Angel. Life for all slowed and became more solemn. The violins, when they played around the fires in the evenings, wept their songs of love and death and partings. No one married, no one danced, few made love. It was as if the world had stopped in its orbit, awaiting some final decision from on high as to the old queen's fate.

Only one activity remained unaltered. Practice continued daily, with Mateo—careful now to keep Charlotte at arm's length—instructing her in the graceful art of bareback acrobatics.

They no longer talked of love or marriage. Their sole purpose lay in perfecting Charlotte's act so that she would be ready for a special performance a few weeks off. She would put in minor appearances in the ring before then, to get the feel of riding in costume and before an audience, but her big moment would come when the circus went to Fort Leavenworth to entertain the cavalry and their families.

"We have only a short time left, but you are coming along wonderfully, Charlotte." She basked in Mateo's praise, but she would have preferred his kisses. "Has Tamara finished your costume yet?" he asked.

"The scarlet and gold? Yes." Charlotte was glad the sun was hot this morning and grateful the workout had been strenuous. The heat and exercise disguised the blush that crept into her cheeks just thinking about the tights and scanty bodice and skirt he spoke of. "Mateo, don't you think it's a bit daring to wear in public?"

"Not for a Gypsy."

"But I'm not—"

"I know that, but our audiences will not. They expect a certain display of the bizarre from us. We must not disappoint our paying public. Now let me see your hand-stand once more and then your dismount."

While they'd talked, Charlotte had been astride Vela-core, riding around the ring. Now she leaned forward, resting her head on the horse's neck and bringing her legs up gracefully, toes pointed, until she was reclining on Velacore's broad back as she might on a couch in a parlor.

"Slowly, now," Mateo directed. "You must make it look as if the motion is totally effortless."

That was easy enough for *him* to say, but she would try. After posing for a moment in her reclining position, she sat up, both legs dangling over Velacore's right side. He continued his steady canter. Charlotte spread her arms wide and smiled. Mateo had taught her to play to the audience.

"Lovely!" He applauded. "Now the final move. Take it slowly."

This was the tricky part—the dangerous part. One slip and Charlotte could easily break her neck or fall beneath the horse's hooves and be trampled. She took a deep, steadying breath before beginning the maneuver. Kneeling carefully, she placed the flat of her palms at the very center of Velacore's backbone. Then slowly . . . gracefully . . . ever so carefully, she raised her body and then her legs until they were fully extended, again with her toes at a perfect point.

Mateo clapped loudly. "Bravo! It is perfect! Now down . . . easy, easy, don't let your weight shift. That's it. Beautiful!"

Just as Charlotte was almost back to her normal position and safety, Phaedra came running toward them. Velacore shied at the unexpected movement, destroying the tenuous unity between horse and rider. Charlotte felt herself slipping and cried out.

Mateo was there in an instant to catch her in his arms. She clung to him, shuddering at the thought of what might have happened had he not reacted so quickly. She felt his eyes on her and looked up. What she saw in his face triggered a familiar quiver deep inside her. The mask he had worn for so many days melted away. Here was the Mateo she loved . . . the Mateo who loved and desired her in return.

"*Sunaki bal*," he whispered, and his lips parted, readying themselves for a kiss.

"Mateo *darling*," Phaedra broke in.

Still holding Charlotte, Mateo turned on her. "Damn you, don't ever do that again! You know I don't allow anyone at the practice ring. You could have caused a tragic accident!"

Phaedra only smiled and tossed her long, unbraided hair back over her bare shoulders. "You don't seem to be suffering from my actions, Mateo. And certainly your little *gajo* helper is enjoying it immensely. Look at her, all trembly and blushing. She's exactly where she's been scheming to be all along—in the arms of *my man!*" Phaedra's smile narrowed to a threatening grimace.

Mateo set Charlotte on her feet at once and moved away from her. So it had been between them since Queen Zolande took ill. He seemed to believe that if he so much as touched Charlotte, he could in some way harm his mother—perhaps even bring about her death. His attitude pained Charlotte, but she did not give up hope. Whatever feelings they had experienced they still shared. And as Phaedra clutched at him possessively, Mateo's distaste for her grew more evident every day.

"Why have you come?" Mateo snapped at her.

"Since I'm going to be your wife, I feel we should share everything—not just a bed." The last part of her statement was aimed directly at Charlotte. "Your precious beasts will simply have to get used to me. I may even decide to return to the act."

"Never," Mateo muttered under his breath.

"I see you're finished here," she continued, "and you promised to take me to the market today. I'm ready to go."

"I said I would drive you in only if my mother is better. She had a very bad night. How is she feeling now?"

Phaedra scowled at him and shrugged. "How should I know?"

"You mean you didn't even bother to look in on her this morning, as I asked?"

"You didn't ask; you commanded. I don't take orders, Mateo! The sooner you learn that about me, the better off you'll be."

Mateo, his face flushed with anger, drew back his hand as if to strike her.

Phaedra only laughed. "Hit me! Go ahead," she taunted. "It wouldn't be the first time." She turned to Charlotte. "Did you know that this great *Rom* you so desire is a woman beater? Yes! He may be gentle with his horses, but he takes his vicious temper out on his women." She looked back at Mateo, her full lips twisting in a cruel smile. "Can you deny it?"

A nerve twitched under Mateo's eyes, but he held his peace. Finally, he turned away from both women and went to tend his horses. Would Phaedra never let him forget that one time in the ring when his perfect control had faltered . . . when his hand had slipped? The very memory of it pained him.

Phaedra had been inept at best with the horses. During one performance, she'd dashed between the Black Devil and Velacore, terrifying the pair and throwing all his *grai* into a panic. Velacore had stumbled, and Mateo, in a nightmare flash, had imagined the great stallion's leg broken. Flailing the air with his whip—out of fear, rage, frustration—he'd tried to restore order in the ranks. The tip of the slashing whip had caught Phaedra's back, tearing her costume and drawing a thin line of blood. She wore a scar to this day and claimed that Mateo's aim had been true. Perhaps she was right. He'd certainly felt like taking a whip to her . . . more than once! If ever a woman deserved it . . .

Phaedra whined on to Charlotte, accusing Mateo of one injustice after another. The woman's voice and her complaints reminded Charlotte of her own mother. How often she had heard Jemima Buckland complain of the hardships of life, even before the war when times were good. And always the object of her mother's scorn had been Charlotte's father. There was no justice in life when a man must be saddled with such a wife.

For the first time in a long while, Charlotte Buckland

thought of her home, her mother, and Granny Fate. What had become of the two women and Fairview? She longed to know, but her old life now seemed like something she'd only imagined—a dim shadow in the back of her mind.

Ignoring the irritating drone of Phaedra's voice, she glanced toward Mateo. Here was her reality—this sad, sweet man. He could be angered to the point of violence by a woman's foolishness, but his dark features took on an angelic glow when he was alone with his horses, tending them with gentle hands and speaking with them in secret whispers. She ached to tell him that she understood, but she knew that would not be wise. Even if she had sole claim on him, he would never accept words of sympathy from her. It was not in Rom Mateo to show weakness; therefore his woman should not see any in him. Such was the Gypsy way, she had learned.

"Charlotte," Mateo called suddenly, "I'm going to see about my mother now. We're finished for the day. Tomorrow we will not practice. But on the following day, wear your new costume."

He strode off toward the camp without a word to Phaedra.

"Poor darling!" Phaedra called after him in a mocking tone. "Tonight you must keep your rendezvous with the moon, eh? I will pray to Sara-la-Kali for you, if I happen to think of it."

Charlotte felt a chill race through her. She had forgotten that this would be the night of the full moon. On the last such night, she had come to this place. But by the time Petronovich had stolen her away, Mateo had recovered enough to rescue her. She had no idea what exactly happened to him when the moon was full. He had called it "madness," but beyond his own vague explanation, she knew nothing.

"Will it be bad for him tonight?" she asked of Phaedra.

The other woman laughed. "Mateo is a great actor. And as good a liar as any one among us. In my opinion, he and his dear mother concocted this whole tale of moon madness to keep the others under their control. You'll see tonight the way they cower in their tents, almost afraid to breathe." Phaedra fingered the purple scarf tied about her neck and added, "But I have my own plans, and I don't intend to let Mateo's act interfere with them."

The full moon rose that evening, blood-red in the death-black sky, from behind the skeletal line of trees to the east. Charlotte sat alone in the brides' tent. Tamara would stay with Queen Zolande to see her through this fearful night. It seemed hard to believe that the same moon that Charlotte and her father had wished upon so happily together could bring such terror into the Gypsy camp.

But it was as Phaedra had predicted. Supper fires were kindled early so that the last man, woman, child, and dog would be finished eating before dark. Now only embers glowed outside. Not a soul was in view. And only the lonesome west wind howled its mournful song in the night. Violins and guitars lay abandoned, their owners too terrified to sing in the face of such evil and suffering.

Somewhere near the tent an owl hooted. Charlotte shivered and pulled her shawl more closely about her shoulders. For the first time since she'd left Kentucky, she felt totally alone. The emptiness and silence were not pleasant companions. She gazed out across the encampment toward Mateo's tent. The flap was secured and no light gleamed from within. She closed her eyes and tried to imagine what he must be going through . . .

but it was no use. Sighing, she shook her head and stared down at her hands, feeling as if they were tied and useless.

The full moon sailed higher, turning from red to orange to tarnished gold. But still the night was dark as heavy black clouds scudded low across the sky. Thunder rumbled far off in the distance. The wind shifted and rose, whipping the tops of the trees until they looked as if they were whirling in a devil dance. A jagged streak of lightning ripped asunder the black garment of night. Thunder shook the earth, followed a moment later by a scream of agony.

"Mateo!" Charlotte cried.

She didn't think about what she was doing. She only knew that she must go to him . . . that he needed her. Hurrying out of the tent, she was met by great sheets of driving rain. The wind tore at her clothes, whipping her shawl away and making a blindfold of her storm-tossed hair. But she would not be held back.

"Mateo!" she cried again. "I'm coming, Mateo!"

As she neared his tent, she saw that the wind was beating at the canvas. Then she realized the motion was coming from within. It looked as if some wild animal were trapped inside, trying desperately to fight its way out.

She knelt and called through the flap, "It's Charlotte, Mateo. I've come to help you."

Only an unearthly snarl answered her. She drew back, afraid for a moment. Then her courage and determination returned.

"Untie the flap, Mateo. I'm coming in."

The thrashing inside ceased, and, for a while she heard nothing. Again terror touched her, this time because she feared Mateo might be dead. Then the groaning began anew—a terrible, heart-wrenching sound of one in pain. But Charlotte rejoiced. He was still alive!

Quickly she reached under the flap and untied the laces. Minutes later she was inside, her eyes aching in the darkness.

"Mateo?" she whispered.

She could hear his labored breathing and judged that he was only a few feet away—off to her left. On hands and knees she crept toward him. The tent was not large; it contained only a pallet of skins, a chest, a brazier. And a chair. She bumped it, hurting her shoulder. She must have light. How could she help Mateo if she was blind?

Slowly she rose to her feet, feeling for the ridgepole and the lamp she knew she would find there. Before fumbling for the matches in her pocket, which she had wrapped in oilskin to keep dry, she turned the wick down low. When she struck the match, Mateo screamed and shied away.

She looked at him, and her heart sank. There, tangled in wolf skins, lay a panting, wild-eyed stranger. The gentle lines of his face were contorted as if in rage or pain. His eyes were bloodshot and bleary. Deep scratches on his throat and chest oozed fresh blood, evidence that he had injured himself in his anguish. His beautiful dark hair was tangled and matted as if he were some wild mustang whose mane had never known a currycomb. Clenched between his teeth was a twist of rawhide, and leather thongs secured to a heavy wooden pole bound his wrists. As another spasm racked his body, he strained in these restraints until the leather grew dark with his sweat and blood.

Recovering from her shock, Charlotte drew closer and whispered, "Mateo, I've come to help you."

He looked at her, but his eyes remained unfocused. Spitting out the rawhide, he gasped, "Go away! Get out of here!"

Another scream escaped him. The moon was turning from gold to silver. Charlotte composed herself as best she could and bent down to retrieve the badly chewed rawhide. Carefully she slid it back between his teeth. It muffled his next cry of pain.

She looked about and spied a pitcher. Pouring spring water into a basin, she knelt beside Mateo and began to bathe his face, neck, and heaving chest.

"I'm going to untie your wrists, Mateo."

She reached carefully for the leather thongs, wondering if she was doing the right thing. A moment later, she found out. His freed right hand lashed out as if of its own volition, striking her across the breasts. A sharp pain shot through her and she gasped.

Mateo, meanwhile, had spat out the rawhide once more. His face contorted painfully as he tried to form words. At last they came. "Go, Charlotte . . . before . . . before . . ."

Tears filled her eyes. He knew who she was! At least that was something. Bending over him, she took hold of his shoulders and forced him to lie back.

"I'm not going anywhere, Mateo. Not until you're better."

"I hurt you," he managed to say.

"You didn't mean to."

She continued bathing his brow while he was calm. Busy at her task, she never noticed that the wind had blown open the unlaced tent flap and one silver streak from the full moon was inching its way in. Slowly it crept, feeling its way—searching, probing, intent on evil.

When Mateo's body strained in another spasm, Charlotte leaned forward, pressing with all her weight to hold him still. She wrestled with him, pinning his arms to his sides. She was heaving with exhaustion by the time the spell had passed.

Then, for a time, he grew too still. His eyes were closed. His body felt cold and there was a silvery pallor about his face. Charlotte leaned close to his open mouth, terrified that he might have stopped breathing. Suddenly his arms closed about her, bruising her ribs, and he ravaged her with a brutal kiss. She struggled against him, but there was no freeing herself from his crushing embrace. He seemed to be trying to draw the last breath from her body. She felt dizzy, disoriented. This was not Mateo, but some savage stranger, unleashing his brutal lust upon her. Clawlike hands tore at her clothes. she felt her blouse being ripped away, felt her bare breasts cool against Mateo's fevered chest. She fought desperately. But she might as well have been a day-old kitten fighting a raging lion. Mateo was a strong man. His moon madness tripled that strength.

She lay against him panting, not knowing what she could do or what he would do next. For the moment, he seemed calm again. Although he still held her prisoner in his arms, his head was thrown back and he was breathing deeply and evenly. He appeared to be recovering himself.

"Mateo?" she ventured.

At the sound of her voice, his head shot up again. He glared at her with wild, unfocused eyes. Letting his big hand slide down her body, his fingers bit into her waist and he forced her onto her back beside him. The skins that had been tangled about him fell away. For the first time, Charlotte realized that Mateo was naked. A harsh beam of moonlight silvered his belly and made a thick, gleaming dagger of his erect penis. She gave a startled cry. He echoed and intensified the sound with another pained scream. Doubling up, he fell over her, writhing and clutching at her breasts with pain-cramped fingers. Charlotte could only lie there and pray that the moon would wane before Mateo destroyed them both.

Again he forced her mouth to obey his savage will. Still his hands kneaded her soft, bruised flesh. Then, slowly, his fingers moved down her torso, gripping the waistband of her skirt. She heard the sharp rip before she realized what was happening. An instant later, Mateo raised himself from her long enough to yank the rest of her clothes away.

Flesh met flesh with a shattering impact. Charlotte's resistance was feeble at best. Her body ached from trying to fight him off. It was no use. Besides, wasn't this what she had wanted all along? If he was less than gentle, did that matter so very much?

Yes, dammit, it did matter!

The man Charlotte desired was the tender, passionate Gypsy *Rom* she had come to love. If this savage, lust-filled stranger took her, it would mean nothing. Would Mateo even know that he had made her his when the last moonbeam faded with the dawn? That was what hurt most of all.

"Please, Mateo, love me, but love me gently," she begged.

Already he was poised for the thrust. Through her tears, she could see the outline of his hard body straining above hers. He hunched over her—a beast about to mount its mate. The hot pulse pressed between her thighs jerked and prodded at her in anticipation. A moment more and it would be done.

"Mateo, can you hear me? It's Charlotte. Please don't hurt me!"

He hesitated, seemingly trying to understand or make up his mind. Charlotte took hope. Perhaps the madness was wearing off. Perhaps he had some inkling of who she was and what he was about to do to her.

"Charlotte?" he said, his voice sounding almost normal.

"Oh, yes, Mateo!" she cried, frantic now with relief and happiness. He was coming around.

Just then, a vicious gust of wind whipped the tent flap back. Squarely framed in canvas, the small, pale silver sphere cast its dying light upon them. Mateo gave an anguished cry. Charlotte watched the muscles bunch in his shoulders, gathering strength—shuddering, straining, making ready.

This is Mateo, she told herself. You have nothing to fear.

Charlotte closed her eyes and gripped the coarse fur rug beneath her, steeling herself. She forced her mind to think of him as he had been that night by the stream—as he had always been . . . except for now. She could endure anything at his hands. She loved him. She would welcome him; for to fight him would be madness on her own part. She willed her body to relax. Now, though still crying softly, she smiled. She was ready.

A strange fever seemed to enter her mind the moment Mateo forced his way into her body. Her senses reeled crazily. She felt disoriented and filled with a wild, inexplicable panic. This was a torture like none she had ever imagined. But oddly enough, as this terrible spell seized her, Mateo grew calm. It was almost as if through her love she was drawing the torment from his body and soul into her own.

Soon her terror vanished with her pain. Each new thrust soothed her torn flesh and righted her confused mind. She tensed once more, but this time with a new sensation. Mateo had brought her through the cruel gate to some new and fantastic realm. Here they walked together, hand in hand, body in body, and the sun, not the moon, shone down on them in all its glory. Charlotte had no idea where he was taking her, but she knew that she had been searching for this unknown paradise all her life.

He rode her expertly, with the same combination of

fiery command and loving gentleness that he used in handling his Black Devil. And Charlotte responded to the great *graiengeri*'s touch.

His lips and tongue had lost their harshness. His hands on her breasts no longer bruised, but pleasured. She felt her nipples straining to be stroked. And the battering of his hips had become an undulating series of waves, smashing on her ready shore. She rose and fell to meet him. She welcomed him, drawing him deep into her body, feeling his caresses in the very core of her.

Suddenly, the sun inside her head and heart became blinding. She thrust at Mateo with a fury, begging him for something—she knew not what. And then she felt it coming—ever nearer, ever sweeter. A tidal wave of sensations rose within her, dashing all else in its wake. Her sweating, love-scented body quaked under the impact. A feeling totally new to her surged through every muscle, bone, and sinew. She shuddered against Mateo, holding him close, kissing him, adoring him for what he had given her.

Her lover clutched her tightly, and she could feel the throb of him deep inside her. Suddenly he held very still. A tremor ran through him. A spasm jerked his hips. The next instant she felt the precious deluge filling her with his princely seed. A new kind of pleasure washed over her and trembled through them both. Now, as never before, they were one.

Mateo held her a moment more, then rolled away. He lay on his back, breathing heavily, one arm thrown over his eyes. He sighed and reached out to touch her breast. For a long, silent time he stroked the full nipple. She lay very still, marveling at the way she felt—full, warm, *loved*.

The sun's first rays penetrated the opening of the tent. Charlotte heard birds outside chirping their waking songs.

Somewhere a Gypsy mongrel barked, a kettle clanged, a horse neighed sleepily. The terrible, beautiful night of the full moon was past.

Mateo reached out and took Charlotte's hand. "Oh, my *sunaki bal*, what have I done to you?"

"Only what Fate intended, my darling."

She leaned over and touched his lips in a gentle, loving kiss.

Chapter 11

Major Winston Krantz stood in his sparsely furnished quarters at Fort Leavenworth, perspiring mightily as he donned his battle garb. The whole idea of this expedition irked him. He wouldn't have minded so much if a band of scalp-stealing Indians had been the day's intended quarry. That was what he was out here for, after all. But this . . . *this was uncivilized madness*!

Krantz pulled on his new fringed buckskin jacket, identical to the one Colonel Custer always wore. He looked at himself in the mirror over his washstand and grimaced. His mother, back home in Boston, would have shuddered in horror at the sight; his father probably would have said Winston looked like a red-skinned savage himself. The garment certainly did nothing to enhance the outdoorsman image he had hoped to create. Even if no one else thought so, he'd hoped to make the damned buffalo they were about to go after think he looked threatening, if not downright dangerous. But the picture he presented—at least to his own eyes—was more that of an overstuffed deerskin with tassels.

"Blasted fringe!" he muttered as his sleeve tangled in his cartridge belt.

This was just the latest in a series of frustrations since he'd joined up with Custer's 7th Cavalry. He was half glad Charlotte Buckland had run out on him before the wedding. Fort Leavenworth, with all its pretense of civilization, simply wasn't his idea of the proper place to begin a happy marriage. The rough quarters, the heat, the constant threat of Indian attack . . . well, he wasn't sure what he'd expected, but it certainly hadn't been what he'd found.

He'd never dream of bringing a wife here to endure such hardships. But many of the men had wives, children, sisters, even mothers living on the post. Mrs. Custer wasn't in residence at present, but only because the 7th Cavalry was here on temporary duty. Still, the colonel swore that his Libbie might just pop in any day. He vowed that she loved every minute of army life and hated being left behind when her "Autie" rode out.

The "boy general" himself, as Custer had been called after his field promotion during the war, was Krantz's second shock. The man was not made of the tall, muscular stuff one envisioned in connection with heroes. In fact, had it not been for George Custer's manly swoop of mustache, those long golden locks might have made the officer look quite effeminate. Granted, he was a keen strategist when it came to fighting these bloody savages. His idea last year of mounting a campaign during the winter months, when the Indians were off their guard, had been a stroke of genius. But Custer's interests were so unorthodox for a West Point man—writing poetry, taking part in amateur theatricals, holding mule races. Why, some of the men even whispered that he consorted with Gypsies! It all smacked of the bizarre to Krantz. And perhaps the man's strangest quirk was the menagerie that always traveled in his company.

Krantz harrumphed loudly into his fist and reprimanded his own thoughts. "Not including Mrs. Custer, of course."

Winston didn't mind the dozen or so dogs—although he was sure some of them were full-blooded and still vicious wolves—or even the assorted raccoons, squirrels, and smaller furry vermin. It was that damned obnoxious pelican that got his goat. The thing was always following Krantz about, flapping its big wings and begging in its irritating, voiceless fashion at the mess.

Krantz was trying on his new broad-brimmed felt hunting hat when a voice outside his door announced, "Mail call, Major Krantz, sir."

A sudden pang of nostalgia raced through him. He thought of home and the cool New England fall that would soon be descending upon his beloved Boston. The first letter from his mother must have arrived with all the latest news and gossip about family and friends. He could hardly wait to read her detailed account.

"That dear lady," he murmured, thinking of his prim, gray-haired mother as he hurried to open the door for the mail orderly.

The soldier thrust one envelope into Krantz's hand and said, "Colonel Custer says we'll be mounting up in ten minutes, sir."

"Thank you." Krantz turned away, anxious to read his letter before joining the others.

A strong waft of verbena perfume pervaded the room. Odd! He'd never known his mother to wear scent. He glanced down at the evelope—a woman's dainty handwriting, but certainly not Prudence Barclay Krantz's clean, economical, no-nonsense script. He tore into it, most curious now.

Fairview Plantation
September 1, 1870

My Dear Major Krantz,
  I cannot begin to tell you how devastated I am over Charlotte's unforgivable behavior. The only excuses I can offer for such rash, unfeeling rejection of you and your most kind and generous offer are her youth and impetuosity. I fear, too, that her grandmother aided and abetted her in defying me and disappointing you. Their actions are inexcusable! Were I not a Christian woman, I am sure I should never be able to find it in my poor, sad heart to forgive either of them. But you and I must trust in the preordination of all things and believe that this has happened for the best.

Winston Krantz stopped reading for a moment to nod his head in agreement. Hadn't he thought these same things only moments before? He must write to Jemima Buckland and put her mind and heart at ease.

A warning bugle sounded outside. He hurried back to the letter, anxious to read all that Charlotte's mother had to say before it was time to leave for the hunt.

  I am sure you must realize, dear Winnie, that I thought my daughter too young and too flighty for you from the beginning. Such a strong, distinguished, and honorable gentleman, in my humble estimation, should have a wife fit to the task of helpmate as well as heartmate. Such was the relationship between myself and my dear, departed husband. I hope, if I ever decide to marry again, I will find a man very much like yourself—with your courage, strength, virility, and understanding.

Krantz stopped to reread that sentence. He was smiling broadly—fairly preening. He hadn't realized before what a keen judge of human nature Jemima Buckland was. Perhaps he should have spent more time gazing at the mother instead of the daughter.

Charlotte is still unaccounted for. Her grandmother tells me she took the train for California to seek her fortune. Neither of us may ever see her again, I fear. But whatever she finds in that wild country, she richly deserves!

In conclusion, I would like to plead with you to stay in touch with me. I worry far more about you than I do about my unfeeling daughter. How have you taken all this? What kind of life are you living in that dangerous, heathen land? Do you ever think of Fairview—of us? Please write, Winnie. A scribbled note will be met with heartfelt gratitude. I promise to answer back.

Until that time, I remain . . .

Ever sincerely,
Jemima Lewis Buckland

He stared at the page for a long time, breathing in Jemima's perfume and visualizing the golden hair that framed as pretty a face as her daughter's. The added maturity was no detriment, he decided. He could even see her blue eyes. Funny, until this very moment he hadn't realized that Jemima Buckland had blue eyes. Perhaps he'd taken more note of her than he'd thought.

A second, louder bugle call aroused him from his reverie, thrusting him back into the unwelcome reality of camp life and the buffalo hunt about to take place. Groaning slightly, he hoisted his gear and started out of his quarters. He turned back, smiling suddenly, and took the letter, slipping it inside his shirt. It would be nice to feel Jemima Buckland's warm words close to him during the coming hours.

Fort Leavenworth was caught up in a flurry of activity. Horses, in their anxiety to be off on the chase, tramped the parade ground into an all-encompassing cloud of dust. Soldiers shouted back and forth to one another. Scouts lounged about, chewing tobacco and looking bored, waiting for more taxing sport. Custer's ever-present pack of hounds added to the morning's confusion, chasing this way and that and yapping excitedly. In the midst of it all, Col. George Armstrong Custer, his golden locks and red neck scarf blowing in the breeze, sat his favorite hunter, Custis Lee, issuing orders right and left. Only Custer's pet pelican looked totally unconcerned, perched on the railing outside its master's quarters where it could view the whole scene without fear of being trampled or getting nipped by an excited hound.

Krantz shook his head, wondering how this bunch of farmhands and city boys could ever be whipped into shape. The batch of raw recruits that had arrived at Fort Leavenworth just days ago knew nothing of army life. Many of them had never even been on a horse. But that's what he was here for, to help train them. And Colonal Custer swore that the best way to keep a brand-new cavalryman in the saddle was to take him buffalo hunting.

"Damned if they don't learn how to ride mighty quick when they see that herd thundering down on them!" he'd said, laughing.

"Here's your mount for the day, sir," said a young soldier to Krantz, handing over the reins of a horse as dark as Custer's own Custis Lee.

"Soldier!" Winston Krantz barked at the private's retreating back. "This isn't my palomino. Bring me Old Ironsides."

"Begging your pardon, sir, but I can't do that. You see, Colonel Custer's ordered the troops divided into two groups today as a sort of contest. Those riding with him will be mounted on dark horses like Jock here. The others will be on light ones. That way everybody will know who's riding with whom, and we'll know which side won when it comes time to count tongues.''

"Count tongues?"

But the private never got a chance to reply as Custer called through the chaos, "Major Krantz! Mount up! I'm ready to lead them out.''

Winston Krantz pulled himself up into the saddle and urged his horse through the mob until he was alongside Custer.

"I'm ready, sir,'' he said, feeling anything but ready.

Custer looked at him with cool blue eyes and said, "By God, sir, you are *not*! Where's the Hawken rifle I had issued to you?''

"I'm used to my old Kentucky. It got me through the war without so much as a scratch.''

"That might have been fine for Johnny Rebs, but not for buffalo. Myself, I prefer to ride in close and count my coup with a pistol. But that's not for someone new at this game. You'll want the best you can get. The new Hawken's shorter barrel and larger bore can drop one of those great furry beasts at two hundred yards. And believe me, you won't want to get much closer once you see the size of them. Besides, if those ragged hunks of cloud off to the west turn into a prairie storm, a percussion rifle's going to be a lot more use to you than an old Kentucky flintlock. Go get the Hawken, Major Krantz.''

With a huff of annoyance, Winston climbed down from his horse and headed back for the new rifle. He'd never been much of a hunter, and the thought of going out on a strange horse with an unfamiliar weapon was sorely trying. But an order was an order, and Custer was his superior.

Moments later, Winston Krantz was back in the saddle, Hawken in hand. Colonel Custer gave the signal and the entire troop headed out at a smart clip. Even Krantz couldn't deny a certain feeling of exhilaration now that they were on their way.

The troop hadn't ridden many miles before they came over a small rise; suddenly, the brown-and-tan range turned black. Before them stretched a herd of buffalo, a sea of dark, dusty shapes, their great humps like waves moving restlessly all the way to the horizon.

"Hellfire and damnation!" Winston Krantz cried. "I never saw anything like it!"

"Quiet!" Custer cautioned in a harsh whisper. He passed the same word back through the ranks, then motioned for his men to follow.

"They don't even seem to see us," Krantz observed in a monotone.

"They won't spook as long as we stay downwind. Buffalo are stupid beasts. I've shot a dozen or more in a small group while the others just grazed on, watching their mates fall dead around them. As long as they don't pick up our scent, they won't budge from their feeding."

When Custer had his men in position, halved into two troops by horse color, he gave the signal to fire. The great, hulking beasts dropped like flies—a shot, a bellow, a thud, then a cloud of dust and it was over. To Winston Krantz, it seemed almost too easy to be sport. But the roar of his rifle, the smell of blood, and the confidence brought on by man's superiority to beast soon warmed him to the hunt.

Suddenly Custer yelled, "Okay, boys, let's go get 'em!"

Having given the raw recruits and Winston Krantz their chance, Custer and his veteran buffalo hunters whipped out their pistols and galloped at breakneck speed into the midst of the herd. The earth shook as the buffalo herd stampeded. Krantz watched, amazed, as Custer and his men rode close enough to reach out and touch the charging beasts, firing at deadly point-blank range. Custer himself dropped three . . . four, and was riding down a fifth large bull. Krantz watched, transfixed by the man's daring.

Custer was almost up close enough now to put a bullet in the animal's brain. He gave a war whoop and took aim with his revolver. But the next moment, the buffalo veered directly into Custis Lee's path. The horse reared, and Custer's pistol—cocked and ready for the kill—exploded, sending a bullet through his mount's head. Winston Krantz felt his breath stop for an instant as the dying horse pitched and Colonel Custer flew through the air. Hitting the hard-packed earth with a thud, he sprang immediately to his feet, gun still in hand. He came up eye to eye with the startled bull buffalo. Only a few feet separated man from beast.

Except for the thunder of the retreating herd, silence reigned. Then the bull gave a low, dangerous-sounding snort. Custer stood his ground but held his fire. Krantz wondered if the man was paralyzed with fear or simply knocked senseless from his fall. The buffalo pawed the earth and seemed about ready to charge his former pursuer. Then suddenly the huge beast swung away and galloped off after the rest of the herd. A great cheer went up from the ranks. Custer let the noble animal depart without firing a shot, then ambled back toward the others.

"Damned if I ever saw anything so brave, Colonel!" Krantz said.

Custer gave him a weak smile and a wink. "Don't tell the others, but I hope I never see anything like it again! And if the truth be known, it was about one part brave and nine parts scared shitless!" He grinned a bit sheepishly. "That, of course, is strictly between you and me, Major."

"Certainly, sir," Krantz answered, glancing about to make sure no one else had heard.

"I think I'll call it a day now. The boys have had their fun, don't you think, Major? Time for the tongue count."

"I hate to sound like a complete novice, Colonel, but what on earth are you talking about?" Winston Krantz squirmed with discomfort at having to admit his ignorance.

"Simple," Custer answered. "Those carcasses are too heavy to haul all the way back to the fort. They'll be butchered on the spot. Then, to total up our kill, the men will cut out the tongues and bring them back to see which side won. Besides, the tongue of a buffalo is the tastiest part."

Winston Krantz held back any comment, afraid of what he might say. But the thought of eating buffalo tongue dispersed any appetite he'd worked up during the hunt.

An orderly came running, leading Custer's spare hunter, Dandy. The colonel mounted and sat watching as his men butchered the buffalo. His horse neighed impatiently and Custer patted its neck.

"Damn fine horse I lost," he muttered to Krantz.

The two men hung their heads in an unofficial moment of mourning for Custis Lee before heading back toward Fort Leavenworth.

That night, the mess tent was decked out with battle flags for the festive occasion. Long tables, set with bottles of wine, seated officers and men alike. Krantz and Custer's troop had won the tongue count, so they were feted by the soldiers of the opposing force. Much kidding and telling of tall tales was the order of the evening as the meal passed down the ranks: steaming platters of hump stew; soup made of buffalo bones and marrow and seasoned with milkweed buds, rose hips, and prickly pear; broiled ribs; and, of course, the pièce de résistance—smoked tongue.

"Sweet and tender as veal, eh, Krantz?" Custer asked jovially.

Winston had to agree that it wasn't half-bad, although he passed on the raw liver, which some of the men actually fought over. A brash young lieutenant named Lance Delacorte won the largest portion. Winston looked away as the man devoured it with relish.

Well into the evening, when the meal was over and both the talk and the wine were almost exhausted, Winston Krantz felt a kind of warm glow steal over him. It had been a strange day and a stranger night, but all in all this was a good life—a man's life.

He looked across the table at George Armstrong Custer and smiled his approval of the man. Suddenly he wanted to say something to let his superior know he respected him as an officer and liked him as a friend. A man needed a friend in this wild country.

"You certainly handled yourself well today, Colonel."

"You've got to, if you want to stay alive out here, Krantz. If one thing's not out to get your hide, something else will be. That's the first lesson you learn out west: be ready for *anything*! Right, men?"

The other officers voiced their full agreement.

"I see your point, Colonel. It's a far cry from humdrum duty, teaching at West Point, or even riding into bloody battles as we did during the war. At least then all we had to fight were the Rebs. Out here you've got beasts, redskins, and, so I hear, even Gypsies," Krantz finished in a whisper.

Custer gave a great laugh. "They're here all right, but not to do battle. I don't think those Romanies have a word in their language for *fight*. I sent a troop of six men to their camp when they first got to these parts. I told my horse soldiers to rout them out, even if they had to use their guns to do it."

"They're still here, though, sir. What happened?"

Custer leaned back from the table and patted his full belly in a pleased manner as he continued, "Picture this, Major. My men ride up on the camp and all the Gypsies are singing and dancing around the campfire—those lovely, dusky women in their bright skirts, their faces reflecting the flames as if they were chiseled in bronze and copper. My men were struck dumb at first. When they did get around to issuing my orders, the Gypsies ignored them—acted as if they weren't even there. They went right on laughing, singing, and dancing. Finally, one of my men fired a warning shot to get their attention. He got attention, but not the kind he'd expected. One of the young women came to him, disarmed him, and led him into the dance. Four days later, I went myself to see what the hell the Gypsies had done with my men. I figured I'd find them all dead. But no! There those happy fools were—all six of them—drinking brown ale, dancing, singing, carrying on like no decent soldiers I ever saw before. I was damn mad, I can tell you! But a day and a night in that Gypsy camp and I was tempted myself to stay the rest of my life."

"Colonel, you don't mean . . ." Winston Krantz could hardly believe such a thing of the man he'd witnessed staring down a bull buffalo.

"Don't get me wrong, Krantz." Custer laughed, guessing what the major must be imagining. "I know my duty. I rounded up my soldiers and hauled them back to camp. But I had a damn fine time doing it!"

"And you allowed the Gypsies to stay?"

"I hadn't much choice. They refused to hear my orders. Even that Prince Mateo, who's certainly nobody's fool, turned deaf on me when I told him to vacate. They live by their own rules. As long as I don't get any complaints, I'll leave them be. But the minute I hear of any trouble, out they go. You can count on it!"

"Well, that's reassuring," Krantz said.

Custer threw back his head and laughed aloud. "Major Krantz, why don't you ease up a bit? This isn't Boston, or even Kentucky. We live by a different code out here. As for the Gypsies, I think you'll change your mind about them once you see them perform."

"That good, are they?" Krantz asked, not quite convinced that anything could change his mind about a dirty, thieving bunch of vagabonds.

"You'll see. They say a Gypsy *Rom* can put on an entertaining show with no more than a dog, two fleas, and a fly. When you see that fellow, Mateo, and his matched stallions, I'd be willing to bet your staid Bostonian eyes will bug right out. You'll probably be haggling with him to buy one of his horses as soon as he finishes his act. But you might as well save your breath. I think he'd sell his own mother—the old queen—before he'd part with one of those beauties."

"I want to see his new woman!" Lieutenant Delacorte put in with an unmistakable gleam in his gray eyes.

"Ha! You'd better not let your wife hear you say that, Lance!" Custer laughed. "But I'm with you. I'm anxious to see this unusual lady he's added to his act as well. I've heard she's a blonde Gypsy, with skin as light as yours or mine, Krantz."

"Do tell?"

Custer nodded and smiled a bit wickedly. "Mind you, I have nothing against dusky ladies. I've been forced to accept the hospitality of more than one Indian chief with an accomplished daughter. But the thought of one of those fiery Gypsy women with fair skin is somehow exciting, don't you agree, gentlemen?"

"I'll drink to that, sir!" Delacorte answered, raising his mug.

Winnie Krantz had no idea whether he agreed or disagreed. He'd never seen a Gypsy as far as he knew. And as for golden-haired women, he already had two in his life—Charlotte and her mother. That was enough to occupy any man's thoughts and senses. He'd leave the Gypsies to Custer and young Delacorte, although Krantz had to confess he was curious to see their show when it came to camp in a couple of weeks. He would bide his time and reserve final judgment until then.

He pounded his chest with his fist to dislodge a belch, and in so doing felt Jemima Buckland's letter inside his shirt. A new warmth crept into him and he had a sudden urge to reread it.

"If you gentlemen will excuse me?" he said, rising. Several others had already left for their bunks. The party was breaking up.

As Winston Krantz sauntered across the parade ground, he thought about Charlotte Buckland. He wondered where she was . . . how she was . . . and if he'd ever see her again. Suddenly he felt a deep sadness that she had refused to become his wife. Maybe it was the wine, or it could have been the moonlight. Whatever the cause, he felt a pressing need tonight for a woman—no, a *wife*, he corrected himself.

How nice it would have been to trudge home to Charlotte Buckland's waiting caresses. He sighed and staggered slightly as he made for his bunk.

Chapter 12

During the next few days, as Charlotte and Mateo worked closely together perfecting their act for the performance at Fort Leavenworth, she came to view him through different eyes. Indeed, Mateo was a different man when surrounded by his mighty black stallions. He was even more masterful and all-powerful—a god in the forty-two-foot ring that was his professional domain.

The memory of their one night of tumultuous love-making remained with Charlotte, waking and sleeping. But she found it difficult to equate this magnificently self-assured master of the horses with the tortured soul whose moon madness had claimed them both. Once that night was past, Mateo had never spoken of what had happened. He even seemed not to remember that he had taken her to him during those dark, stormy hours by the light of the full moon. But often when she turned toward him quickly, she would catch him gazing at her with a look of love and wonder in his dark eyes.

Charlotte stood at the edge of the outdoor ring now, watching as Mateo, poised on the Black Devil's back, prepared to execute a new maneuver. He was a marvel. As he initiated his move, she thought once more that he must surely have invisible wings.

"Hi-yiah!" he whooped, and somersaulted over the horse's hind quarters.

Charlotte applauded. "You're more than ready for the show. I only hope I don't disappoint you."

For the barest instant, an intimate look passed over Mateo's dark features. It appeared and was gone so quickly that Charlotte couldn't be sure she had seen his change of expression at all. But if indeed she hadn't imagined it, she knew in that moment that Mateo did remember their night together, that he both gloried in the thought of having loved her and hated himself for having caused her pain.

She longed to tell him that she forgave him, although there was nothing to forgive . . . that she would love him, no matter what. But there was no need. He knew without hearing her words. Still, speaking these truths aloud would have helped her a great deal. She desperately needed to have this thing between them—this dark shadow—lifted.

"I have come up with a name for you, Charlotte," Mateo announced, striding toward her, hands on hips. It was a problem they had both been pondering. Certainly she couldn't use her true name in the ring. "We will call you the Golden One. And I have directed Tamara to alter your costume accordingly. No scarlet, only gold. You will shine like the setting sun as you ride. You will blind their staring eyes with your radiance even as you warm their hearts. What do you think?"

Charlotte smiled and a twinkle lighted her eyes. "I like that, Mateo. Yes! The Golden One. And will the ringmaster claim that I, too, have performed before the crowned heads of Europe?''

He threw back his head and laughed. ''Would we tell such a lie to the unsuspecting *gajos*? No!'' He came toward her and brushed back a stray lock of hair from her cheek in an intimate but casual gesture. ''We will tell them,'' he whispered, his dark eyes dancing with merriment, ''that you come of the Gypsy stock of Ireland, and that a leprechaun king once took you for his own. His gift to you was your skill with the horses, and to honor him, you wear his gold.''

''Blarney,'' Charlotte whispered back, laughing softly. ''They will love it!''

''They will love *you*, Golden One.'' He was leaning down to her, his lips parted, his face serious. ''Even as I do.''

Mateo's kiss, as light as a butterfly's wing on her lips, came as a shock to Charlotte. This was the first time, since the night of the full moon almost two weeks past, that Mateo had failed to remain cool and distant with her. She hardly knew how to react.

Drawing away, Charlotte said, ''Mateo, please. There are things that need to be sorted out. Do you know what happened between us in your tent? Do you remember anything of that night?''

Mateo's smile vanished. He looked away from Charlotte, far off toward the distant horizon. ''I know. I remember. I experienced anger and fear. Not my own, but that of someone else. And I felt a desire so strong, so uncontrollable, that it could not be denied. It is a dreadful anguish passed down through the ages. You should not have been there, Charlotte. You might have spared yourself by staying away. I couldn't save you from the terrible passion, even though I experienced your pain as if it were my own.''

''Then you're saying that night meant nothing?'' His

words twisted like a dagger in her breast. Charlotte felt faint and knew that tears were brimming in her eyes. "It was simply an urge you couldn't control and I just happened to be the willing victim of your lust?"

"No, Charlotte!" He grasped her arms in a gesture of desperation. "That's not what I mean at all. You know I've wanted you, *loved you,* from the beginning. But do you think that if I had been in my right mind I would have forced you in such a way? Never! I am a man of appetite, but not cruelty. What I'm trying to tell you is that I don't know what that night meant to either of us. For me, it was as if my body were only the tool of some long-dead ancestor whose lust is too powerful to die. Somehow, the full moon allows this ghostly passion to revive itself in my body. That night, it was almost as if I lay there, helpless and tormented, watching a stranger take the woman I love. That is, until the last few minutes . . ." His voice trailed off.

Charlotte was confused, disappointed. She couldn't understand. *Mateo* had held her and loved her, no other. How could he say these things to her and expect her to accept them?

"So what does it all mean? To you and me, Mateo?"

The desperation in Charlotte's tone pleaded for an answer. But Mateo could give her none—not yet.

They were not the only two in the Gypsy camp left puzzling over events that had taken place on the night of the full moon. Even as Charlotte and Mateo stood silently searching for answers in each other's eyes, Queen Zolande sat alone in her tent, pondering life's meaning. Somehow she knew the answer to what had occurred on the night of the full moon was within her reach.

"But where . . . *where*?" the old queen muttered to herself.

A strange thing had happened to her during those storm-whipped hours of the full moon. She had felt Death lurking outside her tent that night. In her troubled dreams, she had been visited by her mother, her father, her dead sister, and many others much more ancient—some she had never known in this life. They had spoken to her. Even now, she could remember their words:

"Come! There will be no pain, my daughter," her mother had assured her, looking young and happy.

"The tunnel of light, my child," her father had said. "Follow it to the place where there are no questions because all the answers are known."

A beautiful woman with hair like the raven's wings and great, sad eyes had told Zolande, "Soon the moon's pain will cease forever. The blood of the virgin will be avenged. You and I will find peace together, sister."

But this apparition had not been Zolande's dead sister—Phaedra's mother. The old queen had pondered long and hard over the identity of the sad-eyed woman. She was Romany by her bright skirts and peasant blouse, the hoops at her ears, and the coins around her neck. But she seemed to be of some ancient tribe. Her skin was darker, her features more chiseled and sharply defined.

Zolande had thought at first, when she awoke from her dream, that she had been visited by Sara-la-Kali herself. But of course not!

"I am a foolish old woman, no longer right in the head," she'd chided herself. "That holy saint has better things to do than soothe the passing of a nothing . . . a *nobody.*"

But the ghostly woman's mention of the blood of the virgin seemed such a fitting thing for the Gypsies' patron saint to say—after all, she had been handmaiden to the sisters of the Virgin Mary.

And this was not the only mystery left over from that night. While the wind had whipped at her tent and the flame of her lamp had guttered threateningly, casting ominous shadows over her sickbed, Zolande had felt Death enter. More than that, she had *watched* it enter! It had crept in slowly, riding a silver beam from the full moon. With it had come a chill that had gripped her instantly. She'd lain in her wolf skins and shivered and ached with the death-dealing cold. And, odd as it seemed, Tamara had sat beside her bed, drowsing, in only a thin nightshift with never a chilblain on her smooth flesh.

But so it was with Gypsies. They felt neither the parching heat of summer nor the frigid winds of winter. So why had Death's cold breath so affected her? Zolande wondered. Why indeed, unless her time had come that night?

Therein lay the mystery. Her time *had* come. She knew it! Her earthly tasks were done and her loved ones awaited her on the other side. She herself had been ready—even willing. She had opened her arms to Death that night as a maiden would welcome her lover. Death had leaned close enough to kiss her brow, her lips, and to touch her heart. She had felt the weak flutter of its final beat. And in that instant, she had seen the tunnel of light her father spoke of. She had entered it, fearful at first; then her silent heart had taken flight, hurrying her footsteps, which trod nothing more substantial than the air she had once breathed.

Suddenly, from out of the midst of the bright white light, voices had spoken to her. No, not to her, but to each other. She'd heard a man say, "What have I done to you?" And a woman, with great tenderness and love in her voice, had answered, "Only what Fate intended."

At that very instant, as if the distant words had been some cue from on high, Zolande had felt herself jerked back from the tunnel of light. She was in her bed once more, her heart beating, the cold vanished. And the pain—the awful, soul-gnawing pain that had racked her body night and day for so many moons—the pain had gone. She'd no longer felt old and feeble. She'd felt reborn, as if the marrow-deep cold and the searing white light together had worked some magic to cleanse her of a terrible evil.

She had arisen with the dawn that morning, going about her chores as any Gypsy woman would. Her joints were limber, her heartbeat strong, her head and eye clear. No pain, no weariness, no regrets for the past or fear of the future. And thus it had been since that night.

The others had stared at first, then smiled. They asked no questions of their queen. That was good, because their queen had no answers to explain away the miracle. She had only the gladness in her heart that the miraculous was still a part of life.

But now she had four questions to ponder: Who was the woman in her dreams? How had she been snatched back to life from beyond the grave? Who were the couple whose words had rescued her?

"And why, *why*?" she wondered aloud. Surely she had been pulled back from the other side to accomplish some great service. But what?

Zolande shook her head to clear it. Weary now from puzzling over so many questions, she closed her eyes and let her mind drift. Back, back, back in time she journeyed—to the old country and near-forgotten memories. Suddenly she smiled, thinking of the golden-haired woman who had joined her father's caravan in Zolande's thirteenth summer to travel with them through Bavaria. They had all been so sure that this was the golden Gypsy who would dispel the ancient curse. How different Zolande's own life would be even now, if such had been the case. Her own betrothed, Strombol, had been the carrier of the curse in those years. As such, he would have taken the light-skinned woman as his bride.

"And what, then, of Mateo?" Zolande wondered aloud.

"Would he still have come from my womb, but with no taint of moon madness?"

She shook her head at her own foolishness. Without Strombol, there would have been no children. She had loved him far too much to marry any other. But Fate had seen to her needs. The woman had caught a chill and died of a fever during the first snowstorm that winter, proving that she was not of Gypsy blood. She had left Zolande her legacy—Strombol, and Valencia's curse for her only surviving son.

"Ah!" Zolande cried aloud, clutching her throat suddenly. *"Valencia!"*

There was no need to struggle with one of the questions any longer. Every Gypsy knew the story of Valencia and her curse. But now the woman herself had appeared to Zolande in her dream. The raven hair, the ancient look about her, her very words—the queen should have realized her identity at once. Still, there had to be a reason for the vision. This one answer gave birth to yet another question: Why had Valencia come to her?

Zolande tried to rest, but once more faces and voices from her dreams drifted back. "Blood of the virgin . . ." "The moon's pain will cease . . ." "Only what Fate intended . . ."

The old queen might have slipped into a well-deserved repose at last, if Phaedra's strident tones hadn't penetrated her sanctuary.

"I know you went to his tent the other night. You needn't deny it. I'm just curious, since we were supposed to be married. How was he?"

Charlotte hadn't meant to get trapped like this by Phaedra. She'd come back directly from the practice ring and had been on her way to bring Queen Zolande some fresh berries when the other woman had barred her way and demanded conversation.

"He was quite ill, Phaedra," Charlotte answered honestly, but blushing nonetheless.

Phaedra's lips curled in a smirk. "Oh, come now! I saw you as you sneaked back to the brides' tent at dawn—hair tangled, blouse ripped, skirts wrinkled. You're not going to tell me all that came of tending Mateo while he was out of his head."

"You might say so, Phaedra."

"Nothing happened between you, then?"

"I really don't see that that's any of your concern."

"No, I suppose not, now that I've decided I don't want him yet."

Charlotte's eyes widened with surprise. "Don't want him? I'm not sure I understand."

"Well, it was my idea to press for a wedding date. But once I got what I wanted, I changed my mind. Besides, Queen Zolande is better now. There's no hurry. She'll last the winter at least." She laughed. "That's probably more than you can say."

"Maybe you're right, Phaedra. Maybe I won't be here for the winter. Maybe Mateo won't be, either."

"Don't tell me he's spinning wild tales to you again about taking you away from all this. You know he'll never leave his people."

Charlotte didn't know what to say. Mateo had made no further mention of such a move in the past few weeks. Maybe Phaedra was right—maybe she was only living in a dream world.

"Besides," Phaedra went on, her voice barely more than a whisper, "you haven't done what every Gypsy woman must do to prove her loyalty and love for her man."

"What are you talking about?" Charlotte was frowning now, growing uneasy. Had she failed Mateo in some way without knowing it?

"Were you a Gypsy woman, you would know without having to be told," Phaedra said haughtily. "Before the man offers the brideprice, it is good for him to know that his woman can earn gold herself if it is ever needed."

"But I am earning my keep. Mateo is paying me to work with him."

Phaedra laughed. "Stupid little *gajo*! What sense does it make for a woman to earn money from her own man? What if he is sick or hurt and cannot work? Then who will pay either of you? No. You must know how to earn *gajo* gold."

"You mean *begging*?" Charlotte was horrified. Hadn't her mother predicted that she would end up doing exactly that if she didn't marry Winston Krantz?

"If that's all you can do. But there is a far better and faster way to bring in money. I've been quite successful at it in Leavenworth."

"Then tell me! Certainly if *you* can do it, Phaedra, I'll be superb at it," Charlotte replied, matching the other woman's sarcastic tone.

"Very well. There is a code among the *Roms*. Their women must never give themselves to other men for pleasure, but it is quite acceptable to do so to earn gold when it is needed."

Charlotte gasped. "No!"

"You said you were willing to do *anything* for Mateo." Phaedra shrugged. "And yet you refuse the least suggestion. When I tell him, he'll never look on you with favor again. But very well. We all know you are no Gypsy. You've only proven it by your refusal."

Phaedra swished her skirts and started away, but Charlotte caught her arm.

"Wait! Why hasn't anyone else told me of this before?"

"Perhaps they guessed you would refuse. I gave you the benefit of the doubt. But I was wrong."

Fear and panic seized Charlotte. What Phaedra was suggesting was unthinkable. But if the Gypsies . . . if *Mateo* expected it of her, how could she say no?

"Don't tell Mateo, Phaedra!"

"Don't tell him what?"

"That we've even talked about this. Please!"

"Then you've changed your mind?"

Charlotte still hesitated. She could talk to Tamara about it, but her friend might feel compelled to tell Mateo. Charlotte didn't want him to find out, for fear she might back out at the last moment.

"Yes!" Charlotte answered after taking a deep, steeling breath. "I will do it . . . for Mateo."

A catlike smile curled Phaedra's lips. "I give you credit, little *gajo*. You have more gumption than I thought. Meet me at the edge of the forest tonight. Petronovich will drive us to town."

"Petronovich?" Charlotte said uneasily.

"He should not concern you. I am more than enough woman to keep him occupied!"

Phaedra stalked away, leaving Charlotte in a quandary of fear and worry. She stood there, watching the other woman disappear into her tent. What had she gotten herself into?

Kentucky and her old, ordered way of life seemed far away and near forgotten. She was not the young girl who had run off in a fit of impassioned rebellion. Charlotte Buckland was a woman now.

"But what kind of woman?" she whispered aloud.

Just a few feet away, inside her tent, Queen Zolande was wondering the same thing about Charlotte Buckland. She had heard everything that had passed between the pair. Her first impulse had been to rise from her bed and scold Phaedra severely. But why should she? Every word Phaedra had spoken to Charlotte was the truth. During lean times in the old country, Zolande's own mother had been forced to sell her body to the *gajos* in the towns to feed her family. It was every Gypsy woman's duty.

Still, this Charlotte Buckland was not a Gypsy. Zolande could tell by the quaking of her voice that the very idea was repulsive to the girl.

The queen pondered the problem. She could go now and tell Charlotte that Mateo would never expect this of her, a *gajo*—in fact, it would no doubt provoke his wrath rather than earn his respect.

Then the old woman nodded to herself. "Yes," she whispered. "This is as it should be."

Zolande had sought a means to convince Charlotte to return to her own people and leave Mateo to his duty. Now Phaedra, with her wicked cunning, had come up with the perfect scheme to accomplish that end.

The queen sighed and closed her eyes in sleep.

Outside, Charlotte stood where Phaedra had left her, staring blankly down at her basket of berries. She couldn't face Mateo's mother right now. The old queen, she knew, could read thoughts. Charlotte was too ashamed of what was in her mind at the moment to want anyone to know. Her body felt stricken with cold at the very idea of what she had committed herself to do. How could she let another man use her body when it belonged to Mateo by word and deed?

Slowly, she walked toward the front of Queen Zolande's tent. She peeked through the flap and was relieved to find Mateo's mother napping. The old queen looked noble even in sleep. These Gypsies were indeed a proud people.

Placing the basket of berries just inside, Charlotte rose and squared her shoulders. Suddenly a great resolve gripped her—a feeling of honor, duty, and the rightness of things. She knew what she must do.

But when the actual time came, could she really bring herself to lie with a strange man, even if it was part of a Gypsy woman's obligation?

Yes! She could and would do *anything* for Mateo!

"I am *Mateo's woman!*" she said, turning, her head held high.

Chapter 13

The Star of the West saloon was busy for a week night. Besides the usual locals and soldiers from Fort Leavenworth, a wagon train headed for California had come in at almost the same time a rowdy bunch of cowboys hit town. Their pay from a trail drive would be burning in their pockets until it was all spent on liquor and paid-for love.

But Solange certainly had no complaints about booming business. This was the type of night every saloon keeper dreamed of. She would make more money in a few hours than she normally did in a week. As she poured more whiskey for two dusty drovers at the bar, she smiled to herself, thinking that she might even clear enough to give her girls a bonus. They would deserve it before this night was through.

"How much longer?" demanded the good-looking cavalry officer at the end of the bar. His temper, she could tell, was growing shorter by the minute.

"I'm sorry, Lieutenant Delacorte," Solange said with a winning smile. "I know you've been waiting a long time. But all my girls are still upstairs, and who can say exactly how long love takes?"

He muttered a curse into his drink and tossed down another whiskey. Solange frowned. He was getting very drunk. She hoped one of the girls would be down soon. Lieutenant Lance Delacorte could be surly when sober, but he was impossible when inebriated. He came here once a week, always for the same thing—a bottle of whiskey and a woman. Usually, he was quiet and kept to himself—a real loner. But when crossed, he could get ugly.

She wished that he would take his business elsewhere. Handsome as he was, with his night-dark hair and smoke-gray eyes, he was a strange man. At times, according to her girls, he could be brutal in bed. Not one of them desired his company. Still, he had never done any permanent damage. She had no real reason to turn him away.

"How about you, Solange?" Delacorte said suddenly. "You keep saying 'some other time.' What's the matter with me? I know you take other men upstairs. Why not me? Why not right this goddamn minute?"

The lieutenant was on his feet, coming down the bar toward her. His step was unsteady. His eyes looked bleary. His face was flushed from the whiskey. Before Solange could reply, he reached across the bar and grabbed her wrist in a painful grip, pulling her toward him until his lips were almost touching hers.

She remained cool. "You're hurting me, Lieutenant. Please let go."

"Dammit, woman, I'll do more than that if you don't get this show under way! I want you . . . *now*!"

"I can't leave the bar. There's no one else to tend to

the customers. Besides, I decide upon my own customers. They do not choose me.''

"Meaning you don't choose *me*!"

"However you wish to put it, Lieutenant.''

Delacorte was truly angry now, and Solange was feeling a rise of panic. She hadn't handled the situation well. But then, she didn't care for the way he was manhandling her. Perhaps she should have Farlow, the bouncer, throw him out. But she didn't want a scene on such a busy night. It was bad for business.

"Lieutenant Delacorte, please be reasonable. I'm sure that either Bella or Rosalie will be down any moment.''

He made an angry sound in his throat. "Bella's a bitch! And Rosalie's old enough to be my mother.''

"Then perhaps you prefer Lydia?''

"I prefer *you*!" Delacorte tightened his grip on her wrist.

Solange nodded almost imperceptibly toward Farlow. The huge, burly bouncer, who resembled the Gypsies' performing bear, ambled toward the bar.

"Take your hand off the lady, mister,'' Farlow said in a quiet, deadly voice.

Lance Delacorte hesitated, then slowly uncurled his fingers from Solange's wrist, exposing angry red marks where his grip had bruised her flesh.

"You want I should throw him out, Miss Solange?'' Farlow asked.

She stared at the lieutenant for a moment. He seemed subdued now. She didn't think he would give her any more trouble. Besides, he had been waiting a long time. She waved Farlow away.

"No. Thank you. I'm sure Lieutenant Delacorte will behave himself now.''

*   *   *

Charlotte felt queer—woozy. The full impact of what she was about to do was just beginning to seep into her consciousness. Squeezed in next to Phaedra on the front seat of the caravan, she hung on for dear life as Petronovich whipped his horses into a gallop. She prayed that a wheel would come off and wreck the wagon. Maybe she would be killed in the accident and wouldn't have to go through with this. Her earlier façade of brave self-assurance fled as they approached Leavenworth.

They hit a bump, which nearly unseated all three of them. Petronovich and Phaedra whooped and laughed. They were having a fine time. Charlotte sat in silence, utterly miserable.

"How are you doing, little mouse?" Petronovich asked, still laughing.

"I'm fine, thank you," Charlotte replied stiffly.

"She will loosen up when we get there, Petronovich. Don't worry."

"Oh, I'm not worried. I only pity the poor *gajo* who will pay good money for her bad-tempered bites and scratches. As I remember, this one is anything but willing in bed."

Charlotte's cheeks burned and her stomach twisted uncomfortably. The last thing she wanted to be reminded of right now was that night in her hotel room with Petronovich.

"Mateo didn't seem to have any complaints," Phaedra taunted.

"Ah, but the moon madness was upon him at the time, love. Under those circumstances, he could have found pleasure with one of his mares."

Charlotte ached with embarrassment. Until this moment, she hadn't realized that Petronovich knew of her night with Mateo. Did everyone in the *familia* know? The thought was mortifying.

The caravan rumbled into Shawnee Street. The broad

thoroughfare was lined with hard-ridden horses tied up at the hitching posts. Loud music blared from the saloon. Inside, people were singing, laughing, and Charlotte thought she heard a woman's muffled screams. The hair rose on the back of her neck.

"Where are we going?" she ventured, wondering why she hadn't thought to ask before.

"To the Star of the West," answered Petronovich. "The best bawdy house in town. Looks like a good night, too. Solange must have her hands full with all those customers."

"A *bawdy house*?" Charlotte gasped. "But I thought..."

"You thought what?" Phaedra challenged her with a stony stare.

"I don't know," Charlotte whispered, looking down to avoid the other woman's gaze. "I thought there was a gentleman you knew and you were taking me to his home and that it would all be very discreet."

Both Phaedra and Petronovich howled with laughter, making Charlotte feel even worse.

"Whoring is not a discreet profession," Phaedra said coldly. "You go where the men and the money are."

"Don't call it 'whoring,' love," Petronovich added sarcastically. "Do you want to offend the little *gajo's* delicate sensibilities? Call it 'sacrificing in the name of love.' After all, she is doing this for Mateo."

"Right," Phaedra said, laughing, "for Mateo! I can hardly wait to see the *pleasure* on his face when you give him the gold and tell him how you earned it."

Charlotte wanted to believe Phaedra's words, but she didn't like her tone. There was something ugly and menacing in Phaedra's voice. Maybe this whole thing was a setup to degrade her and get even. Certainly neither Phaedra nor Petronovich had any feelings of friendship toward her.

"I've changed my mind!" Charlotte said suddenly. "Turn the horses back, please."

More laughter from the two of them greeted her plea. Petronovich jumped down to tie the team to the hitching post outside the saloon. Hearing the bells on the Gypsy caravan, several customers had already come outside to take a look. Charlotte noticed that one dark-haired cavalry officer seemed particularly interested in the bizarre trio. He approached Petronovich and spoke to him quietly. Gold changed hands. The lieutenant came to the wagon and motioned for Charlotte to get down.

"Come with me," he commanded.

Charlotte shrank away from him, but Phaedra gave her a shove. She lost her balance and fell into the strange man's arms. He held her for a few moments, staring into her wide, frightened eyes. She was very aware of her breasts crushed against his hard chest in the punishing embrace. He was holding her so tightly that she had difficulty breathing. Her head felt light.

A slow smile spread over his face. "Yes, this one will do fine," he said to Petronovich.

The next moment, Lance Delacorte had his arm locked around Charlotte's waist and was dragging her toward the swinging doors of the saloon. The other men parted to let them enter but stood gawking and sniggering.

"No! Please, let me go," she cried. "This is a mistake."

"There's no mistake. I know what you Gypsy women come to town for. I've already paid your man . . . probably more than you're worth."

"Let me go! He's not my man. And I'm not a Gypsy."

"But you *are* a woman. That's all I care about at the moment."

As Lieutenant Delacorte pushed Charlotte into the saloon to face the curious stares of a multitude of gaping cowboys and soldiers, she heard Phaedra call out with a laugh, "Remember! It's for Mateo."

Solange didn't like the looks of this at all. She didn't recognize the woman in Gypsy garb whom Lance Delacorte had hauled in off the street, but she had a feeling the pretty blonde was not a Gypsy, not a prostitute, and not a willing partner for the lieutenant's bed.

"Give me a key, Solange," Delacorte demanded.

"You know all the rooms are occupied right now, Lieutenant."

The ploy didn't work. "Yours isn't! The key dammit!"

Solange hesitated a moment longer, staring at Lance Delacorte's companion. The girl was wild-eyed with fear. She seemed to be in a daze. Maybe she was drunk. She appeared not to know where she was or what was happening.

"Mademoiselle, are you all right?" Solange asked Charlotte.

"Everything's fine, Solange," Delacorte cut in. "Just give me the goddamn key before I take this place apart."

"I would prefer you wait for one of my own girls, Lieutenant. It's not good to bring strange women in off the streets. It's against the house policy."

"To hell with your policy. Either you give me that key right this minute, or I swear to you, Solange, I'll take her right over there on top of that poker table! How does that fit in with *house policy*?"

To prove he meant the words, Delacorte yanked the peasant blouse from one of Charlotte's shoulders, exposing a creamy expanse of breast. His action was greeted by hoots and whistles of approval. A gang of cowboys moved in, egging him on:

"Go to it, soldier boy!"

"Yeah, show us your stuff!"

"Ride 'em, cowboy! Whoo-e-e-e!"

Charlotte felt very odd. She was aware of everything that was happening, but she seemed to be viewing it from afar. Her head throbbed and she felt alternately burning hot and chilled. She tried to fight her way out of the lieutenant's grasp, but her muscles seemed to be made of water. Her limbs refused her commands. It was almost as if she'd been drugged. Then the realization hit her. She had been!

Earlier in the evening, Phaedra had come to the brides' tent. At that point, Charlotte had decided against accompanying the two Gypsies to town and had told Phaedra just that. At first the woman had flared at her in anger, calling her an assortment of vile names. Then she'd left the tent and returned a few moments later with a bottle of wine—a "peace offering," she'd called it. She had insisted that they have a glass together.

Charlotte knew the strong, sweet taste of Gypsy wine. She had never tasted any that had such bitterness and bite as this one. It was after the second glass that she had once more agreed to this mad scheme. At that moment, it had seemed the most logical thing in the world to do.

"Well, Solange? Where will it be?" Delacorte demanded. "Upstairs? Or . . ." Abruptly, he shoved chips, cards, and glasses from a table and lifted Charlotte— none too gently—onto the green baize cover.

Solange glanced nervously about. She'd sent Farlow on an errand; he was nowhere to be seen. And all her customers seemed to be siding with Lieutenant Delacorte. There were many impatient customers in the crowd who had been waiting overlong for her girls to get to them. In another few moments she'd have a riot on her hands, and only heaven knew what they would do then to this poor girl.

"Here, Lieutenant, take the key. My room is at the end of—"

"I know!" Delacorte snapped.

The next moment, Charlotte was being hauled up the stairs, accompanied by the whistles and lewd comments of the men in the barroom. She put up a valiant struggle, but it was no use. The lieutenant meant to have what he had paid for.

"What do you mean, 'Charlotte's not here'?"

Mateo stood outside the door to the brides' tent, demanding information from Tamara. It was well past dark. Surely Charlotte hadn't gone roaming in the woods alone at this hour. Something was very wrong.

"I'm sorry, Mateo. I don't know where she is. When I came back here from the queen's tent, she was gone. There were two wineglasses on the table, but no other clues as to who was here with her or where they might have gone. It's not like her to leave without telling me."

Mateo stared long and hard at the pretty, velvet-eyed woman and decided she was telling him the truth. But Tamara the fortune-teller knew many truths. She always seemed to know without being told what was going on. Something in the taut lines around her mouth told Mateo that she was aware of more than she was willing to say, and that she didn't like what she knew.

"Tamara, where is she?" he demanded.

"It is not my place to say, Mateo. Speak to your mother."

Tamara's reply sent a rush of anxiety through him. Had his mother finally sent Charlotte away to try and break the bond between them? He felt a deep rage filling his chest. Then, as he neared the queen's tent, he noticed something that turned his rage to dread. Petronovich's caravan was gone!

He stormed into his mother's tent and demanded, "Where is she?"

"Were is who?"

The old woman matched his fire with her own. Her eyes glittered with defiance. Mateo realized immediately that the information he sought would not be easily come by. Certainly loudly voiced demands would get him nowhere.

"Tamara told me Charlotte is gone. She said you might know where she is."

"Yes, I might."

"Then, *tell me!*"

"Some things are better left untold until after the fact, my son. It would do you no good to know where she is. She is out of your reach for the moment."

"She's safe, then?"

The old queen nodded.

"She will return?"

"If she chooses. I certainly did not drive her away, if that's what you're thinking, Mateo."

"I'm sorry, Mother. I should have known you wouldn't do such a thing. But it isn't like Charlotte to just disappear . . . to go off all alone."

"You needn't worry. She isn't alone."

A heavy silence hung in the tent for a few seconds. The dread that had gnawed at Mateo a short time earlier returned with far greater impact.

"You didn't let her go off with Petronovich?"

"I told you, son. I had nothing to do with her leaving. As for who accompanied her, I had no say in that either. I haven't spoken to Charlotte all day."

Mateo frowned. "But she told me she was coming to visit you. She had a basket of berries she'd picked."

"She meant to, but Phaedra intercepted her before she got here—just outside, in fact. The two of them talked for a long time."

"And you overheard their conversation?"

"I had little choice in the matter."

"Then you know exactly what's going on."

"I do. At first, I considered putting a stop to it. But after all, Charlotte Buckland is not one of us. I have no say in what she does. Perhaps Fate willed this. At any rate, it was not my place to interfere. You must not either, Mateo. It would only shame her and prove nothing.''

''*Shame her?* Mother, what in God's name are you talking about? What's going on? I have to know!''

Queen Zolande was silent for a moment, considering. She had heard Petronovich's caravan leaving some time ago. Surely, by now, that which they had set out to accomplish was done. She could not see putting her son through further needless worry. Besides, he would learn the truth sooner or later, and perhaps it would not hurt so much coming from his mother.

''Very well, Mateo. I will tell you. Charlotte Buckland has returned to Leavenworth. It seems she and Phaedra have certain plans for the evening. Phaedra explained to her one of our ancient traditions, and Charlotte expressed a desire to experience the Gypsy way of life. Tonight your Golden One has lain with a *gajo* in order to earn her own gold.''

For several moments, silence reigned in the tent. When Mateo finally spoke, his voice was cold, hard, deadly. ''How could you allow this?'' He turned away from his mother, afraid of what else he might say if he stayed a minute longer.

''Mateo, let her go!''

The queen's words followed him from the tent as he raced for his horse. He leaped into the saddle, dug in his heels, and headed at a gallop toward Leavenworth. His face was grim, his heart and soul torn with a black fury. Maybe he would be in time. If he wasn't . . .

''You need not be afraid of me.''

The lieutenant had brought Charlotte to a lavishly appointed bedroom, where he'd tossed her unceremoniously into the middle of the large featherbed. He'd locked the door. Now he was taking his own good time—toying with her.

He fixed himself a drink and offered her one. Charlotte declined. Sipping from his glass in a leisurely manner, he strode about the room, touching the dainty pieces of gilt furniture, stroking the purple satin bedspread, smiling at his reflection and Charlotte's in the mirrors overhead. Suddenly he reached down and stripped the blouse from her shoulders, still staring at her reflection. His hand fondled her breasts casually. Charlotte went rigid.

"Relax!" he ordered in a stern voice. "I told you, there's nothing to be afraid of. I'm sure this isn't your first time. That bastard in the fancy cart who brought you in would have charged far more for a virgin. So we won't have that to worry about, will we?" He looked down, his cold gray eyes measuring Charlotte's reaction, and added, "More's the pity! Still, I can't say I have the patience tonight that it takes to deal with a virgin."

Charlotte could see in the mirror that her cheeks were flaming scarlet. She had to escape. She glanced toward the window. Maybe she could get out that way.

Lance Delacorte guessed her motives and gave a low, humorless chuckle. "You're here to stay until I've had my fill. Doors locked, windows barred. Solange's one great fear is of thieves stealing her precious things." He leaned down close, pressing a hand on Charlotte's skirt until it slipped between her legs. Then he whispered, "If you want to know the truth, I think she keeps some of her other valuables barred up as well. I wouldn't be at all surprised to find out that the woman wears a chastity belt to guard against thieves in that area, too."

He gave his hand a quick twist, then pinched her

through the layers of fabric. Charlotte cried out as much from shock as pain.

"Good!" He smiled down at her. "No chastity belt there!"

He left her for a moment, going back to the portable bar on the bureau. Pouring a stiff whiskey, he tossed it down, then a second and a third. With his back still to her, he began undressing. He slippped off his shirt, displaying a lean back bulging with muscles. He tossed the shirt onto a chair near the door.

Charlotte eyed him cautiously. The key was in the pocket of that shirt. If she were quick enough, she might be able to make a dash for key, door, and freedom. But there was no time to think about it. She must move like lightning.

In one fluid motion, she was off the bed and at the chair, fumbling in the shirt pocket until her fingers closed on cool metal. She had the key in the lock and was turning it when powerful arms gripped her from behind. He threw her across the room to the bed with the bellow of an enraged bull. She lay there, panting, terrified. All was lost.

His eyes blazed with rage as he shouted, "I was going to be nice to you. Yes! I fully intended to make this a pleasant experience for both of us. But no! You don't want that. You want to make things difficult—unpleasant. Well, Gypsy woman, I can arrange that, too!"

He fell on her then, tearing at her clothes while his mouth ravaged hers. She tried to scream, but he swallowed the sound. Meanwhile, his hands worked her flesh—kneading, gouging, bruising.

Frantic to be away from him, she bit down on his lips. He howled in pain and rose from her, but only long enough to slap her hard across the mouth. The blow stunned her. She lay still for a time, her whole body aching and refusing to respond. Lance Delacorte took advantage of her immobility to strip away the rest of her clothing. When her head cleared, she was staring up at her own naked image. She screamed so loudly that the crystal droplets on the wall sconces tinkled together, threatening to break.

Mateo leaped off his Black Devil even before the horse came to a full stop. Already he had spotted the caravan in front of the saloon. He found Petronovich and Phaedra in each other's arms in the back. Pulling his cousin out into the street, he yelled, "Where is she?"

Petronovich, hurriedly hauling up his trousers, replied, "How should I know? In there somewhere with the *gajo* who paid for her."

"You slimy son of a diseased dog!"

Mateo smashed his clenched fist into Petronovich's jaw and sent him sprawling in the street, his blood mingling with the dust and filth. The enraged *Rom* never even noticed the half-naked Phaedra scurrying from the caravan to go to her downed lover. Mateo stormed into the saloon and pounded the bar.

"Where is she, Solange? The woman the Gypsies brought in?"

Solange turned to him with a startled look. Never had she seen murder in this man's eyes before. Prince Mateo was a man of peace. But now . . . She shuddered and said, "Upstairs in the end room."

Matco heard nothing past her first word. He took the stairs in great leaps and started down the hall, kicking in one door after another. Women's screams and men's curses filled the Star of the West. Soon Solange's girls and their customers, in various states of undress, crowded into the upstairs hall.

"He's crazy, that one!" Bella shrilled, her ample pink body quivering with indignation.

Lydia—tall, dark, and entirely naked—strolled after Mateo, a wanton smile on her full, wine-colored lips. "Crazy or not, he can kick in my door *anytime*! That one is *all man*!"

Mateo heard none of their comments. What he did hear was Charlotte's screams. He charged the length of the hall and battered down the door to Solange's private apartment. The sight that greeted him chilled his blood. Charlotte lay naked on the bed, a trickle of blood oozing from her puffy mouth. Over her knelt a dark-haired man, aiming his first plunge.

At the sound of the crash behind him, Lieutenant Delacorte turned his face toward the shattered door. The next instant, Mateo was upon him. His first blow sent the officer sprawling to Solange's thick white carpet. The next bashed the lieutenant into a table beside the door. A moment later, the two men were brawling their way down the hall amidst screaming women and men, who were hurrying to dress and get away before they were recognized.

"I paid for that whore!" Delacorte shouted as he landed a right jab to Mateo's midsection.

Neither the blow nor the remark was well placed. Mateo, with a roar of renewed rage, charged the other man, sending him through the balcony railing with splintered wood flying. Delacorte landed below on the very poker table he had cleared for Charlotte earlier.

Breathing heavily, Mateo stared down. The bastard, whoever he was, lay on his back, his arms and legs—among other things—now limp and useless. Solange hurried forward with a red-and-white-checkered tablecloth to cover the naked, unconscious officer.

"Leave him!" Mateo bellowed.

Solange looked up. She smiled, nodded, and dropped the cloth to the floor. The crowd cheered.

"Prince Mateo," Solange called up to him. "If you wish, you and the lady may use my room for the night."

Mateo returned her smile. "Exactly what I had in mind!"

He turned and stalked back down the hall. When he reached the room, Charlotte was still on the bed. But she had pulled the purple quilt up to her neck. He stood in the doorway—hands on hips, fight-tousled hair in wild whorls framing his face, while his black eyes glittered with a mixture of accusation, jealousy, and smoldering desire.

Charlotte was far more afraid of him in that instant than she had been during the entire night of his moon madness.

"Mateo?" she whispered uncertainly. "You aren't going to do anything rash, are you?"

His black expression never softened as he strode toward her. Suddenly he reached out and snatched the quilt away. She gave a startled cry. He stood beside the bed and stared down, his gaze traveling from her face to her full breasts, her smooth belly, and the silky golden triangle dividing her thighs.

"Mateo, please," she begged, "say something."

"What I have to say you won't enjoy hearing, Charlotte Buckland!"

He reached a hand toward her bruised face. She shrank away. She had never seen him this way and had no idea what he was about to do to her.

She would find out soon enough.

Chapter 14

Still without speaking to Charlotte, but never taking his eyes from her, Mateo stepped back a pace and loosened the money pouch from his belt. He stood holding the leather bag in one hand, balancing it on his open palm as if to measure the contents.

"How much?"

Charlotte was confused. "What do you mean, Mateo?"

"How much gold did that man pay you?"

She shook her head in furious denial. "He paid me nothing!"

"Don't lie to me. There is always gold exchanged when a man buys a woman's body."

"Petronovich took it." She hung her head, unable to meet Mateo's eyes. Suddenly, the full weight of what she had done hit her. She felt ashamed, sick, *dirtied*.

"How much do you think you're worth, then?"

Charlotte could feel tears brimming. She stretched out a pleading hand. "I don't know, Mateo. Please don't talk about it."

A grim smile curved his full lips. "But only a moment ago you wanted me to talk. Now I'm willing. *Answer me!*" As he shouted the words at her, he caught her upper arms, dragging her toward him across the bed until their lips almost met. But a kiss was not his goal at the moment; that much was very clear to Charlotte Buckland.

Her fight against tears was lost. "Please, Mateo, you're hurting me. I don't have an answer. Maybe I'm not worth anything. At least, that's how I feel right now."

He released her so abruptly that she fell back on the bed. She clamped a palm over her mouth, trying to stifle a sob. He was staring at her now in a different way—his manner cold and appraising.

"A pretty face . . . nice skin . . . breasts, not quite as large as they might be, but ample for a *gajo* woman, I suppose." His eyes traveled once more down her torso. "Too thin. No belly at all!" He glared at her suddenly and accused, "A man likes some softness in his woman. You're all skin and bones!"

Charlotte's tears stopped suddenly and she bolted upright, shaking a fist at him. "If you think I'm going to go to flab and paunch just to please some man, you *are* crazy! I'm the way I want to be. If you don't like it, you can go to . . ." She tried desperately to think of the *Romani* word for hell, but it eluded her.

Mateo smiled grimly. "So, you do think you're worth something after all. How much?" She didn't answer, only stared as he opened his pouch and poured a heap of gold coins onto the bed in front of her. "That should be enough."

"Enough for what?" Charlotte was horrified, guessing his meaning.

"Enough to buy your favors for the night. I want to be fair. I don't want to pay any less than your other customers."

"Mateo!" Charlotte wailed. "I don't want *your* gold." She stared up—mouth open, eyes wide. "What are you doing?"

He never answered, merely stripped off his shirt and trousers, showing her his readiness. His intention was all too clear.

He scorched her with blazing eyes. "My money's not good enough, eh? After the other night, I can't even buy your favors. Well, then I'll take what I want."

He came to her suddenly—an animal seeking its mate. Instinctively Charlotte struggled against him, but only briefly. She wanted Mateo as much as he wanted her.

His weight crushed her down into the soft mattress. He pinned her shoulders with his hands and entered her without preamble. The sudden penetration made her gasp, but not from pain. She had waited so long for this. It was as if she were suddenly filled and warmed and made whole.

She stared up at Mateo. His eyes were wide, looking down into hers while a sneer curled his lip. His hips worked at her with powerful, determined thrusts. She could see his strong, pale buttocks in the mirror above, the muscles bunching and straining before each plunge. His body was damp against hers. The hair on his chest scratched her breasts. She felt every touch of flesh to flesh a thousand times over, until her nerves tingled and her muscles and thighs ached.

Her pleasure was rising to its highest point when, suddenly, his eyes narrowed, almost closed. He drew in a ragged breath and his entire body shuddered over hers. She watched as his eyes came open again—black, hot, glazed. He paused in midstroke. His tongue darted out to lick his dry lips. He stared down at her, groaned, and gave a final, spasmodic thrust. Charlotte felt his liquid warmth flood through her, firing the passions that throbbed deep in secret parts of her body.

He rolled onto his back away from her and threw one arm across his brow, shielding his eyes from the sight of himself and the woman he had just used for his own pleasure.

"You've earned your gold, Charlotte Buckland. Every coin of it!"

"I don't want it." Fresh tears made her voice husky. "Your gold doesn't count."

"Take it! Then you'll be able to get away—to leave this whole unpleasant experience behind. Isn't that what you want?"

A sudden cold, sick feeling gripped Charlotte. Is that what he thought she wanted gold for—to escape from him? She sat up, hugging her knees, staring at but not seeing the far wall.

"Phaedra says the gold must come from another man . . . that I must give it to you to prove my loyalty and my love." Tears flooded her eyes. She had thought Mateo knew why she'd come to Leavenworth and to the Star of the West. Could he really believe she only wanted to be rid of him and his *familia*? How could she imagine such a thing after everything they'd been through together? It was all so foreign to her . . . so painful for her to explain to Mateo. Surely there must be better ways to show their love for one another.

Mateo turned and stared at her. He sat on the edge of the bed, sagging the mattress. The gold coins spilled off onto the floor, clinking softly against each other in the silence before they sifted down into the deep carpet. His rage shifted from Charlotte to Phaedra. He reached out for Charlotte, tenderly now, drawing her close and kissing the tears from her cheeks.

"Why did you do it, little one? Don't you understand that you don't have to prove anything to me? I love you. I believe that you love me."

"But what about the tradition? Phaedra said—"

His voice flared to an angry roar. "The Devil take Phaedra! Do you think she did this out of kindness? No! She did it for two reasons: to humiliate you and to infuriate me. As for the tradition—yes, it existed in the old country. But it is so ancient that no one follows it any longer. It is only something passed down in our history. I don't know of a woman in our *familia* who has ever done such a thing."

"Not even Phaedra?" Charlotte stared up at him, her eyes wide with innocence.

Mateo gave a cynical laugh. "Oh, she's done it all right, but not for the reasons she told you. She tricked you, my little darling. I'm sorry I've put you through this. But perhaps it wasn't as bad as what might have been. If Mother hadn't told me what was going on, I hate to think what would have happened."

"The queen knows?" Charlotte's horror was evident in her voice.

"Little goes on in our camp that escapes her."

"But she'll never accept me now! Oh, Mateo! I've ruined everything!"

She collapsed into his arms, sobbing against his chest. Mateo held her, letting her cry it out. All the while, his large hands rubbed her quaking shoulders and stroked up and down her bare back. He could feel her skin quiver beneath his touch. Her back arched to meet his fingers. Soon, her whole body was making inviting, undulating motions. Mateo felt new desire rising within him, but he refused to give in this time. No, this would be their first true experience. He would do everything possible to wipe the memories of his night of moon madness and his earlier selfish use of Charlotte from her mind forever. He wanted her to remember, after tonight, that he could be gentle, loving, giving.

Charlotte trembled against Mateo's hard chest as he kissed her forehead, her eyelids, and the tender flesh beneath her eyes and around her mouth. He avoided her lips, maddeningly. And all the while, his big, warm hands played over her back—fingering her ribs, tracing her spine, teasing the sensitive skin about her waist and below. She felt a pleasant numbness creeping into her legs. Heat seemed to radiate from deep inside her until it warmed the entire surface of her body. She felt fevered. She ached. She clutched at him. She throbbed for him.

"Mateo, oh, Mateo!"

In answer, he let one hand slip between them to cup her breast. She sucked at the air, filling her lungs like a drowning victim. His callused thumb scraped across the nipple, charging it to pulsing life. He repeated his manipulations on the opposite side, then let the flat of his palm smooth down over her rib cage to her belly. He pressed, released . . . pressed, released. Soon Charlotte could feel new vibrations set up inside her. Her body seemed caught up in sensual waves set in motion by his caresses. When his hand slipped farther down, stroking the silkiness between her thighs, Charlotte all but stopped breathing. One questing finger sought out her tender flesh, teasing it to fullness, torturing it with hesitancy. Charlotte gasped softly and writhed against his palm. The finger, made bold by her actions, plunged into her moist, hot depths.

For what seemed an eternity, Mateo played with her as if she were a toy created for his exploration and amusement. He searched her body with hands, mouth, and eyes, seeming to know without being told what would bring her the sweetest pleasure. When he changed positions—laying his lover back against the pillows— Charlotte stared overhead, fascinated by the sight of the tender homage being paid her.

Mateo's own body, she noticed, had renewed itself. She reached a trembling hand toward him and ran her fingers lightly along the dark, velvety skin. It pulsed and swelled in her hand. She started to pull away, but Mateo's hand stayed hers.

"No, please," he whispered.

Then they were lying side by side. He found her waiting lips at last and gave them their due. This was the final pleasure before the ultimate act of love. With tender skill, Mateo's tongue sought and was granted entrance. His mouth tasted of sweet, warm wine and desire. Suddenly, his eager tongue brought every individual longing in her body into focus, gathering all together in a consuming, soul-wrenching need to be filled.

Mateo rolled onto his back, holding Charlotte firmly in his arms. She stared down at him, puzzled.

"Do with me as you will, my Golden One," he whispered. "I am the stallion to be ridden in your ring—at the command of your whip. Mount me."

Charlotte felt at once embarrassed and thrilled. Carefully, she lowered her body over his—slowly, precisely, at her own pace. Mateo allowed her to take the lead, meeting each stroke of her slim body with an answering thrust. To spur her passions, he fondled her breasts, her belly, and her thighs, murmuring to her tenderly.

"Gently, darling. Do not rush your pleasure. Ride your mount slowly to start. The canter before the full gallop. Get the feel of the saddle."

The feel of the saddle! Charlotte thought. She had never felt such a thing in her life! Her heart was threatening to burst from her chest. Her blood raced like the wind. Every nerve *zing*ed with sensual static. Her flesh burned, melding itself to Mateo's.

"Mateo. Oh, God!" she cried out.

He gripped her hips, afraid she might flee from him in the final, ecstatic moments.

"Pace yourself, darling. Let it come naturally—rising, flowing, flooding over you like the warm waters of a river in summer. Bathe in the feeling. Drink deeply of it.''

Charlotte Buckland did more than Mateo instructed. She nearly drowned in the ecstasy. It came, as he said, rising until it flooded her—working from her toes up and her head down to meet at the very core of her in an explosion of tingling, gripping, other-worldly sensations. At the grandest moment of all, when starbursts were flashing in her head and all that is wonderful in the universe was pulsing through her body, Mateo clasped her to him in a fierce grip and cried her name aloud. They were one . . . forever . . . come what may.

Afterward, they lay in each other's arms, sated, exhausted, in awe of what had passed between them. Mateo continued to stroke Charlotte's breasts and kiss her lips lightly from time to time, but they said nothing for a long while. Words seemed pointless after what they had just shared.

Finally, Charlotte broke the comfortable silence. ''What now, Mateo?''

''Now I will see to it that our marriage is hastened. Love as sweet as we have just given each other must have created a new life. There is no other explanation for the way I felt . . . the way I feel even now.''

Charlotte had to admit to herself that she had thought the same. But that was not what she'd meant by her question.

''No, Mateo. You misunderstand. What can we experience from here on through the rest of our lives that will be better than tonight? Is there anything more to look forward to?''

He raised on one elbow and smiled down into her face, tracing the delicate line of her lips with one finger.

''Oh, my love, with one such as you there will always be something to look forward to—the coming of darkness each night to shelter us as we make love, the sunrise of a new day to light the love in your eyes, the sight of you bathing in a clear stream, the sound of your voice crooning lullabies to our child, the taste of your lips, the feel of your breasts, the glow on your face this very minute. Oh, yes! There is much to look forward to still."

She closed her eyes and smiled. "Yes," she whispered. "And I can always look forward to being in your arms the next time. Each time will be better for us. I know it will."

But even as she breathed in his closeness and drifted off into her dreams, she wondered how many more times she could look forward to having Mateo make love to her. Things were not as simple as he would have her believe. And the more she came to love him, the more complicated their lives became.

What if she were carrying his child even now? Even that might not be enough to force Queen Zolande to sanction their marriage. *Mateo must marry a Gypsy!* The words nagged at Charlotte's mind and heart. But if she let him take her away somewhere so that they could be married, what would it do to him? Would it change him so that he would become someone other than the man she now loved so desperately? Could she bring herself to be that selfish?

She tossed and moaned in Mateo's arms. He kissed her tenderly and her arms closed about him. This was not the time to ponder all the questions of the world, she decided. This was a time for love.

Lieutenant Lance Delacorte, too groggy to sit his horse, hitched a ride back to Fort Leavenworth that night on one of the army's quartermaster wagons. He was certain at least two of his ribs were cracked, and he was visibly bruised and battered all over. But he felt lucky at that.

The fall from upstairs at the Star of the West could have broken his back or cracked his skull.

That Gypsy fellow might have worn earrings, but there was nothing sissy about him. No sir! He was hard as a rock and mean as a rattler! But since when did those *Roms* start taking up for white women? Lance wondered. And the little whore most assuredly had been white—from the bright yellow of *all* her hair to the little pink nipples crowning her creamy breasts. The thought forced him to adjust the throbbing crotch of his borrowed trousers for more comfort. Damn, he'd wanted her! And that Gypsy bastard who'd brought her to town had run off with his money to boot. It sure hadn't been his night!

He mulled it all over—as best he could with his head aching as if he'd just been caught lying down in the middle of a buffalo stampede. When he'd come around, there on the poker table, the first thing he'd grabbed for was that checkered tablecloth on the floor. Those sonsuvbitches in the saloon had sure gotten their jollies at his expense. He'd wanted to belt every grinning, gap-toothed face in the bar, but his fists were so torn up from slugging it out with that Gypsy that he'd squirmed in pain at the mere thought of socking another jaw.

The ill-fitting work clothes he wore now were a parting gift from Solange. He could hear that sexy French accent of hers still: "You needn't bother to return them, Monsieur Lieutenant. In fact, it will please me for you to find another place of amusement from now on."

He put his elbows on his knees and let his head sink down between his palms.

"Shit!"

"You ain't feelin' so hot, Lieutenant?" The crusty old mule skinner sitting beside Lance on the front of the wagon gave him a sidelong glance. His voice held an unmistakable trace of humor.

"Oh, I feel just great, Sarge! Why, I couldn't feel any better if I'd been kicked in the head by one of your army mules!"

Sarge—his hair, body, and eyes all bleached the color of desert sand from long service in the West—chuckled out loud.

"Lord-a-mercy, you young fellers really get yourselves into some scrapes. I'm glad I ain't spry enough to be interested in females no longer. Tossed my last skirt seven years, two months, thirteen days"—he paused and looked off toward the lightening horizon—"and I reckon about twenty-six minutes ago. Then I swore off for good. From the looks of you, Lieutenant, you might think about taking the oath your own self. Might be a helluva lot healthier."

"How do you know the fight was over a woman?"

"Always is. There ain't nothing much else out here worth fighting over. And hellfire, I don't see no sense to it. Get off in the dark with 'em and one's good as another. Course now, them Gypsy women is the best! Lord, Lord!" he said, rolling his eyes heavenward and smacking his lips. "I tell you, I had me one of them a couple of times. A real gouger and biter, she was. But I ain't never had another one like her. That gal, once you got her primed, could of sucked the Rio Grande plumb dry." He gave a visible shudder to demonstrate his remembered pleasure.

The sun was coming up, turning the landscape to coral and gold as the men rode on at a slow pace behind a pair of brown mules. Lance Delacorte sat up straighter, forgetting some of his aches, at the sergeant's mention of Gypsies. The light dawned in his fogged mind. The woman he'd been with *was* a Gypsy after all. She was the light-skinned one that all the soldiers were talking about.

"Sarge, have you ever heard of such a thing as a blonde Gypsy?"

"Well, hell, yes! They ain't all real dark. Blood gets mixed, you know. Say one of them dark ones gets knocked up by some towheaded soldier. Their kid's gonna be lighter. They's all colors. I hear tell there's a white one with that tribe camped out by the river now."

"Do tell!" Lance Delacorte arched one eyebrow thoughtfully. Sure as hell, she was the one he'd been with!

"Yep, we gonna get a chance to eyeball her real soon, too. I ain't got no other reason but curiosity, mind you, but I'm looking real forward to it."

"What are you talking about?" The sergeant had babbled on while Lance was remembering the woman.

"The circus! Them folks are bringing their show right out to the fort in a few days. Where you been that you ain't heard about it?"

Lance's mind was working now at a feverish pace. "Nowhere. I guess I was just thinking about something else."

"Well everybody's talking about it, from Colonel Custer on down. They say she's a right smart rider for a woman. Call her 'the Golden One.' Fits her, so I hear. They claim she hails from Ireland and that's how come she's so fair. I reckon she must make a real startling contrast to that Prince Mateo she rides with, and him as dark and wild-looking as Satan's pitchfork."

Lance stared at the sergeant for a moment, absorbing his words. So, that's whom he'd tangled with tonight—the legendary Prince Mateo. No wonder he'd gotten his ass kicked.

"When did you say they'll be at the fort, Sarge?"

"Didn't! But I was fixin' to. Be there a week from yestiddy, 'bout noontime. You goin' to see their show?"

Lance grinned in spite of his busted lip. "I wouldn't miss it for the world."

Sarge whipped the reins with a sudden vengeance.

"Giddap, you goddamn lazy jackasses! We ain't got all day!"

Lieutenant Lance Delacorte settled back into quiet contemplation of his own scheming thoughts.

Mateo and Charlotte were hardly prepared for what awaited them back at the Gypsy camp. They had lingered in Solange's bed until dawn blushed the sky. Their ride back, together on Mateo's horse, had been at a leisurely pace. Mateo had said he didn't want to tire the great black stallion, but Charlotte knew that he simply wanted their time alone together to last as long as possible. She agreed and loved him all the more for it.

When they neared the camp, Mateo sniffed the air, then stood in the stirrups and shielded his eyes against the sun's rays to get a better view.

"What is it?" Charlotte asked, seeing the deep frown that etched his features.

"Council fires," he replied. "I don't understand it."

"I don't either. What do you mean, Mateo?"

"On extremely momentous occasions, the *familia* piles logs high and sets torch to them, signaling any *Rom* who might pass that his wisdom is called upon to make some serious decision. All the elders, headed by the queen or king, gather to consult with one another. But there is no reason for such a meeting. At least, there was none last night when I left here to find you."

"What sort of reason would be needed?"

"Oh, any number of things—the discussion of a move, the transgression of a member of the troupe, war with someone, or the death of a very important personage."

Charlotte glanced up at Mateo, but he didn't seem to be taking these last words personally. Apparently he wasn't as worried about his mother as he had been a short time ago.

He spurred his horse. "We'd better hurry. I should be at the council."

"But not me." Once again, Charlotte felt like an outsider.

"No, little dove, not you. I'm sorry. Go to the brides' tent as soon as we arrive. Stay there until I come for you."

But when they rode into the outskirts of the camp and dismounted, they were surrounded by members of the clan dressed in their best ceremonial finery.

"You will both come with me at once, please," Tamara said in a serious, almost ominous, tone.

"What's going on?" Mateo asked.

"A meeting of the council," was the only answer he received from his cousin as she bustled him and Charlotte toward the largest campfire, which had the queen's throne set before it.

Charlotte was suddenly gripped with terror. Surely her mission in town had something, if not *everything*, to do with this high court. As they passed, every Gypsy to the last small child looked through her as if she were entirely invisible. She shuddered inside, remembering stories in old books she had read as a girl that told of ancient, barbaric customs, even cannibalism, among the Gypsy tribes of Europe.

The queen knew where she had gone and for what purpose. Glancing about, Charlotte saw, too, that Phaedra and Petronovich had returned. His painted wagon stood in its usual place. So they would have brought back word that a man had paid the required gold to lie with her. Her heart sank. She should never have trusted that pair.

But why should she be punished for acting out one of their own traditions, even if, as Mateo said, it was no longer practiced? The answer came to her in a sickening flash—because she was not a Gypsy. A *gajo* carrying out the same time-honored tradition of the Romany folk came off as nothing but a prostitute, a person of low and tainted morals. She was no longer good enough to associate with the others. She was about to have her punishment pronounced; she knew it.

Feeling her tremble beside him, Mateo squeezed her hand reassuringly. "Do not worry, little dove. You have nothing to fear."

But the very fact that he did not include himself in that statement made her all the more fearful. What if Mateo was to be punished on her account? She could bear whatever torture they chose for her. But she could not endure seeing him suffer. She bit her lip to keep silent and hold back the tears that were threatening.

Tamara led them to Queen Zolande. The old woman was dressed in stark black instead of her usual scarlet. A veil of thick black lace partially covered her features. About her throat she wore a necklace of charms—a shining silver nail, a dried snakeskin, the foot of a rooster, the horn feathers of an owl, and locks of human hair. Mateo bowed before his mother and indicated with a tug on her hand that Charlotte should do the same.

"So, you have found her, Prince Mateo."

"And brought her home," he answered in the same somber, impersonal tone as his mother.

"Not *home*! Never *her* home!"

Mateo drew up beside Charlotte and his voice boomed. "Then it is no longer *my* home, either!"

Queen Zolande's eyes narrowed until only a faint, hard glitter showed between the lashes. "You will hold your tongue! We all know where she went and what she has done. Witnesses have spoken against her. Now it is only left for the council to judge."

"Bring forth your witnesses," Mateo demanded with a sneer.

The queen raised her gnarled wooden staff and tapped it three times. "Witnesses!" she cried. "Come and be heard!"

Phaedra, also dressed in black, came through the crowd, followed by Petronovich, washed and showing nothing more from his bout with Mateo than a swollen lip. Both wore the gold trappings of minor royalty. They bowed before the queen; then, in a move of alarming speed, Phaedra whirled to point a bejeweled finger directly into Charlotte's face. Charlotte cringed, then straightened and stared hard into the other woman's face, steeled to hear the charges.

"This one begged to be taken to town. 'I'm so lonely for my own kind,' she whined to me. 'I will die of it. Please, if you are my friend, help me to get to Leavenworth.' " Phaedra turned from Charlotte to the elders and forced a demure look to her face. "I am not one to turn away from such a plea. She seemed so pitiful. I would die if I were taken away from my people, I know. I could only sympathize and try to help her." The Gypsy woman lowered her voice to a whisper. "The rest Petronovich must tell." Phaedra bowed and backed into the crowd while her lover came into the open circle.

Mateo once more squeezed Charlotte's hand and whispered, "Be brave. They cannot hurt us. The truth is on our side."

For a moment, his words gave her strength. But was the truth on their side? How would the others feel when they found out that their prince had spent the night with a *gajo* in a bawdy house?

"This one," Petronovich said, pointing at Charlotte, "convinced me to take her to Leavenworth—I thought to meet with an old friend at his home."

Charlotte flinched. Petronovich was twisting her own words to use them against her!

"But I was sadly mistaken," he went on. "She is not our kind. And I do not mean by that simply that she is not a Gypsy. She lies with men for pleasure. She is a whore!"

A murmur ran through the crowd; the word whispered like a foul wind through broken branches. When the voices quieted, Petronovich continued.

"Hardly had I hitched my team in town before she was in the arms of a man—a horse soldier. He forced gold on me and said he would buy her body for the night. I argued, but the crowd became angry and shoved me away. She hissed at me to leave her alone and let her have her night of pleasure before she had to return to Mateo and his harsh embraces."

Charlotte felt Mateo stiffen beside her. This time it was her hand that squeezed his compassionately.

"And did you see what went on between the soldier and this woman?" Queen Zolande asked in an unemotional voice.

"Only part, but enough. He took her inside the saloon, to the bar. There, I think she had several drinks of strong whiskey."

"I never!" Charlotte cried. The queen scorched her with a dark look.

Mateo whispered, "Please, *sunaki bal*. You will only make it worse by speaking out."

"Go on," the queen said to Petronovich.

"Even as they drank, she could not wait for him to take her. She pulled the blouse from her shoulders, baring her breasts for all to see. I shudder with embarrassment for her even as I speak the words, my queen. Would any decent woman do such a thing? She is a whore by birth and nature, I tell you all. But it was worse still. She could not wait for him to carry her upstairs to one of those pits of degradation they call bedrooms. She pulled him with her to a tabletop, lay back, spread her skirts, and begged him to take her there for all to see."

"And did he?" the queen asked dispassionately.

"All thanks be to Sara-la-Kali, my queen, the man refused her. But moments later she followed him upstairs. Beyond that point, I can only guess at what transpired. I repeat: The woman is not fit to be among us!"

Petronovich backed away and lost himself in the crowd, never looking at Mateo or Charlotte. The queen turned her attention back to her son and the accused.

"You have heard the witnesses. Did the woman go to Leavenworth for this purpose?"

"Yes, but—" Charlotte began.

"Tell the woman to be silent, Prince Mateo. My question is directed at you alone. Did she go?"

Mateo was caught. He looked from Charlotte to his mother and finally down at the ground as he murmured. "Yes. But you know why she went."

"The truth has many faces. Did a soldier pay gold for her?"

Mateo brightened for a moment. "I saw no gold."

"Here is the gold," Petronovich volunteered, producing the damning evidence.

"Did he lie with her, Prince Mateo?" demanded the queen.

Suddenly Mateo's temper flared as bright as the fire. He pulled Charlotte into his arms protectively and shouted, "He did not! But I did! Charlotte Buckland is my woman and no one will touch her without dealing first with me. It is good that you have formed this council, for I have an important announcement to make. I hereby renounce my title of prince." He paused while another wave of shocked murmurs passed through the *familia.* "Choose whom you will to take my place. I have already chosen where I wish to be—by the side of Charlotte Buckland, the woman I love, the woman I will marry, the woman who even now carries my child in her womb."

"Mateo!" Charlotte gasped, shocked.

Shouts of outraged protest burst from the crowd. Queen Zolande silenced them by raising her hands.

"You are sure of this?" she asked of her son.

"Yes, Mother," he said softly. "As sure as I am that the curse will strike me with the next full moon."

Charlotte was torn. Mateo's declaration had filled her with hope for a happy future, but seeing the old queen's reaction, her feeling changed to guilt. The woman sagged on her throne, looking frail and ancient. It was as if Mateo had taken away her last hope for happiness.

No! Charlotte thought. I am the one who has robbed her of that.

At that very moment, Charlotte Buckland decided what she must do—for Queen Zolande and most of all for Mateo. She would have to be careful and choose her time carefully. The very thought filled her with pain.

But I must! she told herself. I must leave him because I love him.

Chapter 15

Lance Delacorte glanced up at the entrance to Fort Leavenworth and groaned. As if last night hadn't been bad enough, he knew that two confrontations awaited him inside those log walls that would make his bout with Prince Mateo look like child's play by comparison.

"I reckon Colonel Custer will be wantin' to have a word with you right off, Lieutenant, you missin' muster and all." The old mule skinner seemed to be reading his passenger's mind. "Want I should drive you right over to headquarters?"

"No thanks, Sarge," Delacorte answered. "I'll go by my quarters first and clean up a bit. It wouldn't do to present myself to the colonel dressed like this."

Sarge squinted against the sun to cover a grin. Lordy, but this young buck was in for it! That wife of his was one of the devil's own. She'd probably draw and quarter him the minute he walked in. Nobody crossed Annabelle Hampton Delacorte and came away unsinged . . . least of all her husband. Sarge nodded to himself. Yes sir, that'd be a sight to see—him walking in wearing borrowed britches this time of the morning. That would take some explaining!

"Thanks for the ride, Sarge," Delacorte said, easing his aching body down from the wagon seat.

"Don't mention it."

Lance's head throbbed. He'd tried all during the ride back from town to come up with some explanation that he thought Annabelle might accept. If there was anything he didn't need this morning, it was her viper's tongue slashing at him.

He grinned dourly. "Wonder if she'd believe I was kidnapped by pirates on the Missouri River, who beat me up, stole my clothes, then dumped me on the far shore," he muttered. "Not likely!"

Lance mounted the wooden steps and crossed the narrow porch, walking as lightly as he could. No need to attract Annabelle's attention any sooner than he had to. He certainly didn't want another scene out here in front of everyone, like the last time he overstayed his time in town. Lord, she'd made him the laughingstock of the whole fort—screaming at him like a fishwife and threatening him with everything from divorce to castration.

Carefully, he turned the knob and pushed the front door open. The tiny living room, with its horsehair settee, side chairs, and coffee table, was immaculate but deserted. He frowned. Surely Annabelle wouldn't still be in bed at this hour. It wasn't like her.

He tiptoed through the room and across the narrow hallway. The bedroom door was closed. He could hear humming coming from within. His frown deepened. Annabelle might sing for company, but she never hummed. What the hell was going on?

He started to knock on the closed bedroom door, then changed his mind. This was his house, his bedroom, his wife. If he felt like walking in unannounced, by God, he'd do just that!

Giving the door a healthy push, he looked in. "*Annabelle!*" His shocked cry rattled the mirror she stood before.

"How dare you burst in on me?" she snapped, whirling toward her husband. In that moment, her narrow green eyes took in his battered face, his ill-fitting clothes, and his uncombed hair. She smiled. "Poor darling," she crooned, "whatever happened to you? Were you kidnapped by river pirates?"

Her sarcastic mention of the very excuse he'd planned to try out on her made him all the madder. "Never mind what happened to me! What do you think you're doing—fawning and primping in front of the mirror in your underwear and smearing lip paint on your mouth? I demand an explanation!"

She sniffed and turned back to her reflection, continuing to smooth the rose-tinted cream over the thin line of her lips. He had to wait for an answer until she'd finished.

"I'm going riding with Colonel Custer, if you must know. He has asked me several times before this and I've always declined. But since you chose to get into mischief again last night, I thought it might be helpful to your career if I accepted his invitation this time. Not that I haven't wanted to all along. He's quite a fascinating man."

A rumbling jealousy roared through Lance Delacorte. Colonel Custer's rides with young ladies were legendary and much whispered about on post. He'd had no idea the man had sought out his own wife for such a dubious honor. Annabelle might not be a prize, with her thin, pale face, mousy hair, and flat-chested figure, but she was his wife. The thought of another man paying attention to her infuriated him. It also made her look far more enticing to him than she had only a few hours ago. Standing before him in her thin, beribboned camisole, tight-fitting corset, and pantaloons, she seemed almost as arousing a morsel now as she had that first time, on their wedding night four years before. She certainly seemed a far cry from the cold little prude she'd proved to be since that night.

"I forbid it!"

She flicked a limp wrist toward him, dismissing his words. "La, aren't you the masterful one! I'd like to see a lowly lieutenant march into the colonel's office and announce that his wife isn't *allowed* to ride out with the gentleman." Her eyes narrowed once more as she turned on him. "Besides, I'm on to your weekly trips to Leavenworth. Special scouting duty, bah! Scouting out whiskey and women—that's what you do best!"

"Annabelle!" he gasped.

"Never mind the outraged protest, darling. Some of the enlisted men stopped by the Star of the West last night. I know all about your fling with the little golden-haired Gypsy. The whole camp knows. And from now on, Lance Delacorte, I plan to do just as I please. You go your way and I'll go mine. Now, if you will excuse me, I'd like to finish dressing. I don't want to keep George waiting."

Lance Delacorte stumbled backward and fell to a sitting position on the bed, his mouth agape. *George*, she'd called him!

Annabelle continued preparing herself, ignoring him completely. She pulled on a linen blouse with a lace ruff that gave the illusion of more bosom than she actually possessed. The hunter-green riding habit snugged itself close to her tiny waist, making her look tantalizingly dainty and feminine, before it swirled into a full skirt. Fetching, he thought miserably. Designed to make a man crave what lay underneath.

Slipping her long fingers into soft kid gloves, Annabelle offered him a false smile and said, "Ta-ta, darling. I shan't be too late. George says we'll simply ride out to a private place he knows and read poetry together while we lunch on pheasant and champagne." She scowled at Lance suddenly. "You really should clean yourself up. You're a dreadful sight in those baggy old britches. Did your little Gypsy steal your clothes as well as your wallet?"

With that, Annabelle Delacorte swept past her husband and out of the room. Lance slumped on the bed, miserable, defeated, and determined to get even with Prince Mateo and his blonde whore if it was the last thing he ever did.

It wasn't that George Custer sought any dalliance with Annabelle Delacorte, even though he had become aware of her flirtatious glances. Surely there were more attractive women on post than this little mouse whose own husband didn't seem to have any interest in her. Still, he enjoyed the company of women in general, and with his own wife away, he often invited his officers' ladies out to ride. Nothing gave him greater joy than to swing into the saddle next to a pretty woman on horseback and gallop out over the plains on a fine day.

He glanced up at the wide expanse of blue overhead and smiled, stroking his mustache. "Fine day indeed! Now if only the woman were a bit prettier."

"Colonel Custer," called a musically feminine voice.

He looked across the parade ground, toward the green-clad, lace-jaboted figure sweeping toward him. A low, appreciative whistle escaped him. Could this be Annabelle Delacorte? He smiled and offered his buckskin-gloved hand.

"Madam, you look fetching."

Annabelle executed a smart curtsy and flashed him a winsome smile. "Why, thank you, Colonel."

"Please, call me George."

She nodded and blushed slightly, thinking that she had been calling him George secretly for some time now. But flirtation was not her main objective today. No. She had much more serious business on her mind.

Having accepted the colonel's assistance in mounting, she watched admiringly as he swung onto the back of his own horse and spurred the animal to action. For a long time, they raced toward the distant horizon, too windblown and exhilarated to engage in conversation. But Annabelle never ceased rehearsing her speech to him in her mind. Only when they reached a distant hillock covered with a copse of trees did she get her chance.

They had dismounted, nibbled at lunch, and toasted the day and their newfound friendship with sparkling wine before Annabelle finally broached the subject uppermost in her thoughts.

"George," she began in a whispery voice.

He turned admiring eyes on her. "Yes, Annabelle. What is it?"

"Well, this might not be the time or place, but I must speak to you about a personal problem."

His hand, which had been inching toward hers, drew away. "Feel free to discuss anything you like, madam."

"This is something I *don't* like. Those Gypsies."

He frowned at her, slightly confused. "I had no idea you'd had occasion to meet any of them."

"I haven't, but my husband has, most regrettably."

Custer laughed and ran nervous fingers through his long yellow hair. "Ah, you mean the talk about last night. I wouldn't let that bother me, if I were you. It's probably like any other gossip on an army post—exaggerated and not worth the breath to repeat it. Let's not allow it to spoil our outing, Annabelle."

"I don't want it to spoil anything. That's why we have to talk about it. Did you see Lance this morning when he came in?" Custer shook his head and Annabelle hurried on, the wind at her back now. "His uniform was gone."

Custer jerked upright. "*Naked?* By God, I won't have that of one of my officers!"

"No, no, no! He was in a horrible, threadbare suit of borrowed clothes."

"Well, I should hope!"

"But don't you see, it was just as embarrassing for me as if he had been nak— Unclothed. He was with some Gypsy woman last night, drinking and who knows what else. He goes to town once a week and stays all night. Until I heard the rumors flying around this morning, I believed what he'd always told me . . . that he was on some sort of special duty. Now I feel like such a fool! And those very Gypsies he's been consorting with are coming here next week. I simply can't face them!"

Tears coursed down Annabelle's cheeks and choked her words. Custer patted her hand compassionately and made murmuring sounds of comfort, finally drawing her against his chest to hush the racket. Crying women always confounded him. His own wife never wept or made such unseemly female noises.

"There, there, my dear. Don't take on so."

The moment George Custer embraced her, Annabelle felt all her pent-up yearning burst forth. Here she was— "unattractive little Annabelle"—being crushed to the hard bosom of a hero, a man of iron. The thought made her feel faint. She stared up at his lips, wondering how it would feel to have them pressed to her own. Her heart thudded and heat flowed through her.

"George?" she breathed.

But instead of kissing her, he released her, saying, "I really don't know what I can do, madam. As long as your husband breaks no army regulations, he is his own man.''

She sat staring at him, gasping softly, before she could find her voice to reply. ''But he did break the rules! He missed muster this morning. Doesn't that count?''

''Well, yes, I suppose so. Are you suggesting I have him locked in the guardhouse?''

The thought pleased Annabelle, but she dared not say so. ''No! I want Lance with me, not away from me. It's the Gypsies I want you to deal with. Can't you send them away?''

George Custer stroked his chin thoughtfully. A helluva lot of good it would do Annabelle Delacorte to have the Gypsies and their women sent away. Her husband would simply search out other women for his carnal gratification. Still, Custer knew he couldn't say that to the man's wife.

''If you could only do something about the blonde one. She seems to be the troublemaker,'' Annabelle spat out. The wild stories about last night varied with each telling, except on one point—the lusty beauty of the woman her husband had been with.

''We'll see,'' he muttered, trying to appease her.

Annabelle threw herself into George Custer's arms and sought the lips she had longed for. He tried to extract himself from her impetuous embrace, but her fingers were twisted through his long hair. He was her prisoner. Finally, he left off fighting and simply allowed himself to enjoy it.

By God, she was a fiery little temptress, he decided. What the hell was Delacorte thinking, fooling around with other women when he had this one at his beck and call?

*   *   *

Later that day, Colonel George Custer faced Lance Delacorte across his desk, feeling no small amount of embarrassment. Granted, what had passed between himself and this man's wife was only one kiss—and that not of his choosing—but still, the memory of her ardor made him squirm in the presence of her husband.

"Lieutenant Delacorte, Colonel, reporting as ordered." A smart salute accompanied the man's words, and his uniform and military bearing were impeccable. Only the discoloration around one eye and his swollen lip hinted at last night's escapade.

"At ease, Lieutenant Delacorte." Custer sorely wished that he could say the same for himself. "Now, what do you have to say for yourself?"

"No excuse, sir," Delacorte answered in routine military fashion.

Custer leaned across his desk. "Off the record, Lance. What happened? You look like hell!"

"It was Gypsies, sir. I'm not trying to excuse my own actions, but I go into town once a week for a night out. I've never had any trouble until those Gypsies turned up."

"How many of them jumped you?"

Lance Delacorte's voice dropped an octave. "Well, there were four in all."

"Four against one! Those are sizable odds. You're lucky they didn't beat you to death." Custer was shaking his head, thinking that getting rid of the troublesome band might not be such a bad idea.

"It wasn't exactly like that, sir." Delacorte was aware of a flush rising to his face, and his collar felt extremely tight. "Two of the four were females, and the second man had disappeared by the time the fight broke out."

"So the truth comes out. One Gypsy whipped the likes of a U.S. Cavalry officer." Custer shook his head again sorrowfully. "More combat training, that's what we need around here."

"Sir, if I could say a word in my own defense?"

Custer nodded.

"They tricked me. The first man tempted me with one woman and then sold me another. I paid far more than I usually do."

"You *pay* for women?" The very thought was repulsive to Custer. Any self-respecting officer should be able to seduce a woman, not have to buy her favors.

Delacorte shrugged. "Well, occasionally, sir. Anyway, I took her upstairs and found out she wasn't willing. I don't know what their game was, but I'd paid and I meant to have the goods. Then this crazy Gypsy kicked the door in, started pounding me to a pulp, and damn near killed me before it was over. They're a dangerous lot! I think something should be done about them. Do you really believe it's safe to let them come on the post next week? They might turn on us and take us by force."

"Not if we're ready for them, Lieutenant."

"Then you have a plan?"

Custer winked and grinned. "We'll see their circus and then we'll show them a few tricks of our own."

Forgetting himself, Delacorte placed his hands on the colonel's desk and leaned toward his superior officer. "What are we going to do?"

"*Nothing*, so far as you know. Dismissed, Lieutenant," Custer barked.

"Yes, sir!" Delacorte snapped another smart salute, turned, and marched out.

George Custer leaned back in his chair, weary from the day's events. He wasn't actually sure what he would do, but it was clear that some action was called for. There had been no trouble with the Gypsies until recently. What had happened? What was different now? His brow knit as he pondered. Suddenly, he slapped the desk top. That was it! The whole mess had begun with her arrival.

"The Golden One," he said aloud. "This is all her doing."

Charlotte dreaded the coming performance at Fort Leavenworth—not because she was unsure of her ability with the horses, but because she knew what else she must do that day: she must throw herself upon Colonel Custer's mercy and beg for his help in getting her back to Kentucky. She had no other choice.

She had worried that she might truly be carrying Mateo's child, as he had told the queen. But she was not, so nothing bound her to him. Nothing, that is, but a deep fullness of love that tore at her heart every time she thought of leaving him. And she thought of little else these days.

"Charlotte, concentrate!" Mateo shouted, seeing that she had obviously allowed her mind to wander while she balanced on the black stallion's back. Her lack of attention had nearly caused her to slip. He was a patient man, but that patience grew short when he was in the ring.

What was wrong with Charlotte? She'd been acting distracted for days.

"I'm sorry, Mateo. Maybe we'd better call it quits for the morning. I just can't seem to get the feel of it today."

The solemn look on her face wounded Mateo. He shouldn't have yelled at her. Even he had his bad days in the ring. She would be fine by the time of the show. She knew her act and she was good . . . *really* good.

"You're right," he said, helping her down. "There's no need to overtrain you. We'll take the next two days off and rest before the performance."

When her feet touched the ground, Charlotte leaned against Mateo's strong, bare chest, savoring the feeling and the smell of him. The blood raced in her veins, as it always did at his touch. Just two more days! Then she would never know his touch or experience this warmth in her blood again. How could she ever survive without him?

But neither of them would survive if she stayed. Already the others in the *familia* were treating him as an outcast. So far, Mateo had been able to ignore their censure, to pretend that it made no difference to him. But how long could he keep up this false front, when even now Charlotte could see the deep hurt in his eyes? Above all else, Prince Mateo loved his people. She could never make up for the loss their marriage would inflict upon him.

"I'm so sorry, Mateo," she whispered, not looking up.

"You have no reason to apologize," he said. "I was the one who lost my temper. I've worked you too hard. Forgive me."

He had misunderstood her apology. Just as well, she decided. If Mateo knew what she was planning, he would never let her go.

"Come, walk with me," he said.

She took his hand and even managed a smile for the man she loved. After all, time was too precious to let one remaining minute slip away unsavored. She must store up a lifetime of memories to see her through. For after having loved Mateo, Charlotte Buckland knew in her heart that she could never love another.

They walked hand in hand in silence toward the woods. The fall sun warmed Charlotte's face just as Mateo warmed her soul. Suddenly, he stopped and turned her to face him, a grave expression on his face. A muscle at the side of his square jaw twitched with nervousness. His eyes looked black in the sunlight.

"I've made a decision. I know you are unhappy here, Charlotte. Immediately following the performance the day after tomorrow, you and I will leave together. This is not your home, so it can no longer be mine. We will be married and move on westward, perhaps to San Francisco."

"But Mateo . . ."

He covered her lips with his fingers and shook his head. "I will hear no objections. My mind is set. It is time we found our own way."

His lips replaced his fingers on her mouth. Soon Charlotte was lost in a hazy golden aura of pleasure and longing. He kissed her thoroughly—long and deeply. Each passing moment shook her resolve to leave him and made his plan sound more enticing. Perhaps, if there was love enough between them, it would work out.

When Mateo finally broke the embrace, but held her still with his warm, loving gaze, Charlotte was more than convinced. She smiled up at him while her heart sang a new and thrilling song.

Yes, they would be together! Forever! She had been foolish to think anything else was possible.

"Two more days, my Golden One," he whispered.

"Yes, two more days, my darling."

Then all was silent in the woods except for the songs of birds and the gentle sounds of their kisses.

Chapter 16

Dawn was no more than a hint of orchid and vermilion in the sky when Charlotte awoke the morning of the performance. Leaving Tamara still sleeping, she slipped soundlessly out of the brides' tent. Outside, the cookfires glowed as always, and around them sat a few ancient souls who never seemed to sleep. She knew they saw her; nothing in camp escaped them.

Quickly, she darted around the side of the tent and sped into the woods heading toward the stream. Although the Gypsy women took communal bathing for granted, Charlotte had never been able to overcome her modesty and join them. So she hurried to the stream early each morning, before the others woke up. That way she had the icy waters all to herself.

The woods were still black and only faintly stirring with the sounds of creatures up and about. She glanced over her shoulder before stripping off her blouse and skirt. She had learned that as the weather grew cooler it was wise not to test the water with her toe, but to simply dive right in. That way the shock was brief and took her breath away only for a few moments. Once her body grew accustomed to the first frigid plunge, her bath could be almost enjoyable.

But this morning, the water hit her with such a shock that she gasped and came up sputtering, her teeth chattering. Her skin ached. Goose bumps popped out all over her arms and legs. She took deep breaths to try to control the shaking. When physical efforts failed, Charlotte closed her eyes and used her mind to banish the chill. She thought of Mateo, how warm and smooth his body felt next to hers, how they seemed made to fit together. Her blood pounded, sending waves of heat through her. She lay back in the water, letting it massage her scalp with its icy fingers.

"Mateo," she breathed. "My Mateo. Today is our day."

She had given up her plan of leaving him. It was foolish to think that she could live without him. Hadn't he once said that Fate had meant them to be together? She must believe that. She must trust his instincts in his decision to take her away with him after the performance.

Where would they be by nightfall? she wondered. Would they be man and wife before the sun set? Would they lie in each other's arms this very night, wedded for all eternity?

Suddenly, she felt a terrific urge to get on with the day. Even now the sun was gleaming through the trees, warming the rocks and her face. She splashed out of the stream and rubbed herself all over with a length of coarse cloth. Checking to make sure no one was headed down the path, she stretched out for a few moments on a large, flat rock beside the stream. It felt warm as down and smooth as silk. She could almost fall asleep again right here.

"But that might lead to embarrassment," she said aloud.

Sitting up, she looked down at herself. She had filled out since coming to the Gypsy camp. Perhaps it was the good spicy food they fed her or the exercise in the ring. At any rate, her legs were firm, her belly smooth, and her breasts full and peaked from the cold water. Her skin, too, had changed. It was tanned a rich gold from working in the sun. She laughed, thinking how horrified her mother would be at her "Golden One."

That thought of family and home produced another: she and Mateo could return to Fairview after they were married. Mateo could add his fine stallions to the stock and produce a whole new strain at the horse farm. He could put Fairview back on the map. Yes, it was perfect! Her mother could hardly object to a husband who had good horse sense and gold in his pockets.

Charlotte laughed. "I wonder what she'll think of the gold in his ears."

Still, the idea sent a thrill through her. She could hardly wait to mention it to Mateo. Even if he did have a few problems gaining Jemima Buckland's acceptance at first, Granny Fate would love him on sight.

Then, as she thought about it, she realized her idea would never work. Prince Mateo was not a man to settle down on a farm for the rest of his life and tend stock. There was a wildness in his blood and a restlessness in his spirit that would never permit it. And those were the very qualities she loved most about him. Perhaps San Francisco was the best idea after all.

Her thoughts in turmoil, Charlotte hurriedly pulled on her clothes and set off back toward the tent. She met the other women on the path and moved aside for them. Only Tamara acknowledged her presence. The fortune-teller caught Charlotte's arm and pulled her aside.

"We must talk," she said, a grim expression marring her pretty features.

"What's wrong? Is the queen ill again?"

"Sick at heart, as you and her son well know! But this is only part of the problem we must discuss. I have had dreams these past nights. They were good dreams, filled with hope. But last night . . ." Tamara paused and made a sign against the evil eye as a shudder went through her. "Last night, Charlotte, all the demons of hell plagued me while I slept."

Two of the older women had paused on the trail, curious to hear what Tamara had to say to the *gajo* woman.

"Come," Tamara said, nodding toward the eaves-dropping pair. "We cannot talk here."

Once they were alone inside the tent, Tamara poured tea to ward off the morning chill and took a seat across from Charlotte. The lovely Gypsy still looked tense and nervous. Dark circles under her eyes plainly showed that she had slept little the night before.

"What is it, Tamara?" Charlotte asked, covering her friend's hand with her own.

The Gypsy woman shook her head sadly. "I only wish I knew. I have tried divining my dreams, but they make no sense to me. Has something changed between you and Mateo, Charlotte?"

Charlotte Buckland felt a sudden wave of guilt wash over her. *Everything* had changed since yesterday. But how could she admit that to Tamara? She dared not confess that she and Mateo planned to run away together this very day.

"I'm not sure what you mean. Changed how?"

The brooding woman swept up out of her chair and stood with her back to Charlotte, her forehead resting in her palm. "Oh, I don't know. All I know is that I have never had dreams such as these that did not presage disaster. Something terrible is about to happen, but how can I do anything to stop it if I don't know what it is?" Her voice was a wail of desperation.

"Tamara, please try to calm down," Charlotte begged. "Maybe there's nothing you could do, anyway. I thought you believed in Fate running its course."

"I do. But now there is some evil outside force working against us all. If only I knew its source, I might be able to stop it."

Charlotte sighed. She felt so helpless. There was nothing *she* could do to relieve Tamara's troubled mind.

The other woman spun toward her suddenly and grasped both Charlotte's hands. "I do not want you to ride today! It isn't safe. Stay here. Don't even go to Fort Leavenworth. Please! I beg of you, Charlotte!"

Tamara's urgent tone was so unnerving that Charlotte squirmed in her chair. Was the fortune-teller saying that there would be an accident in the ring?

"You know I can't disappoint Mateo. We've both worked so long and hard to be ready for this day. Besides, what could go wrong?" Charlotte asked.

"A thousand things and more. You *must not go!*"

As gently as she could, Charlotte replied, "I have to go. I'm sorry, Tamara."

"I am afraid we will all be sorry before this day is through."

The pall that Tamara's doomsaying had cast over Charlotte's bright mood did not disperse even as she donned the glittering golden costume she would wear in the ring. Perhaps Tamara's dreams had come because of her plan to run away with Mateo. But somehow, even though Charlotte hated to admit it, she felt the meaning of those nightmares ran deeper. And she had lived among the

Gypsies long enough to realize that each dream held its own message of good or evil.

Charlotte decided not to think about it any longer, since there was obviously nothing she could do. She would force herself to concentrate on the coming show.

Wearing the gold tights, she stood back and looked at herself in the mirror. They were spangled all over with tiny gold coins, throwing out sparks of reflected light in all directions. The bodice was tight and cut fairly low in front with more coins at the neckline. Carefully, Charlotte tied on the stiff little skirt of gilded netting. She twisted her long hair back and up, forming a halo braid on top of her head. The final touch was a tiara of gold in the shape of a sunburst. The total effect, when she finished, was almost blinding. Charlotte Buckland was, indeed, the Golden One.

Feeling eyes on her, she turned to find Mateo standing in the doorway, his muscled torso bare, his hips and legs encased in form-fitting scarlet satin trimmed in gold to match her costume. An admiring smile lit his face. Slowly the smile vanished, replaced by an expression of smoldering desire. He came toward her, never taking his eyes from hers.

Charlotte felt her nerves tingle, starting at the base of her spine and working upward. Breaking his gaze, she turned to give him the full effect of her costume.

"Do you like it?"

His hands were on her shoulders then, spinning her back to face him. Hot black eyes danced before her. His lips parted as he drew her near, and his tongue darted out to moisten them. His breathing was heavy, almost labored. She felt herself trembling in his grasp. The touch of his lips on hers gentled her. His breath warmed her. His hands on her bare arms soothed her.

The kiss came slowly, starting as he caressed her lips with his. His big hands moved up over her shoulders to settle about her throat. His thumbs circled downward, dipping into her bodice to massage the tops of her breasts. At the same moment, his tongue found passage to moister depths, making her sigh and tremble.

"Do I like it?" he said against her parted lips. "The only thing I will like better is stripping it off you later, my darling. But for now we must be satisfied with this."

He never let her respond with words. Prince Mateo took his woman back into his strong arms and devoured her with hungry lips, sending tidal waves of longing surging through her gilt-clad body.

As Winston Krantz thought back on the night of the buffalo hunt, he wondered if it had been the wine at the banquet or simply the moonlight that had cast its spell. Whatever the cause, he had done a most impetuous thing when he'd returned to his room after the banquet. He had written a long, sentimental letter to Jemima Buckland. He flushed even now at the thought of some of the phrases he had used. Why, it must seem to the woman that he had penned a love letter!

He had admitted to "dearest Jemima" that he was utterly homesick and distraught in this wasteland. He had extolled the virtues of marriage and told her how envious he felt of the officers who had their wives on the post to ease their loneliness. He had confessed to her that her "sapphire eyes" often gleamed before him in unguarded moments, and that her golden hair was not unlike "an angel's shining halo" in his mind.

On the subject of her rebellious daughter, he had written only that "there is no fool like an old fool" and that he now "begrudged the hours I spent gazing so fondly on the child when they might have been spent adoring the woman."

He had asked Jemima to return her thoughts by the

next mail. And he had signed the letter "Your foolish but ardent admirer."

He lay in bed the morning of the Gypsy circus, muttering recriminations to himself as he awaited the call of the bugle. She would have his letter by now. Whatever must she be thinking of him? Certainly nothing more derogatory than what he was thinking of himself. One would suppose he'd been raised in the gutter, to treat a lady so insensitively! She would undoubtedly be shocked and repulsed by his forwardness. What a cad he was!

Certain that he would sleep no more now that the sun was creeping up, he rose, washed his face, and pulled on his trousers. At least the Gypsies would be arriving soon. Perhaps their circus would divert his mind from Jemima Buckland and that cursed letter!

Lance Delacorte and his wife, Annabelle, were still maintaining a frosty silence this morning. She had not yet forgiven him for his escapade in town with the blonde Gypsy. He, on the other hand, felt himself the injured party. In spite of his lecherous intentions, nothing had happened that night. And he was furious with his wife for accepting Colonel Custer's invitation to go riding—alone, with only Custer's hounds to chaperone. Annabelle had been taking great pains with her appearance since that day, walking about with her pert little nose in the air and humming constantly. The Lord only knew what had transpired between the two of them!

"Must you keep up that infernal humming, Annabelle?"

She turned a sugary smile on him and continued making the bed in which they had slept—but not connubially for quite some time now. "I hum when I'm happy. And this morning I have a special reason to feel pleased and gay."

"Oh?" he responded, trying not to sound as curious as he felt.

"Several reasons, actually. George has asked us to sit with him for the performance."

"Are you sure he invited *us*?"

Annabelle giggled. "Well, actually, Lance, he invited me, but he did say that you would be welcome to join us."

"That was big of the colonel!" Lance bellowed, stamping angrily about the bedroom. Then, wheeling on his wife, he demanded, "Dammit all, Annabelle, when is this going to stop? I'm sick and tired of you mooning over Custer this way. It isn't decent! You'll have the whole post talking about you."

"My darling husband," she said in a sweetly sarcastic tone, "how could they possibly find time to gossip about me, when your name is still on everyone's lips? At least George Custer is a gentleman. I daresay even you would be hard-pressed to call your little blonde Gypsy a lady." She resumed humming while Lance held his silence and scowled at her. "Cheer up, darling! You'll get to see her again today. We'll *all* get to see her!" Annabelle taunted him.

Lance didn't wait for any more slashes of his wife's sharp tongue. He stormed out of their bedroom and out of their quarters, pounding his way across the dusty parade ground, where even now the soldiers were setting up wooden bleachers and marking off the ring.

Annabelle watched him from the front window. She hated treating him so badly, but maybe he would learn his lesson once and for all. She'd put up with four years of him always having his way—always refusing to answer her questions—always taking, never giving. She loved him, but love had to go two ways, if it was going to work. She had a feeling this was her last chance—and she meant to make good on it!

She had Colonel Custer's promise that he would do something about the Gypsies, and she certainly had her husband's attention now that she'd spent three days primping for and flirting with Lance's commanding officer. She'd never seen a man so jealous. Now maybe he was beginning to understand what he'd put her through all these years.

Annabelle Delacorte let the lace curtain drop from her fingers when Lance disappeared into the stable. She sighed wearily and wiped a tear from the corner of her eye. She only hoped all this pain was worth the effort.

George Custer strode about his living room, trying to get his thoughts in order. Everything had to work today with split-second precision, or it would fail and he'd have a riot on his hands.

He stopped by the piano and caressed the gilt frame containing his wife's picture. He wished Libbie were here today. But in another way, he was glad she wasn't. He missed her terribly, but at least he wouldn't have to worry about her safety when all hell broke loose after the performance. He didn't mean for anyone to be harmed. He only wanted to throw a scare into those copper-skinned devils so they would leave his territory of their own accord. At first, he considered cutting only the blonde Gypsy from the herd and sending her away. He didn't think that would work, though. She was sure to have a man among the group—probably Prince Mateo himself—who would fight to the death for her. He finally decided it would be safest to arrest them all. But one never knew; anything might happen if some of them panicked.

A knock at the door interrupted his thoughts.

"Come," he called.

A soldier in parade dress uniform stepped inside, saluted, and said, "The lookout just spotted them, sir. They should be approaching the gate in a few minutes."

"Thank you, Corporal."

The door closed and Custer took a deep breath. He glanced up at the hunting trophies mounted about his walls as he tied his red neckerchief. The moose, the elk, the mountain lion—he had faced them all fearlessly. Now he must do the same with this wild band of Gypsies.

Charlotte felt more nervous than she would have liked as she rode next to Mateo at the head of the circus parade. Up ahead, she could see the high wooden walls of Fort Leavenworth. Soon they would be inside, in a world that had become alien to her over the past weeks. She didn't feel like one of them anymore. She thought like a Gypsy; she felt like a Gypsy. How would it feel to be among the *gajos* once more?

"We're almost there," Mateo said as much to himself as to Charlotte.

"Yes," she replied. "Mateo, I'm so nervous."

He looked down into her wide brown eyes and flashed her a broad smile. "That is good! You'll put on a better show that way. The horses are keyed up, too. They know what is about to happen. They look forward to going through their paces and to hearing the applause that follows. Just remember, Charlotte, that not one of those watching can do what you can do. They will think you magnificent!" He leaned down and kissed her cheek. "You are, my love, you truly are."

Behind them trailed the rest of the troupe—the ringmaster in his splendid suit of shiny black; Petronovich and Phaedra, the silver gleaming on their emerald-and-purple costumes; Lantro, the juggler, with his glittering orbs and plates; the old dog woman with her dancing mongrels; and, of course, Poor Little Pesha and her band of ragged beggars, ready to work the crowd.

Charlotte hadn't mentioned Tamara's fears to Mateo, but deep down he knew. Never before had the fortune-teller refused to accompany them. But today Tamara had chosen to stay in camp by the bedside of the ailing queen. It was only an excuse; Mateo saw that. Something was worrying Tamara. He tried not to think about it, but he, too, could feel clouds gathering, although the day was fine.

A great cheer went up from the wall of the fort as sentries swung the heavy gates open for the Gypsy troupe. Women, children, and soldiers scurried about, choosing their seats. Custer's pack of hounds yapped and howled. And his pet pelican found its favorite perch outside the colonel's quarters, flapping its broad wings and opening and closing its huge beak soundlessly in excitement. To all of the Gypsy band, including Charlotte Buckland, the army post seemed a strange, exotic place.

Mateo led his troupe to the reviewing stand, where Colonel Custer rose from his seat to greet them. While the yellow-haired officer delivered a brief speech of welcome, Mateo scanned the crowd and frowned slightly.

Sitting beside the Colonel was an attractive young woman in a red-and-white-striped gown, who seemed set on killing Charlotte with her look. Next to her was the officer who had paid to bed Charlotte. He directed his gaze anywhere but at the two of them. And right behind him sat Major Winston Krantz. He, too, was staring at Charlotte, his mouth sagging open, his pale eyes almost popping out of his head. Perhaps, Mateo thought, she reminded the poor man of the woman who had left him at the altar.

"And now, Prince Mateo, if you will be so kind as to show us your wonders." Colonel Custer smiled and took his seat.

Mateo noticed that the woman next to the colonel leaned close to him, whispered something, and nodded toward Charlotte. Custer nodded back and shot a quick glance at the Golden One, his smile vanishing. Mateo's frown deepened. Something was afoot.

Meanwhile Charlotte was having trouble breathing. Lord, what had she gotten herself into? It couldn't be, but it was! Winston Krantz, in the flesh—all of it! And he was staring at her. He had recognized her immediately. Her instinct was to put heels to horseflesh and take off out of the gate as fast as the stallion could carry her. But where could she go? Now that Krantz knew she was here, he would track her down. It was only a matter of time. Of all the army posts in the country, why did Winston Krantz have to be stationed at Fort Leavenworth? This must be what Tamara's nightmares were all about. Why hadn't Charlotte heeded her friend's warning and stayed in camp?

"There will be no trouble," whispered Mateo. "We will put on our performance and then we will leave . . . *quickly!*"

His words stunned Charlotte. "But how did you know?"

"I'm the man who hauled him out of your bed and threw him over the balcony railing, remember?"

"Oh," she replied, realizing suddenly that they were anticipating trouble from different areas. She wondered if she should tell Mateo about Krantz, then decided there was no reason to if he planned to whisk her out of the fort as soon as they'd done their act.

The Gypsies used the stable at the far corner of the post as their staging area. Mateo and Charlotte waited as act after act preceded theirs—he pacing, she growing more nervous by the minute. The horses seemed to sense their disquiet and stamped impatiently. Mateo soothed them with quiet words, but there was nothing he could do to help Charlotte. She fully expected Winston to come out of the stands and grab her, laying his claim, the minute she entered the ring.

Suddenly, male voices roared. Whistles and applause filled the air.

"Phaedra," Mateo said, and Charlotte nodded, knowing that the woman would be playing to every man in the audience, seducing each one with a smile, a wink, a twitch of her shapely hips.

The four people seated on the main stand—Custer, the Delacortes, and Winston Krantz—were all caught up in their separate thoughts.

Annabelle, her head turned slightly away from the ring so that she wouldn't have to witness the wanton performance of the woman and the trained bear, was watching her husband out the corner of her eye. He was eating it up! She'd been mistaken about the blonde Gypsy. It wasn't just that one who interested him; it was any of them, perhaps *any other female*. Maybe she'd been wrong to try to save her marriage. Maybe there were some men who simply could not survive on the love of one woman alone. Seeing his reaction to Phaedra—his sweating brow and wide eyes, his trembling hands, and the bulge in his uniform trousers—she was convinced of it.

Custer and Krantz, although quite taken with Phaedra's sensual beauty, were impatient to see the Golden One again. To Custer, she had looked like a beautiful, startled doe, with those large brown eyes and her smooth, sun-gold skin. She was indeed exquisite. Her cape had covered her form as she'd ridden in and sat before him on the great stallion. He was fascinated by her. Surely she could not be total perfection. But the way Prince Mateo devoured her with his eyes made the colonel suspect that she had few flaws. He was anxious for her to enter the ring so that he could judge for himself.

Winston Krantz's curiosity ran far deeper than Colonel Custer's. Was this some trick of his mind—some guilty reaction to the letter he'd written to Charlotte's mother? Surely the Golden One and the shy young woman he'd planned to marry couldn't be one and the same! What would a refined Kentucky belle like Charlotte Buckland be doing with a wild band of Gypsies? But that face . . . those eyes! Could it be she had a double? Either thought was staggering.

The major mopped his brow with his handkerchief and hardly took any notice of the bear-baiting beauty in the ring. His eyes remained fixed on the stable door, hoping for another glimpse of the Golden One, as the Gypsies billed her.

Then, in a swirl of green-and-heliotrope gauze and a flash of silver spangles, Phaedra swept out of the ring, followed by the whoops and cheers of the soldiers. The ringmaster reappeared and began to introduce Mateo's act. Eloquently he lauded the Romany prince's expertise with the great stallions. Silence fell over the spectators as he told of the fabulous Gypsy's performances before the crowned heads of Europe.

"And assisting the great master of the *grai*, for the very first time in public, is the beautiful and mysterious Golden One. The lady is a legend in her own time. Wedded to the king of the leprechauns, this Irish Gypsy found the fabled pot of gold, and her wee husband decreed that she should forevermore gleam with riches. He, too, bestowed upon the Golden One her talent with the horses. It is said she speaks in words they alone understand—that she rides like the wind—that she has invisible wings. It is my great pleasure to present to you . . . Prince Mateo and the Golden One!"

A huge wave of applause went up, filling the post and

surrounding landscape like thunder before a storm. Mateo looked at Charlotte, smiled, and took her hand. Bringing her fingers to his lips, he kissed them.

"They are ours," he said. "We will give them our best. And after we have finished and accepted their applause, we will give ourselves only to each other, my dearest."

Charlotte smiled bravely. "I love you, Mateo!"

"And I you, my *sunaki bal*. Now, up with you!"

He boosted her up onto Velacore's back and mounted the Black Devil.

"Hiyah!" he whooped, and the two of them pounded into the arena, their golden capes whipping in the wind as the crowd cheered and stamped.

Chapter 17

The thunderous applause quieted as the two huge stallions galloped into the ring—Prince Mateo, in scarlet and gold astride his Black Devil, and Charlotte Buckland, the Golden One, gleaming like a sunburst on Velacore's broad back. Around and around they rode in opposite directions, the riders bowing and smiling to each other as they passed. An expectant hush awaited their first daring move.

"Hiyah!" Mateo gave his signal.

With perfect precision, he and Charlotte raised themselves until they were standing upright, the reins in their right hands while their left arms reached gracefully heavenward. As they rode in this fashion, the other four stallions filed into the ring—two behind Mateo's mount and the other pair following Charlotte. Perfect timing! It was going well.

Charlotte felt her heart pounding as loudly as the horses' hooves. So far everything was fine, but she could not relax and enjoy it. She heard Mateo's next signal and nodded. Without lowering her head to see it happen, she knew that the pair of stallions had moved into position on either side of Velacore, the horses galloping now three abreast. Her next move looked far more difficult than it actually was. Still, it could be dangerous. One false step and she would slip between the horses to be trampled, if she weren't crushed between their heavy bodies before she hit the ground. She waited and watched for Mateo's nod, feeling her pulse race at the sight of him.

He was so beautiful in the ring—his every move strong, fluid, executed with perfect assurance. He stood now like a gleaming statue upon the Black Devil's back, a broad smile on his handsome face, his dark hair whipping in the wind, the muscles in his arms and back rippling magnificently.

Another signal. Charlotte followed it automatically, sliding down to a sitting position with her legs over her mount's right side. She raised her arms high, smiling at the crowd and accepting their applause. Then slowly, carefully, she eased her body down. Soon she was facing the sky, her head on the inner horse, her back on Velacore's, and her toes on the other, pointed toward the audience. She raised one leg and then the other, careful not to shift her position too drastically. Mateo, she knew, was performing the same maneuver on the opposite side of the ring. She remained as she was, waiting for his whistle.

It came, and she tensed her stomach muscles to lift her head and legs, balancing now on her back alone as the other outside horses picked up speed and moved ahead of Velacore. The four spare horses spaced themselves perfectly in the ring and continued circling.

"I'm almost there." She heard Mateo's voice over the hoofbeats.

A moment later, her head leaning far back, she saw the Black Devil move in beside her. Mateo's face looked into hers as he reached for her hands. His grip was sure and strong. Anything less would have brought them both tumbling from their mounts. Now they circled, hands locked tight, balanced precariously on their stallions' backs.

"Up!" Mateo ordered.

With practiced timing, the two of them rose once more to sitting positions. The crowd screamed its approval. Charlotte felt the applause drumming through her body. It felt marvelous! She smiled broadly, waved, and bowed as she continued riding around the ring.

From Charlotte's vantage point, the audience was only a blur of color and indistinct faces. She couldn't have made out Colonel Custer's broad grin, Annabelle Delacort's frown, her husband's smirk, or Winston Krantz's agitation.

"Outstanding!" Custer cheered, applauding the pair enthusiastically. "Have you ever seen anything like it, Annabelle?"

"They are quite good. But frankly, George, I find that woman's costume shocking. Why, she might just as well have painted her body gold! *Everything* shows!"

"And isn't it all gorgeous!" the colonel said under his breath.

"Colonel, I've got to speak with you in private!" Major Krantz was leaning over, shouting frantically in Custer's ear.

"Not now, Winston. Later, after they finish. That woman is the most enchanting creature I've ever seen!"

"That woman," Krantz continued in a shrill voice, *"is my fiancée*, Colonel!"

Custer turned in his seat, his smile fading. "You're joking, of course!"

The perspiring major shook his head. "No, Colonel. That 'Golden One' is none other than Miss Charlotte Buckland of Fairview Plantation in Kentucky."

"You can't mean it, Major!" Annabelle shrilled. "George, they've kidnapped the poor girl! We must save her!"

"Yes, Colonel, we must!" Krantz agreed. "Why, her dear mother has been half out of her mind worrying over what's happened to her."

"Very well," Custer said at last. "But after the performance."

He wasn't about to forgo a moment of Charlotte Buckland's act. Besides, now that there was a white woman involved, he would have to alter the plans he had made earlier. Somehow he would have to get her away from the others before he made his move. He needed time to think.

"George?" Annabelle tugged at his arm, once more disrupting his concentration. "Did you see where Lance went?"

"No, my dear. But I'm sure he'll be right back."

Coming right back was the furthest thing from Lance Delacorte's thoughts at the moment. Never mind the Golden One, he'd decided as he'd watched Phaedra tease her bear to a frenzy. He had slipped out of his seat and around the back way to the stables while the crowd was cheering Mateo and Charlotte. It hadn't been difficult to lure Phaedra away from the others. Now the two of them were in the safest place on earth—the bedroom he shared with Annabelle. She'd never look for him there.

"So you liked my act?" Phaedra said, beaming into

Lance's flushed face. "Many men have told me that they would like to change places with my Boski—especially during the part when he licks my body all over."

Lance was trembling, sweating, aching to do just that. He put his hands on her bare shoulders and brought her close, breathing in the strong earthy odor of her body.

"I'd like that, too. You're a beautiful woman, Phaedra. The most beautiful I've ever seen."

She laughed. "Tell me something I haven't heard before, horse soldier!"

He whispered an obscenely phrased suggestion into her ear, then said aloud, "I want you, woman!"

Her hands were on him now, pulling his shirt free, opening it, running her long nails tantalizingly over his chest. He groaned and clutched her close, crushing her hips to his thighs and holding her there to feel his heat.

"Oh, you *do* want me, don't you, soldier boy! You're like a stallion ready for his mare. I like a man who knows what he wants. But if my Petronovich catches us together, you may find yourself a gelding. He is one jealous *Rom*!"

Lance pulled quickly away from Phaedra and saw the laughing light in her eyes. He wanted her, yes! But he'd already tangled with one of these wild Gypsies; he wasn't sure he was willing to take on another—not even to have Phaedra.

"Where is this Petronovich?"

She laughed and hooked a finger in the top of his trousers to pull him back to her. "I am only joking with you, O brave one! You have nothing to fear from my man. He has left to go back to our camp already. Besides," she said huskily, "I do as I please. And right now, you please me."

Made bold by Phaedra's words, Lance caught her in his arms and kissed her deeply. She moaned into his open mouth, arousing him beyond all limits. Still holding the kiss, he fumbled at the lacing of her silver top. In no time at all, he had a full, ripe breast in each hand. Phaedra's large, berry-colored nipples distended, welcoming his touch. When she battered his tongue with her own, it was Lance's turn to moan and quiver. He'd never been with such a bold woman.

Suddenly she pushed him away and ordered, "Take off your clothes!"

He stared at her. She stood there, her huge breasts bare and heaving, her hands on her hips, ordering him to disrobe in broad daylight before her. She was outrageous, but ever so exciting.

"Do it! Now!" she demanded. "I want to see what you have to offer me. Do as I say or I'll leave this minute!"

Lance was out of his boots, britches, and drawers in no time. Phaedra walked around him, appraising him from all angles. At last she came back to stand in front of him, her dark eyes unmistakably focused on the main point of her interest. He had the urge to cover himself with his hands, but he knew if he did so, she would either laugh or leave. So he stood perfectly still, embarrassed, but at the same time strangely aroused by her frank gaze.

"You are not the best I've ever seen." She shrugged. "But you'll do."

"Well, thank God for that!" he answered in a mocking tone. "Now you!"

Phaedra feigned modesty, pulling the silver top back up and turning away. "No! Never!"

"Like hell, woman!" He lunged at her, catching her laces in his fingers. They pulled tight about her waist and she gasped for breath.

"Let me go!"

"When I'm damn good and ready!"

He shoved her down on the bed, but she slipped away

from him. A moment later, the naked man and near-naked woman were tumbling about on the bedroom floor in a lusty love-fight.

Charlotte and Mateo were once more astride their mounts, galloping around the ring. Mateo's Black Devil caught up with Velacore. He flashed Charlotte a blinding white smile and reached out to squeeze her hand.

"You are superb, my darling!"

"You'd better wait until we finish this final maneuver before you start handing out the praise, my love."

He blew her a kiss. "Not to worry, my *sunaki bal!*"

Their moves perfectly in tune, they stood on their horses' backs, with no reins this time to steady them. Charlotte dared take only shallow breaths. The Black Devil moved in so close to her horse that their flanks were almost touching. Like lightning, Mateo switched horses, leaping onto Velacore's back behind Charlotte. He slipped his arm about her waist to steady them both, and she leaned into him, savoring the feel of his hard body.

The crowd grew silent, waiting to see what would happen. When Mateo slid to a sitting position, a general gasp went up. They thought he had slipped. But no! This was all part of the act.

A moment later, he leaned forward. Ever so carefully, Charlotte straddled his shoulders. He straightened. The horse picked up speed. Charlotte waved with both hands as she sat high above the prancing horse. The audience went wild.

"Well, George, that must be it," Annabelle said. "I'm going to find Lance. He's been gone a dreadfully long time."

"As you wish, my dear, but you really shouldn't miss any of this."

Annabelle was already out of her seat, heading toward their quarters. She knew Lance wouldn't be there, but she wanted to wash her face and hands after all the dust those horses had kicked up.

The door was not locked, but that wasn't unusual: they seldom felt the need of such security measures within the safe confines of the fort. She went into the orderly living room. No, Lance wasn't here. When he came in, he invariably dropped his riding crop or his hat on the sofa, in spite of all her complaints about his untidy habits.

Spotting the sherry decanter on the sideboard, she decided she might benefit from a bit of fortification. The dust was clogging her throat so she could hardly speak or swallow. And heaven only knew what kind of a row she and Lance would have when he did turn up . . . *if* he turned up! Yes, a drop of sherry would help in either case.

She walked to the front window and looked out, shielding her eyes against the blinding glare from the Golden One's costume. What she saw almost took her breath away. The handsome Gypsy prince was still standing on his horse's back with the woman astride his shoulders. As the great stallion continued a steady gallop around the ring, the blonde Gypsy maneuvered upward until she was standing on Prince Mateo's shoulders. Annabelle held her breath, sure that the woman would never be able to maintain her balance. But she did it! Soon the two of them stood erect, towering over the people in the bleachers. It was a spectacular trick indeed. Annabelle felt she should have stayed to see it at closer range.

Once more the applause was like thunder. One hand occupied holding her sherry glass, she did not clap for the pair, but she did smile broadly and nod her approval.

Then she took a seat, exhausted from the excitement of watching the daring performers. For the moment, all thoughts of her errant husband were forgotten.

While his wife sat sipping sherry in a most civilized manner in the outer room, Lance Delacorte was in a most uncivilized predicament on the floor of their bedroom.

Somehow—he wasn't sure how it happened—the Gypsy woman had gotten hold of his rope and tied him up like a calf at branding time. He lay flat on his back, unable to move, as the half-clothed beauty taunted him beyond endurance. He had often had fantasies about being in just such an exciting position, but actually living it was something else altogether.

At the same instant that Annabelle had unstoppered the sherry decanter, Phaedra had tired of riding her hobbled mount. Now she was licking him all over in imitation of Boski's attentions to her in the ring. Lance was writhing and almost choking to keep from screaming.

"Phaedra . . . Phaedra, don't do that . . . please. Let me loose. Come on, now. I've had enough of this. What if someone comes in?"

She raised her head from his quivering belly and grinned at him. "Then I'll go out the window and you'll have one helluva time explaining yourself, my pretty horse soldier."

"Oh, God!" He rolled his eyes and tried to think of an appropriate prayer to save him. He almost made a promise never to look at another woman again but decided that was *too* drastic. "You wouldn't leave me like this?"

"Well, I am certainly not going to stay here and get caught!"

"Phaedra, *please!*" he moaned. "Untie me!"

*   *   *

Annabelle cocked an ear. She thought she heard sounds from the bedroom, but she couldn't be sure: there was so much cheering coming from outside. She tipped her glass to her lips once more, but it was empty.

"Maybe just a spot more," she murmured.

There was that noise again from the bedroom—a moaning sound. She started to get up, but the sherry had made her drowsy and her limbs felt heavy. She couldn't force herself to move.

The moan she'd heard had come when Phaedra finally eased herself down upon her victim. She still hadn't untied him, but at least she had tired of her torture and was ready to satisfy him.

And by damn, the woman knows her business! Lance thought happily, feeling his release fast approaching. Yes, sir, this one was every bit as good a rider as that little blonde out there in the ring. And a helluva lot more willing!

He was on the brink now . . . he felt himself coming. His eyes shot open and he was staring right into her big, dark nipples. He tried to reach one with his lips, but he was just short of it. He stuck out his tongue and lapped at it. At his unexpected licking, Phaedra gave a back-wrenching jerk with her body and vocalized her pleasure, now very near her own ecstasy. Throwing caution to the wind, they rode it out together.

"Horses' hooves in the bedroom?" Annabelle turned in her chair and squinted at the door as if to see what was making the loud thumping noise.

"Lance, is that you in there?"

*   *   *

They both froze, but only for a moment. True to her word, Phaedra dismounted, grabbed up the rest of her costume, blew him a quick kiss, and climbed out the window, leaving Lance to his uncertain fate.

He was struggling against his bonds and had wriggled all but his lower torso out of sight when Annabelle came in.

"Oh, my Lord!" she screamed, seeing his bound naked ankles and hairy legs sticking out from under her bed. Immediately she turned and fled the house, shouting hysterically, "Murder! Murder! Someone's killed my husband!"

Colonel Custer ran to her. He caught the sobbing, near fainting woman in his arms. "What's happened, Annabelle?"

"There's a body in my bedroom. I think it's Lance," she cried.

"Close the gates!" the colonel yelled to one of the captains. "Don't let anyone else leave the post."

Charlotte and Mateo didn't hear the excited shouts coming from the parade ground. They were back in the stable, locked tightly in an embrace of joy and love. The show had gone off without the slightest mistake. Now they were free!

"Let's change quickly and be on our way." Mateo's words had the ring of a boy setting out on a great adventure.

"Yes, before anyone can stop us," Charlotte agreed.

He frowned slightly. "Who would try to stop us, love?"

She tried to shrug off his question and the nagging

feeling that had been twisting her stomach since she'd first spotted Winston Krantz.

"Oh, no one. I'm just anxious to be away with you . . . alone together."

The very next instant, it seemed as if Charlotte's thoughts had conjured up her adversary. Major Winston Krantz, his usually serious demeanor especially solemn, came walking into the stable just in time to interrupt a kiss. He gave Charlotte a searching look but spoke to Mateo.

"I'm sorry, but we'll have to detain you on the post for a time."

Mateo put on his "laugh, Gypsy, laugh" face for the major. "Why should you want to do a thing like that? We performed for you. Now we go back to camp to celebrate and then to sleep."

Again the major's pale eyes were on Charlotte, traveling the length of her golden tights but shooting up to her face when he saw that she was watching him. This was the moment she had dreaded. He was about to tell Mateo who he was and lay claim to her. But when his words came, they couldn't have shocked her more.

"There's been a murder. We're holding everyone."

"A *murder*?" they both cried in unison.

He nodded and grimaced. "Messy business. Seems the corpse was found bound and naked. Oh, excuse me, ma'am." He flushed deeply.

Meanwhile, the "corpse" was truly in danger of losing his life. If he couldn't come up with a satisfactory explanation for the embarrassing circumstances under which his wife had found him, he'd have to tell them all the truth. And that was the last thing Lance Delacorte wanted to do.

"Darling, darling! Are you all right?" Annabelle, made

mellow by the sherry and finding her husband still alive, was sobbing all over him.

"What happened here, Lieutenant?" Custer demanded.

Lance clutched the army blanket covering his nakedness and held his head with his other hand, pretending he'd been hit.

"I'm not really sure, Colonel. I remember coming back here to find my pipe."

"But Lance dear, you haven't smoked that pipe in over a year."

"Well, I wanted it. I needed a smoke." He glared at his wife, then looked at the colonel again. "I came into the bedroom and they . . . they jumped me. Yes, that's what happened. It must have been some of the Gypsies. I probably walked in on them while they were looting the place."

"See, I told you, George!" Annabelle said vehemently. "They are no good! You shouldn't have let them come here!"

"Have you noticed anything missing, Annabelle?" Custer asked.

She glanced about. No, everything seemed to be in place. Even Lance's money clip, which contained a wad of bills, was lying on the bureau in plain view. Surely they would have taken that. She shook her head, looking slightly bewildered.

"You seem to have a difficult time lately keeping track of your uniform, Lieutenant Delacorte," Custer said sarcastically. "Did these brigands strip you as well?"

Lance nodded vigorously. "Yes, yes, they must have."

"You mean you don't remember?" Custer demanded.

"Well, everything's very hazy in my mind after they hit me, sir."

"How many?"

"I'm not sure. They must have been hiding behind the door when I came in. I never saw them."

Maybe Delacorte hadn't seen them, but George Custer had spotted telltale bits of evidence the moment he'd come into the room. The lieutenant had strange red marks all over his neck and chest—almost like teeth marks. Then there had been the triangular scrap of silver material caught on the windowsill. And the knots in the rope that bound Delacorte had been of peculiar Gypsy fashion, but too loose for a man to have tied them. Custer's guess was that a Gypsy woman had been with Lance Delacorte . . . and there was only one in the troupe dressed in silver.

"Well, as long as nothing is missing and there's no real harm done, I suppose we can just let it pass," Custer said.

"*Colonel!*" shrieked Annabelle Delacorte. "They nearly killed my husband and you aren't going to do anything about it?"

He was furious at being caught in such a position by Delacorte's feeble lies. It was one thing for the lieutenant to cheat on his wife, quite another to ensnare his commanding officer in his treachery. Custer was fed up! It wasn't the Gypsies who were causing him all this trouble: it was his own people!

Just then, Winston Krantz came bustling through the door. "I've detained the rest of them, Colonel." His eyes went wild, his lower jaw drooped. "Delacorte! You're *alive!*"

"*And well!*" Custer added. "Go and tell the others they can leave now, Krantz. There's no need to hold anyone."

Winston and Annabelle both turned shocked gazes on Custer.

"Sir, remember what I told you about the woman? Well, I'm sure of it now. I've seen her close up. She is Charlotte Buckland, the young lady I intended to marry.

We can't just allow them take her away again against her will," Winston protested.

"And what about your promise to me, Colonel?" Annabelle shrilled. "You said you'd do something about this situation."

Custer mopped his brow, wishing that they would all leave him alone. He wanted peace and quiet on the post, no more Gypsies, a long ride with Libbie at his side, and maybe a few redskins to take his frustrations out on.

"How many are you detaining, Major?"

"I have five of them, not counting Charlotte Buckland. Prince Mateo, three of his horse handlers, and the woman who performed with the bear."

Lance paled and drew deeper into the folds of his blanket.

"Very well," Custer replied with a sigh. "Bring them all to my quarters immediately."

Mateo's horse handlers were released after only a few minutes' interrogation. They were instructed to leave the stallions but return immediately to their camp.

Colonel Custer, who found this whole matter boring, senseless, and a damned nuisance besides, perked up noticeably when Phaedra sauntered into his office. There was no denying that she was a real beauty. Looking into those smoldering black eyes and seeing those pouty lips and the sultry way she carried herself, he could almost forgive Lance Delacorte for this stupid debacle. Goddamn if she wasn't some piece of female!

"Name?" he asked tonelessly.

She hiked one shapely thigh onto the edge of his desk and leaned close to his face. "Phaedra," she said in such a manner that her breath fanned the long yellow hair framing his face.

Custer sat back in his chair, away from her, but she

could tell by the gleam in his eyes and the way they scrutinized her that he was not unaffected by her charms.

"Well, Phaedra, it seems you've stirred up quite a hornets' nest here on post."

"I?" she said with exaggerated innocence.

Custer pulled the silver scrap from his pocket and flipped it across the desk to her. "Looks to me like this just about fits that piece torn out of your bodice."

"Oh, thank you, Colonel!" she enthused. "Wherever did you find this? Boski tore my gown after our performance today. I've been searching everywhere for this missing piece. Silver cloth is *so* dear! You have no idea. Queen Zolande would have been very angry with me if I'd come home with my costume ruined. But now I can mend it. You are a dear, dear man!"

Custer uttered a disgusted sigh. "Young lady! Please don't say any more. I've had my fill of lies today. I know what you and Lance Delacorte were up to. This scrap came from the windowsill of his bedroom. I'm not blaming you. Certainly, no man strong of body and right in his mind could refuse your charms."

Phaedra leaned close, smiling, and caressed the colonel's flowing hair. "How sweet!"

"Never mind that!" He brushed her hand away. "But dammit, woman! To tie him up naked and leave him that way for his wife to find? Have you no sense of decency?"

Phaedra's dark brows shot up dramatically and she leaned close again, shrugging and smiling. "He enjoyed it, Colonel!"

Custer harrumphed in his embarrassment. "Be that as it may, it isn't a decent sport for a cavalry officer to be engaged in."

"You have a better idea, yellow-haired one?" She leaned so far over that her breasts nearly popped from their silver confinement.

Custer stood abruptly. "I think that's quite enough,

young lady! I want you out of my office and off this post in five minutes! Otherwise, I won't be responsible for what happens to you with all these woman-hungry soldiers about!''

"Ooh! Sounds nice!"

"Out! Out, do you hear me?''

Phaedra slunk through the door, tossing the colonel a kiss over her shoulder as she left.

Custer stared after her, making strange rumbling noises in his throat, then adjusted his uniform as he poured himself a stiff drink. He tossed it off quickly and took a deep breath.

"Thank God that's over with!"

He was still trying to regain his composure when Mateo and Charlotte came in. They were still splendidly in costume.

Custer resumed his seat and motioned them to the sofa. "Sit down, won't you? Let's get this over with in a hurry.''

"That sounds like a good idea, Colonel," Mateo agreed.

"Miss Buckland!"

Charlotte sat forward and answered, "Yes, sir?"

The colonel slumped in his chair. He had hoped against hope that his trick would fail, but . . .

"I understand that you came here from Kentucky."

Charlotte knew Mateo was staring at her, but she dared not meet his gaze.

"Yes, I did."

"And just how is it that you happen to be performing with a Gypsy circus?"

Charlotte stammered uncomfortably, trying to frame a suitable answer.

"Were you kidnapped?"

Charlotte's head snapped up, as did Mateo's. "Who told you that?" she demanded.

"Never mind. Just answer my question, young lady."

She looked down at her hands. "I can't. It's not that simple."

Custer rose and walked around his desk. "Oh, I think it is. Either you came to the Gypsies by choice, or you were taken by force. Which is it?"

Charlotte stood, too, unwilling to allow the colonel an unfair advantage by towering over her. "How I came to them no longer matters. I intend to stay with Mateo. He is my man . . . not Major Krantz!"

Custer's eyes narrowed as he looked into hers. He had heard white women, taken as squaws, speak in much the same manner. But they could be rehabilitated. Perhaps there was still hope for Charlotte Buckland.

"Major Krantz is very concerned for your welfare, Miss Buckland. He says your family is worried about you, too."

Charlotte laughed. "My mother cares only for herself. As for my grandmother, she sent me here." She turned to look lovingly at the man seated next to her and pressed his hand with hers. "Besides, Mateo is my family now."

"I'm afraid that won't do, Miss Buckland. I mean to see you safely back in society and reunited with your real family."

"You mean you're sending me back to Kentucky? No, I won't go!"

Mateo was on his feet, glaring at Custer. "You have no right. Charlotte and I are going away together . . . tonight!"

Custer whipped out a pistol and leveled it at Mateo's heart. "Stay right where you are! You and the others will be leaving tonight, but Miss Buckland will remain here under my protection. Now get out of here, round up your clan, and move on. This woman is going back to her family and her fiancé!"

Mateo rushed the colonel, struggling to wrest the gun from his hand. A shot rang out, and Charlotte screamed.

The next moment half a dozen soldiers poured into the room, subdued Mateo, and hauled him away. She tried to keep the men away from him, but they pushed her aside into George Custer's arms. All she could do was sob helplessly and watch the man she loved be taken away.

"Calm yourself, Miss Buckland," Custer said soothingly. "It's all over now. You're safe. He can't force you against your will any longer."

Charlotte stared up at the colonel, unable to believe what she was hearing. Mateo, *force her*? Never! It was Custer and the other *gajos* who were doing the forcing. She would fight them with everything in her until they let Mateo go.

A mousy-haired woman entered the room and took Charlotte's hand, smiling sweetly.

"Come with me my dear. You're back with your own kind. No need to worry about that wild Gypsy any longer. He's out of your life for good!"

Charlotte went with Annabelle Delacorte, but she swore silently that Mateo would never be out of her life. She would bide her time. And when the right opportunity presented itself, she and Mateo would ride the wind.

Chapter 18

George Custer frowned as he watched Annabelle Delacorte lead Charlotte Buckland out of his office. Things certainly hadn't gone as he'd planned today. That young woman had fouled him up royally.

Originally, he had instructed his men to round up the Gypsy group as soon as their performance was over. He'd meant to lock up the lot of them in the guardhouse overnight and give them a stern lecture on staying clear of his soldiers and their wives. Then he'd planned to offer them their freedom, but only if they were ready to pack up their caravans and move on.

Well, he had one Gypsy in the guardhouse all right! But what the hell was he supposed to do with him? Prince Mateo could prove to be a dangerous prisoner. These Romanies truly believed that one of their own would die if confined. They certainly weren't going to sit by passively and let Gypsy royalty wither away in his jail. Of that Custer was certain.

But the man had threatened him—fought him for his own gun and damn near shot him. He couldn't just open the bars and let Mateo walk out. Besides, if he did that, what would happen to Charlotte Buckland? He'd probably kidnap her again and her family would never know what happened to her.

Lord, it was a mess!

The colonel flopped down in the chair behind his desk and heaved a weary sigh. Taking pen and paper, he started a letter to Libbie. If he couldn't talk to her, at least he could pour out all of his troubles to his sweet wife in writing.

Short of fighting the woman off and taking her chances at running the gauntlet of soldiers to escape by the main gate, Charlotte had no choice but to go along quietly to the Delacortes' quarters.

"My husband won't be sleeping here tonight, Miss Buckland. He's had a bad time of it today and the surgeon thinks he should spend the night in the infirmary. So it will be just us girls."

"How exciting," Charlotte muttered. She wasn't paying much attention to Annabelle's words; she was too busy scanning the post to try to spot the guardhouse. There it was—across the compound, tucked in behind the stables.

Annabelle took her key out and fumbled at the lock. "No more unlocked doors around here! Not after what happened this afternoon. The very thought still makes me feel faint. Why, my husband could have been killed by those thieves!"

"I thought you said nothing was stolen," Charlotte said.

"Oh . . . well, that's right. But still, they broke into my house!"

"Not if the door was unlocked."

"Just never you mind!" Annabelle cried in an exasperated tone. "I'm still going to take extra precautions from now on. What if that one they arrested broke out during the night and burst in on us—two defenseless women all alone?"

"Don't I wish!" Charlotte said under her breath.

"Well, here we are, my dear. It's not much, but it's home. And I want you to consider it your home until we can contact your family and make other arrangements."

Charlotte came into the living room but remained very near the door, as if she meant to take flight at any moment.

"Mrs. Delacorte," she said quietly, "I know you're only trying to be hospitable, but I really won't be here that long. I'm about to be married."

"Oh, I know," Annabelle said, beaming. "Major Krantz told me all about it while you were in with the colonel, and I'm so happy for both of you. I think it's just the most romantic thing I've ever heard—you two being separated and then finding each other again way out here."

"We weren't *separated*. I ran away. I didn't want to marry him then, and I certainly don't plan to now. I am going to marry Prince Mateo."

Annabelle took a step back and put a hand over her heart. "You can't mean that wild heathen you performed with in the ring! Why, my dear, he's no more civilized than a red Indian! You come from a fine old Southern family with high standards, traditions, a heritage going back to the *Mayflower*! Major Krantz told me all about Fairview when he dined with us one evening. Do you really think you could take that savage with the gold rings in his ears back to Kentucky to meet your dear mother? Oh, it's too outlandish even to consider!"

Charlotte saw that she was getting nowhere convincing Annabelle Delacorte of her intentions, so she dropped the subject.

The other woman was surveying her now. "Hmm, I think the first thing we'd better do is get you some decent clothes."

Charlotte spread her cape wide and looked down at herself. She didn't think she looked indecent.

"Oh, please, no!" Annabelle cried, covering her eyes. "I don't want to see. The feminine form should at all times be covered and protected, not exhibited in such a vulgar, unnatural manner. Those Gypsies are tasteless heathens to make you display yourself so."

"Mrs. Delacorte, the Gypsy woman who made this costume is neither tasteless nor a heathen. Tamara is one of the most loving, understanding women I've ever met. My mother could take lessons from her!"

"Charlotte, shame on you! You can't mean that."

"No, probably not. My mother is too stubborn to learn anything worth knowing!"

Annabelle patted Charlotte's shoulders. "You're just tired and grumpy after all you've been through, dear. You'll feel better once you've cleaned up and changed. I'll go find something for you to put on."

"I had clothes," she called after her hostess. "Winston Krantz took them when he searched the stable for your husband's *murderer*. Can't I have those back now?"

Annabelle leaned her head out of the bedroom door, an apologetic look on her face. "Oh, I am sorry, dear, but those had to be burned."

"*Burned?*"

"Major Krantz's idea. He was afraid they might be . . . infested."

Charlotte narrowed her brown eyes and took a step toward the woman. "What are you talking about?"

Annabelle glanced this way and that as if afraid someone might overhear. She looked most uncomfortable.

"Oh, you know how unclean those Gypsies are, Charlotte. They never bathe or change clothes. The major only wanted to guard against their lice spreading about the post."

Charlotte exploded. "*Lice?* Those were *my best clothes*! Are you saying you think I might have bugs?"

"Well, of course you don't, my dear. But those others . . . We can't be too careful, now, can we?"

Charlotte thought of the icy water in the stream and the sounds of women laughing and singing as they bathed every morning. She vowed to get even with this petty *gajo* woman and all like her. Suppressing a smirk, Charlotte reached her hand up to her head and scratched vigorously.

Annabelle Delacorte paled. "Oh, dear me! I'd better heat some bathwater immediately!" She left Charlotte scratching and scurried into the kitchen to fire up the old black cookstove.

A dozen armed soldiers shoved, poked, and prodded Mateo to the guardhouse. He considered putting up a fight, but that would have been madness. They all had their guns trained on him, and he guessed correctly that a few of them would have cherished his scalp as a trophy. So he went along quietly, not giving one of them the chance to act the hero.

But once he was inside the guardhouse, a scheme began to form in his mind. The sergeant on duty had been drinking—not heavily, just enough to make him drowsy and less than interested in his new prisoner. Streaming curses across the room, the jailer hustled Mateo into a cell.

Before he could lock the door, Mateo said, "You might as well leave it open. The others will be coming for me soon."

The tall, rangy man squinted at him, seeming to sober up in an instant. "Huh? What'd you say?"

"My people will be here to collect me from your jail anytime now."

"Well, by damn, I don't reckon they'll get you, mister!"

Mateo, still in his scarlet and gold tights, lounged against the back wall, crossing his arms over his broad bare chest, and laughed. "Oh, you don't know my men! Nothing can stop them. I'll be free before dawn."

"Like hell you will! I got my rifle right here and enough ammo to cut down a whole tribe of redskins. Ain't no mangy pack of Gypsies getting in my jail or even near it." The soldier was shouting now.

"I didn't mean to alarm you," Mateo said quietly. "I shouldn't even have mentioned it. At any rate, you won't know when it happens. The *Rom* come on silent feet. Barred gates and locked doors mean nothing to them. One moment you will be sleeping in your chair— snoring, perhaps, and dreaming. The next moment your dreams will vanish, because your throat will be cut from ear to ear."

Smiling broadly, Mateo drew a finger across his own throat while making a slitting sound.

The jailer shuddered. "Je-e-sus!" he breathed. Then he straightened and shook off his look of fear. "You might as well settle yourself down and get some shut-eye, mister. Ain't nobody coming in here tonight to disturb anybody's sleep, much less do any throat-cuttin'."

Pretending to ignore Mateo, the soldier took his seat at the desk.

"You go on and take a nap. I'll wait up for them."

The man whirled back toward the cell door, which he had forgotten to lock since Mateo had drawn his attention away from it. "I ain't shuttin' one single eye as long as you're awake. You hear?"

"Then I'm afraid, my friend, that we are both in for a long night. Unless they come early, that is."

"*They ain't coming!* Now you just shut up about it!"

Mateo did shut up. But by this time, the man was so unnerved that he was jumping at shadows and popping out of his chair at the slightest sound. Pretty soon, after first checking the front door to make sure no one was coming, he pulled a flask from inside his jacket and took a healthy swig to calm his nerves. Mateo watched as the man leaned back and closed his eyes.

Very softly, Mateo began singing an old Gypsy lullaby. The jailer sighed and slipped lower in his chair. Mateo continued singing as he edged toward the unlocked cell door. His time was running short. This was the night of the full moon. He must escape from here, find Charlotte, and be away before it rose. He reached for the door. It creaked on rusty hinges and the jailer was out of his chair in an instant—wide awake.

"Here now!" he shouted. "You get on back in there! How'd you get that door unlocked?"

Once again, Mateo found himself at the business end of a gun. He backed away, his hands up. The lock clicked shut, putting thick bars between him, his freedom, and the woman he loved.

Charlotte felt as if she were locked inside some medieval torture chamber. Her breasts and ribs, accustomed now to loose clothing and natural circulation, chafed inside the corset Mrs. Delacorte had insisted she wear. The bleached muslin gown was starched so stiffly that it could well have stood alone. And the tight little borrowed slippers were blistering her feet. She longed to kick them off but knew the action would only bring on another tirade on propriety from her hostess.

So Charlotte sat ramrod straight on a chair in the

living room, trying to sip her tea daintily while her head whirled with plans of escape. There was no way she could endure this torture for more than a few hours. Besides, she had to free Mateo.

"Charlotte dear, you look charming." Annabelle offered her a motherly smile. "One would never suspect that you've been living with that wild band of Gypsies all these weeks. Why, my dear, you would fit right into any Bostonian drawing room!"

At the mention of Boston, Charlotte's head shot up and her eyes narrowed in suspicion.

"I have a surprise for you. Major Krantz is coming to pay a call this evening."

Charlotte sprang to her aching feet. "I don't want to see—"

There was a knock at the door.

"Too late," Annabelle said brightly. "That's probably your fiancé now. I'll just let him in and then leave the two of you to get reacquainted."

Mateo's jailer was snoring. One hand dangled limply over the side of his chair. The empty flask lay where it had dropped on the floor. Not even the fly buzzing around the man's face woke him. The time had come.

Without making a sound, Mateo slipped a thin dagger from its sheath inside his boot and walked to his cell door. The sun was just going down, which meant he had enough time before the moon rose. Quietly he slipped the blade of his knife into the lock and turned. It clicked and opened.

The whole post was celebrating tonight. Custer had decided to make a day of it—first the circus and then a barbecue for his soldiers. There were a few sentries posted around the walls, but their watchful eyes were turned outward, searching for Indians or for Gypsies coming to rescue the prisoner. The layout of the fort was such that Mateo could slip out the back door of the guardhouse, steal around behind the stables, and reach the back window of the Delacorte quarters. He had heard Custer say that Charlotte would be there. In no time at all, the two of them would be away and safe again in each other's arms.

Mateo met no resistance as he made his way around behind the buildings. For a time, it looked as if one of Custer's hounds might give him trouble. But the half-wild dog responded to Mateo's *Romani* words and let him pass. When he was in back of the officers' quarters, he checked window after window before finding the right one.

It stood open the barest crack. The room was dark, but the door was open and he could see through the hallway into the living room.

He heard Charlotte's voice before he saw her. "Winnie, it's very good to see you again."

"Charlotte, my dear!"

Mateo felt his heart twisting as the two of them moved into his line of vision. The officer took Charlotte into his arms and held her for a moment, kissing her cheek. She seemed to welcome his affection.

Mateo studied her for a long time. The *gajos* had stolen her from him already. She was no longer his Golden One in loose blouse and scarlet petticoats. She wore her own kind's stiff clothing along with their closed, smug expression. She looked every inch the *gajo* with her waist drawn in, her breasts bound and pushed up unnaturally high. She appeared the way she had at their very first meeting—foreign, like someone not of his world.

"I've heard from your mother, Charlotte. She's very distressed over your disappearance. You gave her quite a turn, leaving that way."

"And what about you, Winnie? Were you distressed when I left?"

"Charlotte, my darling, you know I was! Why, I expected to be your husband by the very next day!"

Mateo watched Charlotte's head droop in a dejected manner and heard words that stabbed him deeply. "I'm sorry, Winnie. I've hurt you. It was a terrible thing for me to do. Can you ever forgive me?"

"Charlotte, Charlotte," Krantz crooned, taking her into his arms once more. "There's nothing to forgive. You're here now. Everything will be all right. I promise you."

Mateo's blood boiled. He felt like climbing through the window and tearing her from the other man's embrace. He pulled the window open and poised himself to enter—then froze. The major was lifting Charlotte's lips to his. The next instant, he was kissing her—tenderly, possessively. His white *gajo*'s hands caressed her while their kiss became ever more intimate. Charlotte made no protest.

This, then, was her choice.

Dropping to the ground once more—his emotions running the gamut from heartsick pain to a desire to kill—Mateo stormed away toward the stable. A madness was upon him, but not from the moon. This madness came from the heart, breaking now from the sight of Charlotte in another man's arms.

He found only one of his stallions in the corral, Velacore, Charlotte's favorite mount. The others, he knew, were on the parade ground, being admired and ridden by the off-duty soldiers. One whistle brought Velacore sailing over the fence to him. Before the horse could come to a full stop, Mateo leaped onto its back and urged the animal toward the Gypsy camp.

The ride was fast. The wind stung Mateo's eyes and cut at his bare chest. Twice—blinded by his rage—he guided the horse into low-hanging trees. The branches whipped at him, slashing his flesh, but he never felt them. The pain in his heart obliterated all others.

Charlotte Buckland was gone from him . . . forever.

Charlotte pushed her way out of Winston's embrace. She was trying to contain her anger, but it wasn't easy.

"Winnie, please. No!" she said firmly.

"But Charlotte!"

She looked him squarely in the eyes and shook her head. "There are no buts about it, Winnie. I don't love you. That's all."

He started toward her. "You could learn to, my dear. I'm not a bad sort."

She put her hands out and pushed gently against his chest, forcing him to keep his distance. "Winston, I am in love with Prince Mateo. I thought you would have guessed that when you surprised us in the stable this afternoon."

"But you were another woman then. You weren't Charlotte Buckland. You were the Golden One. I supposed he'd cast some sort of Gypsy spell over you."

She smiled. "Oh, he's cast a spell over me all right! But it's one that is very real and lasts a lifetime. I'm going to marry him, Winnie."

"You can't be serious!"

"I am! I'm going to Colonel Custer this very night to beg for his release. Then we're going away together. Not back to his people. They don't accept me. Funny, isn't it? We're both outcasts. So we plan to make our own world."

"You really mean it, don't you?" The major's voice was quiet now, resigned.

"Yes. And I'd hoped you might help me convince your colonel to free him."

Krantz smiled and took a deep breath. "If you don't want me for a husband, Charlotte, how would you feel about having me as a father?"

"What?"

"Well, I know it's sudden, but your mother wrote to me and I answered her letter with a bit more emotion than was quite proper. I'm afraid that any day now I'm going to get a letter back, demanding that I set a date since I compromised her—verbally, at least. Besides, I think I've been enamored of her since the first day I came to Fairview."

"Oh, Winston!" Charlotte cried, running to hug him. "That's wonderful news!" She stood back for a moment, staring at him. "But if that's the case, why did you put me through all this tonight?"

He shrugged. "It seemed the gentlemanly thing to do, since we were promised to each other."

Just then, a cry rang out through the courtyard. "Escape! The prisoner's gotten away!"

Charlotte whirled, her hand at her throat.

"Oh, God! The man must be mad!" Winston groaned.

"What do you mean?" Charlotte asked anxiously.

"He's going to get himself shot!"

"They'll never catch him," she insisted.

"Would he leave here without you, Charlotte?"

Slowly, she shook her head.

"Then his life is in very real danger, I'm afraid."

Annabelle Delacorte came flying in the front door just then, her face flushed with excitement. "Oh, thank the Lord, you're all right, Charlotte! I was afraid that dreadful man might have come here to take you away with him. But he didn't. I'm so relieved."

"What do you mean, Mrs. Delacorte?"

"Well, he's long gone. He took the one Gypsy horse that was still in the corral and rode off. I doubt they'll catch up with him, but it doesn't matter as long as you're here and safe."

"Mateo's *gone*?" The word came hollowly from Charlotte's lips. How could he have ridden away without her? Had his freedom meant more to him than their promises to each other?

She ran to the front door, scanning the parade ground. What she saw chilled her blood. The moon—full and fiery—was hanging in the black night sky.

"Oh, dear God!" she murmured. "How could I have forgotten?"

"Forgotten what, my dear? I don't understand," Annabelle said from behind her.

But Charlotte never gave the woman an answer. Kicking off the uncomfortable slippers and hiking up her long skirt, she raced out onto the parade ground. Only one of Mateo's stallions stood riderless. It never dawned on her that no one but its owner could ride the Black Devil. She scrambled onto his back and dug in her bare heels. The huge horse screamed and reared, trying to pitch her off, but she clung to its mane and screamed, "Open the gates!"

The soldier on duty had little choice with the crazed stallion bearing down on him. It was either open up or see the horse and rider killed and himself possibly injured in the fracas. The wide gate groaned open and the Black Devil, with Charlotte Buckland hanging on for dear life, shot away into the darkness.

George Custer stormed across the compound. "Why in hell did you let her go, Corporal?"

"Sorry, sir, but I didn't want to see the little lady get hurt."

The two men stood staring as the raging animal with the white-clad woman clinging desperately to its back disappeared into the night.

Custer shook his head. "Well, I guess we've seen the

last of the lot of them now. I just hope she doesn't break her lovely neck on that killer horse. Close that gate, soldier.''

The colonel would have thought his words prophetic if he had been on the scene a few moments later.

Charlotte's whole body ached from trying to stay with the Black Devil. He would gallop, then slow his pace, pitch and rear, sidestep, then pick up speed again. Finally, the raging animal pointed himself toward one of the very limbs that had earlier slashed Mateo's chest and face—and raced straight for it.

She saw it coming, but there was no time to react. The spiky branches tore at her, and the blow to her head knocked her momentarily senseless. Then Charlotte felt herself falling. Her head struck the ground with a sickening thud. She lay very still, gasping for breath.

"Mateo," she whispered. "Mateo, where are you?"

Speaking the words stabbed her chest with pain. Her head throbbed. Her vision clouded. She seemed to be slipping deep into a cold, dark pool. The instant before unconsciousness claimed her, she had one last clear vision. The huge silver moon gleamed down from the blackness, filling the night with evil and Charlotte Buckland with a terrible hopelessness.

Chapter 19

The Gypsies heard a horse's hooves thundering into camp and peered cautiously from their tents. It might have been the Devil himself they saw astride his hellish stallion, horse and rider silhouetted there against the campfire flames. But no. . . .

"Mateo! It's Prince Mateo!" The message was passed from tent to tent in awed and frightened whispers.

Never before had any of them seen him abroad on the night of the full moon. But his appearance—the wildness of his black eyes, the grim set of his features, and his blood-streaked chest—told them all that Valencia's curse was upon him. His mount, too, seemed affected as it reared and screamed, lathering at the bit and pawing the air.

Mateo—half-crazed with rage and grief—searched the clearing, begging silently for some end to his pain. He was here now, with his people, but the place seemed empty and cold. Charlotte had been his *familia*. Without

275

her, his existence was meaningless. He was only a shadow of the man he had been. He was tempted to ride back to the fort and tear her from the major's arms. Why had he left in the first place? What was he doing here?

"Mateo!" He heard his name spoken urgently. A hand grasped his leg.

"Tamara! What do you want?" He looked down into her beautiful face. Her eyes were wide and glittering in the firelight. She was smiling.

"Your mother wants you."

He whirled the stallion away, breaking Tamara's hold on him.

"I can't go to her now. I have to go back for Charlotte."

"No!" she said. "See your mother before you do anything."

He had no chance to decide which he would do. The next instant, the old queen was standing beside his horse, her hands raised toward him in a gesture of benediction.

"Come, my son. There are words you must hear."

Mateo wanted to gallop away, but Zolande's tone of voice and the fire in her dark eyes proved hypnotic. Slowly, he dismounted and followed her toward the tent. She poured wine and told him to drink. He had no power to refuse her. The heady potion calmed him. His breathing and heartbeat slowed to normal. His head cleared.

"Now, my son, tell me what has happened."

"They have Charlotte . . . at the fort. The man she was promised to has claimed her, but I mean to steal her back. *She's mine!*" Again his voice quivered with near hysteria.

"Then why did you leave her there?"

"They would have killed me."

His mother shook her head, letting him know that she didn't believe his words. Her son was not a man who feared death.

"The truth, Mateo," she said gently, touching his cheek with her palm.

His head drooped. He couldn't meet her gaze. "She doesn't want me, Mother. She went to him willingly, with never a thought of my love for her. You were right all along. It was not meant to be."

"Mateo, listen to me and hear me well." The queen raised her son's face, forcing him to look at her. "The truth we see with our eyes is more often than not a lie. Did she tell you that she no longer loved you?"

"No. We never had a chance to speak together."

"Then you only *assume* she wants the other. Is your love for her so shallow that a small wave is able to empty your heart of it? This is not the passionate man I know as my son."

Mateo frowned up at her. Something had changed. Did he understand his mother correctly? Was she urging him to go back to Charlotte? She, above all others, had been against the match from the start.

"Mother?" His searching eyes asked the rest of his question.

Zolande smiled and nodded. "*She* is your answer, Mateo! She is the answer for all of our troubles."

Seeing his confusion, the queen went on, "Mateo, this is the night of the full moon."

"Yes, I know."

"Well, look at you! Are you raving, thrashing, trying to do harm to yourself?"

He looked down at his body. It was not quaking. His hands were steady. His vision was clear. The gashes in his chest still oozed blood, but not because he had raked his own flesh in a frenzy of moon madness.

"No," he breathed, almost unable to believe it himself. "The curse has not come tonight."

The queen smiled and leaned forward to kiss his cheek. "Nor will it come ever again. Mateo, my darling son, if my suspicions are correct, you have found your golden Gypsy!''

"Charlotte?"

Zolande nodded. ''I suspect so. And she still loves you, no matter what you may imagine at the moment. Go to her. Bring her back to be your bride. At last, the curse will end forever!''

''But how can that be? She is not a Gypsy!''

The old queen smiled. ''Are you so sure, Mateo? Charlotte Buckland possesses a strength and a fire that I have never observed in a *gajo*. Trust an old woman's intuition, my son, and do what you must.''

Mateo grasped his frail, little mother in a rib-crushing hug. Then he spun away, out of the tent. He was on Velacore's back and galloping off into the night in the flicker of an eye.

Had it not been for the white muslin gown loaned to her by Annabelle Delacorte, Mateo might have passed Charlotte by. But the same full moon that had caused him such grief all his life reflected its silver glow on her still, white form, drawing his attention.

He leaped down from Velacore's back, murmuring her name. But his relief at finding her turned to heart-wrenching dread the moment he touched her. Her flesh was cold, her breathing labored.

''Charlotte! Speak to me. Can you hear me, my Golden One?''

She moaned softly, but her eyes never opened.

Mateo heard a familiar snort and his head jerked up. The Black Devil stood nearby, head down as if in apology.

''Mother of God,'' Mateo breathed. ''She rode you?'' He had seen more than one man killed simply trying to mount the huge devil horse. And Charlotte had known the danger; he had warned her time and time again. If ever he needed proof of her love, this was it. She had risked death to be with him.

The thought of death spurred him to action. He must get her back to the camp immediately. Tamara would know what to do. He was not dealing simply with the woman he loved any longer. Charlotte Buckland was the golden Gypsy!

The horse that had caused the accident carried them safely toward the camp. It seemed to Mateo that the Black Devil realized what a terrible thing he had done and was now trying to make amends. The big stallion stepped lightly, taking pains to avoid rough stretches of ground so that his precious burden would suffer no further damage. Mateo cradled Charlotte's unconscious form in his arms, talking to her quietly all the way back to the Gypsy camp.

His heart ached with her pain and he prayed silently that Sara-la-Kali would see fit to spare her. As for him, he scarcely deserved any notice from the saint after what he had put this woman through.

All was in readiness when they arrived. Tamara had known before they returned that Charlotte had been hurt. Her twisted nightmares of the night before had come clear to her in a flash. A time of trial was upon them. They would save the golden Gypsy, or they would lose everything.

"I knew you would want her in your tent, Mateo, so I have made a pallet for her," Tamara said. "Bring her quickly, but do be careful with her."

"She's hardly breathing," Mateo said in a pained voice.

"As long as her heart is beating there is hope. Put her down and then go away for a time."

"No! I'm staying here with her!"

Tamara knew there was no time to argue with him. "Very well. But stay out of my way!"

Mateo slumped in a far corner of the tent, his whole body aching as he stared at Charlotte's bruised and battered form. Her face, arms, and throat were torn where branches had hit her. A bright crimson gash in her forehead yawned wide like an ugly grin. And her right arm rested at an awkward angle. He had done this to her. It was all his fault. He felt like tearing his hair, ripping his clothes, rending his flesh. He richly deserved all the suffering the moon madness had ever brought him. If only he could tell her he was sorry and have her hear him and understand.

Tamara bathed Charlotte's face, put a compress on her head wound, then turned to Mateo. "Give me your *churi*."

Mateo clutched the sharp knife, refusing to hand it over. "I won't let you bleed her. She's lost too much blood already."

"You talk crazy, Mateo! Would I do such a stupid thing? I must cut her out of these tight clothes. She can't breathe laced up like this. Give it to me!"

He handed her the silver dagger, remembering how it had once drawn Charlotte's blood. The memory of that night by the stream brought a fresh flood of remorse. Why hadn't he been able to admit to himself that night that she was the only woman for him? His foolishness had cost them both so much. He had wanted her then just as he wanted her now. He ached with his need and his despair.

Carefully, never allowing the blade to slip, Tamara sliced through the soiled muslin. Soon Charlotte lay with her constricted breasts heaving, trying to gasp more air into her lungs.

"Turn away your eyes!" Tamara ordered Mateo, the knife poised to slit the corset.

He glared at his cousin for a moment but finally did as she commanded. But the sound of the tight satin giving way beneath the knife's sharp edge soon brought his gaze darting back. Intent on her work, Tamara never noticed.

Mateo's mouth went dry and his palms grew sweaty when he looked at Charlotte's bare breasts. They were marked from the whalebone ribbing of the corset. As she lay on her back, they seemed like small, battered children, cringing away from more punishment. Could these pale orbs be the same warm, honey-flavored breasts his hands and mouth knew so well? He ran his tongue over his dry lips and a shudder twisted through him.

"Several ribs are cracked," Tamara said after running her hands delicately over Charlotte's sides. "She's lucky, though. She might have broken more than her arm when she fell from that crazed horse of yours."

"She knew not to ride him," Mateo answered defensively.

Tamara gave him a hard look and sniffed indignantly. "That animal should be destroyed!"

"No. No, don't!" The words were a bare whisper—the first Charlotte had uttered.

"Darling!" Mateo sprang to her side, clutching her left hand to his heart. Her eyes opened for an instant and a faint smile touched her lips. Then she lapsed back into unconsciousness.

"Mateo, please," Tamara said. "If you are going to stay in here, you must get out of my way. She needs help, not you pawing over her."

He went back to his corner, thoroughly chastised by his gentle cousin's words, but feeling a lightness in his heart from having heard Charlotte's voice. She would get better. She had to!

But as one day dragged into another, Mateo began to wonder. Charlotte was not recovering as she should. At times, her eyes would flicker open and he would see that familiar spark of life and laughter in their warm brown depths. But it would only last an instant. Then her awareness would fade. She would give him a confused look, frown, and lapse back into unconsciousness.

Once she spoke his name in one of these brief, lucid interludes. His heart took flight. He kissed her and gloried in her passionate response. Then she slept—an almost natural sleep. When she awoke the next day, she stared at him with fear in her eyes and asked, "Who are you? What are you doing in my room?"

After two weeks of this, Mateo sought out Tamara and demanded, "When is she going to be herself again? You must do something!"

Tamara was at her wits' end. She had tried everything. Charlotte's wounds were healing, her broken arm was on the mend, but there was some deeper damage that refused to respond to herbs, compresses, and Gypsy charms. Only Charlotte herself could bring about this ailment's cure. Whether or not she had the will to do it, no one could say.

"I'm sorry, Mateo," Tamara said. "There's nothing more I can do for her. Her fate is in other hands now. We must simply trust that what is meant to happen will transpire."

"No!" Mateo stormed. "I will not allow Fate to be the ruling factor here. I love her. I need her. I won't let her go!"

The two of them had been talking just outside Mateo's tent. They both turned when they suddenly heard Charlotte's voice from inside, calling Mateo's name.

Tamara touched his arm and smiled. "Now is your chance. Go and show her this great and powerful love of yours. Perhaps it is just the medicine she needs."

Mateo didn't have to be told a second time. He tore open the tent flap and went in. Charlotte lay on the wolf skins, looking pale and ever so fragile.

Winter was coming on and the first harsh winds were blowing down from the north. A brazier burned warmly in the tent, casting its golden glow on Charlotte's face. The fire seemed to come from within her as Mateo gazed down at his lover. She reached her hand up to him. He took it in his and knelt beside her to kiss her cool fingertips.

"Charlotte," he whispered, "I've been waiting for you. I wanted to tell you how sorry I am . . . how much I love you."

She stared at him oddly for a moment, as if trying to place him. His heart sank. But the smile that soon took possession of her face warmed him through and through.

"You've been here with me all the time, haven't you?"

He nodded. "I couldn't leave you again, my love."

"Again?" She looked confused once more.

He drew her gently into his arms. "Never mind, darling. It will all come back to you in time. For now it's enough that you remember who I am and what we mean to each other."

The man holding her felt warm and good. Charlotte knew him, yes. She had seen his face hovering over hers every time she'd awakened from her strange sleep. Even in her dreams, he was there. He rode a black horse and shone like the sun. He was a good man, an honorable man. He was not at all like the other dark shadow who haunted her nightmares. But somehow in her mind, they seemed like twins—two faces of the same coin. Who were they, and how had they come into her life? And why did she writhe with pain when, in her dreams, he took her to him by the full moon's glow?

He was kissing her lips now and she responded. His mouth was hot and soft. He tasted of fruit and wine. She knew the taste of him. She remembered the feeling of his hands on her body . . . his hardness pressed close against her. All the fear in her fled when she was in his arms. There was a rightness about being close to him.

"Charlotte, I want to make love to you," he whispered into her ear

She searched his face, his eyes. Was he merely stating a fact or asking her permission? She couldn't be sure. She wanted him, too. But how could she give herself to this stranger? Still, she could see the pain deep in his eyes. It was her duty—and her joy—to draw it from him unto herself.

His hand was on her shoulder, gently easing away the fabric of her robe to bare her flesh to his lips. She closed her eyes and allowed the touch of his mouth on her skin to send a wonderful warmth surging through her. He was so very gentle with her. It felt so good to be held this way. She sighed.

But a moment later, his bold hand ventured beneath the robe. Startled by his intimacy, she tried to pull away. He quieted her with strange, foreign-sounding words, and soon his hand cupped her breast, draining away her resistance. He seemed to know her body well. He knew just where to touch her and how to bring a rush of pleasure surging through her. She had been in pain for so long, it seemed—*forever*. Now she was hard-pressed to deny herself these exquisite sensations, even knowing that in the end more pain would come of it. She gave herself up to him, luxuriating in his knowing caresses.

"Charlotte, oh, my *sunaki bal,* I've wanted this for so long. You'll never know how much I've needed you these past weeks. I was so afraid you weren't coming back to me."

Coming back to him? She wondered where she had been. Her brain was spinning. She remembered now that when she'd awakened a short time before, she had been repeating a name from a dream. What was it?

Mateo! That was it! This man must be the one called Mateo!

She sighed the name aloud and he crushed her close, sure that she remembered everything now. The thought made him bold. He leaned her back against her pillows and opened her robe. She struggled against his hands, but very weakly. The excitement he aroused in her had drained away her small wellspring of strength.

"Be still, darling," he murmured. "Let me love you."

She lay back with her body exposed to his exploring eyes and his caressing hands and lips. Tenderly, he fondled her breasts before dipping his head low to suckle there. She tangled the fingers of her left hand in his dark hair, holding his mouth to the spot while shattering bursts of pleasure surged through her body. What was he doing to her? Could she stand much more? Already her eyes wanted to close, her strength was waning. But she fought to stay awake. She wanted him. She needed the power of his body and spirit to nourish her own, just as she knew he needed her to absorb his madness with her love.

"Please, Mateo," she whispered.

He barely heard the words, but they shot him through with longing.

His hands were on her belly now. He drew them down her legs and up the insides of her thighs. She quivered convulsively and moaned. Her eyes closed. Her hand groped for him, but he was out of her reach.

Then she felt the hot pulse of him, eager and ready to enter her. She relaxed, knowing—without realizing how she knew—that in the next instant she would be filled and satisfied, and Mateo would be cleansed.

He entered her ever so slowly, careful not to put undue pressure on her body. His movements were a tantalizing exercise in slow motion. In . . . and out, in . . . and out. She could feel every inch of him. When he drew away, her body tried to clutch him back. And all the while his hands played over her skin—teasing, exciting, raising her to a fever pitch.

When the moment of exquisite pleasure came, they shared it. Charlotte felt him now—filling her, anointing her, loving her as never before. She felt released from the pain of her body, the confusion in her mind, only to have the awful curse attack her senses in the next instant. But only one thing mattered: she and this man named Mateo were one. The two of them were like a great, soaring bird, flying toward the sun on shared wings . . . in one magnificent body. She could endure anything to have his love.

Then the terrible pain, which had racked her soul and rent her mind, vanished as quickly as it had come. The sheer release brought with it total exhaustion. Before Mateo could speak his love to her in words, Charlotte had once more lapsed into unconsciousness. He stared down at her still form, stricken.

"What did you do to her, Mateo?" Tamara demanded angrily. "I've told you not to disturb her. Now just look. She has slipped away again. Did you upset her in some way?"

Sick at heart, Mateo looked down at the pale woman on the pallet and whispered, "I made love to her."

"Mateo!" Tamara's voice betrayed her shock. "How could you?"

"How could I not? We needed each other."

"Enough to bring on a relapse?" In an unaccustomed tirade, Tamara showered Mateo with a string of *Romani* oaths. "Men! I will never understand any of you!"

"I didn't harm her, Tamara. I was very gentle."

She looked at him as if he were a lunatic trying to

convince her that he was perfectly sane. "Mateo, did she even know who you were?"

"Yes, I think she did."

"*You think?* You mean you aren't even sure? You are mad! Don't you see that you may have done her permanent damage? She may never come out of this."

"But Tamara, she wanted it as much as I!"

"You mean she didn't fight you?"

"No."

"That proves nothing! How does a sick kitten fight off a tiger?"

They both stared down at Charlotte for a moment. Her breathing was so deep they could tell she was at some level beyond normal sleep.

"I think we must send for her family," Tamara said finally. "That major at Fort Leavenworth knows how to reach them, doesn't he?"

"It's that bad?"

Tamara, taking pity on Mateo, touched his arm. "I'm afraid so," she said softly. "And I don't understand her illness. It is as if some terrible evil has a grip on her." She shook her head sadly.

"I won't let them take her away!" Mateo's voice sounded in a sudden boom of rage.

Hearing him, Charlotte stirred slightly in her sleep, but neither of them noticed.

"You don't have to worry about that right now, Mateo. No one is going to take her anywhere. She's too ill to be moved."

Charlotte was someplace far away, but trying desperately to get back. He was there. She had heard him speak. She fought to part a way through the dark storm clouds fogging her brain, but lightning flashed on all sides of her, forcing her back when she tried to surface.

The full moon rose, blinding her and making her cry out and turn away. But the great silver sphere seemed to control her mind and body. Why was the moon so evil now, when once it had been her friend? Nothing made sense anymore. Where was she? Who was she?

Silhouetted against the moon, other menaces threatened. An evil, dark-haired Gypsy and a woman wearing a purple scarf about her throat were coming for her. She tried desperately to get away, but the man lunged at her. The woman laughed and laughed—a terrible sound. She ran and ran, but they were everywhere, blocking her path.

When she did escape at last, she was lost in a forest filled with wild animals. A bear with a ring through its nose chased her. Then she was on the back of a black horse that breathed fire and raced with her at cyclone speed. She screamed and cried. Her body ached from the pounding force of his gallop. Pain shot through her fingers, cramping them so that she had to release her hold. Suddenly she was falling. Down and down and down. The wind buffeted her body. Rain lashed her face. Jagged lightning flashed and she saw Mateo's face. She called to him, frantic now, but he turned away from her once more.

Down and down. Her fall seemed never to end. Her brain whirled and her spirit seemed about to be sucked from her body. If only her feet would touch earth, she might be able to hold on.

Then horror constricted her heart. She saw where she was about to land. The shining, distorted face of the full moon glared up at her, grinning like some demon from hell.

She heard her own scream just before she was swallowed up by the evil, smothering silver mass, which tore her body with pain even as it took possession of her very soul.

Chapter 20

Jemima Buckland didn't waste any time. She was packing to head out west the moment she'd read Winston Krantz's first letter. No one, including her late husband, had ever written to her in such glowing terms. If ever a man's words held an invitation, the major's did.

And it wasn't even his old Bostonian money that lured her, much as she wanted to save Fairview from the auction block. No! She really felt something for the man. In middle age—wonder of wonders—she was experiencing the euphoria of a first-time bride. Her marriage to Charlotte's father had been connived at by her aunt and uncle. Albert Buckland had been a good man; no one disputed that. She simply hadn't loved him. In fact, she had fought her relations tooth and nail, trying to get out of that match. But she had been young then—vulnerable and malleable. She had disgraced herself back home in Maryland, so she'd been forced into a marriage not of her choosing.

But Winston Krantz—here was another matter entirely. The man was refined, understanding, attractive in his own way, *and* he had money. What more could a widow ask?

"You've lost your mind, 'Mima Lewis!" Granny Fate ranted.

"The name is *Buckland*, if you please! And I know exactly what I'm doing! Winnie does everything but get down on one knee in this letter." She waved the fervid missive under the old woman's nose. "By the time he receives my reply and has had a few days to think about it, he'll have a parson in tow when he meets me at the train. I've never been more sure of anything in my life!"

The two women were in Fairview's front parlor, surrounded by half-packed trunks and valises. Fatima Buckland couldn't say she hated to see her daughter-in-law go—it was simply a matter of not relishing the thought of any woman acting like a fool by throwing herself at a man. What would 'Mima do if she got out there and found she'd misread his letter and his intentions? The whole idea didn't make a thimbleful of sense!

"What about Charlotte?" demanded Granny Fate. "Have you given any thought to her feelings?"

Jemima turned a hard look on the older woman. "Did either of you give any thought to *my* feelings or Winston's when you helped her run off in the middle of the night on the very eve of her wedding? No, quite frankly, I haven't bothered to consider her. I don't feel any obligation to do so. Besides, Winston's letter proves that he was clearly interested in me before I offered him Charlotte as his bride. If only he'd been more vocal at the time, he and I might be married already."

"So your plan is to pack up and go traipsing off—just like that?" Granny Fate snapped her golden-ringed fingers.

Jemima snapped hers right back. *"Just like that!"*

"You're acting crazy, 'Mima!" Granny Fate knew her

words were falling on deaf ears, but she had to try. Her Albert would want it.

Before Jemima could answer, the knocker at the front door banged loudly.

"Who on earth could that be?" Jemima said

She hurried to the door and opened it to find a messenger. "Special mail for you, ma'am. All the way from Leavenworth, Kansas."

Jemima snatched the letter and shut the door, dismissing the courier without so much as the offer of a cup of tea. She stared at it, almost afraid to open the envelope when she recognized Winston Krantz's handwriting. Would it be a proposal or a rejection?

"Who was it, 'Mima?" Granny Fate asked

"A messenger," she answered distractedly. "He's brought a letter from Winnie."

"Well, land's sake, girl, open it up!"

Jemima tore into it, feeling her heart race as she scanned the page, then read it aloud to Granny Fate.

Fort Leavenworth
November 12, 1870

My dear Jemima,

I have good news and bad. First, Charlotte has been located. She has been staying with a band of Gypsies all this time. Please do not be alarmed by this news. Although she was apparently kidnapped by them some time ago, they seem to have treated her well. However, she has been injured in a recent riding accident. The bad news is that she is not recovering as speedily as she should. The post surgeon feels that her main problem may be of the mind rather than the body.

Prince Mateo, the Gypsy who has taken over her care, asked me to write to you, pleading that you and Fatima make the trip out here as soon as you can arrange it. The post surgeon agrees that having family members close at hand may well speed Charlotte's recovery. Please come, Jemima! Charlotte, for all her faults as a daughter, needs her mother now.

And, my dearest Jemima, I need you, too. I received your heart-warming letter just this morning. I cannot begin to tell you what your words meant to me. Even before hearing from you, I spoke with Charlotte on the subject (the very day of her accident, in fact). Although she could never accept me as her husband, she agreed wholeheartedly to having me as a stepfather. She has given our marriage her blessing, my dear. Nothing stands in our way now except the miles that separate us. Hurry, dear lady, and fill this empty life with your sweet warmth!

I have taken the liberty of enclosing a bank draft for the amount of two train tickets and expenses. I will be looking forward to your arrival, my dear. Please hurry!

> *Ever your loving and obedient servant,*
> *Winston Krantz*

Jemima Buckland stood very still, clutching the letter to her heart. This was almost too good to be true. Although she would never have let Granny Fate know it, she hadn't been entirely sure that Winnie would accept her. Now that worry was erased from her mind. She would be his bride!

And as much as she had ranted and raved against Charlotte and her obstinate behavior, deep down she had been worried about her daughter. She was relieved to know where Charlotte was at last. As for her injuries, Jemima felt confident from the tone of Winston's letter that Charlotte would recover fully. She needed her mother, that was all.

Jemima was so preoccupied with her own thoughts that she didn't notice the sparkle in Granny Fate's dark eyes or the secretive smile on her face. "Gypsies!" the woman muttered to herself.

Far from disturbing her, the thought that her granddaughter had been kidnapped by Mateo's people seemed the most romantic escapade she could imagine. And Charlotte was "being taken care of" by a Gypsy prince, at that! It was thrilling.

"Well, what are you standing around mooning about, 'Mima? Let's finish packing these bags!" Granny Fate said, interrupting her daughter-in-law's daydreaming.

The two women launched themselves into a flurry of activity.

Queen Zolande, alone in her tent, fretted over Charlotte's condition. If the woman didn't recover, the curse would continue.

"She can't die! She has no reason to. Mateo loves her and needs her." Zolande glared up at an ancient portrait of Sara-la-Kali hanging over her bed and shook a fist at the lovely saint. The queen had given up praying and was now threatening. "I won't have it, do you hear? She *will* stay alive to marry my son!"

The old queen slumped in her chair. She shouldn't let herself get so upset. If she made herself ill, poor Tamara would have two patients to deal with, and she needed all her energy to save Charlotte Buckland.

To distract herself from her worries, Zolande recounted the tale of Valencia's curse in her mind. The Gypsies prided themselves on their verbal accounts. No incident in their history was ever lost, although no written records existed. Tales were told and told again—a thousand times over around the campfires.

The queen thought of Xendar's disgrace and Valencia's fury. Mateo, through his father, was descended directly from the child of the forbidden union. But where did Charlotte Buckland fit into the scheme of things? The girl obviously had no idea she was of Gypsy ancestry. The old queen shook her head. The more she worried over the question, the more muddled the problem became in her mind. She would simply have to trust in Fate.

"And in love," she added aloud.

"Excuse me, my queen," Tamara's voice broke in. "I called from outside, but you seemed to be napping."

Zolande motioned for the woman to come in. "Not napping, only lost in thought. What is it, my dear?"

Tamara's face showed the strain of her constant vigil at Charlotte's bedside. She said, "I don't know what to do, Queen Zolande. Her illness is beyond my comprehension. I have tried everything, but nothing helps her. If she should die . . ."

"Silence! Do not even think such a thought. She *must* live! She will live for Mateo's sake. Now that he may have found his golden Gypsy, she cannot slip away. It would be the end of us all."

"Mateo has returned from Fort Leavenworth."

The queen's eyes widened. "They did not arrest him?"

"No. He is free and unharmed. They even returned his stallions. He says their yellow-haired colonel was most understanding."

"What happened, then?"

"Major Krantz has sent for Charlotte's mother and grandmother. And their physician has come to look at her."

"Good. Perhaps he has thought of some cure we have overlooked. You say her family is coming?"

Tamara nodded.

"That is good! Go back to Charlotte now, child. She needs your strength."

"Yes, my queen."

Unfortunately, the strength Charlotte needed most was being denied her. Mateo, morose from guilt and grief, had kept to himself in the woods for several days—thinking, fasting, and praying to Sara-la-Kali. He remained close enough to camp to find out if there was any change in Charlotte's condition, but he dared not trust himself near her after what had happened. He was sure that his lovemaking had done her grave harm. So now, although he ached for her every moment, he denied himself any thoughts of pleasure, passion, or love. He had cast himself out in much the same manner that Valencia exiled Xendar so long ago. He knew his ancestor's pain.

Twilight was coming on, and great, purple clouds boiled up on the horizon. Mateo strode back and forth, his heavy boots crushing a path through the winter-hard buffalo grass. The day was cold, the air frosty, but he never noticed. His bare chest—crisscrossed with many wounds inflicted by his own sharp blade during the past few days—took the full brunt of the winter wind. He dared it to freeze him! He tramped on, head down, eyes clouded, communing silently with the spirit of the north wind.

Surely there must be something he could do. He felt so helpless. He dropped to his knees before an altar of stones he had erected for his private use. A strange, half-faced image of Sara-la-Kali stared down on him. The ancient icon of ivory and gold—shattered in rage almost a century before he was born—rested atop the pile of rocks. He mumbled a few prayers, but his mind wandered and he broke off in midsentence. Was the holy Handmaiden even listening to him? It didn't seem so. He had offered her everything he could think of. He would give up his right to the throne. He would never perform again. He would leave his *familia* and live among strangers, if only he could have Charlotte by his side. For days now, he had shunned food, shelter, companionship. How much more could she ask? He buried his face in his hands and sighed wearily.

Suddenly, the wind shifted and the aroma of roasting venison drifted to him from the nearby Gypsy camp. His stomach muscles contracted at the smell, twisting and complaining of emptiness. He grabbed his belly convulsively, but he rejoiced in the pain. It was only just! Why should he be free of suffering while the woman he loved lay wasting away?

He sat up abruptly with the crystal-clear vision that often comes from fasting. At last, Sara-la-Kali had answered his prayers! He should have realized his mistake before now. What did the saint care if he slashed his flesh to ribbons, starved it, or froze it to solid ice? These were punishments of the body, not the soul. In order to appease her, he must give up what meant the most to him in all the world. He must tear out his own heart and present it to her as a sacrifice. Only then would she believe in his faith in her and his love for Charlotte Buckland. Only then would she allow his golden Gypsy to live.

But what sacrifice would be great enough to satisfy Sara the Black?

Suddenly, Mateo knew what he must do!

He stripped off his boots and buckskin britches and waded into the icy waters of the bathing stream. Plunging below the surface, he let the current carry him where it would. His body grew numb with cold and his lungs burned for air, but still he went with the flow. Not until the blackness began to close over his open eyes and he had his sign would he return to the world above.

At first he was blind in the cold water, but soon his sight cleared and the holy Handmaiden provided him with visions. He knew a sacrifice must be made. But what? *What?*

As the current dragged him along, pounding him, bruising his flesh against boulder and bank, his life unfolded before him. He saw himself as a small boy—in Russia first, riding over the mounds of snow in a bright red sleigh pulled by a matched team of four gray horses. Silver sleigh bells tinkled in the crisp air, and he could once again smell the familiar odors of leather and lathered horseflesh. Then he was in Spain, riding along the golden beach—the sun on his face, the wind in his hair, a swift cloud-white stallion beneath him. Italy, France, Wales; he relived his adolescent years, his young manhood, his coming of age. And always there were his horses.

His final vision was of himself and the Golden One astride his great black stallions. They rode around and around the ring in perfect step, their timing exact. He saw himself dismount, reach into his pocket, and bring out a lump of sugar. He felt a warm muzzle in his cold hand. He heard his horse whinny its thanks . . . its love. He felt his heart swell with pride and tender affection. And in that awful instant, he knew!

The cold water chilled him through. He thrashed to be out of its clutches. It filled his nostrils and burned into his lungs. Fighting, raging, sobbing, he dragged himself onto the shore. He lay naked and shivering on the bank, pounding the frozen earth with clenched fists.

"No! No! Anything else! You can't demand *this* of

me!'' he cried. But only the wind answered his anguish in mournful, funereal moans.

How long Mateo lay on the bank, he could not guess. When he dragged himself up at last, the sky was blacker than any he had ever seen. So, this was it—the moment of truth! Now—with one single, terrible stroke—he must prove himself.

Slowly, carefully, with every attention paid to the slightest detail, Mateo began preparing. He gathered herbs and sweet grasses from the woods and piled them high upon the altar he had built. Next, he walked to the stream and cleaned his knives of his own blood. ''Useless stuff!'' he sneered. He laid the weapons out on the bank beside the gleaming Gypsy broadsword used only in ceremonies. One by one, he sharpened the blades on a stone. They were in readiness.

He went back to the altar and struck flint to the grasses. They exploded into sweet-scented flame, filling his nostrils with thick smoke and obscuring the one staring eye of Black Sara. Taking his knives and the sword, one by one, he held them in the fire until each was glowing-hot, then he took them to the icy stream and plunged each blade in. Steam hissed and sizzled, rising into the night. He should have tempered the steel in blood, but that would come . . . all too soon.

There was an eerie silence to the night. He could see the dim glow of the campfire through the trees, but it was deserted. No Gypsies sang or danced or even sat about, puzzling over the mysteries of life. It was almost as if they knew of his desperation, his terrible mission.

Slowly, Mateo pulled on his buckskins. Then, standing tall and determined. he split the silent night with a shrill whistle. He heard the Black Devil answer his call. The great hooves pounded the earth as the magnificent stallion plunged through the forest, seeking his master.

The beautiful animal slowed when he entered the clearing. He stood a few feet from Mateo—nostrils flared, flanks quivering—and pawed at the hard ground. The great head tossed, sending a cascade of black mane rippling in the wind. He neighed, sidestepped, and eyed his master, waiting for a command.

Mateo, the broadsword in his right hand, reached out his left and said softly, "Come."

The trusting animal pranced forward and nuzzled him affectionately. The feel of the velvety muzzle against his bare chest shot Mateo through with sadness. His heart twisted with pain. They had shared so much, these two. They loved each other better than brothers. They understood and respected each other without words.

He caught the great horse about the neck, burying his face in the thick, silky mane as he raised his sword.

Suddenly, Mateo looked up at the dark sky. "Just one more ride!" he pleaded. But he knew what he must do. And it must be *now*!

Stepping away from the Black Devil, who still gazed at his master with soft, trusting eyes, Mateo raised the broadsword with both hands. His thrust must be swift and sure. He would sacrifice this dearest of creatures, if he must, to save the woman he loved. But he would not see his friend suffer.

The stallion shifted slightly and drooped his head. He neighed very softly as if telling Mateo he understood and was ready to die. Pain raged through Mateo's body. The muscles of his arms jerked and spasmed. His heart pounded as if it might tear through his chest. His breath was labored, his eyes clouded.

"Now!" he screamed, forcing his arms to move.

Lightning tore through the night sky. The wide blade flashed and glowed as if electrified. Mateo felt it grow hot in his hands even as he aimed for the Black Devil's heart. Wind howled through the clearing, swirling dead leaves and grass in a whirlwind about man and horse.

Mateo tried to thrust downward with his blade, but some unseen hand seemed to be holding his arms. Again the lightning flashed, the sword blazed, and Mateo, palms blistered with heat, screamed and dropped his weapon. He fell to the ground, stunned.

It seemed that he blacked out for a moment. When he was conscious once more of his surroundings, he felt warm breath on his face. He opened his eyes and looked up at the black muzzle nudging his cheek.

He hadn't been able to do it. He had tried. But something—some force beyond reason—had stayed his lethal hand. In the same instant that he rejoiced, he understood what had happened. His depression deepened and a new, heavier hopelessness gripped him.

Sara-la-Kali hadn't been fooled for a moment. Once, his great stallion might have been the most precious sacrifice he had to offer. But no more! There was only one thing in life that he could not bear to part with. But to save her, he must do just that.

At every turn, Charlotte Buckland had suffered at his hands. He had taken her sacred virginity when the madness had been upon him. On a second occasion, he'd used her cruelly. He did not deserve her love, yet she'd given it to him unselfishly. He couldn't ask the holy Handmaiden to spare the woman he loved on his account. And he couldn't appease her with the slaughter of a sacrificial animal. He must make the ultimate sacrifice in order to save Charlotte. He must, though it would be the end of him.

Mateo stood up and walked to the altar. He touched the jagged, broken edge of the icon. Then he raised his arms to heaven. His voice boomed through the night. "Hear me, Handmaiden! If Charlotte Buckland is indeed the golden Gypsy, whose love could take away my curse forever, I give her to you. I will live with the moon madness to the end of my days. If the Golden One recovers, I promise you I will refuse her—turn my back on her. She will never again know that I love her from my words or actions. And I will take no other to my heart. A Gypsy *Rom* loves but once, and he loves for all eternity. I now make you a gift of my love in return for her life." His arms dropped to his side. His head drooped. And his voice became a whispered prayer. "Let her live, Sara-la-Kali. Let her live!"

When Mateo turned away, he felt empty and alone. He was angry with Fate, but what purpose could that anger serve? His destiny had been written in the stars long before his birth. He was only a puppet, with the powers of the universe pulling his strings. As for Charlotte Buckland, she was better off without him.

He mounted the Black Devil and headed north, upriver. They picked up speed and flew with the wind through the black night. Now that Charlotte was out of his life forever, he knew what he must do. Although he could never love another, he was Mateo, prince of the Gypsies, and he must have a wife . . . a Gypsy queen.

"Good Lord! No wonder she's not recovering. It's too damn cold in here!"

The army surgeon, Captain Ira Feldston, stood just inside Mateo's tent, observing the comatose patient. The brazier burned low in the far corner and Feldston noticed that his breath fogged the chill air.

"The cold has nothing to do with her condition, Captain," Tamara responded angrily. "Gypsy blood is impervious to changes in temperature."

He stared first at the dark woman beside him and then down at the frail-looking blonde on the pallet.

"But this woman's no Gypsy."

Tamara saw no need to discuss Charlotte's bloodlines

with this *gajo* doctor. He was wasting enough time as it was. "Can you help her?"

Feldston was already bending down to lift Charlotte's limp form from her bed of wolf skins. He was an average-sized man, but his arms were strong from many hours spent as a battlefield surgeon.

"What are you doing with her?" Tamara demanded.

"Surely you have someplace warmer than this small, drafty tent. She needs to be where she's more protected."

"The brides' tent is larger and more comfortable," Tamara said. "Follow me."

The captain held Charlotte close and trudged across the compound toward the tent with the blue door. Snow was beginning to fall, but as he glanced about, he saw naked children playing in the clearing. The sight made him shiver. How could they stand it?

A few of the large flakes drifted down onto Charlotte's cheeks and eyelids, where they melted quickly. She moaned and stirred in the doctor's arms. He thought her eyes fluttered open for an instant, but he couldn't be sure.

"Hurry!" he called to Tamara. "I think she's coming around."

She sped toward the door and held it wide for him. "Over there, on that pallet, Captain."

Feldston had no sooner settled his patient in the bed of rabbit fur than she began thrashing about, murmuring in her sleep. He flashed a wide smile at Tamara and his blue eyes sparkled.

"I told you. She's pulling out of it! Come over here so she'll see a familiar face if she opens her eyes. Seeing my ugly mug first thing would be enough to frighten her back into a coma, I'm afraid."

Tamara hurried to kneel beside Charlotte and gave Ira Feldston a bright smile. He wasn't ugly at all. In fact, she found him quite beautiful when he wasn't scowling.

"Charlotte, can you hear me?" she asked. "Charlotte, it's Tamara. Open your eyes, please."

But Tamara's soft voice only seemed to agitate her friend further. Charlotte thrashed furiously and kicked off her cover of skins. Her lips moved; she was trying to speak. Tamara and Feldston exchanged hopeful glances. Without realizing it, they both leaned closer, trying to catch her slightest murmur.

"Ma . . . Mateo," she gasped out at last. "Mateo!"

"She's calling for the prince," Feldston said. "Where is he?"

"I'll go and find him."

"Quickly, Tamara!" he said, using her name for the first time.

She turned for an instant and looked into his eyes. "As fast as I can, Ira."

But Mateo was nowhere to be found. Tamara searched and searched, trudging through the snow, which was coming down fast now and blowing into deep drifts. She called until her voice grew hoarse against the wind. Although she did not know it, Mateo was many miles away by now. Finally she gave up and returned to the tent.

"Mateo . . . Mateo . . . Mateo!" Charlotte's frantic cries greeted her the moment she entered.

Feldston turned an anxious face toward her. "Is he coming?"

"I'm sorry," she said dejectedly. "I couldn't find him."

"Good God! Where could he be? She's wild. She's going to hurt herself if he doesn't come soon and quiet her."

"I searched everywhere. He simply isn't here."

"What about that other chap?"

Tamara frowned, not understanding.

"The fellow with the bear. Is he anywhere about?"

Tamara stared at him, dumbfounded. "You can't mean Petronovich! Surely Charlotte hasn't been calling for him!"

"No, no. But I noticed during the performance at the post how very much he and Prince Mateo resemble each other. Perhaps if he were to come, she would think he was Mateo in her present state and calm down."

"I don't think it will work."

"It's worth a try, Tamara," Ira insisted.

"I really don't think it's wise."

"We don't have time to argue about it. Just go and get him. Hurry!"

"Mateo!" Charlotte's frantic cry followed Tamara as she dashed out into the snow again.

Charlotte was fighting for survival with everything she had. For a long time, she had been far away, drifting in some netherworld. It was a cold, dark place, peopled by strange forms and filled with terrifying sights and sounds. Always, the cruel light of the full moon followed her. She wanted desperately to escape. Now, at last, she could feel herself drifting toward the surface, but her path was uncertain. Obstacles—distorted and unearthly—loomed in her way. If only *he* would come again to guide her toward the sunlight . . . to soar with her on their powerful, shared wings.

"Mateo," she murmured. "Mateo, Mateo!"

She heard voices far away. A woman and a man were hovering over her, speaking in hushed tones. Strong hands gripped her shoulders, trying to hold her where she was, not allowing her to come out of her nightmare. But where was *he*? Where was Mateo?

"Charlotte." The voice calling to her was rich and deep, colored with the exotic accents she knew so well. "Charlotte, can you hear my words?"

Was he real, or was this another of their tricks? More often than not, they allowed her to see his image, hear his voice, then banished him from her dreams before she could reach his arms.

"She's not responding," Charlotte heard the woman say.

But she wanted to respond. Yes! Yes! She wanted Mateo to hear her . . . to hold her.

"Mateo!"

"I am here beside you, Charlotte." The words touched her heart at the same moment his hand brushed her cheek.

She must open her eyes. She must see him . . . make sure that he was with her. They had tricked her before. But not this time, she was sure. The rich voice . . . the gentle caress. This had to be Mateo!

Summoning all her strength and willpower, Charlotte forced her eyes open. For a few moments, everything was blurred. But she could see well enough to make out his dark curls and the bronze cast of his skin. She reached out a trembling hand to touch his face. He caught it in his and brought her fingers to his lips.

"Mateo!" she whispered, convinced now that this was her lover.

He caught her in his arms and held her close, letting his lips find hers. But the kiss was wrong. It felt hard and cold to her. She pulled away and stared up at him. Slowly, her vision cleared. An instant later, she screamed and fell back on the pallet. They had deceived her again. But this was a more terrible deception than those her troubled dreams had played on her senses. This was real. Petronovich was real!

"Get him out of here!" she moaned. "Get him away from me! Mateo. Where's Mateo?"

"I told you it would not work," Tamara whispered to the doctor.

Feldston only shook his head.

"I thought I put on a rather good act," Petronovich said, his face smug. "The little *gajo* witch simply does not appreciate the finer things in life."

"Leave us, please," Tamara ordered, trying to control her temper

"Gladly! Phaedra and I were about to get on with more interesting business when you so rudely interrupted us, Tamara."

"Oh, Petronovich," his cousin called after him, unable to resist, "tell Phaedra she had better bring in her purple scarf. The snow might ruin it. Then how would she call in her dog to toss him a scrap?"

Petronovich threw her a snarl and then was gone.

When she turned back, Ira Feldston was staring at her quizzically. "What's all that about a purple scarf?"

She set about trying to make Charlotte more comfortable as she answered him matter-of-factly. "Petronovich and Phaedra are lovers, but she makes all the rules in the game. Whenever she wants him, she hangs a purple scarf outside her tent. If it is not there, he is not allowed to enter."

The doctor's eyebrows shot up. "And he comes . . . *always*?"

"Always, when summoned. He is her instrument of pleasure. There is no love between them, only lust."

Ira Feldston stared at Tamara, his mouth slightly open in astonishment. He'd never had a woman speak so plainly to him, not even one of his patients. These Gypsies were indeed a breed all their own.

Tamara's voice brought his thoughts back to the woman they were tending. "She seems to be sleeping now. I don't think she has slipped away from us this time."

"I agree. And at least now we know what the problem is. We have to find Mateo and get him here as soon as possible—he should have been with her all along."

Tamara's head drooped and her long hair hid her face from the doctor. "It's my fault. He wanted to stay nearby, but I sent him away from her."

"Why would you do a thing like that, Tamara? You must know that the nearness of a loved one always helps a patient."

"Yes. But he got too near. One day I left them alone and he made love to her."

"My God!" Ira knew he was blushing from his boot tips to his high hairline. Did these Gypsies answer any and all questions so frankly? "How did he accomplish that, when she had a broken arm and two cracked ribs?"

"Well, you see, he—"

"No! Don't answer. I don't think I want to know."

The two of them lapsed into silence and took up their vigil once more. All night they sat side by side, watching for the slightest change, starting at any movement or sound. There didn't seem to be much improvement, but at least Charlotte was holding her own.

"Time will tell," Ira whispered as dawn crept into the tent.

"Yes." Tamara nodded. "Time and Fate."

Chapter 21

"I have the brideprice!"

Mateo, absent for more than a week, plunked down a heavy bag before his astonished mother. It clinked with the sound of gold, and she stared up at his face—a stranger's face, bearded with many days' growth and carved deep with lines of weariness and anguish.

"Where have you been?" she asked quietly. "We have searched for you all this time. I thought you dead."

"Only half-dead, Mother. I went upriver to buy and sell horses. Here are the fruits of my labor." He indicated the leather pouch between them. "Two thousand dollars in *gajo* gold."

"By the saintly Handmaiden! Mateo, that is more than twice the required brideprice!"

"A future queen should be bought with a king's ransom, Mother."

"Well, of course a generous husband is much respected, Mateo. But *two thousand*! It is a staggering amount, even for such a prize wife."

Mateo uttered a humorless laugh. "Yes, such a prize!"

Queen Zolande was confounded by her son's strange attitude. She had never seen him this way. He seemed angry, bitter, even hostile toward her. But why should he be? The day a man paid for his bride should be the happiest of his life. And Charlotte was much improved.

"Don't you even want to know how she is, Mateo?"

Again the sardonic laugh. "I know full well. She is passionate, alluring, lusty, dangerous, and given to wicked excess. In a word: a *man-eater*! But she's strong and healthy, a good breeder. She will give you many grandsons, my queen."

"Mateo! How can you speak in such a way of Charlotte Buckland? She is none of these things you call her. If she were, you would not love her. And she has been anything but strong and healthy of late. Thanks be to Sara-la-Kali, she is almost herself again."

"Yes indeed, we have the good black saint to thank for Charlotte Buckland's recovery." The thought of his promise to Sara-la-Kali tore his heart with pain. So Charlotte was better. He rejoiced in that but raged inwardly to think that he could not go to her . . . not ever again. "But this bag of gold is not for her purchase. I will take Phaedra as my bride."

"Phaedra?" The queen bolted out of her chair, staring hard into her son's wild eyes. "Have you gone mad, Mateo?"

"Not yet, Mother, but I have no doubt my wife will do her best to drive me there in short order."

"You can't be serious! Why would you ask for Phaedra? You know she shares her pallet with Petronovich—with any man who will have her. You've fought this arranged marriage for years. Why would you suddenly decide to accept her now? Especially now when it seems that Charlotte Buckland's love may have ended Valencia's curse?"

The muscles in Mateo's jaw tensed before he answered. "I do not believe it!"

"How could you not? Have you been visited by the curse of late? No! There is your proof. But you should need no other proof beyond your love for each other."

Mateo picked up the bag of gold and dropped it once more in front of her, emphasizing his determination. He refused to discuss the matter any longer. He couldn't admit to his mother that since Charlotte would never be his, he planned to marry a woman he despised to punish himself for all that had happened. "I will have Phaedra. I am going to her tent now to claim her."

He stalked away from the queen, leaving her speechless and stunned. He was mad! There was no other possible explanation.

The other Gypsies stared after Mateo as he covered the distance from his mother's tent to Phaedra's in long, angry strides. The gold-handled whip, clutched in his right hand, whacked with threatening regularity at the top of his boot. Children scattered before him, and even vicious dogs whimpered, tucked in their tails, and slunk away to hide. This was not good Prince Mateo, but some coarse and ruthless stranger.

Mateo's upper lip curled in a sneer when he came to Phaedra's tent. Bright against the white frost on the canvas, the purple scarf fluttered nervously in the breeze—her blatant invitation to Petronovich. Mateo took a few steps back, uncoiled his whip, and lashed at the thing. The sharp report brought a scream from inside, followed by a stream of curses.

Phaedra threw back the tent flap and glared up at Mateo. Her eyes glittered like black fire and her teeth were bared in seething rage. She saw the shredded bits of purple fabric in Mateo's hand.

"How dare you?" she spat at him.

"Petronovich is lucky he did not heed your signal so promptly this time. Had I found him lying with you, he would be in ribbons instead of your scarf."

"Give that to me!"

She charged out of the tent and lunged, trying to grab what was left of the scarf. But Mateo was too quick for her. He seized one slim wrist and twisted it behind her back, bringing forth a fresh stream of obscenities from her lovely lips.

"No more purple scarves and no more Petronovich, my pretty whore! You are *my* woman now. I've paid a fortune for you and I mean to get my money's worth, starting this very minute!"

Phaedra twisted around to stare up at him, her mouth wide in astonishment. "What are you saying?"

"I have delivered your brideprice to the queen. Now I intend to bed you. If I find you satisfactory and you prove to me that you can produce an heir, I will make you my wife."

Before she could say a word, Mateo shoved her back into the tent. She landed, sprawled in her wolf skins, staring up at him with wide, frightened eyes. But her look of fear soon turned into a wanton smile. "Then I will be queen! I knew you would tire of your pale little *gajo* and come to me sooner or later!"

The look she gave him and the words she spoke filled Mateo with renewed rage. How he detested the woman he would wed!

"Mateo, no!" she cried as he came toward her, his whip poised to strike.

Charlotte's periods of unconsciousness had ceased, but still she slept most of the time. Being awake and facing reality was too painful to endure for more than brief periods. Her whole world seemed to have crashed in upon her. She had no idea why Mateo had deserted her at the fort. Vaguely she remembered having him with her for a time while she was very ill, but it seemed almost as if that had taken place in one of her dreams. And now he had disappeared. No one had seen or heard from him in days. She had never felt more alone in her life.

Where could he be? And why had he gone away? No one knew. A melancholy pall had hung over the camp these past days. Charlotte's mood reflected the same deep depression.

She sat by the window of the brides' tent, looking out at the snowbound camp but not really seeing it. Her mind searched the past, trying to understand all that had happened to her since she'd left her home in Kentucky.

Suddenly, a change in the slow rhythm of camp life caught her eye. There seemed to be a great deal of activity around the campfire—people running, shouting, waving. The mob of brightly costumed Gypsies parted for a moment, giving her a clear view of Phaedra's tent and the man standing before its entrance. Petronovich, she thought, losing interest. She'd noticed the purple scarf waving its invitation earlier.

She turned her eyes away, but something drew them back—the way the man stood with his feet wide apart, the tilt of his head, the tight cut of his buckskins. She looked again and her heart leaped into her throat.

"Mateo!" she breathed, not quite believing what she saw.

When the mighty whip cracked, however, there was no denying the truth. He was back. Her love had returned.

Charlotte bolted up from her seat and grabbed for her shawl. She couldn't wait for him to come to her. She would fly to him and into his arms. Her heart and head felt light. Her world had reassembled itself miraculously in an instant. Then, in the next moment, all her dreams came crashing down around her. She watched, poised at the door to hurry to him, as Mateo followed Phaedra into her tent. The very life seemed to be flowing out of Charlotte. No man—not even Mateo—entered Phaedra's tent for any purpose but one.

Charlotte slumped back in her chair. At first, the tears refused to come. Then, when they did, it seemed there was no staunching the flood.

"Get out of my tent!"

Phaedra was terrified of a man for the first time in her life. Still, she tried to hide it, issuing her order to Mateo in her usual imperious manner. He leered down at her, still clutching his whip, and laughed.

"*Your* tent? You forget. I have paid your price. Now you and all your belongings are mine. And I plan to claim them all . . . *immediately*!"

He moved toward her and Phaedra drew back, raising her hands before her as if they might bar his way.

"No, Mateo. Please," she whimpered. She was used to issuing orders, not obeying them. Without her usual command over a lover, she knew only terror.

He fell to his knees beside her pallet, his mind black with anger and hopelessness. Grasping her shoulders in less than gentle hands, he drew her full lips toward his. Once he set his brand to her, his fate would be cast. His relationship with Charlotte Buckland would end for all time. He must take Phaedra now!

"The sooner the better," he said through clenched teeth, then he crushed his mouth down hard over Phaedra's.

She fought him at first—scratching, clawing, biting the lips that were ravaging hers. But soon her muffled sounds of anger became willing sighs. She turned pliable in his strong arms. Her hands kneaded his bare shoulders and chest, and her thrusting hips invited him to do as he would with her. The kiss lingered, their hot mouths and tongues doing intimate battle until both were gasping for breath.

Suddenly Mateo pulled away, shoving Phaedra back to the pallet. He stared at her, half of him feeling the lust she aroused, the other half knowing nothing but disgust for himself and this woman. She was smiling, her eyes almost closed. Her whole body writhed before him like a snake in search of its mate. She tempted him, lured him, dared him to possess her body.

"I know of no heirs produced by one kiss, Mateo," she taunted. "Come to me. Take what you have purchased. Let my body sip the wine of your loins."

She raised her arms to him. When he made no move to respond, she slipped the blouse from her shoulders, tempting him with her full, bare breasts.

Mateo felt the hunger that shone in his eyes as he stared at the large, plum-colored nipples. No wonder Phaedra maintained such a hold over Petronovich. Her body was truly magnificent. What man could resist such temptation? He leaned toward her and cupped the satiny globes in his hands. She closed her eyes, ran her tongue over her lips, and moaned. Her hands groped for him, finding her prize and stroking the bulging heat in his britches.

He dragged himself over on top of her and found her breast with his mouth. The taste of her flesh—like bitter fruit—came as a shock. He drew away and stared at her. Her curving lips dared him to try to leave her now. She was the spider, spinning her purple web, and he was the hapless fly.

"We will be good together, you and I. King Mateo and Queen Phaedra. I am better than your little *gajo*. No?"

She writhed beneath him, thrusting her breasts and

her hips hard against him, but her words hit the wrong
mark. Suddenly, he was snapped back from the heat of
passion to the realization that this was not the woman he
loved. Charlotte was in camp somewhere, waiting for
him, needing him even as he needed her.

He started to stand up, intent upon leaving, but Phaedra
caught his leg and held him fast.

"You cannot go now, Mateo! You told me yourself
that you have offered the brideprice and it has been
accepted. I am yours!"

He stood where he was, looking down at the self-
satisfied smile on her face and the invitation of her
heaving breasts. In spite of himself, he felt a surge of
blood pulse downward. He hesitated and she rushed on.

"You say you want an heir. I am willing to give you
the little prince your pale lover has denied you. You told
us all that she was with child, but it was not true.
Perhaps she is incapable of conceiving."

Mateo frowned. He had been so sure that Charlotte
was carrying his seed. What had happened? But it made
no difference now. He could never have her.

"We both know that I am not barren. Pesha is my
proof, the child of my own childhood, and as crafty a
little wench as ever was born." Phaedra saw that she
had his full attention now and went on, pleased to find
the opportunity at last to confess a long hidden secret to
Mateo—one that would give her power over him even
after he was king. "But then how could she be other
than a true thoroughbred? Her bloodlines are of champi-
onship stock—out of Princess Phaedra, sired by King
Strombol—*your own father.*"

Stunned, Mateo jerked away from her. He had known
that Poor Little Pesha was Phaedra's child, but the father
had never been revealed. Her words twisted through
him as painfully as a knife through flesh. Then anger

replaced that pain and he raised his hand to strike her lying mouth.

She smiled up at him. "Go ahead! Hit me! It will not change the truth. Strombol maintained the fire in his loins to his very last days. He was a powerful, compelling lover. Ask your mother, if you don't believe me."

His eyes narrowed to dark slits. "No more! Do you hear me?"

She shrugged, making her breasts quiver tantalizingly. "I only thought that since we are to be man and wife there should be no secrets between us. The fact that your father loved me so well, it seemed to me, would make you want me all the more. And it would be interesting to compare the son to the father. But in every thoroughbred line there is one throwback to a weaker strain. Perhaps that is you, Mateo. You've always been a hesitant lover. You may never be able to produce an heir. Still, I am willing to give you the chance to try. A king *must* have princes from his queen."

It seemed to Phaedra that her confession and her taunting words had the desired effect. Mateo fell upon her once more. There had been little tenderness in his touch before; there was none at all now. His strong fingers bruised her flesh; his teeth bit at her nipples until she cried out in delicious agony. His hips ground against hers, crushing her down into the skins.

Phaedra felt a fever in her womb. Never had any man charged her with such fire and longing. She would die of it if he didn't enter her soon. He tore away her skirt and she lay very still—holding her breath, waiting for his first, fierce thrust. Her whole body quivered with exquisite anticipation. But still he lingered over her lips, her breasts—still he tortured her with need, bringing her to the very brink but denying her the fulfillment of possessing him.

"Mateo!" she screamed at him. "By the holy Handmaiden, take me now before I die!"

At once he drew away and stood towering over her naked form. A cruel smile twisted his unshaven face. When he spoke, his voice was cold, devoid of any emotion.

"No, Phaedra. I will not bed a woman my father has lain with. You will be my wife, but there will be no heirs. Not of my loins or any other's."

"Mateo!" she gasped, her face a tortured mask of disbelief. "No! You can't mean that. You want me. I know it!"

Ignoring her words, he went on. "And there will be no lovers! My father died many years ago. If the wicked tale you have told me is true, you have used your body for wanton pleasure too long already. From this day forward, you will be a chaste vessel. You want to be queen? Very well. But these are my terms. Go against them and . . ." He fingered his whip meaningfully.

He left her then—aching, seething, scheming, and vowing revenge.

Charlotte—not wanting to see, but unable to tear her gaze away—had watched Phaedra's tent all the while Mateo was with the dark-haired woman. Charlotte sat, hurting inside and crying softly, wondering what was going on between them. She didn't understand any of it. Then, when she thought she couldn't stand the suspense for another moment, Tamara came flying in the door. Seeing Charlotte up and staring with tear-flooded eyes out the window, the fortune-teller tried to hurry past. But her attempt to evade her friend failed.

"What's happened, Tamara?"

Flushed and flustered, the Gypsy woman waved Charlotte's question away. "Mateo has finally returned."

"I know that. He's in Phaedra's tent this minute." She turned a searching gaze on Tamara, pleading for an explanation. "Why did he go there instead of coming here to see me? He's been away so long."

"Who knows?" The fortune-teller shrugged eloquently.

"*You* know!" Charlotte said quietly. "Please, tell me, Tamara. The truth!"

"I wish I knew the truth myself. Oh, Charlotte, nothing makes sense anymore." There was pain in her voice. "Mateo has paid the queen an exorbitant brideprice."

"But not for me." There was something close to acceptance in Charlotte's tone.

"For Phaedra, a woman he despises. Who can guess what is in his mind? He looks like a wild man. His eyes hold a mad gleam. In the days he's been gone, he has turned from the man we all knew to a vicious, raging savage. Something terrible has happened to him."

"He's been in her tent a long time," Charlotte said wistfully, as if she hadn't heard Tamara's impassioned words. "But then he is always very thorough when he makes love."

"Charlotte, don't say such a thing! Don't even think it! How could he lie with her when he still loves you?"

Charlotte turned to look placidly at her friend. "Does he love me?"

Tamara came to her and hugged her compassionately. "You know he does!"

"I don't know anything any longer. As you said, something has happened to him. Something has changed him. It's time I made some decisions, Tamara."

"Don't do anything hasty, Charlotte. Wait and see. This will all work itself out."

Charlotte laughed softly, but there was little humor in it. "As Fate wills, you mean? I'm afraid your precious Fate has been against me from the start. No, I've been a foolish, starry-eyed girl. It's high time I learned to face reality. I have no future with Prince Mateo."

"You're tiring yourself, Charlotte. Come back now and lie down. You shouldn't get yourself so upset."

"I'm perfectly calm. And I plan to stay right here until he comes out. At least I can look at him from a distance. There's no Gypsy law against that, is there?"

"No," Tamara answered quietly, feeling totally defeated and powerless to help her friend. She wanted desperately to tell Charlotte of Queen Zolande's suspicions. She wanted to reassure her by letting her know the wonderful secret—that it was possible Charlotte could banish Mateo's curse forever with her love. But the queen had forbidden Tamara to speak of these things to Charlotte. The decision was up to Mateo. If he chose to wed Phaedra—even against all reason and in spite of his mother's will—then Charlotte would never be told. Her family was coming. Charlotte Buckland would return to Kentucky with them, and her brief passage in the oft told family history would become a closed chapter.

"He's coming out," Charlotte said in a dull tone.

The two women watched in silence as Mateo stalked away from Phaedra's tent. When he turned toward the brides' tent, they both held their breath.

Even from a distance, Charlotte thought she could see the harsh lines of his face soften when he looked at the window where she sat. Her heart ached for him and she felt unbidden tears gathering in her eyes. He took two steps toward her, then turned and strode off toward his horses. Soon he vanished from their line of vision.

"Yes," Charlotte whispered. "It's time I made other plans."

Chapter 22

Queen Zolande, weary from days of trying to reason with her son, took great pleasure in an opportunity for celebration. Hearing of the imminent arrival of Charlotte Buckland's family at Leavenworth, she sent a message to Major Krantz, inviting him, Charlotte's mother, and Fatima Lee Buckland to a reunion with Charlotte. They would join the Gypsies for a *patshiva*—a sumptuous feast with much singing and dancing.

All day long the cookfires blazed, filling the clearing with mouth-watering aromas. Venison stew flavored with wild garlic bubbled in a huge black pot. A roast of buffalo hump sizzled to a crusty golden color on the spit, its juices making the fire hiss and sputter. And dozens of plump hens stuffed with dried plums browned to a turn in their bed of hot rocks.

"If only we had a few hedgehogs," a hefty cook said to the queen as she passed through the work area, inspecting. "My mouth waters at the thought of their sweet, tender flesh."

"Ah, yes, that would be nice," Zolande answered. "But we must be content with what Fate has provided in our new land, Rishna."

Zolande walked on toward the huge silver samovars that brewed the thick, sweet coffee. Beyond those she saw large tubs where chunks of ice broken from the nearby stream kept chilled crocks of brown ale, blackberry wine, and *pivos,* Gypsy beer.

Already the *prima* was rehearsing his strolling musicians. Their violins wept magnificently, while tambourines and drums throbbed out their soul-felt rhythms. A few of the children, dressed in many-colored costumes, whirled and pirouetted in time to the music.

Yes. Zolande nodded to herself. This night will be special.

This was the night Charlotte had been waiting for. Although her arm was still in a sling of red silk, she had recovered her strength. And her mind was made up. These past days she had only been biding her time, waiting for the arrival of her family. She would not leave without seeing them: she owed them that much.

But that was all she owed anyone. She was her own woman—capable of finding her way alone. She would not look back, she vowed. The past was over. Once more, the uncertain future was all she possessed.

As for Mateo, perhaps she had never really known him. Or perhaps his Gypsy blood was fired with such passion that one woman would never be enough to satisfy him. Still, if that were the case, why had he not come to her? Since his return, he had avoided her. When she saw him it was from a distance, and usually Phaedra was by his side. The whole *familia* now knew and seemed to accept that Phaedra was to be Mateo's bride and their future queen. Charlotte had no other choice: she must accept that fact, also. If only she could be certain that he *had* loved her—for a time, at least—how much easier it would be for her to face the bleak, empty years ahead.

She closed herself away behind the amethyst curtains at the far end of the brides' tent so that Tamara would not see her packing her small trunk.

Her friend called out suddenly, startling her. "Hurry, Charlotte, and finish dressing. Already the music and dancing have begun. Your family will arrive at any moment."

Charlotte was dressed. She wore a snow-white blouse, a fine silk skirt of shifting rainbow colors, and new scarlet petticoats underneath. Large golden hoops dangled from her ears. Chains of coins dripped from her throat and wrists. And the ruby-eyed snake encircled her upper arm. She would meet her family dressed as what she had become in her heart—*a Gypsy*.

"Tamara, if I ask you a question, will you tell me the truth?"

Her friend looked at her oddly. "I have always been truthful with you, Charlotte."

"I know I have no chance with Mateo now. He will marry Phaedra, as Fate wills. I accept that. But do you think he ever loved me? Or was it all just a Gypsy charade?"

Tamara's expression remained passive even as her heart ached for the other woman. "Why would you ask such a thing, Charlotte?"

"Please. Tell me the truth. I deserve that much, don't I? You're the fortune-teller, Tamara. So now tell me of my past and my future." Charlotte was fighting tears. "Look into your crystal ball and, through it, into Mateo's heart. Did he give me even a small piece of his heart when I gave him my love?"

The silence between the two women stretched uncom-

fortably. Tamara could not answer. There were some
questions too deep, too private, for even her magic ball.
Still, her friend was hurting, and she must try to soothe
her pain.

Tamara took Charlotte's arm. "Come with me. We
will speak with the queen on this matter."

"I don't want to bother her." Mateo's mother was
the last person she wanted to discuss this with; she had
been against them from the first.

"Never mind. Just come along."

As they crossed the clearing, Charlotte spied Mateo.
He was dressed in a fine, ruffled shirt of scarlet and tight
black trousers. His boots were new—made of soft leather,
tooled in silver. He had never looked more handsome or
more unattainable as he stood leaning against the corral
fence, fondling his Black Devil's soft muzzle. She ached
inside, wanting to go to him. But Tamara kept a firm
grip on her arm and steered her toward the queen's tent.

Charlotte noted a certain excitement in Tamara as
they entered. The woman was up to something.

"Queen Zolande, Charlotte Buckland has asked me a
question that only you can answer. She wants to know if
your son ever loved her."

The old queen, decked in black lace and golden ban-
gles for the *patshiva,* raised her head and gazed at them
for a long time without speaking. Finally, she nodded
and spoke directly to Charlotte.

"How could you doubt it, my child? You know he
loves you. We have all known it for some time."

Charlotte's heart quickened with happiness for the
barest moment before sadness overtook her once more.

"Thank you for telling me, Queen Zolande."

The old woman reached out a frail hand to touch
Charlotte's cheek. "But my dear, why do my happy
tidings make you look so sad?"

"How else do you expect me to look . . . to feel?

You've all let me know from the very first that I have no right to your future king. Now he will marry Phaedra, by your command. I must leave the man I love . . . the *only* man I will *ever* love!"

"Not by *my* command, Golden One." The queen's voice was so gentle that it startled Charlotte. It was almost as if she were speaking to one of her own *familia*. "I would have my son wed the woman whose love for him is great enough to take away the curse."

The queen paused, allowing her meaning to sink in. She watched the light of realization replace the dull, sad darkness in Charlotte's eyes.

"I believe *you* are that woman, Charlotte Buckland," said Zolande.

Charlotte stared at the old queen—dazed, uncomprehending. Her words came slowly. "You would allow Mateo to marry a *gajo*?"

"*No! Never!* My son *must* marry a Gypsy!"

Charlotte stared down in confusion, wondering if she could have misunderstood. Was the queen saying that *her* veins ran with Gypsy blood? When she looked up, Queen Zolande wore a shining smile of acceptance.

"But . . . it can't be!" Charlotte stammered. *"How?"*

"I'm not sure how. But it must be true, my dear. I had not meant to tell you just now. But perhaps our little fortune-teller knows something we do not. She is wise for her years. Not only are you a Gypsy, Charlotte, but it seems that you must be the golden Gypsy my Mateo has been searching for all his life. Your love alone can lift the curse from him."

Charlotte's head was spinning. Could any of this be true?

"Does Mateo know?" she asked.

The queen nodded. "He has been aware of my suspicions for some time. I did not know myself until the night of your accident. That was the time of the full moon, but Mateo suffered no madness. Your love for him had purged him of Valencia's curse."

Every sort of emotion went tumbling through Charlotte as she tried to grasp all that Queen Zolande was telling her.

"Yes—he must have left me at Fort Leavenworth, thinking that the moon madness might overtake him at any moment. He didn't want anyone to see his suffering." Charlotte paused, frowning. "But if all this is true, why has he turned away from me? He can't love me any longer. I've seen him with Phaedra—the way he clings to her arm whenever he's near her. It's as if he's afraid to let her go."

The queen and Tamara exchanged glances. Charlotte could not imagine how near the truth she was. They knew of Mateo's vow to see that Phaedra never bedded another man, not even her husband. Phaedra had sworn to escape from him the first chance she got. Mateo seemed to have lost all other urges, so determined had he become to punish Phaedra. He refused to listen to reason. Even his mother couldn't talk to him any longer. The man was obsessed.

"Queen Zolande," Tamara said, "we passed Mateo on our way here. He was alone with his stallions. Don't you think, if Charlotte went to him now, she might be able to talk to him?"

The queen nodded. "What harm could it do? Are you willing, my dear?"

Sudden hope swelled in Charlotte's breast. "Oh, yes, Queen Zolande! I *must* talk to him."

"Go, then. And Sara-la-Kali be with you, my child."

Charlotte Buckland was not the only woman in the Gypsy camp plotting a new course that night. Phaedra had escaped Mateo's watchful eyes for a time by going to bathe in the ice-clogged stream. No *Rom* would dare intrude while the women washed themselves.

The others hurried to be out of the cold water, but Phaedra lingered, allowing all of them to drift back to the camp. Finally she was alone. When the last woman disappeared around a bend in the trail, she gave a shrill whistle. Immediately, boots came stamping through the woods.

"Hurry," Petronovich urged, tossing clothes to her. "When the others get back to camp and he sees that you are not with them, he will come searching for you."

"Well, he won't find me," she hissed. "Not ever again! We'll hide in the woods and wait until the full moon rises and the madness seizes him. Then we'll make our move."

"Hide in the woods? Wait? Have you lost your mind, Phaedra?" Petronovich grabbed her arm and jerked her sharply as if to shake some sense into her.

Her free hand lashed out and slapped him sharply across the face. "Don't you ever handle me that way again! I am no man's property. Not Mateo's and not yours!"

Instead of shying away as he would have done in the past, Petronovich caught her in an even tighter grip and pulled her to him, forcing her head back until his lips were almost touching hers.

"No more, Phaedra! I've submitted to your will for the last time. If you go with me tonight, I am the one who says what we do and when we do it. And you will speak to me with respect from now on. Otherwise, I will take you to Mateo this minute and tell him that I caught you trying to sneak away. Let him deal with you as he will."

Phaedra could see by the cold look in his eyes that he meant every word. She softened her tone.

"Please, Petronovich, you're hurting me. I have a

reason for wanting to wait. I know where the bag of gold is hidden—my brideprice. Don't you think it only just that we should take it along? After all, it *is* my dowry."

The cruel lines around Petronovich's mouth turned to a smile; then he was laughing out loud. "You are a scheming witch, my love! Yes, we shall have your brideprice to finance our escape. And while we await the rise of the moon . . ."

He captured her lips and let his free hand glide up her naked body to her breasts. He crushed the tender flesh with his palm and Phaedra quivered against him. She had feared that she might never again feel a man's hands upon her. As much as she had wanted to be queen, she wanted this more. She welcomed his bruising caresses in a frenzy of wanton passion.

"Yes," she breathed into his open mouth. "Oh, yes, Petronovich! Until the full moon rises . . ."

Mateo was still standing alone, talking softly to Velacore, as Charlotte approached. She caught a few words.

"You miss her as much as I do, don't you, old boy? Well, I am sorry for you. You gave her only your honest affection. There is no reason why you should be deprived of her company. Even my stallions must suffer because of me."

Charlotte started to say that no one—neither man nor horse—need suffer from wanting her near. Then she remembered that Mateo hated anyone to eavesdrop when he talked to his stallions. So she stopped some paces away and waited for him to become aware of her presence.

He turned slowly, never taking his fondling hand from Velacore's muzzle. When he spotted her, the old look of love lit his dark eyes for a moment. Then he composed himself and forced any trace of it from his countenance.

"You are looking fit," he said without emotion.

"I have recovered . . . as much as I ever will."

"The arm?"

"Dr. Feldston advised me to wear the sling for a few more days. But the pain is gone. He says I will ride again."

"I'm sure you will. You are a fine equestrienne."

There was a certain charged force darting between them. Charlotte could feel it as surely as she had ever felt Mateo's lips upon her own. Why were they speaking this way? Were they strangers now? Did her injured arm or her riding expertise matter? So many more important things needed to be said.

"Mateo?" The way she said his name told him that she was about to ask questions he didn't want to answer.

"I'm sorry, Charlotte. I have to go find Phaedra now."

He started away, but she caught his sleeve.

"Mateo, don't do this to us."

"To *us*, Charlotte?" His black eyes bored into her, and something deep inside her shivered with a mixture of love and dread. "There is no *us*. I am going to marry Phaedra."

"You don't love her," Charlotte said matter-of-factly, trying to keep her voice from trembling.

"And you, Charlotte?" His voice was harsh. "Do you love your *gajo* major?"

His question took her totally by surprise. She couldn't find the words to answer him for a moment.

"So. It is as I thought. Good-bye, Charlotte Buckland. Live long and be happy!"

Mateo strode away from her before she could deny his startling allegation. He left her feeling emptier than she had felt before. Charlotte cursed herself a thousand times over. Why hadn't she just told him she loved him and needed him and would never be happy with anyone else? Why hadn't she confronted him with his mother's information about her ability to break the curse? Why? Why? Why?

She had wasted her last chance. Now there was nothing left to do but follow through with her earlier plan.

The sound of approaching horses caught her attention. Shouts of welcome rang out from the Gypsies. She looked toward the trail and saw Winston Krantz driving a buggy into the clearing. Two women rode on the seat beside him—one as fair as Charlotte herself, the other as dark as a Gypsy.

Granny Fate *is* a Gypsy! Charlotte thought suddenly, startled at the realization. Fatima Lee Buckland had given her granddaughter the Romany fire that ran in her veins. In that instant, Charlotte loved the old woman more than ever before. But why had her grandmother never told her? She ran to meet them.

"Charlotte, my dear girl!" her mother cried.

Jemima Buckland looked like a bride; there was no disputing that. Her face shone with a youthful glow that her daughter had never seen before. Her mother's blue eyes sparkled, reflecting the sapphire color of her gown. And something else sparkled almost as brightly—a diamond ring on her finger. Winnie certainly hadn't wasted any time!

Charlotte embraced her mother and assured her that she was recovering nicely. Then she turned to the other woman, who was standing back to allow mother and daughter their reunion.

Fatima Buckland's eyes were as wide as a child's as she took in the whole setting at a glance. She, too, looked younger than her years. Charlotte was relieved to see that the long trip had not been too hard on her.

"Granny Fate," Charlotte whispered, feeling tears

tighten her throat. "Oh, I never thought I'd see you again."

The old woman closed her arms around her beloved granddaughter. "Do not talk foolishness, child! Would I have left this world without finding you again? Never!" She drew away and smiled into Charlotte's eyes. "Where is this Gypsy prince of yours? I want to meet him. Now! We need to discuss brideprice and how many sons he will give you."

Charlotte's smile faded. She glanced about the clearing, but Mateo was nowhere to be seen.

"Granny Fate," she began, about to break the sad news to the woman. But Queen Zolande came on the scene just then and interrupted.

Her eyes widened at the sight of Fatima Buckland. So, here was the missing link—the final puzzle piece fitted into place! It had been many years ago and half a world away, but Queen Zolande would have recognized Charlotte's grandmother anywhere. There was the same laughter lurking deep in her dark eyes, the same smile, the same noble beauty she had admired in a lovely Gypsy bride over fifty years ago. At last she knew Charlotte Buckland's heritage. She was, indeed, the golden Gypsy! The old queen could have wept for joy. Instead, she went to Fatima and embraced her.

"So this is the pretty young bride I saw wed to her handsome Rom Slome so very long ago. Fatima, do you remember me? I was the child who came to you for your bride's blessing. You took a stem of lupine from your bouquet and gave it to me. I have treasured the memory all these years."

Granny Fate's lips parted in surprise and moisture gathered in her warm black eyes. "Little Zolande? Can it be?"

"*Queen* Zolande now," Winston Krantz pointed out,

but neither woman heard him as they clung to each other, weeping with happiness.

"Come to my tent, Fatima. You and I have much to discuss."

"As soon as I meet my granddaughter's prince."

"Now!" Zolande tugged at Fatima's arm and whispered for her ear alone, "My son, Prince Mateo, is to be the main subject of our discussion."

The two women hurried away, arm in arm, leaving Charlotte with her mother and Winston Krantz.

"Have you set a date yet, Mother?"

Winston answered for Jemima. "We thought this very Sunday. The chaplain will marry us at his sunrise service, and immediately afterward we'll leave by stage from Leavenworth on our honeymoon. Of course, we hope you will be there, Charlotte."

Charlotte would not, but she couldn't tell them that. Instead, she answered, "You know I want to see the two of you married, Winnie. I'm very happy for you." She offered the major a coy smile. "But you aren't going to insist that I call you 'Daddy,' are you?"

He bellowed with laughter and hugged her.

"Now, Winnie," Jemima cautioned, "let's not get carried away. What will people think?"

He pulled his fiancée into his arms. "They'll think I'm the luckiest so-and-so on the face of the earth, with two beautiful ladies all my own."

The three of them laughed together. Yes, Winston Krantz was exactly right for her mother. They would be very happy together. The thought relieved Charlotte.

After showing them to their seats of honor and seeing that they had wine and food, Charlotte left them watching the Gypsy dancers and slipped away to the brides' tent. Very soon now she would be leaving. But first she must see her grandmother and bid her farewell.

*   *   *

Fatima Lee Buckland's heart filled with an excitement she hadn't felt in years. For so long she had kept her Gypsy heritage a secret. Afraid of the same sort of persecution in America that had driven them from Spain and then from England, she and Slome had never told a soul in their new land that they were Gypsies.

To think of it! This queen had witnessed her marriage to Slome. That had happened a lifetime ago . . . a world away. And now here they were, two old Gypsy women, sitting in a tent, sipping strong tea, and exchanging memories while violins sang their mournful tales just outside. She could hardly believe it wasn't a dream.

"So tell me, Fatima, how has life been for you?" asked the queen.

"Too short, too sad at times, but Fate has not cheated me, Zolande. I had a good man in my Slome. He gave me a fine son and a granddaughter who means the world to me."

"Yes, your Charlotte is a lovely woman. But more than that!" Zolande leaned close and whispered, "She is more valuable than gold to my Mateo."

"Ah, he loves her that much. That is good to know."

Zolande reached for Fatima's hand and gave it an excited squeeze. "She may bring my Mateo more than love. If my suspicions are correct, she may also bring him peace at last by taking away the curse of moon madness."

"*Valencia's* curse?"

"You know of it, Fatima?"

"What Gypsy does not know that terrible tale? I heard it first at my mother's knee, long ago in a cave in Spain. But what does this have to do with Charlotte?"

Before Zolande could answer, a sudden light gleamed in Fatima's eyes. "*Mateo*—son of Strombol, grandson of Lassim, and descended from Croate, the child born of the unholy union between Kavà and Xendar? *Your* Mateo, Zolande?''

The queen nodded. ''You know our history well, Fatima. So you must also know that Valencia tempered her curse by promising that someday a golden Gypsy would come.''

''Yes, but . . .'' Fatima stopped in midsentence. Her mouth opened, and her eyes went wide. ''You mean my Charlotte? *She* is this golden Gypsy?''

Zolande smiled. ''She is! My son has suffered long. But now, because of Charlotte's love for him, the curse has left him.''

''But this is too wonderful!''

The old queen shook her head sadly. ''There is a grave problem.''

''Nothing that two old *dukkerers* like us cannot solve, Zolande. Tell me!''

''Mateo no longer suffers his moon madness, but another kind of insanity has seized him. He loves your Charlotte as she loves him. Yet he has forced upon me the brideprice to purchase another wife. If he goes through with his foolish plans, the curse will return and plague him forevermore.''

''And Charlotte will live out an empty, loveless life,'' Fatima said. ''We women of the Buckland clan love fiercely, but only once.''

Zolande nodded and reached for Mateo's leather pouch. She poured out a mound of gleaming coins on the table. Fatima stared, amazed.

''No! On the breast of the Handmaiden, so much gold for another! How could he do such a thing?''

''I have no notion as to what is in his mind. He despises the woman he plans to marry. In fact, he has told us all that he will never bed her. She is . . .'' Zolande paused and looked up at Fatima, her eyes narrowing. "I will put it delicately. She is a *lusty* woman. She wants no part of Mateo and his plans for their celibate union."

"And who can blame her? A woman has needs!"

"I feel something in the air tonight, Fatima, Perhaps it is the full moon coming on. It has always been a dreadful time for my people. Whatever it is, there is evil abroad. You and I must act quickly, if there is to be any hope of saving my Mateo and your Charlotte."

"What can we do, Zolande?"

"I have summoned Mateo. He will be here any moment. He must tell me the truth of this situation! And you must speak with Charlotte. I know she loves my son, but he has rejected her. That is not easy for a woman to accept, especially when there is another woman involved. And, too, something is brewing in Charlotte's head. I sensed it earlier when I spoke with her. You must convince her not to do anything rash until I can bring Mateo back to his senses."

"I am on my way to her already, Zolande. May Sarala-Kali give us both the strength and wisdom to bring these lovers together again."

"As a token of my confidence in our combined abilities, Fatima, take the brideprice. It is meant for your Charlotte's purchase."

Fatima quickly scooped the coins into her own bag, leaving Mateo's pouch empty.

"You are very wise, Zolande. The holy Handmaiden will look kindly on your gesture and give us her fullest blessing now."

"Let us pray so!"

Fatima paused at the tent flap and flashed her friend a wily smile. "It has been some time since I saw a real Gypsy wedding. I do not intend to fail in this mission!"

"Nor do I," the queen assured her.

Once alone, Zolande sat staring at the table for a long

time, her mind working over what she would say to Mateo. He would arrive soon, she was sure. Suddenly she noticed the empty pouch. She could not let her son see it; he would question her about the gold.

She started to put it away, then stopped. What if he asked to see if the gold was safe? She could not show him an empty sack.

Stooping to the dark earth beneath her feet, she gathered up enough stones to fill the bag. Then, smiling at her cleverness, she tucked it away behind her chest where the gold had been hidden for safekeeping.

She was just taking her seat again when Mateo entered.

"You wished to see me, my queen?"

"No, Mateo. Not your queen. Your *mother* would have a word with you."

He stood before her—tall, strong, and handsome. How could such a perfect man act such a perfect fool? She wondered.

"If this is about Charlotte, I don't want to hear it."

She rose from her chair, glaring at him. "You will hear it. *Sit!*"

Mateo did as she ordered but slumped in the chair, sprawling his long legs out before him with a weary sigh.

His mother was not about to be discouraged by his reluctance to discuss the matter. "Mateo, you are a fool!"

"I know, Mother. You've told me that before."

She went to the tent flap and threw it open. "Look out there and tell me what you see."

He leaned slightly forward and gave the campsite a cursory glance. "I see Gypsies dancing, children playing, the forest beyond. What is it you want me to see?"

"The *full moon*, Mateo! It is high in the trees, shining brightly, and look at you! You are the same as you were today, yesterday, or the day before that. The curse is gone!"

"I know that. Do you think I'm not happy about it? All these years of misery. I can hardly believe my good fortune."

"But you refuse to believe that Charlotte Buckland is the golden Gypsy . . . the one who has saved you with her love?"

Mateo sat up straight in the chair and stared down at his hands, clenched in his lap. When at last he looked up, there was much pain in his face. He reached out and took his mother's hands in his.

"I do believe it. I do love her," he said quietly. "I ache with wanting her every time I see her."

"Then why are you telling me? Why are you not on your way to her this minute to tell her?"

He smiled in spite of his anguish, thinking how Solange had once spoken almost the same words to him. Then the smile faded. "Mother, I made a promise that now keeps me from her."

Zolande huffed angrily. "Your promise to marry Phaedra means nothing, Mateo!"

"Not to Phaedra, to someone else."

"Who on earth?"

"No one on earth, Mother. In *ravnos*. When Charlotte was so ill, I promised Sara-la-Kali that if she would spare the woman I loved, I would give her up. It came to me after much prayer and soul-searching that I must give up what was most precious to me. Charlotte is almost well now. But my promise, which saved her, now keeps me from her."

Queen Zolande slumped back in her chair. Mateo's confession left her breathless; her head was spinning. Of all the things she'd imagined might have happened, this had never entered her mind. But there had to be a way around it.

She leaned forward and smiled at her son. "Well, it seems we do have a problem, Mateo," she said gently.

"Whatever are we going to do? You see, I made a promise to the good saint, also. When we thought the Golden One might die, I promised Sara-la-Kali that if she were saved, I would see that the two of you were wed. And since I have known the Handmaiden a good many more years than you have, I think my promise means more to her than yours. We can't both abide by what we told her. So, I feel sure that she will forgive you for breaking your vow."

A slow smile kindled in Mateo's eyes; soon, the spark turned to flame. He leaped out of his chair and caught his mother in a bearlike hug.

"Then we're free to wed! I can go to her and tell her?"

"You had better go soon. She's probably getting a little tired of waiting!"

As Mateo dashed away, Queen Zolande turned toward the picture hanging over her bed. "Forgive me, dear Sara. I meant to give you my promise. It must have slipped my mind."

She smiled—and Sara-la-Kali seemed to be smiling back.

Chapter 23

"Oh, Granny Fate, I'm so glad you've come!"

Charlotte snapped the lid of her trunk shut and ran to her grandmother the moment she entered the brides' tent.

The old woman's eyes missed nothing—a packed trunk, Charlotte's hair tied back instead of hanging loose as it had been earlier, her colorful skirts exchanged for riding britches.

"Are you going somewhere, Charlotte?"

She hung her head, not wanting to meet Granny Fate's piercing gaze.

"Yes. But I wouldn't have left before seeing you again."

"And did you plan to tell your prince good-bye?"

"He told me good-bye some time ago." Charlotte searched her grandmother's eyes. "Didn't Queen Zolande tell you that Mateo plans to marry Phaedra?"

"Not the woman's name, but she told me. We both

338

agreed that should not happen. *You* are the golden Gypsy, Charlotte! You have an obligation here. Mateo needs you."

Charlotte went to Granny Fate and led her to a chair. The woman looked old, frail, and suddenly very weary.

"I need him, too," Charlotte told her gently. "But what can I do, Granny Fate? I tried again tonight to let him know how much I care, but he turned away. I can't take any more of this. The sooner I leave, the better for everyone concerned. I don't know why Mateo has rejected me. But I can see the torture in his eyes whenever I'm near him. I don't want to cause him more pain by staying here."

Fatima sighed. "Ah, how difficult love can be nowadays. It was so simple back when your grandfather decided he wanted me for his bride. He simply stole into my father's cave and carried me off. There was no 'Does he love me . . . doesn't he love me?' I fought him, yes, but only for tradition's sake. I knew he was my man."

Charlotte smiled. "Yes, that must have been nice. If only Mateo would come and carry me away!" She sighed heavily. "But there's no use talking about it. His mind, if not his heart, is set on Phaedra. He's already paid her brideprice."

Granny Fate patted her heavy handbag. "Ah, yes! The fabulous brideprice. Two thousand, wasn't it? A pity he didn't offer that for you. That much money would mend a lot of fences back at Fairview."

"Will Fairview be saved?"

Granny Fate shrugged in the same manner Tamara so often did. "Who can tell? It is in the hands of Fate, my child."

"I wish I could help."

The old woman patted her granddaughter's cheek affectionately. "Don't worry your pretty head over it.

You have only to take care of yourself and find your own happiness. It's out there somewhere, Charlotte. Perhaps you and Prince Mateo were never meant to be. But someday some man will steal into your cave and claim your heart for all time. Believe me!"

Charlotte looked at Granny Fate oddly. "Are you saying you aren't going to try and stop me?"

The ancient Gypsy woman smiled, and fires burned deep in her eyes. "Would I try to stop the wind from blowing? No! Your will is your own. Go, if you must!"

Charlotte hugged her grandmother and kissed her on both cheeks. "I love you!" she said.

"Not nearly so much as I love you. Go now, quickly!"

Smiling, Fatima Buckland watched from the door of the brides' tent as Charlotte slipped away into the night.

"There is nothing that will make a man go after a woman faster than her flight away from him," she murmured.

Closing the door softly, she went back to her chair to wait for Mateo. He would come from his mother's tent any time now, she was sure. She would have to be ready for him.

With a determined effort, she forced tears to her eyes. She tore her blouse, pulled her hair, and raked anguished streaks down her throat. Surely no time was more an occasion for mourning than the disappearance of one's beloved granddaughter. Mateo would be convinced.

Phaedra and Petronovich, their passions spent for the moment, huddled close together in the shadows behind Queen Zolande's tent, waiting for her to join the celebration.

"You're sure you know where the gold is?" Petronovich whispered.

"Yes! She hides her valuables in a special place. It will be there, I promise you."

Petronovich pulled Phaedra closer and captured her full, pouting lips. His kiss was hungry, hot, and deep. He would never get enough of this woman! And now that they were about to be rich, he knew what he wanted to do. They would head for San Francisco and live a life of ease there. With two thousand dollars in gold, he would never have to work another day of his life. He would have all the time in the world to partake of the pleasures of Phaedra's lush body. There were so many things he wanted to do with her . . . to do *to her*, he thought as his blood pulsed hotly.

"Stop it, Petronovich," she protested, shoving his hands from her breasts. "She'll hear us."

"You mean my heavy breathing?"

Phaedra didn't answer him. She had her ear against the canvas and could hear the queen moving about inside. A moment later, all was silent.

"She's gone," Phaedra whispered. "You keep watch. I'll slip under the bottom of the tent and get the gold."

It is said that a Gypsy is more slippery than an eel. Phaedra seemed proof of that as she wriggled into the queen's tent and fetched out the leather pouch. In moments she was beside Petronovich once more, holding her prize up high for him to see.

"Two thousand dollars!" he said in a voice hushed with awe.

"And all ours, my lover! Quickly now, before anyone spots us."

The pair of thieves slipped away, hugging the shadows and moving soundlessly. The caravan's departure would only have drawn attention, so they left it behind with all their other belongings and rode off into the night on Petronovich's two horses.

"We won't need that old wagon or anything else from

our past lives," he assured Phaedra. "We'll buy everything new! We'll live like royalty!"

Phaedra laughed and whipped her horse to more speed. "I always wanted to be a queen!"

It was many miles and hours later before they stopped to rest the horses, make love, and count their ill-gotten treasure.

Phaedra was still lying naked with Petronovich at her breast when she reached for the leather pouch and poured the contents out between them. A cold hand closed over her heart and sharp teeth bit her nipple.

"*Rocks?*" she screamed, unbelieving.

Petronovich could only stare at the pile of stones in sick silence. They were in the middle of nowhere, with nothing. How would they ever survive?

When Mateo rushed into the brides' tent, he found a strange woman in a sodden, sobbing heap on the floor. She looked as if a close family member had just died.

Lifting her gently, he said, "Please, try to calm yourself, old woman."

She glared up at him through eyes stained with tears. "Don't order me about, and don't call me 'old woman,' young man! Who are you to intrude upon my grief?"

He looked and felt bewildered. Since he had been off in the woods searching for Phaedra when Major Krantz had arrived, he had no idea that this woman was Charlotte's grandmother.

"I am Prince Mateo. I came here looking for Charlotte Buckland."

Fatima flew at him, her long fingers curved into claws. "*You!*" she screamed, lunging at him as if she meant to tear his eyes from his head. "Because of you, she has gone away . . . *forever*! I will never see my granddaughter again. She is as good as dead to me now. And I have you, you prince of darkness, to thank for all my misfortunes. Perhaps even as we speak she is out there somewhere being torn to bits by a pack of hungry wolves. You devil! You toad!" She went for him again but pulled back when she saw that he did not mean to defend himself.

Her words sank into him like an arrow sinking into tender flesh. He had heard wolves howling in the woods. The old woman could well be right.

"Which way did she go?" he demanded. There was not a second to lose.

"Off to the west."

"How long ago?"

"Not long. The amount of time it takes a stallion and a mare to mate."

He smiled at her. She was most certainly of Gypsy blood. Only a Romany would tell time in such a manner.

"Don't worry. I will find our precious Golden One."

Fatima caught his arm and stayed him for an instant. Opening her bag, she showed him the gold. "I have accepted your brideprice from the queen. When you find my Charlotte, there will be a wedding, Prince Mateo?"

"There will be! That I promise you."

"And little princes?"

He nodded. "And princesses as well!"

With a whistle that split the cold night, he summoned his mount. The Black Devil charged to a snow-scattering halt before the door. Mateo leaped onto his stallion's bare back and galloped away, leaving Fatima Buckland looking on, smiling and feeling almost like a bride herself.

Charlotte had counted on the full moon to light her way. For the first half hour of her ride, all had been well. But now clouds had moved in to obscure her guiding beacon. The wind whipped at her furiously. The temperature was dropping fast. And large, wet snow-flakes were beginning to fall. She tried not to admit it to herself at first, but now there was no denying the fact that she was lost.

She had never been frightened of being alone. But here in this wilderness the leafless trees cast eerie shadows across the snow, creating nightmarish visions before her eyes. She tried to tell herself she was only imagining things—that the monstrous presence off to her right was only a tree trunk that had been shattered by lightning. But the more she stared, the more her skin crawled and her heart pounded.

One frightening factor had nothing to do with her imagination, however. *Wolves!* She had been conscious of their howling far off in the distance for some time. But now the sound was moving ever closer. Velacore could smell them. The great stallion neighed nervously, and she could feel his flanks quivering beneath her.

"Steady, boy. They won't bother us as long as we keep moving."

Her voice trembled with the cold and her fear. How could she reassure her mount when she found no comfort in the sound of her own voice?

She pulled her shawl more closely about her and bent forward into the driving snow. She might have Gypsy blood in her veins, but not enough to keep her warm in a blizzard.

Velacore slowed. "Come on, boy, please!" she said through chattering teeth. "We have to keep moving."

She scanned the landscape but could see only a few feet in any direction. The wind had picked up and was lashing them now with stinging flakes. She thought she saw a shadow move, off to the right. Her head jerked that way, but there was nothing.

"Jumping at phantoms, now, are you? Mateo would have a good laugh over this. Oh, yes! The Golden One, the brave one . . . lost in a storm, quaking with fear at the slightest sound."

But the next sound she heard was not so slight. The shadow had not been imagined—the wolves were closing in. She heard their low snarls before they came close enough for her to see them circling.

Velacore jerked and sidestepped. When the leader of the pack lunged at them, the horse reared and Charlotte screamed. Soon the night was filled with sound and fury. The huge stallion fought the pack for all he was worth—sending one after another of the scavenging wolves flying through the air with his powerful kicks.

Charlotte held on for dear life, but not even Mateo's Black Devil had given her such a ride. Her injured arm ached with cold; her other arm was growing numb from holding on to Velacore's neck. Suddenly, the whole pack charged at once. She felt the horse buck beneath her, and the next thing she knew she was lying in the snow, a ledge of rocks to her back and Velacore putting up a brave defense before her.

Mateo heard the screams of both woman and horse. He put heels to his stallion and sent him hurtling through the blinding snowstorm.

"Find her, you Black Devil! That's our Golden One calling for help!"

He could hear the wolves. He knew the pack was attacking. But how far away were they? The wind carried the sounds in strange directions and added its own distorting moans.

Mateo forced his mount to breakneck speed. This was suicide on such a night, but what good was life without her? He was so close now. But a single second one way or the other could mean life or death for her.

Grinding his teeth, he forced himself to pray to Sara-la-

Kali once more. But this time he made no foolish promises. He *demanded* she save his woman!

Suddenly, the stallion broke out of the forest into a
clearing. Mateo could see them now, silhouetted against
the snow—Charlotte clinging to a rocky ledge and
Velacore fighting off the snarling, snapping villains as if
he were protecting his own mate instead of his master's.

Mateo dismounted in one great leap. His whip uncoiled and whistled its warning through the air. There
was a sharp crack, the howling of a wounded wolf. A
few more strikes and the pack admitted defeat. They
dragged themselves off through the snowdrifts, whim-
pering and whining to one another.

"Mateo!" Charlotte cried, running to his arms. "Oh,
thank God, you came!"

"Thank Sara-la-Kali, too!" he whispered against her
cold cheek. "And my mother and your grandmother, my
darling. They are quite a pair, and they love us both
very much."

Charlotte offered her lips to him. "As much as we
love each other, Mateo?" she whispered.

"No. Not that much," he said before he kissed her.

The blizzard continued all night, but Charlotte and
Mateo never noticed. Finding a tiny cave in the rock
ledge, they took refuge there, leaving the stallions to
shelter in the nearby trees. Mateo built a small fire
inside and spread out his wolf-skin coat to make a bed.
Charlotte lay down, exhausted from her terrifying experience but happier than she had been in a long time.

She watched Mateo as he worked over the fire. His
face was so fine and beautiful. The golden rings gleamed
in his ears and his dark eyes danced with reflected
firelight. Could all this be real, or was her imagination
playing tricks on her again?

"Mateo?"

He turned to her, smiling. When the smile narrowed

and became an intense look of longing, he touched her . . . and she had no doubts left about reality.

They came together with great tenderness, savoring a reunion too long postponed. His hands played over her body, testing to make sure she was unharmed. The feel of his flesh, warm against hers, sent a million thrilling sensations dancing through her. She drew his lips to hers, but his hands took possession of her breasts. Their kiss lingered, growing more fervent as he sought the sweet honey of her mouth with his tongue. She pressed close to his hard body, feeling the heat she kindled there.

"Your grandmother wants princes," he whispered. "I promised her we would do our best."

"I never like to disappoint Granny Fate," Charlotte said, then she laughed softly.

"What is it?"

"She told me before I left that someday a man would come to my cave, claim me for his own, and steal me away. She couldn't know of this place. She must be a Gypsy fortune-teller."

His hands trailed down her body as they talked. "And do you want me to steal you away, after all that's happened, Charlotte?"

"Not this very minute," she answered, snuggling closer and guiding his hand downward.

He glanced toward the cave's opening. "Not until the snowstorm stops."

"How long will that be?" she asked. Her voice quavered as he found her special spot and stroked her gently.

"All night, at least."

A wolf howled in the distance, and she shuddered at the sound. "We'd better not go to sleep. They might come back."

"Mmm," he sighed into the softness between her

breasts. "I hadn't planned to. Since stealing is out of the question, I thought I might claim you instead."

A moment later, he slid her beneath him. Neither of them could wait any longer, though the whole night was theirs. He entered her with a sure, quick thrust and found her moist and ready to receive him. The wind and the wolves howled outside, but inside the cave all was warm and scented with love.

They rode to the summit and poised there, basking in the golden glow of exquisite fulfillment. Then, ever so slowly and gently, they spiraled downward in each other's arms.

All the long night through, Mateo worshiped his Golden One and she lavished him with love.

Near dawn, when the wind had died and the storm was past, Mateo gave up his lover's lips to whisper into her ear, "What shall we name our little prince?"

Charlotte smiled up at him, her face aglow and her eyes asparkle. "Why don't we call him Fate?"

Mateo nodded. "I like that. It's a man's name. I can hear it now, being told around campfires for generations to come: 'Born of the Golden One and Prince Mateo, the prince of Fate. Let it be said of the *Rom* named Fate that he never feared the full moon.' "

Charlotte turned Mateo's face to hers. "Nor did his father," she added.

"Not ever . . . so long as he had his golden Gypsy's love."

Mateo took her back into his arms, and once more the cave was filled with sighs and warmth and love.

Chapter 24

"Mateo!" Charlotte shrieked. "What are you doing?
Let me go!"

They'd been headed back toward the Gypsy camp,
riding in the early-morning sun—talking quietly, touching occasionally, smiling into each other's eyes as they
savored the memory of their night of lovemaking—when
suddenly Mateo's arm had shot out, grabbing Charlotte
around the waist.

Now she felt herself being dragged from Velacore's
back onto his mount. A moment later she was lying
across Mateo's hard thighs, staring down at the patches
of snow on the ground. She kicked and screamed and
threatened, but he held her fast, urging the Black Devil
to more speed.

"Have you lost your mind?" she yelled. Turning her
head slightly, she could see through the hair flowing
down over her eyes that he was wearing a magnificent
grin.

"That's very good, Charlotte." He demonstrated his pleasure with a sharp swat upon her rear. "Only louder—yell louder!"

"Oh, *you*!" she seethed. "Let me down this instant! Who do you think you are, treating me this way?"

"I am the man who is about to be your husband, my love," he answered calmly. "But you aren't acting like a proper bride-to-be. Can't you really let go for me a time or two? Scream, my darling, scream!"

Charlotte was fuming, furious, so angry and humiliated that she would have liked to scratch his eyes out. He wanted a scream? Very well, she would give it to him! She let fly such a shrill cry that blackbirds perched on a nearby tree took wing in a panic. She screamed and screamed until her lungs burned and her throat ached. But Mateo only held her fast and laughed as if this were the grandest joke in all the world. Well, it was no joke to Charlotte. She was damn good and mad!

"You turn me loose! Do you hear?" He ignored her. "I'm warning you, Mateo!" He laughed harder. "You can't treat me this way." He swatted her again and she went for his leg with her teeth.

"Ow!" he howled. "Stop that, woman!"

"And don't call me *woman*!" she hollered. "So help me, Mateo, when we get back to camp, I'm going to tell the queen how you've treated me. Everybody's going to know about this!"

"I sincerely hope so, my golden beauty!"

When they rode into camp, Charlotte was still shrieking her rage, pounding her fists, and by that time swearing she hated him and would never marry him. Everyone from the queen right down to the tiniest toddler converged on the clearing. They stood staring at Charlotte, draped unceremoniously across Mateo's horse. And they were cheering, laughing, and congratulating their prince while they passed around bottles of wine to toast the occasion. Charlotte watched from her upside-down vantage point as Granny Fate took the bottle, tipped it up, and then gave a delighted cheer

"They've all gone mad!" Charlotte muttered.

Suddenly Mateo righted her and turned her in his arms. She drew her fist back to land a blow to his jaw, but he caught her hand and pulled her tightly against his chest, locking her in such an embrace that she couldn't fight him. The next instant, his mouth came down hard on hers, silencing her angry protests. The unexpected intensity of his kiss drained the fight from her. He released her at last, and she stared up into his eyes. He was smiling down at her, love pouring from his beaming face.

"You did well, my Golden One," he whispered. "You are a true Gypsy woman—filled with passion and spirit."

Charlotte suddenly realized what was happening, even as Mateo turned her to face the crowd and shouted, "I have stolen my woman from her cave. Here is my bride, Charlotte Buckland!" This was all part of the wedding ritual. He had to steal her and bring her into camp still fighting him, so that his *familia* could be witnesses as he subdued his woman.

She looked up into his shining face. Her anger had given way once again to love. Her heart pounded. Oh, how she wanted him at this moment! They smiled at each other, then she leaned her head against his chest. The Gypsies burst into loud applause.

"Come now, Charlotte." Granny Fate reached up and took her hand. "It is time for you to prepare for your wedding."

Charlotte gave Mateo an uncertain look.

"Go with your grandmother," he told her. "Make ready to be my wife. My love goes with you."

He helped her down from the Black Devil's back. The crowd parted, making a path to the brides' tent. Granny

Fate led the way, with Charlotte following a few paces behind. At the blue door, Charlotte paused and turned. Mateo stood watching her, his eyes burning with the light of love. He blew her a kiss and suddenly she felt very small and shy. She hurried inside and closed the door on the cheering throng and the man she would marry.

The wedding was set for the next full moon. In the interim, Charlotte did not lay eyes on Mateo. She felt almost as if she'd been locked away in a nunnery. The brides' tent became her entire world. She was not even permitted to leave to attend her mother's wedding to Winston Krantz. She spent long hours being tutored by Tamara in the ways of a Gypsy woman and by Granny Fate in the traditions of marriage. She learned the story of the curse from beginning to end. After two weeks of this, Charlotte became rebellious.

"I want to see him, Granny Fate!" She stood with arms crossed angrily over her chest and stamped her bare foot on the earthen floor.

"Tsk-tsk!" The old woman made a sign to ward off the evil eye. Brides were especially susceptible. "No, you can't see him! What a thing to say! Nothing is more taboo, Charlotte. The very idea!"

"But we've been separated almost the whole time since my accident. It's not fair!"

"Charlotte, listen to your grandmother," Tamara put in quietly. "She is wise in these things. You don't want to go against the ancient customs, do you? It would spoil everything. It would shame Mateo in the eyes of the others."

Charlotte flopped down on the rug with a sigh of resignation and dropped her chin into her hands. "Oh, all right!"

"Good," said Granny Fate. "Now I want you to concentrate on your weeping."

"I don't see why I have to cry on the happiest day of my life."

"You will cry because it is expected of you!" Granny Fate told her.

Charlotte sat there, trying to think of the saddest things in all the world—a broken china doll, a lost kitten, a horse that had to be destroyed. She'd just about had herself worked up to tears when her thoughts strayed back to Mateo. A smile crept over her face. She glanced up at Granny Fate. The woman was frowning down at her.

"You are impossible!" Fatima threw her hands up in disgust. "You will disgrace us all. Who has ever heard of a *smiling* Gypsy bride?"

"I'm sorry, Granny Fate. Maybe if you explained to me why I'm supposed to be sad. I simply can't cry for no reason."

Charlotte's grandmother—her patience strained, but still intact—knelt beside the bride-to-be. "Close your eyes and think about what I'm saying, please. You are very, very young. A mere child. And, of course, a virgin. A man—a tall, fierce-looking stranger—has come to take you away. You love your father and your mother, your brothers and sisters. You do not want to be snatched away from the bosom of your beloved family. What if the man is cruel to you? What if he is not gentle on your wedding night? What if he starves you . . . beats you? How will you ever know another moment of happiness once you are taken from your family by this terrible stranger? There is so much for a bride to weep over."

Granny Fate stopped and looked at Charlotte. Her eyes were still closed, still dry. She was still smiling.

"You are hopeless—not a fit bride at all!"

"I'm sorry, Granny Fate, but none of those things

apply. I'm not a child. Mateo is not a stranger. I have no brothers and sisters, no father to miss. Mateo would never beat me or starve me. And I can hardly wait for my wedding night, whether he is gentle or not!''

"Every virgin weeps on her wedding day!"

"I'm not *that,* either," Charlotte admitted quietly.

"On the holy breast of the Handmaiden, bite your tongue! What are you saying? Not a virgin? We will get *nothing* for you!" Granny Fate closed her eyes and began making a mournful, keening sound.

"Well, you told Mateo you wanted princes!"

"You are blaming this on *me*? Fatima Lee Buckland, who went to her husband's wolf skins pure as the driven snow—knowing *nothing* of men and love?" She raised her bejeweled hands to heaven and pleaded, "Slome, Slome, what have I done in this life to deserve such a granddaughter?"

"Granny Fate," Tamara said softly, "perhaps she's just tired. Why don't you go out for a walk? I'll watch over her."

Tamara, the eternal peacemaker, soothed both women that day and for the rest of their confinement prior to the wedding. With marvelous understanding and diplomacy, she kept the peace while Charlotte learned of the henna ceremony, the haggling over the brideprice, and everything else it took to become a Gypsy bride.

And during the period of instruction, Tamara's skilled hands fashioned the bridal costume. Charlotte would wear the traditional *salvar,* the billowing harem-style pants of diaphanous white material, and a matching full-sleeved blouse. Other costumes of similar design had to be created out of equally fine fabrics to serve her during the days before the actual ceremony. And even as Tamara worked, the *lohari*—the blacksmith—was busy hammering silver coins into thin sheets to be wrought into fanciful jewels, or *peche,* to adorn the bride's forehead and hair.

As the time drew near, Charlotte grew more and more nervous. Although she wasn't allowed outside, she could hear the bustle of activity. All day and all night, it seemed, the Gypsies sang and danced and laughed and loved. She longed to join in the celebration. Mateo was there with the others. But Granny Fate had told her that she must stay hidden from everyone until the groom's family came to them to perform the first henna ceremony.

Just before the full moon, Queen Zolande and several of Mateo's female cousins, bearing a pan of the sacred henna, knocked at the door of the brides' tent.

"We have come to insure the piety of the bride," the queen called out.

Charlotte shuddered slightly at the sound of Zolande's voice. She wasn't sure what to expect, but she was ready. She stood in the center of the room, dressed in a *salvar* of turquoise satin with a sheer pink blouse. A thin, silver flower *peche* adorned her forehead, and the thick gold ring sent by Mateo encircled the middle finger of her left hand.

"Enter!" Granny Fate said solemnly.

The women, led by Queen Zolande, filed in, looking as somber as pallbearers. Again, dread touched Charlotte's heart. But the moment the door shut behind them, they all began singing, laughing, and teasing the bride good-naturedly. They danced around the bowl of thick reddish-brown paste—the sacred henna brought from their homeland, which had been beaten to powder and mixed with water.

"Ah, she looks fine!" Zolande whispered to Fatima.

"I shall remember your words when it comes time to settle on a brideprice, my old friend."

Mateo's gold had been returned to Zolande. It would be needed for the haggling. Two thousand would be the price, they all knew that. But what was a Gypsy wedding without a good argument over money between the two families? Horse traders were horse traders, whether their object be a mare or a bride.

With much giggling and joking, Mateo's cousins went about their work—dyeing Charlotte's long golden hair with the henna concoction. While they waited for it to dry, they ate little meat pies and goat cheese and drank wine, all the while teasing Charlotte about the wedding night until she was in tears.

Granny Fate smiled and pointed this out to Queen Zolande.

"A good sign, a weeping bride," the queen agreed, nodding sagely.

Then, for the first time in nearly three weeks, Charlotte was allowed out of the brides' tent. To her disappointment, Mateo was nowhere to be seen. In fact, the entire camp was deserted.

"No one must see you, Golden One," the queen told her. "All the others have been sent away for the day."

The women led Charlotte to the stream. There they all stripped, amidst much giggling and singing. For the first time, Charlotte was forced to join the others in the frigid water for their communal bathing. She had no choice.

"It is *tradition*!" her grandmother bellowed when Charlotte objected.

The women took turns running their hands through Charlotte's long hair until the last of the henna had been washed away. But the dye had done its work, turning her pale gold tresses to a rich bronze. And according to the queen, her piety was now assured.

That night, Charlotte felt exhausted. She had been the center of attention all day, with not a moment to herself. All she wanted was to fall down on her pallet and sleep. But as darkness fell, Granny Fate came and shook her awake.

"They are coming to take you! We must defend ourselves!"

Charlotte stared up at her grandmother, convinced that she was still asleep and dreaming. Fatima held several brooms and sticks. Draped around her neck were chains, two heavy skillets tied together with leather thongs, and a sack filled with rocks.

She rubbed her eyes. "Granny Fate, what on earth?"

"Hurry, Charlotte! The groom's family is almost here. We must put up a good fight!"

She dragged her granddaughter from the bed and hauled her out through the blue door. The table from the tent was turned over like a barricade just outside. Overturned chairs flanked its sides. More sticks, rocks, and old pots were piled nearby.

"They plan to take you tonight so that they do not have to pay the brideprice, but we will see about that! Here take this bag. When they come near, throw the rocks at them."

"But Granny Fate—"

"Don't argue, girl. Do as I say!"

Sure enough, in a matter of moments, a mob had formed and was coming across the clearing toward them, armed with sticks and pots. They yelled and threatened as if they were out for blood.

"Fire!" Granny Fate screamed, jumping to her feet and waving one of her wooden broom swords.

The mob charged, yelling and brandishing their weapons. Following her grandmother's orders, Charlotte began hurling the small rocks into their midst. One of the attacking women got past their barricade and was matching her broomstick against Granny Fate's. Charlotte kept firing her missiles. There was no way they could win, but she had to do something.

Suddenly, Granny Fate forced the other woman back out of their territory.

"Victory is ours!" she yelled. "Be gone with you before I give you all a taste of my blade! You will pay dearly for this woman!"

With much grumbling and many angry shouts, the mob fell back. Charlotte stared, shaking her head. She had to smile moments later when the musicians struck up a tune and the angry mob began to laugh and dance.

"It's all over," her grandmother said firmly. "We can go back in now. You're safe."

Granny Fate no doubt thought Charlotte was sleeping when she slipped out to join the revelers who had opposed her during the mock battle. But when she was gone, her granddaughter crept to the window and looked out. There was Fatima Buckland, whirling her colorful skirts and stamping her feet in a frantic dance with the others. Charlotte shook her head, wondering at the strange ways of her people. The whole episode had been a sham—simply another part of the involved bridal ceremony. She went back to bed and fell into an exhausted, dreamless sleep.

The next morning—the day of the wedding—Charlotte awoke to find Granny Fate looking weary and ill. The old woman lay on her pallet, holding her head and moaning, *"Matto, matto! Mandi dinilo!"*

Charlotte ran to her, truly alarmed. "Granny Fate, what's wrong?"

But the old woman just kept up her muttering—words that her granddaughter couldn't understand, although she thought she recalled having heard Phaedra call Mateo *dinilo*. She frowned, trying to remember. Yes, that was it! That first day in Leavenworth. Mateo had said it meant "stupid." She was still trying to soothe her grandmother when Tamara came in.

"Oh, thank goodness you're here! Granny Fate's ill."

Tamara looked at the woman and laughed softly. "Do you understand what she's saying?"

"No. Only something about someone being stupid."

"She's cursing herself, saying she got *matto* last night from too much wine. She says, 'I am stupid!' I'm afraid she's not the only one with a hangover this morning. That was quite a battle last night and quite a celebration afterward."

Charlotte frowned. "Tamara, didn't I see you waving a stick at us with the others during the attack?"

"Of course! I'm part of the groom's family. I would never have passed up the opportunity to join in. I don't want to miss out on a moment of this fine wedding."

Tamara fixed a healing potion for Granny Fate that had her on her feet again in no time. Then the two women set about preparing the bride for the actual wedding ceremony. They bathed her and helped her into the white *salvar*, blouse, and bolero. An intricately wrought *peche* was placed across her forehead, and swirls of silver were draped in front of her hair to frame her face. Her grandmother's lace *mantilla* completed the costume.

"*Now* do I get to see Mateo?" Charlotte pleaded.

"Oh, not just yet," Tamara answered, laughing at the bride's impatience. "Soon the others of his family will come to complete the henna ceremony."

Charlotte touched her darkened hair and looked horrified at the thought. "But they can't! I'm all dressed."

The women came as they had before. But this time they dyed Charlotte's hands and wrapped them in clean white linen.

"A most pious bride," Queen Zolande observed solemnly. "Darkness is falling, so now we begin."

Granny Fate went to Charlotte and lowered the *mantilla* over her face. "Weep!" she ordered.

But there was no need to instruct the bride. Tears

were streaming down Charlotte's face. Tears of happiness! She was about to become Mateo's wife.

The wedding walk would take Charlotte from the brides' tent to the queen's tent, where Mateo awaited her just outside. Again the Gypsies parted for her. Tamara walked before Charlotte, carrying a mirror to reflect her image and so confuse any evil spirits that might be lurking about. Granny Fate led the procession, looking sullen and jeering at the well-wishers.

"There is not enough gold in all the world to buy this woman!" she called out. When someone tried to give her a bottle of wine, Granny Fate turned on the generous Gypsy. "Don't offer me your bribes! She will not marry him, I tell you!"

But she would, of course. They all knew it and rejoiced in the fact.

Suddenly, the bright waves of the sea of Gypsies parted and Charlotte saw Mateo standing before her. He wore a silk, ruffled shirt as orange as a sunset, open to the waist so that the wealth of gold he had draped about his neck gleamed like fire against the dark hair there. His tight britches were shiny black, his waist swathed in a colorful sash. His high boots, blackened with soot, shone from a wax polish. His eyes held hers, speaking to her of love. Everyone else seemed to fade from Charlotte's vision.

"Come, my darling." He took her hand and helped her mount the pile of many-colored rugs provided for the bride and groom. Here they would sit, and listen, and wait through the interminable night while the brideprice was offered, refused, argued over, and finally agreed upon.

The two old women—Granny Fate and Queen Zolande—stood toe to toe before the bridal couple. Their beaklike noses and narrowed, glittering eyes made Charlotte think of two birds of prey in pitched battle over a bit of carrion.

"She is a puny thing, not fit for carrying sons!" Zolande screeched, poking the air with one long talon. "Why, you should pay my son to take her off your hands!"

Granny Fate drew herself up to eye level with the queen. "Does madness run in your entire family, old woman? She is strong enough for any man. Would you want an ox as your son's wife?"

"He will give one hundred gold pieces. No more!"

Fatima whirled away toward the onlooking Gypsies, her arms spread wide in supplication. "Did you hear her?" she said to them. "She would have me sell flesh of my flesh, blood of my blood, for a paltry hundred gold pieces!" She walked toward the blankets and motioned to Charlotte. "Come! The deal is off. We will leave now. There will be no marriage!"

Queen Zolande caught the arm she extended toward the bride. "You rob my son, but very well. Five hundred."

"You would pay more for a good brood mare!"

"I would get more from the mare!"

On and on they haggled. The moon sailed high and then began its descent. The price edged up—nine hundred, twelve, fifteen. Mateo and Charlotte sat atop their throne of bright rugs, holding hands, smiling into each other's eyes. Charlotte wanted desperately for her groom to kiss her, but the lace hiding her face acted as a barricade against his lips.

"How much longer?" she whispered.

He stroked her palm with his fingertips. "Who knows? I thought my mother was the most stubborn woman in the world, but your grandmother wins over her. We could be here until dawn."

Just then, Queen Zolande took a deep breath and

shouted, "Two thousand is my son's final offer for this timid and sickly bride!"

Every voice in the clearing hushed. It was as if the whole world and time itself stood still, awaiting the other woman's decision.

"Done!" Granny Fate boomed at last.

The two women fell into each other's arms, laughing and crying at the same time. They had put on a magnificent show. The other Gypsies applauded and hugged one another, too.

Then silence fell once more. Dawn was streaking the sky with featherlike rays of lilac, gold, and scarlet. Queen Zolande motioned the bridal couple down from their place of honor. She took Charlotte's left hand and placed it in Mateo's.

"Prince Mateo," she said solemnly, "this is the woman you want to be the mother of your children?"

Mateo squeezed Charlotte's hand and looked down into her beautiful face, melting her to tears with his gaze. "She is."

"Then swear that you will leave this woman as soon as you discover that you no longer love her!"

The words shocked Charlotte, but Mateo answered smoothly, "I do so swear."

Mateo then turned slowly and took both Charlotte's hands in his. She was trembling slightly. In a soft, rich voice, he said to her, "Charlotte Buckland, you are the woman I want to be the mother of my children, but you must promise that you will leave me the moment you discover that you no longer love me."

She waited so long to answer that the crowd, growing nervous, shuffled their feet.

"I do so swear, Prince Mateo."

Fatima Buckland appeared at that moment beside Queen Zolande. She was holding a blue satin pillow, cradling a silver knife much like the one Mateo carried in his boot.

"And now we will make you blood friends," Queen Zolande said.

Granny Fate held the pillow out before her, offering the knife to Mateo. He took it in his right hand and held it high for all to see.

Charlotte's heart was pounding. This was a part of the ceremony no one had told her about.

"Give me your right hand, my wife," Mateo ordered.

She did as instructed. Gently, her husband turned it palm up and with the sharp blade made a small cut in her wrist. Charlotte winced but made no sound. She stared down as a tiny pool of blood formed on her white skin.

Mateo then took the blade and cut his own left wrist. Quickly, Queen Zolande took their hands and pressed their wounds together. Granny Fate used a white cloth to bind their wrists in that position.

"Now you are blood friends for life," the queen pronounced. "Even if you should go your separate ways, no longer man and wife, you will always be brother and sister."

Zolande drew the broken icon Mateo had left on his altar from her pocket and kissed it for luck.

"What's that you have there?" Fatima asked, not quite believing what she saw.

"Only a charm, but a very ancient one." She showed the one-eyed saint to Granny Fate.

Without a word, but with a deep inner sense of the rightness of things, Fatima brought forth the other half of the shining relic—smashed by Valencia in her anguish so many full moons ago. Their gnarled old fingers trembling, the two women made the good saint whole again. The final proof!

"So be it!" Zolande whispered.

Fatima answered, nodding sagely, "As Fate has willed!"

Charlotte stared up into Mateo's face. Never had she known such overwhelming love. It seemed that she could feel his life's blood flowing from his heart into hers, while her own veins filled his body with the precious liquid. They were one as they had never been before.

He reached out with his free hand and lifted the lace covering her face. Ever so slowly, he leaned down to kiss her lips. When she felt his warm, soft touch, her body went weak with desire. She would never want any other. Yes, she had sworn to leave him, but only if she no longer loved him. At this moment, she knew that time would never come.

A long day of feasting, dancing, and singing followed. The bride and groom were not allowed to leave but were expected to sit upon their high throne and take what advantage they could of each other's charms with all eyes on them. They hugged and kissed, cuddled and embraced. When the sun began to go down, they were both at a fever pitch.

"When can we be alone, Mateo?" Charlotte begged.

"Now, my love, this minute."

He took her hand and helped her to the ground. Miraculously, the mob of happy Gypsies parted a way for them to Mateo's tent. As bride and groom hurried toward their destination, the wedding guests pressed money on them, saying, as was tradition, "To give a push to the new wagon."

When, at last, they waved to the crowd and entered the tent, Mateo pulled Charlotte into his arms. His eager hands, which had fondled her so discreetly all these hours, sought her breasts beneath the thin fabric of her blouse. She sighed and moved against him.

"Mateo, are there any more traditions to be observed before—"

"None, my darling! No more! Now there are only the two of us, to do as we will."

He drew her down upon his wolf skins and began stripping away her bridal finery. When she lay naked before his eyes, he sat back, caressing her body with his gaze.

He shook his head and smiled. "I have stolen you for two thousand. You are worth millions!"

She raised her arms to him and he came willingly, anxiously.

All the emotions that had been boiling through them for so long now erupted. When Mateo took his wife, she knew him as if for the first time. The tears of a virgin filled her eyes.

Through the long night, they flew the star-strewn skies in each other's arms. They traveled down glowing highways of passion and swam in warm pools of love. And all the while, the Gypsies sang and danced and laughed outside.

At dawn, Mateo stirred from his wife's clinging embrace.

"Don't leave," she begged.

He reached out and stroked her full breasts. "Only for a moment, my love. There is one more tradition to be observed."

Charlotte sat up and stared as Mateo drew on his britches. He went to the tent flap and threw it open. She could see him standing just outside, his feet wide apart, his hands on his hips, his bare back gleaming in the early-morning sun.

His voice boomed through the camp. "Hear me, my *familia*! The woman is true and good and passionate. She will give me many sons!"

His words were followed by a mighty cheer.

The next moment, he was back in his wife's arms and she was sighing and again proving herself more than worthy to be his wife . . . his queen.

Epilogue

1875

The west wind blows through the tall cottonwoods and ripples the surface of the little stream where many full moons ago Gypsy women laughed and bathed together. The clearing, which once knew dancing feet and singing voices, lies in silence except for the sounds of the birds. No caravans, no tents, no devil-black stallions remain. Only a scorched circle of earth, where the women used to cook, marks the spot.

But should another of the *familia* pass this way, he would spot the twisted twigs lying beside piles of stones— the *patrins* left by Mateo's people to guide other Gypsies along the road.

This unspoken language of the *Rom* would say much to the Gypsy stranger of the wanderlust of Mateo's tribe. He might choose a path to east, west, north, south, or any point in between, for so have the descendants of Xendar and Kavà scattered, as if blown by the four winds.

Twin-braided plaits of grass point north to where a pair of old friends ride side by side, gossiping of times gone by, sharing their food, their wine, their ancient laughter.

"Ah, another wintering-over is past, Fatima," observes the woman in black holding the reins. "It is good to be on the road again."

Granny Fate squints at the golden spring sky. "By the holy Handmaiden, I thought the snows would never go this year. But the earth turns, the winds blow, and the Gypsies creep from their caves." She stretches and smiles back at the sun. "I can feel the sap rising in my blood, Zolande. Why, I'm like a flower opening its petals after a long winter sleep."

"Ha! You had better not bud and flower so or you'll, lure some young *Rom* to come and steal us both!"

They laugh together like young girls, giggling over secrets.

"Touch up the team, Zolande. We'd better hurry."

"To where?"

"Anywhere that there's music and dancing! The world is ours. Have some wine?"

"Don't mind if I do, old friend!" The noble old queen, driving the yellow-and-blue caravan with the tinkling silver bells, takes a sip and clucks at the team. "A good *patshiva*, that's what we need!"

"One like when my Charlotte married your Mateo."

"Ah, yes, Fatima, that was a celebration to end all!"

"Do you suppose we will see them soon?"

"Have we missed the spring gathering of the *familia* yet?"

Fatima nods, still smiling. "It will be good to be with them once more."

Zolande agrees.

They chat on—remembering, savoring, weeping at times. But ahead of them stretch the wide rivers and plains, and there is always one more day to live and one more reason to celebrate.

"Life is life!" Fatima cries happily.

"That it is!" Zolande answers. "That it is, my dear old friend!"

Appropriately, a *patrin* made of pyrite rocks—fool's gold—points to the west. Far off, on the coast, two ragged beggars trudge the squalid alleys of San Francisco.

"I'm hungry!" complains the woman in her tattered gown of emerald and heliotrope.

"And what do you expect me to do about it?" The man was probably handsome once, but his dark features are drawn now and a bitter flame burns deep in his eyes. "You know our ways. I have no money to feed us. It is up to you, Phaedra!"

He takes her roughly by the arm and hauls her toward the docks. The many tall masts look promising. The sailors just in port will have money jingling in their pockets and they'll be none too particular what a female looks like or how clean she is.

After shoving the woman out into the street, the dark-eyed man slouches down behind some barrels for a nap.

"No, Petronovich," she whines. "I don't feel like it."

"Go!" he orders. "And do not come back without at least ten pieces of gold!"

She smooths her rags with dirty hands and tugs her silver bodice a bit lower, breathing deeply to show off her full breasts. She struts up and down the dock, giving each passing sailor the eye. One slows and stares at her. She smiles alluringly and beckons to him.

"Are you a hundred years old and no good any longer?" she taunts through pouting lips. "I want you. Can't you tell that? I will be good to you. Only ten pieces of gold to buy my charms."

The bearded sailor grins at her, baring yellowed teeth. "Come along, then, woman! I'm right off the boat, and ain't dipped my wick in near a year. Time's awasting!"

He slips an arm about her waist and hustles her into a reeking alley. His duffel bag serves as a pillow for her head, the hard ground a mattress. He is rough and cruel and loveless, but soon it is over and Phaedra has her handful of gold pieces.

"Here!" she says, adjusting her clothing as she drops the coins into Petronovich's lap

He scowls up at her. "Only *five*? That's not enough! I told you ten. Back to the docks with you, slut!"

He slumps back down to sleep again and dream of a long-lost fortune—two thousand pieces of gold.

She goes back on the street to ply the Gypsies' oldest trade for no more than will keep them from starving.

A smooth chunk of crystal and two sticks placed to ward off evil . . . Hairs from a black horse's tail, a daggerlike stick, and one gleaming pebble.

Two *patrins* point to the east, the first toward neat fences as white as new snow that border green fields, where strong black stallions mount their mares.

The great house on the hill casts a welcoming glow from within, and music floats out on the fragrant night breeze. A ball is in progress.

The mistress of Fairview greets arriving guests. "Dr. and Mrs. Feldston! I'm so happy you could come."

Warmly, Jemima Krantz welcomes the surgeon and his dark-eyed wife.

"We wouldn't have missed it, Mrs. Krantz," answers Tamara Feldston, casting a loving glance up at her Ira. He smiles and agrees.

"You look perfectly marvelous, Tamara!" the hostess adds. "Why, in that Paris gown, no one would ever guess you're expecting your third!"

The pretty Gypsy's eyes glitter happily and she whispers, "Prince Mateo swears that if this one is a daughter, her marriage contract will be sealed at birth. Of course, we'll be on the road when the baby comes."

"How exciting! It must be wonderful traveling all over the country every summer." The older woman, dressed in burgundy silk, eyes the young mother with a touch of envy. But then she shrugs it off and tucks her hand through her husband's arm. She is happy as Winston Krantz's wife. Their life at Fairview is good, rich, full.

"How was your trip, Dr. Feldston?" asks Jemima.

"Too long, but the train was quite comfortable."

"Well, my dear, we've seen the last of trains for a few months," Tamara reminds him.

"And the last of a roof over our heads when it rains," he complains, but then laughs good-naturedly.

The young couple have both been admiring the house as they chat with their hosts. Tamara glances about, eyeing the fine antiques, the new wallpaper from France, and the crystal chandelier.

"You've done wonders with Fairview, Mrs. Krantz. It looks like a palace!"

"Thank you, dear," her hostess answers with a pleased smile. "If I do say so myself, I think the brideprice was well spent!"

"Tamara! Ira!" Suddenly, a familiar voice floats down to the couple from the stairs. The woman standing there looks like a queen. She is dressed in a golden gown glittering with tiny crystals. Her gleaming hair, piled high atop her head, resembles a crown. She sweeps down and embraces them both.

"You're the first to arrive," she tells them, even though the ballroom is filled with guests.

"Perhaps we're the most anxious to be on the road," Tamara answers.

The two friends chat for several minutes. Then suddenly the woman in the golden gown is conscious that someone is watching her. She can feel little shivers along the back of her neck and a familiar heat coursing through her. She turns. The room full of people vanishes. She sees only his dark eyes on her, his face smiling love through time and space. As if drawn by some invisible force, he makes his way across the room to her side.

"Dance with me, my *sunaki bal.*" The tone of his deep voice caresses her, fondling her almost intimately.

He sweeps her into his arms and onto the dance floor. The other couples part for the handsome pair. The candlelight, gleaming from the chandelier and wall sconces, catches the glint of her gown and the golden rings in his ears. The two of them glow as one.

"I want you," he whispers close to her ear, letting one hand stray to brush the side of her breast.

She blushes slightly and whispers back, "Not now, Mateo!"

"When?"

"When the *patshiva* is over, my love."

He squeezes her and pulls her closer.

"Mama, Papa!" A dark child toddles into the ballroom, the bottom of his flannel pajamas flapping in the breeze. He runs to the gilded couple and they scoop him up in their arms together, whirling him about the floor.

"What is it, little Fate?" asks his papa.

"The silver bells . . . I heard them! I heard them, Papa, just like you said!"

"The bells?" his mother asks.

He nods vigorously, the raven locks about his beautiful face dancing a merry jig. "Yes, Mama. Papa told me to listen for the bells when the moon is full. He said it would be my grannies coming."

The Golden One smiles at father and son. Soon it will be time to leave Fairview.

Suddenly the stiff, liveried butler breaks in. "Pardon me, sir, but there are two old women at the front door asking for you." He puts a gloved hand by his mouth and whispers, "Quite a disreputable pair, sir. They appear to me to be a bit tipsy, if you'll pardon my saying so."

Mother, father, and son rush to the door.

"You've come! It's a miracle!" cries the Golden One.

"We've folded our tent from the wintering-over. And now we've come to join the trek, Prince Mateo," the old queen says.

"You will stay here for the night. We've been waiting so long for you to come," the lovely woman says. "Mother has your rooms ready."

"My dear granddaughter, we thank you very much. But every Gypsy knows that when you capture the wind within walls it becomes stale. The front lawn will do nicely. We'll sleep under the stars."

The old women awake in the scarlet-and-golden dawn to the sound of a thousand silver bells tinkling in the bluegrass-scented air. Stretching for miles in all directions, they see the bright caravans converging on Fairview.

Soon their leader appears—black eyes flashing and gold-handled whip snapping signals in the morning air.

He mounts his painted caravan and moves out. Beside him sits his golden-haired woman, her scarlet petticoats rustling in the breeze. She holds a sleepy little Gypsy prince in her arms.

"Let us take to the road!" the prince calls to his followers.

The high-wheeled Gypsy wagons form a bright-colored snake far off into the distance. Their drivers sing, they laugh, they drink May wine. "Life is life!" they call out to friends and strangers along the way. The road is long, but so are the patience and goodwill of the *Rom*. They will live their own way, but they will make many stops along the trail.

Philadelphia is to be their first. The big tent awaits and the crowds with pennies for Poor Little Pesha.

A hush falls over the hundreds in the audience beneath the huge tent. The moment they have waited for has arrived at last. The ringmaster has made his announcement. Anticipation hangs heavy in the air.

Suddenly there is a sound like thunder. Six mighty black stallions charge into the arena.

"Hiyah!" cries the scarlet-and-gold-clad figure on the back of the lead horse. He stands high on the stallion's back, waving with one hand while he grips the reins in the other.

He guides his great, devil-black horse back toward the tent flap and leans dizzyingly downward. When he comes back around, a beautiful blonde Gypsy in shining gold is by his side. The audience thunders its applause for the Golden One.

Vaults and somersaults, dismounts and remounts— the pair put the stallions through their paces. Never a missed step, never a falter; it is as if the riders have invisible wings.

Suddenly the tent flap flies back. The ringmaster's voice booms.

"And now with great pleasure, we introduce to you the Prince of Fate! Soon to be admired by the crowned heads of Europe—the child sired by the wolf and born of the storm, the heir apparent to the Gypsy throne!"

Little Prince Fate, clad in scarlet-and-gold tights and a shining cape, rides his coal-black pony around and around to waves of cheers. The two old grannies in the front row nod with pride and smile to each other.

"He'll make a find husband for our daughter," Tamara says to her doctor as the black-eyed infant in her arms coos softly.

Then the golden trio leap from their mounts to bow before their admirers and smile to one another.

"You are magnificent, my Golden One!" The handsome prince brings the woman's fingertips to his lips while his dark eyes consume her with love.

In that intimate moment, she remembers another time and place, when wolves howled, snow blanketed the forest, and this man taught her with his strong, demanding body what few women are lucky enough to learn about love. A familiar warmth creeps through her limbs. Her breasts ache for his touch. She moves closer to feel the heat of his flesh—to breathe in his leathery musk.

He drapes an arm about her shoulders, drawing her near. Their eyes kiss and exchange a secret promise. Then their attention shifts to the fruit of their love.

The child struts and sweeps his cape for the adoring audience. His parents look on, allowing little Prince Fate center stage. Already their minds are away from the crowds, the ring, the performance. They are thinking ahead to more intimate sport.

"This will be a fine night, a special night," Prince

Mateo whispers to his Golden One. "A night for making love and little Gypsy princesses.

She smiles, shy with him suddenly, and squeezes his hand. "Yes, my love. This is the night of the full moon."

About the Author

Becky Lee Weyrich, a native Georgian, was born on Margaret Mitchell's birthday in a hospital that later became a library, and she is named for Daphne Du Maurier's *Rebecca.* So it seems only fitting that she should have become a writer.

But before taking pen in hand, she spent her early career as a professional navy wife and mother of two. For seventeen years, she moved with her pilot husband from base to base, living in such diverse locations as Maine, Florida, California, and Naples, Italy.

In 1969 she took a job on a Maryland newspaper, writing a weekly column. Since then, she has contributed to several other newspapers and magazines. She wrote, illustrated, and published two volumes of poetry. And since she turned to fiction in 1978, nine of her novels have seen print, including from Fawcett, *Rapture's Slave, Captive of Desire, Rainbow Hammock, Tainted Lilies,* and *Summer Lightning,* which was nominated by *Romantic Times* for their ''Reviewers' Choice Award'' as best Civil War novel of 1985.

Becky Lee Weyrich now makes her home on St. Simons Island, Georgia, sharing her old beach cottage—Unicorn Dune—with her husband and son, one dog, and assorted cats. Her hobbies include golf, clogging, bowling, beachcombing, collecting Victorian antiques, and spoiling her new grandson, Jonathan.

Historical romance with a twist of mystery...

MADELEINE BRENT

TAF-39